PRAISE FOR
Fall Into You

If When Harry Met Sally is the quintessential fall movie, Fall Into You is the quintessential fall book. So many quirky, funny episodes, romantic scenes and steamy, heart-racing moments.

— Amazon Reviewer

I loved, loved, loved this book! It has spice, it has the brother's best friend trope, and it has the instalove, but done in a way that doesn't make me cringe. Liza and Matt's chemistry is over the top awesome, and I'm insanely excited to see that it is book one in a series!

— @RomanceBooksFan

If you're looking for a rom-com with a Fall feeling, look no further 🎃 I'm looking forward to the next installment in the series.

— @Lissthebooklover

PRAISE FOR
Shall We Dance?

This book easily moved to my favorite rom com spot. Barbara and Theo are such a fun couple. I'm a sucker for enemies to lovers and Caroline Frank did a wonderful job nailing this with the perfect amount of banter, spice, and tension. I found myself thinking about this story constantly, and couldn't wait to finish it, but also wanted to savor every word.

— @vicwiththegoodbooks

This book is everything a romance novel should be. It had all the pieces for a perfect love story. Enemies to lovers, grump and sunshine, and a detrimental miss communication. What more could a romance lover want?? I loved the characters and how real and relatable they were. Shall We Dance is a 10/10.

— Amazon reviewer

I'm swooning over this book!

— JenG

Para Andrea, Dani, Diana, y Julieta. Mis OG.
Las extraño muchísimo. XO.

"Winter is the time for comfort, for good food and warmth, for the touch of a friendly hand and for a talk beside the fire: it is time for home."

— Edith Sitwell

Second Chance Snowmance

SEASONS OF LOVE:
BOOK 3

CAROLINE FRANK

Prologue

ROSIE

18 Years Old - New Year's Eve

Lungs burning as I gasp for air, feet aching in the tightness of my heels, toes cramping, calves hurting; I search for him. A drop of sweat runs down my back as I run through the party, eyes desperately bouncing off every face in the crowd in search of the one person I need most right now.

I check the time on my phone and my stomach turns—11:58 p.m. The countdown will begin soon, and I still haven't found him.

Where are you?

Tears puddle in my eyes as desperation floods my system, and I begin to shake. Could be from the blast of chilled air coming from the open doors, or it could be the fear of losing the person I love the most for good. The guests move outside to the patio, ready to ring in the New Year, waiting for the fireworks. They wait for the nighttime ski show that will illuminate the mountain like a blazing trail of fire coming down the slopes as soon as the clock strikes twelve. They gather excitedly, holding onto a balloon with a piece of paper tied to its decorative ribbon. Each guest has written their hopes and wishes for the next year, ready to release them into the sky.

For everyone else, tonight is a night full of hope, of possibili-

ties, of new beginnings and second chances—something I hoped I would get, too. So far, however...

"Ten...nine...eight—"

"No, no, no, no..." I cry under my breath, turning my head in every direction as the crowd cheers. Guests pair up, readying for their midnight kisses, and people tighten their coats around themselves.

"—seven...six...five—"

In a last ditch effort, I decide to run to the bench on the terrace just outside the ballroom. It's where we spent every single New Year together since meeting each other—where I thought I would spend every single one of my New Year's with him.

I race to the bench, trying to see through the crowd of people, hoping to find him before the clock strikes twelve.

A couple moves, and I catch a glimpse of a set of familiar long legs in dark pants and the corner of a red coat sitting on the bench. I smile in relief because I found him.

"—four...three—"

With newfound confidence and energy, I push through the guests towards him.

He's been looking for me, too, hoping I'd show up.

It's why he's there; I'm sure of it.

I smile broadly, trying to get to him as quickly as possible. I want us to start the new year together, to fix this, to be together. But as the crowd parts for a brief second, giving me a clear view, my heart rips to shreds.

It's him. He's there. Sitting on our bench on New Year's Eve —just like every other year before. Only this time, his lips are attached to a blonde woman's, one of his hands in her hair, the other grabbing her waist as he brings her closer into him.

"—two...one! Happy New Year!"

The crowd erupts into loud cheers; they kiss and release balloons into the air, flooding the sky with silver and gold. The band plays Auld Lang Syne, and the guests stop what they're doing to sing along with smiles on their faces, happy that the New Year has begun.

But he doesn't stop. They don't stop.

And I keep on staring like a masochist, completely shattered as he uses the hand in her hair to shift her face to his neck. Someone must've punched me in the chest—the heart—because I swear it stops beating.

As if he can hear my sharp inhale over the music and the loud guests, he opens his eyes, immediately meeting mine. They widen for a split second as he holds my gaze, morphing into an unfamiliar hard and cold amber. Gone are the warm and welcoming eyes that always brought me comfort, made me feel safe.

They harden into stone right before he closes them again; and he pulls the woman's lips back to his.

Somehow, I manage to make my legs work and rush out of the party just as the tears streak down my cheeks. Running as fast as I can, I make it to the hotel's front doors, ready to head back home. I push the heavy doors open, but slip on my way out, my vision blurry and head foggy. With a hair-raising splat, I fall onto my hands and knees on the ice-covered pavement, pain shooting up and down my arms and legs. Sniffling, I sit up and check myself for injuries, cringing at the sight of blood. Feeling completely deflated, I look up at the sky, trying to see the stars just like we used to do together, lying side by side on his truck bed, on clear nights. But from where I sit, the powder and smoke from the fireworks cloud the night sky, depriving me of the comforting view I crave.

I can't see the stars anymore, and I can't help but wonder whether it's a sign.

I look down at the bloody palms of my hands, my skinned knees, and wince. I finally let the misery overtake me, succumbing to sobs that rip through my chest and make it hard to breathe. Squeezing my eyes shut, I hug my legs to my chest, not caring about the snow or the cold—just needing to take a moment to get myself together.

After what could've been just a few minutes or an hour, I hear a familiar voice behind me—not the one I hoped for, and certainly not one I expected. "Are you okay?" he asks.

My breath hitches in my throat as I raise my head to look at him, unchanged. I shake my head slightly, not daring to say a word. He sees the state of my palms and knees and winces.

"You want to come with me? Get you cleaned up?"

His kindness—so unlike him, this man I used to know so well —throws me for a loop. But it's more than welcome after how my heart was broken by the one I truly wanted to spend this night with.

For a moment, I stare deeply into his ice-blue eyes. The last of the New Year's fireworks illuminate his pale face and blonde hair in reds and blues as they burst above us. I consider getting up, and saying no. He's not the one I truly want, after all. I consider going back inside and asking the front desk of the hotel to call me a cab. I consider waiting for someone else to give me a ride.

But I don't want to go home alone tonight. Not after what I just witnessed.

So instead I say, "Yes."

Chapter One

ROSIE

27 Years Old - Present

IF YOU WERE TO TELL ME RIGHT NOW THAT HELL ISN'T A fiery pit of despair, but Denver International Airport during the holiday season, I would believe you. The sheer amount of people running around *Home Alone 2* style, crashing into me, is ridiculous. I get that we're all trying to make it to our final destinations, but *damn*, can't we all just take a couple of chill pills?

Working my pastel-pink hair into a loose braid, I wonder idly where all these people came from. I haven't been home in nine years, but I don't remember the airport ever being *this* crowded, even during the holidays. And that's saying something, considering Colorado is a prime ski location.

A man knocks into me from behind with his duffel, and I nearly fall over, catching myself on my pink carry-on. "*Jeez,*" I mutter under my breath. I just want to get out of here, just want the carousel assigned to my flight to start pumping out bags so I can grab my suitcase, get to my bus, and make it home. I daydream of the scalding-hot shower I plan on taking as soon as I get home. Of the super-high-waisted, buttery leggings and loose top I plan on slipping into. I yearn for the hours of *Buffy the*

Vampire Slayer I'm going to watch in bed with my parents' cat, Manolo, cuddled up next to me.

But mostly I just want that shower. Flying is gross.

Normally, I'm a carry-on-only person through and through. But it just wasn't going to happen for this trip given that I'm coming off of a five-week freelance job on location. *Especially* since I'm a goddamn costume designer with a slight shoe obsession. Not to mention the fact that my little sister is getting married on New Year's Eve, which requires additional outfit changes. Plus, it's Christmas, which means presents, and there was no way I was going to fit every single carefully picked-out gift in my small bag along with everything else.

Honestly, it's a miracle I only checked one suitcase, let alone three.

With a loud and shrill noise, the carousel's overlapping metal slats move as bags start tumbling down from a ramp in the ceiling. A large, red duffel falls heavily onto a black suitcase and I wince, realizing now that there is *no way* the glass ornament I got my parents as a Sorry-I've-been-avoiding-coming-home-like-the-plague-all-these-years-but-it's-really-nothing-personal gift will make it out unharmed.

Fantastic.

Pushing through the crowd to get a little closer to my carousel, I look impatiently at the time on my phone. I have about ten minutes to high-tail it outta here if I'm going to make my bus. I shudder to think of what it would mean if I miss it because *one does not simply hop on the next available one.* The shuttles get booked *weeks* in advance, selling out almost as quickly as they open the reservation slots.

I briefly imagine calling my dad and asking him to make the four-hour drive round-trip just to come get me and wince. No, that's out of the question. There's probably no way I'd be able to get a last-minute rental either. A taxi, then? But then that would probably cost me upwards of two hundred dollars...

"Hey," a familiar male voice calls out behind me. The hairs on the back of my neck rise, every muscle in my body tensing. Suppressing the world's heaviest sigh, I turn to face the backwards-facing cap-wearing frat bro who talked my ear off the entire flight here. "Love the braid—it's cute." He reaches out, but I recoil just out of his reach.

Who does this guy think he is? Can he not take a hint? I never once gave him an *ounce* of encouragement the entire flight and now he's back for more rejection?

"I'm Brian, by the way. I just saw you standing here and realized that I never gave you my name and, well, you never gave me yours." His gaze travels up and down my body, taking me in with an appreciative look in his eyes. Though I honestly don't know *what* he thinks he's looking at, because I'm covered in a bulky pink coat and about ten layers of winter clothing.

I press my lips together in a thin line and keep my eyes glued to the carousel.

"Not gonna tell me your name, huh? Mystery Girl. I like that." I roll my eyes, but refuse to acknowledge him otherwise. "Anyway, Mystery Girl. I may or may not have read one of your texts over your shoulder while I was sitting next to you on the plane and seen that you're headed to Avon?"

I'm sorry—what?

"I'm headed to Aspen, which is kinda nearby, and I've decided that we're going skiing together. Have a little *après-ski* moment, too." Wiggling his eyebrows, Brian leans in closer, and I pull away from him. *Again.*

"No, thanks. Not much of a skier." And I'm not even lying. I know it might seem like a requirement for someone from the area to ski at an expert level, but I am absolutely lethal on the slopes. And not in a That-girl-is-killing-it-way. More so in an

I've-literally-caused-accidents way. Truth is, I moved here from Venezuela when I was 12 and never got the hang of it.

"That's okay. I was more looking forward to the après-ski than the actual skiing, really."

I shoot him a tight smile. "No, thanks. I'm good."

"You're having a drink with me. Non-negotiable," he says with a smirk.

That's it—I've had enough.

Listen, I'm not one for conflict, but I *really* don't appreciate people pressuring me into doing something I don't want to do. The last time I almost caved, things did not end well, I can tell you that. So I finally turn to face Brian head-on, ready to tell him off in a *very* direct and impossible to misunderstand manner. "Brian, is it?" He nods, squaring his shoulders. "The thing is—"

I am so ready to put this guy in his place, but suddenly the words get caught in my throat, when something—or rather *someone*—catches my eye over his shoulder.

Asher.

My throat tightens and suddenly I'm choking.

Wait, *am* I choking? Is it possible to choke on air? It certainly *feels* that way to me, because I can't get my lungs to work. Maybe I'm suffering from stress-induced paralysis. Or maybe this really *is* hell. Maybe the plane crashed, and I was sent here for my sins, and the universe—or whoever's in charge—just *knew* to trap me in this over-crowded airport with a man who refuses to leave me alone, only to be haunted by the worst mistake of my entire, short, twenty-seven years of life.

This is definitely hell. I totally just died.

It's such a tragedy, really. I was *so* young. I still had so much to live for. I mean, I was still waiting to hear back about that promotion! Plus, I had tickets for my friend Barbara's musical in January. I'd even been toying with the idea of adopting a cat! Regret floods my system, filling my head with a sudden influx of missed opportunities and untaken vacations.

But then... Then I pull my head out of my ass and realize that maybe I am being just *a little bit* dramatic, and that there is a 99.99% chance that I really am still alive and standing here like an idiot, staring at a man I haven't seen in almost nine years to the date.

I watch him run his fingers through his dark hair as he looks back to his carousel and remember exactly what it felt like when *I* did it.

A sudden sharp intake of breath, and my chest expands, filling with air.

Yes. Oxygen. Good. I need some of that.

My eyes watch every movement he makes with laser focus, taking in just how much he's changed physically, but also remained the same.

God, he looks good. He's still young, of course, but more of a man now. Broader shoulders, slightly shorter hair, and did he get taller? Or maybe I just got shorter.

I certainly feel small right now...

I watch him as he pulls a forest green suitcase from the carousel slats with ease, making it look as light as a feather. With a heartbreaking smile, he hands it to an older lady. My heart squeezes in my chest at the gesture, because he's still the type of guy that helps strangers out without even thinking twice about it. So much has changed since we last saw each other, but it's nice to know that at least that hasn't.

My eyes glued to him, I watch each of his fluid movements like a hawk. The way he runs the back of his hand over his travel stubble, how he rubs his eyes in a sign of tiredness under his round, tortoise glasses (a nice upgrade from the black, hipster ones he used to wear in high school), and how he readjusts the strap of his backpack over his shoulder.

All of a sudden, it hits me: I look like absolute crap. "Oh my god," I mutter under my breath.

"What? What's wrong?" a voice I recognize asks, buzzing like a mosquito in my ear: annoying and distracting.

I ignore it and take stock of myself, of my disheveled hair, gross from travel, of the fact that I feel puffy and bulky (and probably look that way, too).

He *cannot* see me like this. The first time I see Asher Wolff after nine years *cannot* be like this.

I've thought of this moment about a million times. About what I would say, how I would act. How I would casually greet him, cool as a cucumber; as if I had built a bridge over him and everything that had happened, and gotten over it. I even planned out what I would wear, of course: that black wrap dress that looks like nothing on a hanger, but only does amazing things to my body when I wear it—the one currently neatly folded in my suitcase. The color is really off-brand for me, but the whole outfit makes my legs look longer, my waist snatched, my butt appear smaller. It has *just* the right amount of cleavage that my boobs look fantastic, but still leaves something to the imagination. All this time I had imagined my hair would be in soft waves down my back, my toasted skin would be glowy, and I'd be wearing that one shade of red lipstick he once drunkenly admitted to liking so much.

For Christ's sake, I would have at least worn Spanx!

Asher, on the other hand, looks amazing. The combination of the tweed blazer peaking just under his coat and those glasses make him look like an academic snack I'd love to spread on a cracker. A nerdy, sexy professor I wouldn't mind spending the afternoon in detention with, if you know what I mean.

As I continue to watch him, I wonder what he's been up to these past few years. Normally, I try not to let my thoughts stray there. But when your families are so close, it's hard to isolate yourself completely from any information regarding the man you used to love.

Or currently love.

It's hard to tell sometimes.

Last I heard, he was in a Ph.D. program, but I'm not sure which or where. Did he decide to pursue his doctorate in Astrophysics like he planned on while we were still friends? Or did he decide to focus on a different topic?

After a few seconds' consideration, I decide there's no way he'd ever change his mind about that. He was way too passionate about the topic not to pursue it. Even though years have passed since seeing him, I know who Asher is to his core. I'd bet every shoe in my closet he never gave up on his dream.

Despite vowing to limit my knowledge of Asher's life, I had to prepare myself mentally to see him again. And according to my mother, he wasn't supposed to make it to my sister's wedding *or* the holidays this year.

Clearly, I had been ill-informed.

I watch as he effortlessly pulls another bag from the carousel —this time, a familiar, worn black duffel—and straps it over one shoulder. With a last wave to the woman he helped, Asher makes his way toward the car rental desks... The ones that are coincidentally right next to my carousel.

This is it. There's no avoiding it.

I groan in frustration and horror. I mean, I had a plan. One that did not involve me looking like *this*. I *definitely* wouldn't be wearing a million layers of clothing, have bags under my eyes, and have gross hair that looks like—

Wait... Wait one second. My hair!

He's never seen me with pink hair before! He's only ever seen me in its natural jet-black color.

Yes, perfect. He'll never notice me like this. All I have to do is—

Fuck.

I swear it happens in slow motion—or at least it feels that way. But, as if sensing my eyes on him, Asher slowly turns his head in my direction, his gaze locking on mine. Eyes widening, he stops mid-step. For a second, an expression I can't quite make out flashes through his beautiful, amber eyes. He swallows once, adjusts his glasses on his face, and slowly brings his left hand up to give me a slow wave with one of those lopsided smiles of his I remember so well.

My stomach drops, and I stop breathing again. Feeling like I've been caught with my hand in the cookie jar, I wave back. I do my best to smile in return, but it's like I've forgotten which muscles I need to do so. I'm pretty sure the best I can manage is a mangled grimace of sorts, because his grin wavers slightly.

With a deep breath, he changes course and makes his way to me, each of his steps matching the steady drumming in my chest...

Step. Ta-dum. Step. Ta-dum. Step. Ta-dum.

When his eyes fall to the man beside me, his stride falters—and so does my heart. Mortified, I do my best to call upon the uncanny talent we used to have to read each other's thoughts. *No way. I'm not with him,* I try to tell him. But it seems like our powers of telepathy have disappeared and faded into nothingness, along with our friendship.

Finally—after what feels like another decade—Asher stops a few feet from me.

With those amber eyes never leaving mine, he breathes, "*Rosie.*"

Chapter Two

ROSIE

The sound of my name on his lips is like a starter pistol to my heart. It jumps and races into a full-on spree. So much so, that I unconsciously bring my hand to my chest in a half-assed attempt to slow it down, tell it to chill, begging it to stop aching.

Come on, girl. Don't do this to me.

"Rosie." He says it again, as if getting used to uttering my name aloud after all these years. Without hesitation, Asher drops his duffel and opens his arms broadly in invitation. Suddenly, I find that I can't help myself. I go to him.

Sure, I've spent the past nine years literally doing everything possible to avoid ever seeing him again. But I can't help taking the opportunity to feel his arms around me one more time. Like gravity, his pull is absolute and undeniable.

"It's so good to see you." He murmurs into my hair, arms tightening around my waist. But I can barely process it because the entire time I should be enjoying this moment, I ask myself, "*Is it good to see me? Because I would've bet my life that you hated me*". I'm sure that I'm giving myself too much credit, though, because of course he's over it—it's been nine years.

He drops his arms and takes a single step back before saying, "It's been too long". His voice is deeper than I remembered, but still smooth and delicious. It reaches every corner of my soul, soothing some of the pain I'd gotten used to after all this time.

Asher's enthusiasm is contagious—suddenly, I'm not *completely* mortified to have run into him. And then that sparkly feeling I always used to feel around him makes a surprising reappearance after lying dormant for so long. I feel it shine in my chest, like bright lights fighting to get out, to burst through.

Finally, a huge smile spreads on my face because, *oh my god,* Asher is here. He's *here,* standing right in front of me, and it's been so long since I've seen him and sure, we lost touch because of the whole "incident" but whatever, who cares because *he's here.*

"Asher." His name feels foreign on my lips; it almost burns my tongue.

"You changed your hair!" He laughs, reaching out to touch my braid. He stops himself right before, though, dropping his hand, frowning at it as he clenches it into a fist.

I would have let you touch it. I would have let you undo my braid, run your fingers through it.

He collects himself and grins down at me again, amber eyes bright with excitement. He's so beautiful, I stare up at him, completely awestruck. I have to crane my neck because, at six-four, Asher is a full foot taller than me, making me feel smaller than I already do. As my eyes travel over his handsome, angular face, I realize that my memory didn't do him justice. His expectant smile dazzles me, and I can barely open my damn mouth to say a single word.

"Yeah." She speaks! Now I just need to add a few more words, weave them into a logical sentence, and... "Quite a long time ago, actually." Wow. *Two* whole sentences. Yay me!

Asher bends to pick up his duffel, swinging its strap over his shoulder again. "I shouldn't be surprised. You always wanted to color it, and your obsession with pink always ran *deep.*" He chuckles, and the reminder that we once knew each other so well stings a little. "It's the reason I started calling you Rosie, after all."

I squint my eyes and tilt my head to the side, bringing my hand to my chin in an exaggerated, mock-thinking expression. "Was it? Or was it because you couldn't pronounce my name correctly as kids and thought it would also serve as a great *gringo* nickname for Rosario?"

He laughs softly, his eyes bright. "Hey, necessity is the mother of invention. I didn't know how to speak Spanish well back then, and my pronunciation sucked. And am I to assume that now, suddenly, I'm a *gringo*? Didn't you once tell me I was and forever will be an honorary Venezuelan? Don't I get any points for years of you imposing your *delicious* foods, customs, music, and slang?"

It gets you all the points. Whatever you want.

"Imposing," I scoff. "But, I guess so. I guess you deserve *some* credit," I say as we grin stupidly at each other.

"Plus, the nickname stuck, didn't it?" He's right. Everyone calls me Rosie now—except for Dad.

A throat clears behind me, causing me to jolt. "Hey, man." I feel my cheeks flush crimson red in embarrassment—partly because I *completely* forgot about the other human standing right beside me, and partly because I feel oddly compelled to clarify that I am very single.

Weird.

Brian stretches his hand towards Asher, as he edges himself between us.

"The name's Brian. How's it going?" But it's not really a question, is it?

Asher looks down at my kind-of-stalker's hand with a confounded look on his face. Addressing me with an amused, but tight smile, he asks, "Boyfriend?"

I nearly choke on air again.

My mouth opens to answer him with a big, fat *hell, no*, but am quickly cut off by Brian himself: "Nah, man. We just met. But we *are* going on a date. Right?" He winks at me and then looks back at Asher, who catches me rolling my eyes at Brian. He gives up on shaking Asher's hand and drops his, shoving it inside his coat pocket.

"Um." My eyes flash to Asher's, his smile wavering as he watches me. "I'm flattered, Brian. But I'm here with my family, so that's going to be a hard pass for me."

Frowning, Brian slips his hand into his other pocket, pulls out a white card, and hands it to me with a wry smile. "Here. Call me *when* you change your mind." Brian winks once at me and walks away—but not before shooting a glaring look at Asher, who merely snorts in his direction.

More out of habit than anything else, I slip Brian's business card into my purse, planning on throwing it out as soon as I can. Asher looks down at me with an expression of curiosity in his eyes but says nothing. Meanwhile, I take in his perfect dark, curly hair, his slightly crooked nose with that small bump on the bridge of it from when he broke it in high school. I take in his large hands, the ones that knew exactly what to do with me, even when they didn't.

An awkward pause hangs heavy between us before Asher clears his throat and says, "So, are you taking the bus home or...?"

I stare up at him, completely bewildered. "Huh? The—? *Oh, no!*" I pull my phone out and check the time. "I missed my bus!" I groan, putting my face in my hands. "My bags, too!" I turn back to my carousel and, lo-and-behold, my pink suitcase is the last one on the slats, spinning around, looking lonely and abandoned.

"Wait here." Because even though I've spent all these years

avoiding Asher, it only took one second to never want to say goodbye ever again. I jog the few feet back to my flight's carousel, dragging my carry-on behind me. I wait for my bag to make the trip around one last time but, just as I'm about to reach for it, a muscular arm gets ahead of me and pulls it out with ease.

"Damn, Rosie. This weighs a ton," Asher says, his voice laced with amusement as he sets the bag beside me. "You got a body in here or something?"

"Two, actually. My latest victims." His laughter floods my chest with warmth, and suddenly I feel like crying. This is why I didn't want to come back here. *This* is why. We've spent less than an hour together, and I can already tell it's going to be hell readjusting to life without him again.

Another awkward silence. Not a single word passes between us, but a lot is said, the spark reviving itself from the ashes of two people who burned each other down.

Or maybe it was just me. Maybe I was the only one doing the burning.

Something suddenly grips my heart and the words *"Forgive me"* get caught in my throat, begging to be spoken aloud. Nothing comes out, though. I'm a coward. I'm not proud of it, but them's the facts.

There are... so many things I want—*need*—to say. Overwhelmed with emotion, not knowing what will come out first, I open my mouth to say something, but he cuts me off: "So...I'm guessing you need a ride?" With a smirk, he adds, "It's not like you're *too* far out of my way."

Did I mention we were childhood neighbors?

Chapter Three

ASHER

Rosie Castillo

It might not be the most macho thing in the world to admit, but I'm not gonna deny that seeing her standing there by baggage claim didn't momentarily make my heart stop and then restart with so much adrenaline I legitimately felt like I was having a goddamn heart attack.

But it's fine. I'm cool. *I'm* not freaking out—*you're* freaking out.

"You really didn't have to do this, you know. I could've waited for another bus. Or gotten a cab. It's really not a big deal." She settles more comfortably in the seat of my rental, and I can tell that the travel exhaustion is finally catching up with her.

Her mouth says one thing, but her eyes tell a different tale. I scoff, shooting her a disbelieving glance—because, is she insane? "Like I was gonna let you pay two-hundred bucks for a cab. Are you kidding? And why would you make yourself wait hours for the next available shuttle in that hellhole of an airport when I could just give you a free ride?"

"*Hellhole*, indeed." She suppresses a smile. "At least let me pay for half of the rental fee."

"Not a chance. Besides, you know how much I *love* road

trips with you. They're never uneventful. Which reminds me... Did you remember to use the restroom before we left?" I try to control my laughter, but damn, I can't help it as it bursts through.

Rosie sucks in a sharp breath and narrows her eyes at me. "I *cannot* believe you'd bring our trip to CU Boulder up," she hisses, cheeks flushing a deep red. "I thought we agreed never to talk about it again."

"It's kind of hard to forget." I chuckle, remembering the road trip fondly. It was hours of being stuck in the car, having her all to myself, as she sang—*very* poorly—at the top of her lungs. *Of course* I let her take over the radio, so it was hours of torturous Gaga and Adele, pop music she loved and I couldn't stand.

But fuck me if it wasn't the best trip of my life.

The part where she peed her pants was an unfortunate, yet hilarious, cherry on top of it all. However, it made her look a little more human to me, a little less of an unattainable fantasy. But she doesn't know that. All I tell her is, "It was definitely more memorable of an experience than the prospective students tour we went on."

Embarrassment disguised as rage flashes across her face and spills out through her words. "It wasn't my fault! I can't believe I'm having to defend myself again, ten years later. We were stuck on that stupid highway for *five* hours in bumper-to-bumper traffic with no rest stop in sight. It's not like I *wanted* to pee my pants." Rosie crosses her arms in front of her chest and bitterly looks out the window.

I burst out laughing again. "God, that was hilarious. Thank god Mom's car seats were pleather and not fabric. Easy clean-up."

She groans, putting her face in her hands. "I'm not enjoying this particular walk down memory lane, Asher. But if you're going to insist on it, pick a better moment in our history to revisit. *Please.*" Sharp words slice through me, leaving a trail of paralyzing and painful venom.

I gasp quietly, shocked by her reaction. I was just trying to bring back what I *thought* were good memories from our past in order to avoid the unpleasant ones. Excuse me for misreading things. *Again.*

My jaw tightens, trying not to go there.

Ten years ago, she probably would've groaned, shoved my shoulder, and told me to leave her the hell alone or risk exposing one of *my* dirty secrets. But so much has changed... What did I expect? For things to go back to normal? What even *is* normal now anyway?

"I—I'm sorry. I didn't mean to bring up... *bad* memories between us. But I guess there are always two sides to every story, right? Because I just remember having so much fun. Some of my favorite memories come from that two-week road trip we took to visit schools." The entire time, I keep my eyes on the road. It's a clear, sunny day, but you'd think we were in the middle of a snowstorm from how focused I am on my driving. "I didn't mean to upset you. I guess I remember things being a little different." A pause. "As usual."

Okay, that was a low blow. But I tell myself it's the one and only comment I'll make about everything that happened.

"It's fine," she mumbles. "I—I overreacted. Just tired from travel and work, and I'm a bit anxious about seeing my family again."

I latch immediately onto the topic of her family, wanting desperately to steer the conversation away from us. Correction: from me and Rosie.

Silly Asher. There's no "us" for you.

"C'mon, they're not so bad." The corners of my mouth quirk up a little in a half-assed attempt at a smile, and the tension in the car seems to lift ever-so-slightly.

"You say that because you aren't related to them. Plus, I know for a fact my parents love you more than they love me—you can do no wrong in their eyes. I, on the other hand, am their biggest disappointment."

I *tsk* and shake my head.

"Seriously. I think Mom is proud of me, but Dad..." she sighs. "Dad is... Well, you know. I'm sure they would both rather I had taken a different path in life. Though I don't think they agree on which one."

I frown, wanting to ask her if things have gotten worse, but stop myself just in time. Distance. I need to keep some sort of distance here, or I won't survive the rest of the holidays.

"Just the thought of having to spend the next ten days with them, having to listen to them criticize my work, my life, and even the way I look exhausts me."

"What's wrong with the way you look?" I ask, a sense of protectiveness flaring.

"The pink hair?" Rosie points to her head, with a *duh* expression on her face.

"Ah." I nod before thoughtlessly adding, "Well, for what it's worth, I like the way you look."

Fuck.

I shouldn't have said that, right? That was weird. Was it weird? Okay, it was definitely weird.

Fantastic.

Though it sure as hell wasn't a lie; Rosie has *always* been beautiful. And now, nine years later, she's all curves and big, dark brown eyes—fucking gorgeous. And though her pink hair isn't natural, she's never looked more comfortable in her own skin than she does now. Rosie Castillo is so beautiful, I could barely breathe when I saw her standing there in the airport. Even now, it takes everything to keep my cool knowing that she's sitting next to me. My hands are aching to touch her, just to make sure she isn't some sort of hallucination.

My chest aches as I try to steer my mind away from how my body so easily reacts to hers.

"I just meant, the pink hair suits you," I push out.

Nice save, idiot.

"Thanks," she whispers.

I nod once, clearing my throat. My eyes have never been more focused on the road ahead of me, and still, I see how my one little comment makes her toasted skin flush.

"Anyway. I'm just trying to prepare myself. Mom is gonna do everything in her power to get me to move back home—she'll start by saying things like '*Ay*, Rosie. Aren't the mountains *increíbles?* You definitely don't get this view in New York,'" she says, mimicking her mother's Spanish accent. "Dad is going to lecture me about my career choice and how I made a colossal mistake going into fashion and costume design. He thinks I can still switch into something '*serious*'"—she air-quotes—"like finance." I try to control my smile as I realize she's about to go on one of her impassioned rants I used to love so much, with that sexy, barely noticeable accent. Glad some things never change.

"But Diana will *insist* I find a man and settle down and have a family. She thinks she's being a protective older sister telling me to give up on any professional dreams I may have just like she did, but it's like she doesn't know me at all. I'd give up my kidney before giving up my career for some guy."

I shift uncomfortably in my seat, my fists tightening around the steering wheel at her words. I shouldn't be surprised by them, though; I've learned from harsh experience she means what she says.

"We don't all have to have the same dreams or definitions for success, you know? I'm up for a promotion at *Celebrity Dance Battle*; I'm growing in the industry. Why can't they see that?"

She stops, exhales. "Sorry. It's a touchy subject."

"I'll say," I laugh. The topic of Rosie's family not really approving of her life choices has *always* been a touchy subject.

"Plus, everyone is going to be extra stressed because of Andrea's wedding. I predict this to be far from a relaxing holiday vacation."

"Oh, I could totally see that." I laugh softly.

"I assume you're coming, then?"

I nod and she hums thoughtfully before turning her head to look out the window.

"Why?"

She shrugs. "Oh, nothing. It's just, Mom had said you weren't going to make it, which is why I was a little surprised to see you at the airport."

"Really? That's weird. I RSVP'd months ago." And I've been anxious about seeing her ever since. I knew she hadn't been home in years, but I was positive she wouldn't miss her sister's wedding.

Still, I never expected to run into her *the second* I got to Colorado.

Out of the corner of my eye, I watch as Rosie fidgets with her fingers and mutters something unintelligible in Spanish under her breath.

"Is—Is that a problem?" I ask hesitantly.

"What? No. And what about your sister? Is she coming for the holidays?"

"Jessica's husband got transferred to Ramstein Air Base in Germany last year. They're spending the holidays eating *stollen torte* and whatever the hell else German people do on Christmas. But she'll be back home in time for the wedding."

"Awesome." She smiles brightly. "I haven't seen Jess in ages."

I press my lips together, my jaw tightening.

Don't be a dick. Don't be a dick. Don't be a dick.

I nod and clear my throat. "Yeah, well. I noticed you haven't been home in a while. I mean, I haven't seen you around here in years. Not since—" I cut myself off. "Well. You know. Not since that New Year's, right?"

I regret the words as soon as they leave my mouth and curse myself for acknowledging that night. I should've played innocent.

"Um..." Rosie fidgets in her seat. "I—I've been busy."

"Busy." An ice-cold word so sharp it cuts like glass.

"Yes. Busy. You know. Life. Work. Et cetera."

Et cetera.

The urge to snort is strong, but I manage to restrain myself. With a cold, dark voice that I can't help, I parrot, "Et cetera."

"Yes."

After a few minutes of silence, she speaks again: "I'm gonna call my mom, if that's okay with you." She rummages for her phone in her purse.

"Sure."

"*Aló?*" The volume is up high enough on Rosie's phone that I hear Julieta's voice, bright and enthusiastic. In the background on the other end of the line, I hear voices laughing and chatting away loudly in Spanglish.

"*Hola, Mami.* I'm on my way home from the airport. Should be there in an hour and a half or so."

"Great! So you made the bus, then? Your father was scared you wouldn't make it, but I told him it would be fine."

"Oh, um, actually..." Her eyes flash to me. "No, I didn't make it in time for the shuttle bus. But it's fine, because I... I ran into Asher at the airport. He's giving me a ride home."

There's silence on the other end of the line, the sound of a hand covering the receiver, and a muffled whisper.

"*Ma?*" she asks over the snickers.

"*Sí, amor.* We're—" A truck blares its horn beside us, so I miss what Julieta says. "—with his mom at the house, so you should tell Asher to come and say hi when he drops you off before he heads home. It's been so long since I've seen him."

It doesn't surprise me to hear that my mom is at the Castillos' since our mothers are very close. When their family moved to the United States, my mom befriended Rosie's, and helped her with the acclimatization process. Julieta saw a single mother struggling to balance work and her two kids and took all three of them in.

The Castillos were used to having a big family around them, which they had lost with their move. As I understood it, we not only filled that void they seemed to miss but overflowed it.

Meanwhile, we were in search of love and support after having experienced so much loss in such a short amount of time. First, with my father leaving us, and six months later, with the sudden passing of my grandfather.

Very quickly, our families integrated, sharing holidays and vacations, school pickups—you name it.

Our friendship was inevitable.

Loving her was fate.

"Yeah, I'll tell him. We should be home soon." Julieta inhales sharply, and Rosie rolls her eyes—at what, I don't know. She hangs up with a sigh, shoving her phone into her bag.

"Your mom is at my parents'. She said to stop by before you go to yours." I nod once. She pauses. "They're making *hallacas*."

I do my best to control my facial features from revealing the wave of emotions crashing over me. Is this a joke? Is today just a whole fucking cosmic joke? Is this the universe trying to be ironic or something? Because not only did we just happen to run into each other *at the airport*, but now, the first time I see her in nine years will be on the same day they're making *hallacas*? The first time we see each other happens to fall on the same day—

Is this us coming full circle? The sign of the beginning of the end of my story with Rosie?

Seriously, what did I ever do to the universe to deserve this shit? Is it because it's my life's calling to uncover its secrets? It's like it's laughing at me, wanting to twist the knife inside of me, when I just want to get out of this holiday alive.

Screw you, universe.

I nod once, terrified she'll see the emotions coursing through me, terrified to see hers. Or worse—and the more likely of options—the complete lack of connection or acknowledgment in them.

Does she even remember? Does she even remember what it means to us?

From the corner of my eye, I watch as she rubs her chest along her sternum, tired. Her brows pull together as she exhales deeply. With a frown, my anger melts as concern for her overtakes it. "You can sleep, if you want. I mean, we don't have to talk the entire way there."

I turn to look at her and watch her push back slightly into the seat, her eyes widening in surprise before the hurt takes over. Did she think—? Oh, shit.

"Yeah, you're right. We don't have to talk—it's best if we don't." She blinks back tears and keeps her eyes straight on the road.

Horrified with myself, I quickly try to fix the misunderstanding: "I—I didn't mean it like that." My words come out hurried; I can't say them fast enough. "Rosie, I only meant because you mentioned you were tired and—"

"No, no. I understand. Don't worry." Her voice breaks on the last word and I hate myself for it. She unwraps her scarf from around her neck, bundling it up into a ball into a makeshift pillow against the passenger window. "I'm just going to nap.

You're right—I need the energy if I'm going to deal with a full house as soon as I get home."

"Rosie—" But she holds a hand up to stop me before closing her eyes and laying her head on the bunched-up scarf, shutting me out. I watch her squeeze her eyes shut, lips pressed together.

My gaze turns back to the road with a loud exhale.

What a fucking nightmare. I didn't want this. I didn't want it to be like this. Whenever I thought of seeing Rosie again after so long, I promised myself I wouldn't let her see how affected I was by her presence. I promised myself I would be as friendly and open as possible—that I wouldn't let our past define the present. We wouldn't be friends anymore, but I didn't want there to be any anger or resentment between us.

I thought it had gone well, for the most part. But there's no denying that the damage done will be a little harder to leave in the past than I expected.

But don't I get props for being able to drive and talk all while trapped in this fucking car with her? With her scent and her voice and her face and just everything about her reopening wounds I worked hard to close?

God, this is a nightmare.

My heart races as memories of happier times flash before my eyes. Of Christmases past, of the first one we spent together, the instant we became friends. Memories of laughter, and being understood, and *hallacas*...

Chapter Four

ROSIE

12 Years Old

Papi *says that the best way to get used to this is to make the effort to think in English. He also said that he and* Mami *aren't going to speak to us in Spanish anymore, which I don't like.*

Before coming here, I already spoke English well. I think. But Papi still made sure we took intensive English lessons after school every day before our move. Just like he did when he was our age.

He later went on to study hospitality in this country when he was a college student before moving back home. Or I guess this is home now, and Venezuela... isn't. Not anymore.

I try to shake away the sadness, the fear of being somewhere so different from what I'm used to, praying my language skills get better soon.

Mami *says school starts after the new year, so I'm not even allowed to speak Spanish with my sisters. This morning, I asked Diana for her to pass me the* mantequilla *for my* arepa, *and she yelled at me.*

"We need to do our best to do good—well—here, Rosario. This new job is important for Papi *and our family. This is our new life," Diana had said.*

New life.

Diana is really good at speaking the language—almost as good as Papi. I think it's because she watched a lot of TV in English back home.

Mami says Andrea will learn fast because she's only eight and so young, and that it might be a little harder for me. But I'm twelve and that's young, right?

"Rosario! Come down to do the hallacas!" Mami calls. "And we have company. You have to meet, eh..." she struggles to find the right words. Mami's English is not so good either. "The..." I hear her blow a frustrated puff of air as I walk down the stairs towards the kitchen. "The neigh—neighbor? Jaime and her son."

I turn into the kitchen and see a woman and a boy sitting at the table. The mother smiles at me behind her cup of coffee, while the boy beside her lays his chin on his folded hands, which rest on the table. When his eyes, hidden behind thick glasses, meet mine, I see his cheeks pink, and he sits up in his chair.

"Asher, say hi to Mrs. Castillo's daughter."

"Rosario," my mother clarifies.

The boy fixes his glasses before asking, "Did you know that the grey wolf travels in packs of seven or eight? And even though they have complex communication skills, they don't really howl at the moon like in the movies?"

I stare at the boy and take a seat across from him. "No. I did not know that."

His mother laughs nervously, her eyes moving between the two of us. "Asher likes fun facts like that." She makes a face, and he looks up at her with a hurt look in his eyes.

"It's supposed to serve as a conversation starter," he mutters, looking down at his hands with a scowl.

His mother leans in closer to mine and whispers, "I'm sorry. Asher doesn't have many friends, so he's not used to kids his own age."

"I like wolves," I say, speaking up. It's not like I love them, but I don't mind the piece of information. It's...interesting.

The boy—Asher—looks up and meets my eyes, a broad smile appearing on his face.

There's a moment of silence as we stare at each other. Eventually, Mami breaks the silence: "Would you like to stay over for dinner? We're making hallacas."

Jaime tilts her head in confusion. "What are those?"

"They're like...Mexican tamales? But they're Venezuelan and I think they taste better. They have the stuffing of different meats, wrapped in plátano leaves." Mami winces, struggling to find the right words. "We eat them at Christmas on the twenty-fourth. For us, it's a tradition to have all the women in the family gather to cook them as a group around Christmas." Mami frowns, her eyes watering.

"This year, I don't have my sisters or mother here—just my girls. But would you like to join? You can take some home with you if you like them. Diego—my husband—is shopping with my other daughters for the rest of the ingredients, but they will be back soon. Maybe you can ask your daughter?" It's the most I've heard Mami speak in English at one time, and I'm so proud—I know it took a lot of effort.

Mami looks hopeful, the idea of a new friend bringing some much needed light back into her eyes. Smiling, Asher's mom puts her coffee cup back down on the table. "Sure. Jessica, my daughter, is at a friend's house. But I'd love to help—though I'm not much of a cook, if I'm being honest."

The boy chuckles a bit and shoots me a smirk.

"Will you stay, too?" I ask him.

Asher smiles broadly at me and says—

Chapter Five

ROSIE

"Rosie." I hear a male voice somewhere in the distance. "Rosie, wake up."

Asher.

"Mmmm." I groan, wanting to go back to the beginning.

"Rosie." A warm hand shakes me gently by the shoulder. "Wake up—we're here."

Sitting up with a jolt, my eyes fly open, and our gazes immediately lock. Asher slowly smiles at me as I process my surroundings, trying to remember where I am. "Oh." Just one look out the window tells me that we're parked right in front of my parents' house. "We're home," I breathe.

"You good?" He asks, popping the trunk open. I nod, rubbing the newly-formed knot in my neck as he exits the car with the surprising agility of a jungle cat. Seriously, how can a man so tall be so graceful?

Stiff with sleep, I struggle to pull myself out of the car and help him with our bags. "Don't worry about my stuff. I've got it."

"No, it's fine. I don't mind." He smiles down at me, and for a moment, I feel that light building in my chest again.

"*Finalmente*! My daughter is home!" My mother comes barreling out the front door and down the porch step, interrupting the very brief moment Asher and I were sharing. She engulfs us in her arms, squeezing us tightly together.

I wrap my free arm around her—the one that isn't pressed up against Asher's side—and roll my eyes. "*Mami*, we just saw each other in Florida a couple of months ago. Chill."

"*Sí*, but not like this. It's not the same as having you here for the holidays, *amor*." She pushes back and holds both my arms between her hands in an iron grip. "*Dios mío*, look at all this pink hair," she says, tugging at it. "When are you going to dye it dark again?"

I roll my eyes at her and push her hand away, bracing myself for more. "It's been too long since you've been here, Rosie. And that's not okay. *Mira!* Look how beautiful this place is! And how fresh the air is here. You definitely won't get a view like this anywhere else." I suppress a snort, and look over at Asher, who's smirking.

Told you so.

Turning my attention back to my mother, I say, "I'm here now. Isn't that what counts?"

My mother rolls her eyes and pulls me back into her arms—just me this time. After a few seconds, she lets go and hugs Asher. My heart does that achy thing it's been doing as he happily wraps his arms around her. I rub my chest where it hurts.

"*Ashercito*,"—the *sh* in his name sounding more like a *ch*— "How are you? I haven't seen you since this summer." *This summer?* "I've missed you."

Jealousy shoots through me like adrenaline. My mother gets to so openly express her genuine emotions with him. Meanwhile, I need to repress the sudden onslaught that has overtaken me since seeing him just a few hours ago.

"It's good to see you, too." Asher laughs softly and kisses the top of her head before releasing her. "My mother? Why didn't she come running out to meet me, huh?" He smiles teasingly.

"She went back to your house, *amor*. She had to speak with one of the buyers." Asher nods pensively.

"Buyers?" I stop in my tracks and look over at Asher, who stares back at me with a sympathetic look in his eyes.

"Yeah, ah. Mom's—" He clears his throat. "Mom's selling the store."

A sharp inhale of freezing cold air feels like icicles stabbing my lungs. "She's selling *Seymour's*?"

"Actually, it's already sold. But we have until December thirty-first to clean it up and hand it over."

A wave of disbelief crashes over me, because—No.

"B-B-But—"

No. It's where we grew up; where Asher and I worked for three summers. It's where I had my first kiss, right there in the dark stock room with the one flickering lightbulb.

Asher's pained eyes scan my face because I know he's also reliving an entire adolescence in one place—one we shared. "A new developer wants to make a big condo building there. They made Mom an offer she couldn't refuse."

For the second time today, my jaw drops in surprise. "But Asher... That's—That's your grandfather's shop." As if he didn't already know. My voice cracks on the last word because that place was like our sanctuary—our treehouse, of sorts. I know I have no actual claim to it, but I'm hurt no one felt the need to mention this to me.

Asher can see my pain, though, because he shares it. "I know," he whispers.

Mom pushes past me. "Let's not talk about this now." She turns and waves for us to follow, and he straps his suitcase over one shoulder, lugging mine behind him. "Come inside for a minute to say hi to the girls. We've been cooking all day. Then I'll let you go back to your mother."

Asher chuckles softly but otherwise agrees.

The state of disarray in my mother's kitchen doesn't really surprise me, nor does the loud, collective greeting from the women sitting around the kitchen table. Even if it's been a while, I know for a fact that *hallacas*-making day is all about drinking wine, bonding, and eating—*a lot*.

What does throw me is the unexpected feeling of homesickness brought on by seeing these familiar faces in my childhood kitchen, all while partaking in a deeply significant tradition for our family. We've done it several times over the years, but I obviously haven't been able to be part of one in a while, which leaves me feeling left out.

My little sister is the first one to greet me, abandoning her plantain leaf *hallaca*-wrapping duties, and rising from her seat to pull me quickly into her arms. "Rosie! Oh my god, you're here!"

I wrap my arms around my favorite sister, and breathe her in, letting the happiness of this sweet reunion spread over me like a relieving balm of some kind. It's been a tense couple of hours, and it's nice to have an ally.

Where I'm short and curvy, Andrea is a half foot taller and model-thin. Basically a Latin goddess, with her malachite green eyes and black-as-night long, wavy hair, my little sister has always been considered "the pretty one" in the family. But as if it weren't enough to make her incredibly beautiful, God or the universe or biology or whatever, made her one of the best people in existence, as well. Fiercely loyal, incredibly kind, and absolutely brilliant, Andrea is the whole package, making her fiancé the luckiest man in the world.

"I've missed you so much!"

I hug her tightly, inhaling her sweet coconut scent, squeezing my eyes shut to avoid a tear creeping out.

I've missed her, too.

Growing up, Andrea and I never really bonded or anything. When you're a kid and a teenager, a four-year age gap is pretty big. But a few years ago, just before lockdown began, Andrea had come to New York City for a job interview. What was supposed to be her crashing on my couch for a couple of days became months of being locked in my apartment together. We got to know each other as adults, making the best out of a terrible situation.

For the first time in years, I wasn't running away from closeness to people from my past. Unfortunately, Andrea didn't end up getting the job she wanted, leaving her to take the only one she was offered: a wealth-management position in Miami. Soon after, she met Alex, her soon-to-be husband, and the rest is history.

To say that I was sad when she left is an understatement. I had forgotten what it was like to have someone I could open up to on that level—to have a best friend. And though it felt great to connect again, it only made me realize how much I missed Asher. The fallout from our broken relationship wasn't just about me losing the man I was in love with. It was also about losing the only person in the world who understood me completely.

It's an awful thing to say, but since then, Andrea has acted as a sort of human Splenda over the past couple of years. I love her and she's the closest thing I have to a best friend now, but she's only made me crave sugar more—the true sweetness that was my relationship with Asher.

"Missed you too," I tell her, emotion clogging my throat. "But we saw each other just a couple of months ago."

Andrea releases me from her tight grip and looks down at me skeptically. "That was in May—seven months ago, girl. It's been a minute!"

Oh. I guess it *was* a while ago...

Someone snorts behind me. "Our little Rosie doesn't really have any concept of time, does she? Or familial obligation. You haven't deigned us with your presence for Christmas since you were in college."

I could've, if you'd have celebrated it elsewhere, I want to tell her.

I turn to face Diana, who's never been subtle regarding her feelings about my life choices.

Just like our dad.

Her dark eyes narrow in my direction, curly hair stacked high in a bun atop her head. She sets the glass of wine in her hand down on the kitchen counter.

"Hey." I smile and walk over to hug her just the same, because she's my sister. Though I would happily murder her sometimes, I'd also kill anyone who dared mess with her even a little bit. "I missed you, too, Dee."

She relents, wrapping her arms around me. "Yeah, whatever." But I can sense her grin.

From the corner of my eye, I catch Asher pull a spoon out from the cutlery drawer and stick it in the giant pot of beef stew stuffing, shoveling a huge scoop into his mouth. How he didn't just burn the roof of his mouth is beyond me.

Mom runs over to him and slaps him across the chest with a potholder. "Hey! No sampling!" He playfully rolls his eyes at her, but kisses the top of her head, playing her like a fiddle. "Okay, maybe just a little, then." Asher can do no wrong in her eyes.

He smiles at her and turns to my sisters. With a little wave, he greets them as if he sees them all the time. Andrea gives him a big hug, though, thanking him for coming all the way here. "Although I know you didn't just come here for me. *Duh!*"

He laughs and pulls away, patting her once on the shoulder. My stomach lurches at the contact, my skin burning with envy. Everyone is so open and honest around him, and I'm here measuring every single word that comes out of my mouth, every expression on my face.

Feeling like crawling out of my skin, I change the topic. "Dee, where are Rodrigo and the girls? And *Pa?*" I ask, looking around, expecting to hear the loud, buoyant sounds of Diana's husband chasing their two girls around the house, my father's curt responses and disapproving glances.

Diana shrugs and picks her glass up, taking an unusually long sip of wine. "Rodrigo and Dad took the kids out to the skating rink. *Alex* went with them, too." She shoots Andrea a look.

"Oh my god, Rosie. Can you believe *Papi* is making Alex sleep at the hotel? How ridiculous is that?" Andrea dramatically rolls her eyes with a loud scoff. "I mean, forget about the fact that we're getting married in a week. We've also been *living* together back in Miami for the past year."

My mother frowns, putting her hands on her hips. "Your father and I would like to live in denial, *gracias*. And if he doesn't want your boyfriend—"

"*Fiancé.*"

"—sleeping under *his* roof, then it's *his* choice. Your father is traditional, and he doesn't think it's appropriate for an unmarried man and woman to sleep in the same bed together."

My sisters and mother argue over living in denial, but I tune them out. My eyes fly to Asher's, cheeks burning a deep red as I realize he's looking at me, too. I'd stake my life that we're both thinking of how he would regularly sneak into my bedroom late at night. Of him climbing the trellis up to my window, knocking on the glass and sliding it open, and me letting him slip into bed with me several nights a week. Years of staying up past curfew, falling asleep on his chest after binging shows or movies on my laptop, of late-night talks. Years of offering each other support, when I couldn't stand to be around anyone but him, and vice versa.

And that one final sleepover...

The feeling of his weight on me, the way his fingers grazed the skin of my thigh, how we fought to keep quiet while everyone in the house slept. His soft lips against my ear as he whispered words that, to this day, make my heart ache...

I squeeze my eyes shut, the pain in my chest knocking me breathless.

No, no, no, no.

Don't go back there.

I open my eyes to find Asher's gaze on my mouth, but they quickly flit away.

"Sorry to interrupt, but I'm beat," he says over the sudden Spanglish arguing. "And I should probably go see my mom now before heading out to return the rental."

"Of course, of course," Mom says.

And with a nod, Asher leaves the kitchen, picks up his duffel at the foot of the stairs, and softly closes the front door on his way out without even acknowledging me once.

I stare after him, a little shocked. No *'See you later'*. Nothing. *Nada.* Not even a glance in my direction.

It hurts.

Chapter Six

ROSIE

Soon after Asher leaves, the front door to the house opens once more, bringing with it another shock of cool air into the kitchen.

"We're back!" my father's voice booms, feet stomping on the mat.

Immediately, every muscle in my body tenses, my whole being set on high alert. It's shocking how some people just bring out this response in their presence. One word from my dad, and I turn into a scared kitten, braced for his worst passive-aggressive behavior. Will he comment on my career first? My decision to live in New York? My lack of serious relationship? Or will it be one all-encompassing, heart-ripping comment that will ruin the holidays? (Those are his favorite to make—he has a real talent for them.)

He walks into the kitchen, followed closely behind by Rodrigo, Alex, and the two cutest six- and seven-year-old girls in all of Colorado. "Camila! Emiliana!" I can't help the smile that spreads across my face.

"*Tía!*"

I crouch in front of my nieces and open my arms to hold them at the same time. Savoring the moment, I squeeze my eyes shut and breathe them in. "I've missed you both so much."

"Well, you'd see them more often if you'd visit home from time to time," Dad pipes up.

Here we go.

"Dee lives in Denver, *Papi*, not here. So it's not like I'd see her anyways."

"Yes, but your sister visits at least once a month. Even Andrea, who *also* lives on the East Coast, has managed to come for the holidays."

I release the girls, place a kiss on each of their cheeks, and walk over to my dad, rolling my eyes. "*Hola, Papi.*" He pulls me into an embrace despite his comment, because he is my dad and I love him anyway.

"*Bienvenida, hija.*" He smiles, the tense moment passed as quickly as it came.

I roll my eyes at him once more, and move on to greet Rodrigo, my brother-in-law. "How ya doing, kid?" He pulls me into a bear hug, lifting me off the ground. "How's life?"

"Yeah, it's good." I smile up at him, a little hesitant. Since day one, my sister's husband has always given me this odd feeling in my gut. Though I've known him since their freshman year of college, I still feel like I haven't gotten a read on him.

I continue to make my rounds, moving on to my little sister's man, now. "Alex! How are you finding Colorado? First time here, right?"

"Yeah, it's been a lot of fun! We don't get a lot of snow down in Florida so..."

Crickets.

He smiles expectantly at the group in the kitchen, running his fingers through his light blond hair, but no one seems to acknowledge his "joke."

"Er, right..." Dad lifts an eyebrow and hands a grocery bag over to my mom.

"So, how long you here for?" Rodrigo asks.

"Day after *Reyes*, I think. So, January seventh. And that's *if* I don't get this new job promotion I'm waiting to hear back from." I smile excitedly, staring around at my family, waiting for a reaction.

Nothing.

My mother starts: "That isn't enough time to—" But is thankfully interrupted by Andrea.

"A promotion, Rosie? That's amazing!" She claps softly. "What would it entail?" I throw her a confused glance, because *she already knows* what it's about. We've been talking about it for months.

Andrea winks at me, and suddenly I realize she's trying to throw me a bone, giving me a chance to show off.

I clear my throat, and stand a little straighter, finally shrugging off my coat. "Well, if I get this, I'm going to be head of costume design for the entire show. It's a managerial role with a higher salary, creative control, and—"

"Managerial role? Really?" Dad asks, suddenly perking up.

"Yeah." I smile, hating how much I still crave his approval. "I'll be in charge of the whole team and budgets, too, not just the creative stuff." I suppress a wince, because, though I have full confidence that I can handle that part of the role, I'm not exactly looking forward to it.

"Wait, hold up. I thought you just spent a whole bunch of time working on set of some big fancy movie. Isn't that why you were in Utah?" Diana raises a perfect eyebrow.

"Well, yeah."

"So, you're going to do that and still work for that lame show?"

"Whoa! Shots fired!" Rodrigo laughs. From the corner of my eye, I catch Diana roll her eyes and take another gulp of wine. I glare at him, but do my best to control my reaction.

"The movie was a one-time thing. A fun project my friend Barbara asked me to do."

"Barbara Holt, right? I fuckin' loved her in *Phantom Fighters* as a teenager. She was *hot*," Rodrigo whistles. Dad's eyes widen like he wants to strangle his son-in-law.

"And the show isn't bad," I say defensively.

"Hey, no one's saying that, really. I think the costumes are the best part." I shoot my little sister a grateful smile.

"Yes, *amor*." My mother reaches for my hand and pats it. "You do such amazing work." My eyes widen in surprise. Mom always wanted different things for my life.

"Although it kind of sucks. The promotion is cool, but I was hoping you could introduce me to, like, a celebrity." Andrea stomps her foot in a childlike manner, accidentally stepping on one of Alex's feet. He winces, but doesn't protest. Instead, he stares down at her in adoration.

They're so in love.

Blech.

"Uh, I *literally* work on a show called *Celebrity Dance Battle.* As in, celebrities are part of the cast."

She snorts and shakes her head. "I mean *real* celebrities. Not the old, washed up ones trying to breathe life into their careers."

"Or D-list influencers," Rodrigo oh-so-helpfully adds.

I roll my eyes at them, not wanting to get into it.

Feeling neglected, Camila and Emiliana begin to run circles around the kitchen table, getting rowdier by the second. Diana looks over at Rodrigo, and asks, "Can you take them into the other room, please? Maybe set them in front of a movie while we talk?"

"*Pfft!* Why do *I* have to do it?" The rest of us go quiet as my sister and her husband settle into a standoff. The air in the room grows heavy and uncomfortable as we all pretend to look anywhere but at the arguing couple.

"Because," Diana says between gritted teeth, "my sister, who I haven't seen in seven months, just got here a few minutes ago and I want to spend time with her. Also, you are their father. You can take two minutes out of your day to spend time with your kids."

A tense silence falls over everyone as Rodrigo and Diana glare at each other. My sister's husband breaks away first, muttering a "Fine" under his breath. He calls out to his daughters and leads them to the living room; Diana ignores us and takes a long sip of her wine before serving herself more.

"*Aaaanyway,*" I continue, trying to distract us all from that painful interaction. "This would mean I would be in charge of the whole show's aesthetic and stuff. I'd have a lot of artistic license, which I didn't have before." It's actually pretty awesome. My brain is already buzzing from all the ideas I have to revolutionize the look of the show.

Truthfully, I've been growing bored there. We're very limited in what we can do as stylists on the show.

That was such a fun experience, especially since I was in complete control of how I wanted the characters to be represented. Sure, the director and producers and I discussed how we wanted them to look in general, but I was the one who ultimately designed their costumes. It was me calling the shots and making the big decisions.

"That sounds amazing, Rosie. So when do you find out?" Mom asks.

"I should know by the end of the year."

"You know, we ran into Asher on the way in," Dad changes the topic.

I guess we're done talking about my stuff, then.

"He's such an incredible, smart young man. And successful, too. Now *he's* bringing true value to the world with all the research he'll do." My heart twists in my chest, Dad's one-two punch knocking me breathless. Mom shoots me a sympathetic half-smile as I sigh and shake my head, taking Andrea's wine glass from her hand and throwing it back.

"Hey!"

Dad walks over to the fridge and pulls out a can of beer. Popping it open, he asks, "Do you know if he's staying long?" he asks me.

"I'm not sure. We really didn't discuss it."

"You were in a car with him for two hours and you guys didn't talk about how long you're going to be here?" Dad raises an eyebrow at me, skeptical.

"I—I fell asleep on the car ride here. Didn't really get the chance to talk much." Which isn't even a lie.

Thankfully, Mom interrupts. "Jaime said she doesn't know how long, but that he'll definitely be here for the wedding, of course. So at least until the New Year."

"Amazing! Glad to have him here for that." Dad smiles broadly and winks at Andrea. "This is going to be the best New Year's Eve party *The Inn* has ever seen."

The Inn is the misleading name for the most luxurious and grand hotel in the Vail-Aspen area. It's owned by a conglomerate of high-end hotels, caters exclusively to the rich and famous, and has been managed by my father for the past fifteen years. It's kind of a big deal job in the hotel management industry, even if you wouldn't think so, what with us growing up in a small town and all.

It has a fantastic reputation, and, each year, usually hosts the most incredible (family-friendly) New Year's Eve party for its guests. In the past, the parties were legendary for the glitz and glamor. But since the pandemic, the number of attendees has declined substantially, causing the hotel to bleed money. Because of this, the hotel group decided to cancel this year's party, and gave Dad special permission to host my little sister's wedding as a private party until tourism picks up (which, judging by the amount of people at the airport, might not take long).

Andrea happily claps, bouncing up and down in excitement. I swear, if Alex's arm weren't around her waist, she'd float away.

"This whole week is going to be amazing!" Alex kisses her on the cheek, both so calm and excited for this next phase in their lives.

"So, besides Christmas Eve and your wedding, what other events am I being forced to attend?" I smirk at Andrea, wanting to mess with her a little.

She narrows her eyes at me. "You *know* I sent you an itinerary."

"Did you?" I deadpan.

"Are you serious? Alex's parents get in tomorrow morning. We'll go pick them up at the airport and help them check in before dinner. *You* obviously don't have to be there for that. Then, we have Christmas Eve dinner here. And then—" She stops mid-sentence when she sees the grin on my face. "You're messing with me. You have the itinerary," she says flatly.

"I love you, but you're too easy." Everyone in the kitchen laughs at my strung-out little sister, who just pouts, crosses her arms in front of her chest, and leans into her fiancé. "I promise I read every single one of the six-hundred emails you sent." Alex lovingly wraps his arms around Andrea and gives her a kiss on the nose. She melts into his chest and smiles up at him with a goofy grin.

I smile at the secret moment they're sharing, so happy that my sister has found someone who so adoringly cares for her and her happiness. But I can't help but feel a pang of jealousy at not having that.

I could've easily, though. I was just too scared to reach out and grab it.

After an eternal dinner filled with an uncomfortable line of questioning (*Where's your life going? Is New York really the best place for you? When are you going to start a family?*), we all retreat to our own rooms. Diana puts the girls to bed on the pull-out couch in the den before heading to hers, Andrea runs off muttering something about beauty sleep, and Alex goes back to the hotel. Exhausted, I happily make my way up the stairs with Dad in tow. He helps carry my bags upstairs, refusing my help while Rodrigo doesn't even pretend to offer any assistance, choosing instead to help himself to my dad's finest whisky and the big TV downstairs.

Relieved to finally be alone, my breath catches in my throat as I take my childhood bedroom in. It looks *exactly* the same as I left it that New Year's Day, down to my parents' ginger cat sleeping on my bedspread (although he definitely has a little more white fur than he did the last time I saw him).

I don't know what I was expecting, because turning my bedroom into a gym isn't exactly my parents' style. But I don't think I expected it to look exactly like it used to when I was a teenager.

I feel like I've been taken for a ride on a time machine.

"Hey, buddy." I walk over to pet Manolo and scratch him softly behind the ears, and he responds gratefully with some loud purring.

In a sort of trancelike state, I run my fingers over the pink floral bedspread, walk over to the desk where I spent all those hours filling out college applications to schools my dad insisted on and ones he thought were a waste of time. My eyes peruse my craft and fashion corner, where I find a pile of old sketches beside a covered up second-hand sewing machine that was gifted to me on my sixteenth birthday by my favorite person—Asher. Above it, a corkboard full of magazine cutouts and inspiration, along with other sketches of projects I hoped to complete. In the center of the whole board, a bright blue sticky note with the words, "*Asher Wolff thinks Rosie Castillo is amazing, and everyone else sucks. Period,*" in my former best friend's perfect handwriting.

Laughing softly to myself, my eyes watering, I remember exactly when, where, and *why* Asher passed me the note our senior year. I had made sure to stick it right in the middle of everything else that inspired me. Yes, I've worked hard to get to where I am, but there's no doubt in my mind that I wouldn't be here if he hadn't given me the initial kick in the butt I needed.

With a sniffle and a sigh, I pull the tie from my hair, unbraiding it as I walk to my suitcase to pull out my toiletry bag and clean clothes. Just then, from the corner of my eye, I see the curtain for the window across from mine slide down.

It's him.

I get to my feet quickly, my heart in my throat, as I stare out the window across the joint driveway. Suddenly, the light in the room in front of me switches off, and just like that my heart sinks back down again.

Chapter Seven

ASHER

13 Years Old

ANXIOUSLY, I PACE MY BEDROOM AS I GAZE OUT OF THE *window into Rosie's room. I don't know whether she's realized it yet, but our bedroom windows face each other across the shared driveway between our two homes. It's how I know that, even though it's nearly midnight on a Tuesday, she's crying alone at her desk while scrolling through Facebook on her computer.*

I'm not some creepy kid who pulls out binoculars every night to spy on her while she gets dressed or whatever—gross. Most of the time, either my blinds are down, or hers are—so I've never really seen anything...interesting. Have I thought about it? Of course. I'm 13 years old, not a saint. Plus, it's not like I'm blind. Sure, she's my best friend, but Rosie is beautiful. And the fact that she hasn't even noticed it yet makes it all the better. But I'm not that kind of guy. Unlike some of the other idiots at school who drool all over her, I respect her. I care about her.

Which is why I can't take one more second of her crying like this.

She seemed a bit off earlier today, but said she was fine when I asked. I texted her a while ago, but I don't think she's even glanced at her phone since this afternoon. Normally, I would just go into my dad's old study and use our computer to message her, but it's late, and I'm not supposed to use it past ten p.m. Also, I'm pretty sure Mom would catch me before I even managed to start it.

Scratching the back of my head, I weigh my options. I could just let her cry it out and then ask her about it tomorrow in school. Or I could...? I could what?

With a frustrated huff, I slide my window open and stick my head out. "Psst! Rosie!" But I'm an idiot, because her window is closed, and there's no way she can hear me.

I gauge the distance between my window and the ground, and then the distance between the ground and her window. It's not that high... I could climb my way down the drain pipe, and then use the trellis against Rosie's house to climb up, and—

No—that would be crazy. Asher, you're being crazy.

But suddenly, she hunches over her desk, putting her face in her hands, really sobbing now.

"Okay, that's it," I mutter to myself, quickly slipping on my Converse. It's a struggle at first—especially since the only thing illuminating the way down is the dim streetlamp. But I make it down safely despite the biting cold spring air. I cross the driveway and make my way to the Castillos' trellis, mapping out my free-climb. With a deep breath and my heart in my throat, I carefully make it to Rosie's window.

I knock softly against the glass with one hand, while the other holds on tight.

Rosie yelps in surprise, so I bring my index finger to my lips and shush her. "Open up," I whisper.

Once she realizes I'm not a serial killer, she wipes the tears under her eyes and opens the window for me, helping me pull myself into her room.

"What are you doing here?" she whispers. I adjust my glasses and... *Jesus, how does she look this good in striped pink pajamas?* I blush, trying hard not to notice how good her mussed hair looks, wet from her shower. I gaze up at the ceiling, not wanting to make her feel uncomfortable.

"Are you insane?" she hisses. "If my dad finds you here, he'll kill you, Asher."

"I—I just saw you crying and—" I run my fingers through my hair, suddenly very aware of what I'm wearing (plaid pajama pants and my "Black holes suck" t-shirt). "Not that I was spying on you or anything." I wave my hands in front of her, afraid I sound like the creepy stalker I swear I'm not. "I would never do that. But I was getting ready for bed and I turned around and then I saw you and—" I exhale, wanting to die from embarrassment.

"Oh, I—" she sniffles. "I—I'm fine. I promise. I'm just—" Her voice catches and the dam breaks. She puts her face in her hands and I bring her to me, holding her tightly in my arms.

"What's wrong? Talk to me," I beg. I hate seeing her like this. Since her arrival, we've quickly become best friends.

"Hey Rosie," I whisper in her ear. I feel her smile a little against my chest—she knows what's coming. "Did you know that, on Venus, it rains sulfuric acid and snows heavy metals?"

She snorts and replies with, "No—of course I didn't." We laugh softly and she lifts her head to look at me. "You know, your facts have been trending away from animals and more towards the planets and stuff lately?"

I grin widely because she makes me feel seen. I have been getting more into astrophysics—but nothing too crazy. Still, it feels nice to know someone notices these things; I've never had that before. Even though I know Mom has been trying her hardest, I've seen less of her lately given that she has to support us by herself now and manage the business my grandpa left her. And my sister? Well, she'd rather hang out with her friends than with me. Which... Whatever. I don't care. I have Rosie now. I don't spend my days alone at home reading all the time or playing video games. I don't miss my dad or grandpa as much anymore. And I have someone super cool to hang out with.

Though I know that the move has been extremely difficult for Rosie, I like to think that I've made the transition easier for her.

"You trying to change the subject here? I'm not the one crying my eyes out, alone in my room."

Rosie shakes her head, squeezing her eyes shut. "It's dumb. Don't worry about it." Rosie moves to sit on the foot of her bed and I follow her, wrapping an arm around her shoulders.

"You've been acting weird all day today. What's up?"

She sniffles, and leans into my side. I inhale the scent of her shampoo—some flowery stuff that makes it smell nice all day—as she wipes the back of her hand over her nose. "It's my birthday in, like, half an hour."

"What? It's your birthday tomorrow?" My stomach drops. Rosie and I have been close friends for the past four months now, spending practically every day together, and I had no idea. I say we're best friends, but I'm pretty sure that's something I should've known, right? Why didn't she tell me?

"I didn't know. But... I don't get it. Why are you crying?" I've heard some people get sad on their birthdays, but isn't that something that happens to grown-ups when they realize they're getting old? I think birthdays are pretty cool. My birthday was in February, and mom took me on a trip to Denver for the weekend to check out the Denver Museum of Nature and Science—specifically the Space Odyssey exhibit. It was awesome.

"It's dumb, but I—I'm turning thirteen tomorrow and... Yeah. And I'm super homesick and—"

"Homesick?" I frown. Every time she mentions that she misses home or her old friends, it does something to me. It's completely irrational, I know. But I can't help the jealousy. "I thought you liked it here..." I grumble, forcing myself to remember that this isn't about me.

"I do." She reaches out to grab my face between her hands, forcing me to look at her. The palms of her hands feel nice and warm, and something starts to build in my chest as I stare into her eyes. "I mean, it took a while to get used to things. The freezing weather, American food, the school, new classmates, the language... Though getting used to speaking English wasn't nearly as hard as I thought it would be since being forced to speak it all the time. I know my accent's definitely gotten better."

"Just a little," I tease. But she's right; it's improved. She still struggles with vocabulary sometimes, but it's not as noticeable as before.

She smiles slightly and ignores me. "But I like it here most of the time. I like the fact that it's not dangerous. That I can walk to school without being scared that I'll be kidnapped or whatever. I like that there aren't food shortages. I like that my dad seems to like this job a lot better than his other one. And... and I like you."

I sit up straighter, my brows raised. That feeling in my chest increases just as I feel my eyes widen and cheeks blush. "Uh—"

"God, I didn't mean like that!" She drops her hands and rolls her eyes, laughing once like liking me that way is the most ridiculous idea in the world. "Not that you wouldn't make an amazing boyfriend, but you're my best friend. I don't think of you that way."

Great. That's exactly what every guy with a cute female friend wants to hear.

"Okay, good," I lie. "What does you being homesick have to do with your birthday, though? I don't get it."

"Well." She chews on her bottom lip, shifting on the bed. "Back home, my two best friends and I had planned on having a joint thirteenth birthday party. When we moved here, though, those plans obviously went out the window. But I just logged onto

Facebook about an hour ago and saw that they posted a bunch of pictures from last weekend and—" She starts crying again. "They had the party without me."

I pull her tighter into my side, wrapping both arms around her now, and kiss the top of her head. The floral scent coming from her hair fills my lungs and fogs my brain for a second. God, what is that scent? I want to smell it all the time.

She sobs against my chest as I wrack my brain for the right words to say to her. "I-I don't have many friends, Rosie. Besides you, I mean. So, I don't really know what that's like. But you and I can definitely spend the day tomorrow doing something special. Okay?" She nods against my chest.

"It's like they completely forgot about me. We were supposed to stay in touch, but I can't get them to reply back to my messages, you know? Do people stop being friends if they don't live in the same city anymore?" She fists my t-shirt and presses her face into my neck.

Gently, I release her and cradle her tear-soaked face in my hands, locking my eyes on hers. I just want to make her feel better, to let her know that I would never treat her like that. She's the best friend anyone can ask for, and those other girls are idiots for casting her aside.

"Rosie, I promise you I will never stop being friends with you. No matter where life takes us, okay?"

She sniffs and nods, immediately burrowing herself back into my neck. "Okay."

"Okay, then."

I hold her for a couple of minutes until her crying subsides. Finally, she lifts her head and asks, "Will you stay with me until it's my birthday? Wait until just after midnight to go back, I mean? I want to spend it with you."

I can't breathe and a feeling I don't recognize spreads through my entire body. "Uh, yeah. Whatever you want, Rosie."

"*Okay.*" *She stands and walks over to her desk, picking up her laptop. "We can watch an episode of* The Office? *I only started the show tonight."*

I contain my shock at this brand-new piece of information. How has she never seen it? Has she been living under a rock?

"Sure. We can watch a couple of episodes while we wait for midnight to come around," I say, excited I'll get to watch her fall in love with one of my favorite shows firsthand.

Her smile is blinding even in the low light coming from her nightstand. "Okay." She slides into bed, taking the laptop with her, and pats a spot beside her. But I can't move, because I'm suddenly painfully aware of every bone in my body, every single inch of my skin.

"So...You mean watch it in bed with you?" I practically squeak. Why is this so awkward?

She blushes and hesitates before answering, "It-It's just for one episode, right?"

"Yeah, yeah, of course." Moving slowly, I toe my sneakers off, climb onto her narrow twin bed, and lie down next to her over her comforter. It's so awkward, I almost call the whole thing off completely. It isn't until I wrap an arm around her and she burrows into my side, that we settle in.

"Is this okay?" She asks, her voice low.

I have to clear my throat before answering. "Sure." Closing my eyes, I focus on slowing my heart rate. Why is this so weird?

"So, I'm still on the second episode. It shouldn't be so difficult for you to catch up."

I smirk. "I've seen this before. You're going to love it."

She smiles up at me, sending my heart skyrocketing. "Yeah?"

I find it hard to answer for a minute as the dark chocolate brown eyes pull me in, turning my brain into something resembling mush. Finally, I gather the two functioning neurons in my head and manage to whisper, "Yeah."

Rosie restarts the episode she was already watching and adjusts the laptop so that it's balanced perfectly on both our laps. Unable to help myself, I close my eyes and inhale deeply—being as subtle as possible—letting the scent of her shampoo fill me once again.

After a few minutes, I look down to ask her what she wants to do tomorrow to celebrate, but find her asleep with her head on my chest. I tell myself I'll wait until the episode is over to wake her, that she deserves to rest after such an upsetting night. But soon, I close my eyes to enjoy the feeling of her body close to mine and fall asleep right next to her.

Chapter Eight

ASHER

Building out cardboard boxes has never been my favorite activity. It's not like it's because it's hard and tedious work. Nope. I've been in school now for almost a decade, moving from dorm to dorm almost every year (not by choice), so I've got it down to a science. No, my real hatred towards packing has more to do with the fact that I've always associated it with an ending. And I know what people say: every ending marks a new beginning, but I'm not one to quote Semisonic's *Closing Time*.

So as I stretch the packing tape over the bottom of the large cardboard box, all I can think about is how my grandfather's store is closing after over fifty years of business.

That's half a century.

But life is life, and sometimes things happen around us that are bigger than anything we can control and we just need to deal with it. There's nothing philosophical or deep about it—it's just facts.

"Hey, do you have more empty boxes for me?" Mom peeks her head out from her office—Grandpa's old office—and smiles hopefully at me.

"Yeah, I made a few more. Gimme a sec, and I'll bring them over to you."

"I'll get them." She reaches over to grab one of the boxes, but I quickly pull it away from her.

"Mom, I said I'll bring them to you."

She forcefully pulls the box from my hands, shooting a fiery glare in my direction. With nothing left to say, she quickly turns on her heel back to her office—but not before picking up another empty box on the way.

I put my head in my hands and exhale before running them both through my hair, my patience wearing thin after only a few hours of us working together. How am I supposed to help if she won't follow my carefully crafted system?

The chiming of bells ringing interrupts my thoughts before I let them run on in a frustrated rant. "We're closed!" I yell from behind the counter.

"Oh, I—" I bolt up straight as soon as I recognize the voice. "No, yeah, I saw the sign, but I thought—" Rosie walks around a wall of stacked boxes to stand in front of the counter, right across from me.

My breath catches as I stare down at her, heart racing. "Rosie."

How the hell does she *still* have this effect on me? *How?*

I cut myself some slack yesterday. I mean, how often do you see the woman you thought was the love of your life after nearly a decade? I told myself I was entitled to a mild freakout. Seeing her was like being hit with a freight train of bittersweet memories. But now? No. No more, Asher. You're done. Let it go.

God, but just look *at her.*

Her big, dark brown eyes look up at me from below a fan of full lashes, her hair peeking under a fuzzy, white beanie, pastel pink cascading over her shoulders and down her back. Her perfect, full lips part as if to say something, but she presses them together after reconsidering.

"What—" My voice breaks, so I clear it. Let's try that again, shall we? "What are you doing here?"

"Um." She looks down at her gloved hand, which I just now notice is holding a black cooler. "Mom wanted to make sure that you had breakfast, since apparently you missed out on her invite?"

"Oh, uh." I scratch the back of my head. I just couldn't bring myself to relive what happened the night before in that kitchen. Dinner tonight—Christmas Eve at the Castillos'—is going to be hard enough as it is. The entire week would be torture, if we're being honest. "Yeah, I wanted to get an early start packing up the store, since we're only planning on working a half day. Mom wants to get home early to get ready for tonight."

"Oh." She bobs her head, looking around the store, taking in all the boxes. The corners of her mouth dip into a frown before turning back to look at me. "Well, she made you and your mom some *arepas*."

I smile and take the cooler from her hands, opening it to find two round aluminum-wrapped packets. I peel one open and inhale the mouthwatering scent of one of Julieta's *arepas* filled with butter and grated white cheese, still hot and crunchy somehow.

The corner of Rosie's lips quirks up. "She didn't have *queso palmizulia*, so she substituted it for grated halloumi. I hope that's okay."

I nod with a grin, already on cloud nine. "It's amazing, thank you." I don't hesitate for a second, biting enthusiastically into it. It's so good, I nearly moan aloud.

Rosie laughs softly just as Mom walks in. "Hey, I thought I heard your voice!" Her smile is broad as she pulls my former best friend into her arms. Rosie squeezes her eyes shut as they hold each other in a tight embrace.

"Oh my god, it's so good to see you." Rosie's voice is thick with emotion, her eyes watering.

"If it's so good to see me, why don't I get to see you more often, then?"

Rosie pulls away with a grimace. "We FaceTime like once a month."

What the fuck?

Since when does my mother have regular contact with Rosie? And why don't I know about it?

"It's not enough." Mom puts her hands on her hips, narrowing her eyes.

"Clearly, since you forgot to mention something major." Rosie looks around at the store, frowning. "I can't believe you didn't tell me you sold *Seymour's*, Jaime." Rosie scowls.

Mom just shrugs like it's no big deal, as if she'd sold some random thing on eBay and not my grandfather's legacy. "I honestly didn't think you'd care. I mean, you haven't been around much."

I choke on my *arepa* and look away.

Wow. Go, Mom. But also... Ouch.

Rosie looks nervously at me for a second, before turning back to my mother. "Yeah, well... I'm here now." There's a loaded pause between us, but Rosie moves swiftly to change the subject. "Anyway, Mom sent me over with food. She wanted to make sure you were good since you were packing all day."

"Tell your mother thank you. I'm starving." She walks over to the counter and pulls out her *arepa* wrapped in aluminum foil.

"No problem. She'll be so happy she helped—you know her."

Mom and Rosie grin, but I'm still stuck on the fact that she's been in regular contact with Rosie all these years.

I fall quiet as I stare my mother down, but she blatantly

ignores me. I don't have to say anything for her to know I'm upset.

Rosie senses the tension and hesitantly says, "Well, I guess I'll just—"

"Actually, sweetie. Before you go," Mom cuts her off. "I know you came here to rest after your big job and everything, and I know everyone's going a little crazy with the wedding planning and activities and stuff, but I was wondering..." Oh, no. "Would you mind helping us out a little with the packing? I know it's been a while, but you worked here, so you know where everything is. And I'm sure Asher would be happy to explain his little packing system for you."

I shoot her a look and scoff. "Little packing system," I mutter under my breath.

"Oh," Rosie's eyes flash to mine. "Well—"

"It's just a lot more work than we thought it would be. We could definitely use some help."

"If we just use the packing system I developed, we—"

"Yes, but I need to leave and run a couple of errands, so you'll be one down," Mom cuts me off.

"I can mana—"

"Sure. I'd love to."

She'd love to?

"It would be like my way of saying goodbye to *Seymour's*. To all of the good memories I have." She shrugs, her eyes searching for my permission.

Eyes locked on hers I nod as a particularly amazing memory flashes in my head of the two of us in the stock room. I adjust my glasses and force myself to regulate my breathing. "You don't have to. I'm sure you'd rather go home and relax."

She snorts. "Relax *at home*? Are you new here or something?" She laughs, and the familiar sound wakes something in me. God, look at her laugh. Even her I'm-super-uncomfortable-but-trying-not-to-show-it smile is beautiful. It's like the sun, shining at its brightest.

The light breaks through my carefully built walls, so I smirk. "Family already started offering free advice on how to live your life?"

"Oh, yeah," she laughs half-heartedly. "They're all stressed out about finishing touches, and it's enough to make anyone crazy." Shaking her head, she mutters, "It's been an interesting morning."

"So you don't mind?" Mom asks.

I'm ripped right down the middle, torn between wanting to spend every fucking second together while she's here and wanting to be as far away as possible from her.

"I think I'd enjoy it, actually. I'll help for a bit before hitting the shops. I have some last-minute gift-buying I need to do for the girls. Andrea is currently winning the *Aunt of the Year* award after making our nieces flower girls in the wedding, so I'm trying to find ways to one-up her. I need to buy their love."

I laugh, but it's my mom who replies. "Perfect. I'll head out now, then. Asher could definitely use a couple hands' help." I try not to think about where I'd like Rosie's hands to *help me* exactly.

The thought comes unbidden, and I quickly shake it off.

And with that, we watch as Mom grabs her coat and walks out the front door, a smirk slowly spreading across her face.

Rosie and I stare at each other over the mahogany counter in complete silence for a beat. Yesterday, I was able to fake it—or at least make it work. And now? Now I have no idea what to say to the girl who ripped my heart out.

"I guess I'll just—" Hesitating, she slips her gloves off and unzips her pink ski jacket with a *zrrrp*. I adjust my glasses as I follow the trail of her hand from her neck, over her chest, to the bottom of the jacket until it pops open. It's not like she's wearing a tight catsuit and getting naked or anything, but it's the image that forms in my head that gets to me. The reminder that I've seen her undress in front of me before. That it was *me* pulling down her zipper all those years ago.

The sound of it, the sound of her undressing, causes an electric current to run through me, blood to rush down south.

Fuck.

But that was in a past life.

I look away, busying myself with piling the small packets of hand and toe warmers on the counter, getting them ready to be packed and shipped to another store we resold them to. Without looking at her, I say, "You can just leave your jacket on one of these hooks right here."

Suddenly, a wave of her signature coconut-melon scent hits me, and I snap my head up to see her standing next to me, placing her jacket and scarf beside mine.

Too close. Too close.

"What are you doing?" I panic.

"You—you told me to leave my jacket here?" She looks as anxious as I feel. "Was I not supposed to—"

"No, you're good. You just—I'm just—"

I'm just trying to figure out how I feel about seeing you again, but your scent and your mere presence have completely thrown me off.

"You what?" Her voice is small, scared.

"I just—" I open my eyes and look down at her, exhaling heavily. "Nothing. I'm... Tired." I take her scarf and coat and hang them before facing her again.

It feels like she's moved closer to me, even though I'm positive her feet have stayed right where they were. For such a tiny woman, she sure has the ability to fill up the entire store.

We stare quietly at each other, and there's so much I want to say. The good, the bad, and the ugly. Although sometimes it's hard to tell which is which.

Rosie traps her bottom lip between her teeth and her hands fly to her hair, her fingers working it into a side braid under her fluffy beanie.

My eyes scan her body, and—*fuck*—I've never wanted to touch anything or anyone so bad. "Rosie—"

"Asher—" We speak at the same time.

"Sorry, you—"

"You—"

I hold my hands up. "No, you go—"

"Please, you—"

"*Rosie.*" I sigh, exasperated. I laugh once and rub my eyes under my glasses. I hear her chuckle in relief. "Please. You go first."

She frowns and bites her lip again.

That fucking lip.

She slides her hands into her back pockets and stares down at her snow boots for a moment. "I just wanted to say that... That I'm..." She swallows, looking everywhere but at me. Her eyes finally meet mine, and I nearly dive into them. I'm like Narcissus and her eyes are the mirror in the lake, except it's Rosie that has me enraptured, and I'll soon drown because of her, leading me to my untimely death.

Okay, calm down. You're fine, Asher. Let's not be dramatic.

I get ahold of myself and clear my throat. "Yes?"

Her eyes flicker to my mouth and then back up again. I fidget with my glasses, heart beating so loudly against my chest in anticipation, I barely hear her when she says, "I'm happy to see you again."

My heart stops beating suddenly.

That was... not what I thought she was going to say.

Clearing my head from all the words I imagined—*hoped*—

she would speak, I merely reply, "I'm happy to see you, too, Rosie."

At least part of me is. The other part of me is terrified you'll rip me apart again.

She bites down on her lower lip again—this time to stop a smile from spreading across her face. "Good," she whispers after a pause. "Now put me to work."

Chapter Nine

ASHER

Rosie picks up my packing system in record time (take that, Mom! It really isn't that complicated), quickly getting us into a solid rhythm. After a couple of hours of working in near-complete silence, however, she breaks it with a heaving sigh. Throwing herself dramatically in the armchair by the ski helmets, she groans. "That's it. I need a break." I chuckle as I watch her spread out and throw her head back in an almost cartoonish manner. "I don't see how we're going to be able to finish packing all of this up in just seven days." Her use of *we* surprises me. Is she planning on helping every day, then? "I'm already so exhausted."

"If we follow my plan, it shouldn't take the entire week."

Rosie rolls her eyes at me and sits up. "Aren't you tired, though? I feel like my arms are about to fall off." She lifts her arms and wiggles them in front of her, giggling a little.

I smirk at her, bending my knees to lift one of the larger boxes. "Well, I've been doing most of the heavy lifting, so maybe a little. But I'm more hot than tired." Rosie's eyes land on my arms as I strain to carry the taped-up box closer to the door. I raise an eyebrow in surprise.

Is she checking me out? And being really *obvious about it?*

Nah, there's no chance.

"Yeah, you look hot," she blurts out, almost absentmindedly. Her eyes widen in horror. "I just meant temperature wise. Because you're basically down to your skivvies. Not because—"

Laughing, I carefully place the packed box next to the others. "No, I know what you mean. All those layers didn't really go well with the heavy lifting." I shed my sweater and flannel shirt about two hours ago, leaving only my long-sleeve thermal and dark jeans on.

"Right." She nods. "Well, you did a great job. If the astrophysics thing doesn't work out, at least you know you can fall back on being a professional mover." She removes her white beanie and unbraids her hair, shaking it out. "That is, only *if* you get rid of your ridiculous system," she teases.

I narrow my eyes at her. "It's not ridiculous. It's based on my own personal experience and thorough analyses and facts." I try unsuccessfully to maintain a stern expression, pressing my lips together to keep from laughing. "And I'm hurt you'd ever suggest that there's even the slightest chance *the whole astrophysics thing* would ever not work out."

She laughs once. "I'm *pretty* sure it's mathematically probable for you to end up in another profession."

"*Ooh*, look at you, using science in your argument," I tease, feeling a million times lighter than I did earlier this morning. "I'm impressed." She rolls her eyes at me, with a smile on her face.

Look at us, teasing each other like nothing's wrong. Maybe this is it. Maybe we *can* move forward. Sure, I don't expect things to ever be the same, but maybe that's for the best. Maybe that's the best the universe can offer me now and I think I'm perfectly fine with it.

This new type of relationship might not be the one that I wanted all those years ago, or even the one we had, but at least it's one that would allow us to be civil to each other, to talk without it being so painfully awkward anymore.

"Pretty sure that was meant as an insult, but I'll take it as a compliment." She laughs, the sound of it making my heart flip in my chest. "How are things, by the way? On the school front, I mean. Did you end up going to Stanford?"

I smile. We haven't had the chance to catch up, really, what with the big elephant in the room and not knowing what to say to each other. "Yeah, for undergrad. But I went to MIT for grad school. Am still, I guess." And so close to being done.

She sits up in her chair. "MIT? As in *Massachusetts* Institute of Technology?"

I look at her curiously. "Yeah, why?"

"You've—you've been on the East Coast for the past couple of years?"

Oh. I see.

"Uh, yeah. Well, four and a half." I scratch the back of my neck, feeling suddenly so fucking uncomfortable.

Rosie's face falls, and the vibe in the store shifts from light to heavy. "That's—That's so close to—" She swallows loudly. "I'm confused, though. Yesterday, my mom said you were in California."

They were talking about me?

"Yes, I was. I went to visit one of my former professors and mentor. He's at Caltech now and heading up a NASA post-doctoral fellowship I'm interested in doing after graduation."

Her jaw drops. "Holy shit—*NASA?*"

I feel my cheeks redden because... yeah. NASA.

"Yup. I'd get to study cosmic expansion and gravitational waves. I'd look at colliding black holes and measure the expansion rate of the universe by using data and looking at simulations and observations."

"I don't know what any of that means," she says simply, a huge grin on her face.

I laugh once. "It's a good thing. It would be a dream job. I'd get to do exactly what I've always wanted to do ever since I realized I wanted to go into Astrophysics."

"Oh, good, then." She nods. "And this would be in Caltech? In California?"

"Yeah. Pasadena."

"Amazing," she says softly, before turning her head to look pensively out the store window into the crowd of last-minute shoppers.

I watch her for a moment, taking in the delicate upturn of her nose, her full lips, and her slender neck. Taking in how achingly beautiful she is, her perfect bronzed skin, those deep chocolate eyes...

"What about you?" I ask, aching to know more. "I know the basics. Your mom told me all about you graduating with honors from school and *my* mom won't shut up about how amazing all your work on that TV show is." She smiles at that.

"You been keeping tabs?" Rosie smirks.

"No. Not really." And it's the truth. I don't ever let myself think about her if I can help it. It's too painful.

"Mom just yaps about you constantly. Loves to tell me how proud of you she is."

Now her smile is gigantic. "That's so sweet of her." Rosie looks over at the office door, as if expecting my mom to come out. "Yeah, I'm doing great. The job's okay."

I frown at her, surprised. "Just okay? I thought you said you were up for a promotion."

"Oh, I am. And you're right—it's going better than okay." She shrugs. Confused, I watch her face closely as she starts to braid her hair *again*—her nervous tic. "This promotion is a big opportunity for me."

Eyeing her, trying to meet her gaze, I push her. "What about this last freelance gig you did?"

She lifts her face and grins. "That was so cool."

"Yeah?" A slow smile spreads across my face. The way her eyes light up makes my chest expand and tighten at the same time.

"Yeah. I became super close with one of the actresses on *Celebrity Dance Battle* and she really liked my work, so she asked the studio if they could bring me on as the head of costume design for her movie."

"Whoa, that sounds like a big deal." I'm impressed, but then again, I've always known how talented she is.

"It was!" She laughs, her excitement contagious. "Especially since I had no prior experience whatsoever with that type of stuff." She rushes to explain, excitement clear in her voice. "I got to control the entire look of every character. In, like, a real Hollywood movie. And the pay was incredible for such a short amount of time of work, you know? Plus, the location was breathtaking. We were in Park City; you would've loved it."

I'd always heard there was amazing skiing in Utah, and, like a good Colorado native, she knows I've always been a sucker for the slopes.

I laugh at her excitement, happy to see her in a good place. "Sounds amazing, Rosie. Are you going to do another one of those projects soon?"

Her smile falls again, and she shrugs. "Nah, it was a one-time-thing, you know. Super fun, but not for me."

Frowning, I cross my arms in front of my chest. "Why not? It sounds like you really liked it."

Shrugging, she says, "Because I wouldn't have time with this new job. I would have to pick either *CDB* or going freelance, which is crazy. I mean, yes, going freelance sounds super exciting, but the show gives me financial security. And I like it," she says unconvincingly. "Even if it can be creatively... *stifling* at times."

I scoff and shake my head as I pick up a packed box and set it beside the ever-growing pile.

"I hate it when people say that. Having a job doesn't mean that you have one hundred percent financial security. You could get fired or laid off whenever. Businesses go under, pandemics happen, recessions screw up things. Literally anything can happen at any time and everything or anyone you know could be ripped away from you at any second."

She blinks at me, lips parted before whispering, "Jesus, Asher. That was bleak."

I shrug. "It's the truth." I know this from personal experience. *Experiences.* One day, you're playing catch with your dad, and the next, he leaves your family permanently to go join the other he had on the side. One day, you're learning how to fish from your grandfather, and the next he passes in his sleep from a heart attack. One night, you're in the arms of the woman you've adored for the longest time, making love, and the next morning, she's breaking up with you, screaming every horrible thing you've ever thought about yourself before she disappears.

"I guess you have a point, but still... I feel safer having a salaried job. And working on movies as a costume designer doesn't necessarily mean moving to LA, but I would definitely get more work there, you know? So I would probably have to move, which is something I'm not into. I love New York."

"So you would rather stay in New York than pursue something you seem to really want?" I wince, the words slicing my heart open as soon as they leave my lips. I asked her a similar question almost ten years ago, and it didn't go well. Gutted, the sudden pressure in my chest intensifies, and I struggle to breathe.

I don't miss how the words affect her either. Rosie slumps in on herself and grimaces, looking down at her hands with a guilty expression on her face.

This would be a fantastic opportunity to open up the floor and talk about every goddamn thing that happened. The fact that she toyed with my heart, massacred it, and left me behind. The stupid shit I did after, essentially ruining things for good—sealing our fate, as it were. Because I know I hurt her, too. I'm not ignorant to my role in this.

Though she started it, I definitely ended it. We hurt each other.

Her voice is cautious, yet defensive when she answers. "It's not about New York. I *like* my job." But I'm not buying it. Sure, we haven't spoken in years, but the type of friendship Rosie and I had? It's rare. It's the kind of friendship where, no matter what, we'll always be a part of the other. Which means I know her on a different level than she knows herself.

"Right," I say, turning away from her. And because I've never been able to compete against Rosie's career goals and aspirations, I say, "Well, you know what's best for you in the end," effectively shutting the conversation down.

Busying myself by stacking the boxes we managed to pack up, I focus all of my mental energy on not looking at her, because I can feel her eyes on me, and I just can't handle her right now. I promised myself I wouldn't drag all this up. I promised myself I would find a way to let things go so I could move on. Which is why I force myself to *not* look at her. I almost, *almost* cave when I think I hear a sniffle.

"Asher," she says in a small voice, finally breaking the silence. "I'm so sorry I did this to us."

Chapter Ten

ROSIE

I keep my eyes on Asher, watching as his back muscles immediately tense underneath his shirt.

He doesn't move, doesn't say anything as I beat myself up internally for my imprudence.

I've thought of this moment over and over again for nine years, have gone through every scenario I could think of. I've thought about where it would happen, how I would say it, *when* I would say it, what I would wear, and the words I would use to describe just how devastated I am that I ruined everything about our relationship. I've gone through what I thought was every possible outcome, and not once did word-vomiting a lame apology in his grandfather's store, sweaty from packing and heavy lifting, come to mind.

This is definitely not ideal.

But here we are—the words are out and there's nothing left to do but to push through my apology now.

"I-I'm sorry," I say again, my voice cracking. Tears stream down my face, and I bring my hand up quickly to wipe them away. Crying is the worst thing I can do right now; I don't want him to think I'm trying to make him feel sorry for me.

Asher turns slowly to face me, crossing his arms in front of his chest. His lips press tightly together as he looks at me through his round, tortoise shell glasses with an expression I can't quite pinpoint.

"I'm sorry I left the way I did. I'm sorry I disappeared and hurt you—hurt *us*—and ruined what was arguably one of the best friendships in existence. It wasn't just about the—" I clear my throat. "It wasn't just about us hooking up or my *other* feelings for you. It was about our friendship. And I know that I threw everything away because of my own crap."

He inhales, lips parted slightly. But before he can respond, I push on. "I know it's not an excuse, and I've never really been able to tell you about what happened that day. The fight I had with my dad about my future, why I ran, why I pushed you away and was so, *so* cruel to you, Asher. Because I know that I was. After everything happened and things calmed down, I tried calling you, but you didn't pick up, which I totally get—I was horrible. But then when I came home that winter break... I was going to apologize over Christmas, but your mom told me you were only coming back home from school for a couple of days for New Year's. And then that night..." I squeeze my eyes shut, not wanting to think too much about the details I still remember so vividly. "I looked for you. I looked for you to explain, but..."

"But I was busy," he murmurs.

I laugh once, humorlessly, running the back of my hand over my nose. "*Busy*. Yeah. You were *busy*." Busy mauling a blond on our bench when the clock struck midnight.

"Anyway, I know it might be nine years too late, but I'm sorry. I'm not trying to excuse my behavior, but I was—I was going through it with Dad and shit blew up and you turned into collateral damage. *We* turned into collateral damage."

Asher looks away, running the fingers of his right hand through his dark curls. I watch as he takes in my words, processing them, considering them carefully as he does with everything in life.

"Ash?" I prompt in a small voice.

He stares at his feet for a few seconds before meeting my eyes again. "It was rough, I'm not gonna lie. I can play it as cool as I want, but nothing's going to change the fact that it was a hard couple of months after you left." I watch his Adam's apple bob as he swallows once. Twice. "The things you said... The way you disappeared... It wasn't great. And yeah, I was hurt. I mean, you threw this amazing thing away before it even began as easily as if it were a gum wrapper. You made me feel like literal trash."

I bite back a sob before it can rip through my chest—I deserve the pain currently overtaking my body. "I'm sorry," I whisper as tears spill easily from my eyes.

"I know," he sighs, putting his face in his hands, head hanging low.

We're quiet for a moment as I painfully wait for him to continue. Asher is judge and jury as I wait for my sentence at trial. Have I served enough time of guilt and solitude over the years?

He raises his head as I sniff once more. "I don't know what I was more heartbroken over, you know? Losing your friendship or losing what was only just starting between us."

I gnaw on my lip, trying to still the loud heartbeat in my ears so I can hear his words. "What happened between us that night... It was life-altering, Rosie. And then when you left..." He blows a puff of air through his lips. "I was in pain and badly needed my best friend, but she had been the one to hurt me. It was...excruciating."

I press the heels of my hands over my eyes, crying openly now. Losing every bit of composure I have left, I fall forward a little.

I thought if I apologized, I'd at least feel better. But having every single one of my fears confirmed just made it worse.

Maybe this is my punishment. I deserve this. It was my fault, after all.

"For the longest time, I felt so alone." I sense him take a step towards me, feel him wrap his hands around my wrists, pulling my hands away from my face. "But it's okay. It ended up being okay." I stare in disbelief at the compassion in his eyes. "You hurt me—*a lot*—but I ended up growing from it. If you had gone to Berkeley while I was at Stanford like we had planned before everything—before we even got together—I probably wouldn't have done well in school. I would've wanted to spend every second with you." He takes another step closer, our bodies just inches apart, his hands tightening around my wrists, our breathing fast and shallow. "I would've been on your side of the bay every fucking weekend—hell, probably some weekdays. My grades would've dropped, I would've lost my scholarship. I would've prioritized time with you over joining clubs or doing research. You were already my world, Rosie, and after one night together, I was ready to make you my universe."

My heart stops for what feels like several seconds, only to speed up in my chest. I feel the light grow brighter inside, making it hard to breathe as I look up into his eyes.

"I was too in love with you, Rosie. It would've ruined us in the end."

Was.

I want to ask him how love could ever ruin someone. Isn't love supposed to be the purest of feelings? Lust, for sure—I can see that being someone's downfall easily. But for him to say that the love we had for each other was toxic is almost as painful as the reality that he's actually *happy* we never got together. Whereas I've been beating myself up, living in a world of *what ifs* for nearly a decade.

"I'm okay. Things turned out the way they were supposed to. I got over it."

I bite harder on my lip, trying to hold in what I really want to ask: *How? How* did he get over it? Because I feel like I'm living it every hour of every day.

"You don't need to feel guilty anymore, Rosie."

"How can you be so okay with this?" I ask before I can help myself.

He shrugs, a sad smile on his face. "After a few years, I promised myself that if I ever saw you again I would try to move past it. I realized that it worked out for me and I shouldn't resent you for it. I don't want to hold on to negative feelings for you and taint the friendship we had. Even though some days it's harder to forget than others."

He pulls me into him, using the hold he still has on me to wrap my arms around his torso. I fall into his chest, closing my eyes, inhaling the familiar scent of him.

Torture.

Quiet tears fall from my eyes while I cling to him. "It's okay," he murmurs into my hair. "Don't cry. We're okay."

"I'm so sorry for everything. Especially for ruining your shirt with snot now." I pull back and run my hand over my nose. Asher chuckles and cups my face between his hands, amber eyes on mine. I can see the hint of pain still in them, but he disguises it well.

"I have to apologize, too," he whispers, frowning.

"For what?"

"For hurting you back. I knew you were looking for me—Mom had mentioned it—and I knew you were going to be at the New Year's party. So I... I took a date. And... Well, you know the rest." Asher looks away, guilt clear on his face.

"Oh." I didn't think it would be possible, but I feel my eighteen-year-old heart break all over again. Part of me always thought it had been intentional—the whole holding-my-gaze-while-lip-locked thing was a dead giveaway—but it still hurt to hear it admitted out loud.

"I'm sorry." His frown deepens, mouth twisted.

I nod with a sniff. "I can't really be mad, can I? You were free to do whatever you wanted."

"But my intentions weren't good."

I fist my hands, considering my options: I can choose to be angry, fight it out with him. Or, I can try and let go, acknowledge that what's done is done, and it's time I moved on from loving Asher.

We stare quietly at each other for a beat while I watch him watch me as I process everything. But before I can make a decision, he asks, "Friends?"

The light inside my chest fizzles out, disappearing somewhere within, leaving me cold and empty.

I always intended to clear the air and move forward, yes. All so we could enjoy the next week without feeling like we're walking on eggshells around each other the entire time. But the way he says *friends*... It feels almost worse than being nothing at all.

"Yes. Friends. I'd love that," I lie.

Chapter Eleven

ASHER

I HADN'T PLANNED ON EVER FORGIVING ROSIE. NOT because I held a grudge and wanted to hold it over her head or anything, but because I knew that talking about how we *both* fucked up would reopen old wounds. This afternoon was case in point.

Regardless, it felt good to get things out in the open. After nine years—wounds or no wounds—a part of me felt optimistic we might be able to leave all this built up resentment behind.

It wasn't easy reliving that awful moment in our history. But when I saw her face and I thought about the petty role I played, I knew I didn't have a leg to stand on. Yes, she left me. But if I hadn't purposely tried to hurt her by hooking up with that girl from our class, then... well. Who knows where we would be now? I wasn't lying when I told her I probably wouldn't be as accomplished in my career if we had made it work. I know for a fact I would've made my entire life about her—her hold on me was that strong.

Who the fuck are you kidding? She still has a hold on you.

I groan in frustration as I mull this over, walking to the Castillos' with my mother, a shipping container's worth of gifts in both our arms. Mom shoots me a curious look but doesn't say anything as she knocks on the door and we're greeted by Diego. Suspicion still in her eyes, she watches me as I help her place the presents under the family tree, stopping me when she sees the thin rectangular box in my hand wrapped in festive teddy bear wrapping paper.

"What's this?" she asks, raising an eyebrow at me. "I thought you gave me all the presents that needed wrapping?"

"Oh, uh—" I clear my throat. "It's a last-minute gift I got for the girls from the toy store." It's only half a lie. It *is* from the toy store—just not for Diana's daughters.

Mom smirks at me and leans over to check the tag. "For the girls?" She doesn't hide the smile that spreads across her face as she reads the tag. "You've always been a terrible liar."

"I didn't have a gift for Rosie. I just bought her something silly because I had something for everyone else and not her." Also not a lie, but I'm definitely full of shit. I shrug casually. Pretty sure my beet-red cheeks are giving me away, though. "It's not a big deal."

"No, of course not." She winks at me. I groan and roll my eyes at her. "So, are you back to being friends?"

How the hell am I supposed to answer that question when I don't even know myself? We cleared the air, sure, and we decided we would move on and be friends. But are we really?

"Mom," I warn her. Before she can reply, I get to my feet, rolling my eyes at her. "I'm getting a drink."

I make a beeline for the bar cart in the corner of the room, stopping briefly to wish Rodrigo, Alex, and his parents a Merry Christmas.

"Asher." Julieta appears suddenly beside me with a broad smile on her face. "Merry Christmas, *amor*. You look so handsome."

"Thanks, Julieta. And you look beautiful, too." I grin.

She *pffts* and smooths small hands over her green dress.

"Would you actually mind making drinks for the rest of the night? It's just Andrea's future in-laws are here and Diego has to focus on them while I do the cooking, which your mother is helping me finish. And you know Rodrigo isn't exactly the most *useful* member of the family. I think he's allergic to helping out, from what I can tell. And you're basically family."

I suppress my laughter and nod. "Yeah, I'll be happy to help. I'll make sure everyone's good and drunk," I joke. Julieta pats me once on the cheek before walking away.

As I take a glass and absentmindedly fill it with ice, my mind races with thoughts of earlier this afternoon. My hands shake as I pour the gin over my ice just thinking of having to spend the rest of the week so close to her and having to act unaffected by her presence.

But I'm cool. We're cool. It's fine.

I add a cucumber to my G&T and take a long, refreshing sip just as my eyes fall on her. But because the universe has a sick sense of humor, I choke mid-swallow, my drink running down my shirt.

Jesus Christ, can't I catch a damn break?

Half of me wants to run away in embarrassment, clean up before she can see what a mess I've become since laying eyes on her again. But she's so goddamn beautiful standing there in the kitchen doorway holding a tray of *tequeños*... I wouldn't move from this spot even if you threatened me at gunpoint.

Pastel pink hair waterfalls down to her waist in soft curls, and her hips sway under the skirt of a knee-length black wrap dress—a color I rarely see on her—with every step she takes. The neckline of this sartorial torture device reveals just enough to tease me and make my lizard, caveman brain have to recalibrate. I grab a napkin to wipe the alcohol from my chin praying no one saw that, and adjust my glasses on my nose.

My heart takes off as she draws closer, dropping off the tray of food onto the coffee table, giving me a nice visual of what's under that dress. As she leans down, it shifts slightly and a burst of blush pink lace peaks through.

She hasn't noticed me yet, which makes me feel a little like a creep because I can't, for the life of me, imagine looking at anyone else for the rest of the night. For the rest of my life.

Finally, smoky, dark brown eyes meet mine with a mischievous look. I try to smile but can't really be sure the muscles on my face are working. I'm so caught up in her, it's like my brain's been fried.

I'm a twenty-seven-year-old man with a Ph.D. (well, almost) whose brain has been completely fried just because a beautiful girl—*the* most beautiful girl—is looking his way.

Rosie starts towards me with a soft smile on those red lips, and my breath catches, my heart squeezing in my chest.

Goddamn, this woman makes me crazy.

I'm not sure that I'm prepared to talk to her when she's looking like that. So I take another sip of my drink, needing the liquid courage as each step brings her closer to me—

—until her father pulls her aside and whispers something in her ear. She frowns at him before looking back at me with an apologetic smile. I exhale in relief as I watch her walk away because there's no way I was ready to face her just now. Jesus, not when she looks like *that*.

God, I'm so weak.

I finish off my drink and make myself another, even though I know deep down, I should be pacing myself.

It's going to be a long night.

"Hey, you." Her voice is gentle and tentative when I hear her coming up behind me. "How's it going?"

Well, I'm on my second gin and tonic, and considering serving myself a third in the hopes that it will settle my nerves because I'm a goddamn wreck.

"Good, good." I bob my head, forcing myself not to let my eyes wander down to her chest. Unfortunately, my gaze ends up flitting to her red lips, leaving me wondering whether they feel as soft as I remember. "You?"

Her eyes subtly scan my body up and down and I watch her swallow. "Uh, good. Thanks."

"You look really—" I cough. "You look beautiful, Rosie."

Her cheeks flush a deep crimson. "Thanks," she says, her voice breathy. "You look nice, too."

A loaded silence falls between us, as I'm dying to touch her, to reach out and pull her into my body. To bury my nose in her hair and inhale her scent, wanting to tattoo that look in her eyes onto the side of my brain.

Our talk earlier today helped us start to get past a lot of the pain we were holding onto. But it also enabled the wall I'd managed to build up over the years to start crumbling down at an unbelievably fast rate. It revealed just how big a part of me she still is, how I have never really let her go despite having thought I'd moved on.

My right hand tightens around my glass as I shove my free hand into my pocket—a poor effort to control the primal urge to take her by the hand and declare her mine before taking her to a locked room.

I thought I was over this.

I open my mouth to say something—anything—but am thankfully cut off by my mother. "Rosie, honey, where are our drinks? Your mother and I need fuel for all this cooking."

"On it like a bee on a bonnet, Jaime," she calls back.

I silently exhale in relief, thanking the universe for the interruption.

Just when I thought I was safe, however, Julieta pops her head out, too. "You do know you're both standing under mistletoe, right?" she notes, smiling devilishly at us.

Our heads snap back in unison and look up where there is, in fact, a small bushel of mistletoe tied together with a red bow secured to one of the rafters. It's so tiny, you can barely see it—which makes me think it was done purposefully so.

Suddenly, the room quiets, everyone turning to look with curious anticipation.

"Mistletoe? I don't remember hanging that when I put up all the decorations," Diego muses.

As I feel everyone else's gaze on us, my eyes remain glued to the offending leaves. I can't look down. I just can't. Because I'm suddenly *really* into the whole mistletoe kissing idea. But what if she doesn't want it? What if she turns me down? I'd totally understand why, given everything that we've been through, but can I really take another rejection from Rosie?

"Kiss her, you pussy." Rodrigo, of course. Diana grunts and rolls her eyes at her husband's crass heckle.

He really is an asshole.

A little bit terrified and a lot flustered, I look down to meet Rosie's gaze. To my surprise, it is not met with rejection.

She's... smiling.

"Okay, should we...?" she hesitates.

"I, uh—S-s-sure." I exhale as I place my drink back on the bar cart, panicked. What the hell do I do with my hands? Do they go on her waist? Do I leave them at my sides?

Fuck this.

You know what doesn't make this whole thing easier? Having a room full of people staring at you. The build-up is fucking painful.

"You okay?" she whispers. "We really don't have to do this if you don't want to. It's not like a law or anything."

"*No.*" I protest a little too insistently. Swallowing the massive knot in my throat, I take a step towards her, shaking my head slowly. The tips of my shoes touch the tips of her hot pink, rhinestone-covered stilettos. Just looking at them sparkle makes me smile—they're so *her.*

I collect myself before looking down at her sweet face as she bites into her lower lip.

Sweet coconut floods my senses, the scent of it pulling me farther and farther away from reality. I don't want it—all I want is this moment with her.

It shakes me to my core; I almost lose my balance.

Summoning every ounce of courage I have, I lean into her, sliding my hand over her waist, hiding my smirk as I see the skin on her neck rise in goosebumps. Her breath hitches and she releases her lower lip, which trembles slightly. Suddenly overwhelmed with emotion, I realize that Rosie is just as hypnotized by me as I am by her.

Unbelievable.

I almost groan when her hand slides up my chest, resting just over my heart, fisting gently around my blazer's lapel. I watch in awe as her breathing grows shallower and quicker, and the expression in her eyes turns into need. The thought that she wants this as much as I do? Well, there just aren't words to express how it makes me feel.

Rosie upturns her face, stretching onto the tips of her toes. Even in heels, the height difference between us is still significant, which means having to meet her half way. Not that I mind. Right now, I'd fucking travel hundreds of miles if it meant I got to kiss her again after all these years.

That last thought pops into my head with such conviction, I pull Rosie closer into me, her chest pressing up against mine. My skin practically vibrates in anticipation as I lower my face to hers. My whispered name, so low only I can hear, falls from her lips just before they meet mine. I stop just before, giving her time to back out. She shakes her head slightly in disapproval, and mouths the same words she did over a decade ago: "*I want you to kiss me*".

So I do.

I fucking kiss her.

And it's nothing like our first time.

It's better.

Chapter Twelve

ASHER

16 Years Old

THE JINGLING OF THE BELLS ABOVE THE STORE DOOR *followed by the frantic way she calls my name alert me to Rosie's arrival.*

"I'm in here!" *I call back, putting away the last of the newest hiking packs on the storage shelf.*

If the sound of Rosie's quick steps doesn't tip me off that something's wrong, the expression on her face when she swings the door of the stock room open definitely does. Usually, I can tell in an instant where her head's at, but as I take in her furrowed brows, eyes blazing with determination, and her stiff stance, I realize I'm in new territory.

"Hey," *I turn to face her, reaching out to take hold of her hand. She looks down at where they're joined, and frowns.* "What's up?"

"Tyler Wesley just asked me out."

My stomach drops. Possessiveness washes over me, irrational and unexpected.

When did she even start dating?

"Oh. Okay." *Because what else am I supposed to say?*

She glances over her shoulder before meeting my eyes again. "I-I need to ask you for a favor."

I look down at her, confused. "Okay? Yeah, anything."

"It's—" she blows a puff of air. "It's a weird favor. And I don't —I don't want you to read too much into it, but I don't trust anyone else to do it." I nod hesitantly. The look in her eyes nearly leads me to ask her if she's talking about burying a dead body or something. Not that I wouldn't help her. I'm pretty sure Rosie could talk me into anything at this point. I'd say yes without giving it a second thought.

"Okay?"

The words spill out of her quickly, her nerves getting the best of her: "I just want to preface this by saying that I want to do it already because I'm sixteen, and I think it's ridiculous that I still haven't done it and Valerie and Jenn were telling me how weird it was and I know it's ridiculous, and normally I wouldn't succumb to peer pressure but this isn't that, it's just me going out on my first date ever at sixteen without ever having done it is kind of making me super nervous and I don't want to embarrass myself and—"

"Rosie. Relax." My hands fly to her shoulders, and I shake her. Part of me thinks she may have lost her mind a little. "What are you talking about? What do you mean by "it"?"

"I—" She swallows hard, her eyes bouncing between both of mine. Rosie nibbles on her lower lip before blurting, "I've never been kissed."

I freeze and drop my hands from her shoulders. "O...kay? And how exactly am I supposed to help with that?"

She looks at me like I'm stupid for a minute, and maybe I am, because I would've never expected the words that come out of her mouth to be directed at me. Ever.

"I want you to kiss me."

My eyes glaze over as I process the words.

I. Want. You. To. Kiss. Me.

Something unexpected rushes through me—a surge of adrenaline, a tightness in my chest.

In all the years I've known Rosie, I've tried my hardest to not let myself go there, to never let myself think of her in that way—at least not too much. But it isn't easy when your best friend is attractive and you spend almost every waking moment together— and sometimes even some sleeping ones, thanks to our sneaky midnight TV binges in her bed.

My gaze drops to her full lips, imagining how soft they would feel pressed against mine. I let myself imagine what it would be like to slide my fingers through her dark hair while holding her to me. I let myself think about what she would taste like on my tongue.

No. There's no way this is real life.

Shaking my head, I say. "You can't be serious." *Maybe I heard her wrong. Maybe she didn't say kiss me. Maybe she meant to say... I don't know, but it sure as hell couldn't have been that.*

"Asher," *she breathes.* "Please."

This might be the one time I tell Rosie no.

"I..." *I can't think, so I back up into the stock room, urgently putting some much-needed space between us. Still, she follows me into the small room and closes the door behind her, the sound of the lock clicking into place sucking all the oxygen out of my lungs.*

"Please, Asher? I trust you and I just—I feel like a loser. Like the only person left in our school who's never been kissed." *She raises a shaking hand and places it over my chest.* "You've already done this, right?"

I nod, a knot in my throat. She knows about "Kissy Missy," as Rosie likes to call her, my science camp girlfriend from last summer who only ever wanted to make out. Rosie never met her, and the "relationship" only lasted the two weeks of camp, but it was clear my best friend wasn't a fan.

"Rosie," I choke, looking down at her. "I don't think that's such a good idea." I hate the words even as they leave my mouth. It's the moment I didn't realize I've been waiting for since the day I first met her. A normal guy would take advantage of the situation and let this happen. A normal guy would use this opportunity to get his foot in the door.

But I can't take it.

Rosie slumps, and looks down at her feet, her hand still on my chest. "I'm sorry, I know it sounds so dumb, but I'm so nervous... I'm too freaked out now. I wanted you to be my first kiss. I trust you implicitly, and I feel like I should know this stuff beforehand, and I don't want to embarrass myself with anyone else. I mean, what if I suck?"

I snort. "Believe me, you aren't going to suck."

"How do you know?"

"I just know."

"Come on, Asher," she pleads. "I want my first kiss to be you."

Is this a fever dream or something? Or did something heavy fall on my head while I was putting stuff away on the shelves?

Stuck in a moral quandary, I reach out and cup her face. Her skin is blazing hot, which makes me wonder if she's the one with the fever. It would explain the strange behavior. "I... I would feel like I'm taking advantage of you, Rose. I don't want that."

She meets my eyes, a blush covering her cheeks, and whispers, "But how would that be taking advantage of me if I'm offering myself up? If anything, I'm the one taking advantage of you." She grimaces. "On second thought, maybe you're right. Maybe we shouldn't do this... I'm being crazy—I'm so sorry." She pulls away, but I catch her by the wrist, pulling her to face me.

"No, I—I'll help you."

"Yeah?" She looks up at me, brown eyes bright and hopeful.

My eyes drop to her lips, plump and pink, and an electric current drives through me. Our breathing speeds as my fingers slide into her hair, angling her face towards mine.

"I want you to kiss me," she breathes again, her voice barely audible.

With shaking hands, she fists my smock and gently tugs me forward. Rosie rises to her tiptoes, stretching to get closer. I bend to meet her halfway, stopping with my mouth just an inch from hers. Her lips tremble against mine, her breath sweet on my tongue.

Unable to help myself any longer, I finally press my lips to hers.

The kiss starts off soft, at first. Gentle. It lasts less than a few seconds before we separate. But something lights inside me, and I lean down for another—deeper this time.

Rosie's breath catches, pressing her body into me. Her hands slide up my chest to lock behind my neck, bringing me further down, making it easier for her to reach me. Her tongue tentatively plays at my lips, and suddenly I'm as tense as a tightrope.

I thought we were going more for a peck?

For someone who's never been kissed, she sure seems...eager.

A shiver runs up and down my spine at the low noise that comes from her.

Jesus. I told her she would be good at it.

Wanting more, I part my lips and give in to the kiss. If this is gonna fuck up our friendship, I'm gonna go out guns blazing. My breathing speeds as my hands travel down to her lower back. Rosie responds to the sudden movement with a whimper, and it does something to me.

I break off the kiss abruptly, lips just an inch apart. Panting, we stare at each other, my glasses foggy from our combined heavy breathing. Even through my compromised lenses, with flushed cheeks under the dim light, her lips kiss-bruised, her dark eyes wide and bright, I've never seen her look so beautiful.

"Whoa," she whispers.

"Yeah." My voice is embarrassingly gravelly, but it's all I can manage to say as I try to think of random facts to calm myself down.

"Did you know that barcode scanners actually read the blank spaces in between the black bars instead of the other way around?" I whisper, but she ignores me.

One of Rosie's hands leaves my neck and goes to her lips, touching them lightly. "Is it always like this?" Her voice is soft, full of wonder.

It's not like I have all the experience in the world. But in the limited one that I do have, no. Hell no. It *is* never like this.

"Asher? Was it like that with—you know." She won't say her name, and I'm glad. I don't want to sully this moment by sharing it with anyone else in the universe.

"I—well, no. It wasn't like this, actually." That was nothing, and this was everything.

"Oh." Her face falls and she drops her other hand, falling back on her heels before taking a step back. I miss the contact immediately, having to consciously stop myself from begging her to put her hands back on my body. "Right. I mean, she was your girlfriend." Rosie makes a face. "I guess it must have been better, then."

I want to burst out laughing because nothing has ever felt as incredible as kissing Rosie. I have never experienced anything like that and—even though I'm only 16—I can't imagine anything coming close to it.

"It was just different."

"Different?" She raises an eyebrow at me, looking hurt.

"Not in a bad way," I quickly add. "Just that, each person is different."

"So it wasn't bad?" Her voice is small, insecure.

Is she for real? Was I the only one who had an out of body experience here?

I scoff. "No, Rosie. It wasn't bad." At all. How do I tell my best friend that kissing her was the best thing I've ever experienced in my entire life?

I don't.

A slow smile forms on her face. "Okay."

"Did—" I clear my throat, suddenly nervous. "I mean, did you like it?"

Her toasted skin flushes as she avoids my gaze. I stare at her lips, completely hypnotized. My grip tightens around her, unwilling to let her go. "Yes, it was, um... fun. So. Thank you. For that. I-I think I won't be so nervous when I go out with him later."

"Huh? When you go out with who?" I'm still half in a daze, I think, because nothing she says makes sense. I can't help myself as my mind begins to wander, thinking about the next time I get to kiss her.

God, who would've thought her lips would be so soft and perfect?

"Tyler. My date with him. Remember?"

Shit.

Right. She isn't for me. Friends. Only friends. Only a hot, amazing, smart, creative, incredibly sweet friend.

Who's going out on a date with the biggest douche in school.

Chapter Thirteen

ROSIE

"Did you know that mistletoe is actually super toxic? And that it's a parasitic plant that attaches itself to other trees?"

Those were the first words that came out of Asher's mouth as soon as our kiss ended. He breathed them against my lips at an almost-inaudible level, his eyes on mine.

A little drugged, struggling to keep my knees from buckling, I smiled lazily up at him and whispered back, "No. I didn't know."

As I sit in my parents' living room watching everyone open their Christmas presents, I replay that moment over and over in my head and squirm in my seat. For the hundredth time since, my fingers go to my lips, gently grazing them as I replay the toe-curling moment again.

From now on, it'll forever live rent free there. I spent the entire dinner distracted, thinking about how I really wished we hadn't had to stop.

As if insisting that we kiss under the mistletoe wasn't enough, our mothers insisted we sit next to each other at the crowded dinner table. "Because it's how we always used to do it, and it's important to keep up with tradition." So, with a bashful smile, Asher pulled the chair out for me, and we took our respective seats at the table side by side.

I called upon Buffy Summers for help, but not even the strength from the Chosen One could distract me from the lingering sexual tension. Every accidental bump of the knees under the table or brush of the arms as we ate—every single touch—felt like wildfire, burning away any rational thought from my brain.

It was extremely disorienting.

I sigh and look down at my glass: empty. Just as I start to get up off the couch to serve myself another, Asher gets to his feet, taking the glass from my hand.

"Red, right?" His voice is low, trying not to call attention to us as everyone continues to open their Christmas presents.

"Yes, thank you."

He nods and walks over to the bar cart at the other side of the living room, glancing over his shoulder at me once. My heart does somersaults in my chest at his lopsided smile.

From my seat, I watch the graceful way Asher moves, the way his back muscles look under his blazer, the way he runs his fingers through his hair before uncorking a new bottle of wine for me.

He hasn't changed one bit.

The thought makes me smile, reminds me of how he acted at dinner. How sweet and attentive he was; how we still remembered the little things about each other, even after all this time. I knew he was more of a *pernil* fan than he was turkey, and he knew that I preferred Cholula hot sauce on my *hallacas* instead of Tabasco. We didn't have to ask each other to pass one thing or the other—it was like we were on automatic drive mode. He'd cut me two pieces of *pan de jamón* and I would scoop a large serving of my *abuelita's* famous *ensalada de gallina* onto his plate—all without even saying a word.

It was...nice. Pretty much perfect, actually.

At least for that one moment in time, we were able to slip back into the comfortable and safe version of our relationship from our past. From the outside, it looked as if we were back to being old friends. Truthfully, however, I could feel how delicate the *true* nature of our relationship really was. *Is.*

I try to shake the feeling of foreboding as my eyes follow his return to me. Taking the freshly poured glass of wine from his hands, I smile just before he decides to sit beside me, neither of us interested in the gift-giving happening around us.

"Cheers," he murmurs, lifting his glass in the air.

I raise my glass and clink it to his, holding his amber gaze as he scoots closer to me. Unconsciously, I close my eyes and inhale his citrus scent, only to be interrupted by my mother calling my name. "Here. This present's for you."

I turn to look at the thin, rectangular box with the toy store's wrapping paper in her hands and blush.

Asher's gift.

"No, mom. You read the tag wrong. That's supposed to be from me to Asher, not the other way around."

"You got me a gift?" he asks.

Mom frowns and checks the gift tag once more. "No. It says here: 'To Rosie, from Asher'." She pushes the box into my hands. "See?"

I look down at the package and laugh. "You got me something from the toy store?" I bite down on my lip, trying to control my elation.

He laughs once and scratches the back of his neck, shaking his head. "It's dumb. I just saw it and—"

I rip through the paper, open the thin box underneath it, and gasp when I see its contents. "Oh my god, Asher!" One of my hands flies to my mouth. "Are you serious?"

I turn to look at him but am met only with a perplexed look

in his eyes. "Yes?" He looks down at the gift in my hands and then back up at me.

"Wait, are you fucking with me?" Not able to help myself, I burst out into a fit of laughter, ignoring Diana's "Rosie! Language!"

Asher frowns at me, looking like he's about to have a panic attack now. "Ugh, this was dumb. I shouldn't have—It's not supposed to be like a *real* gift. It was a joke gift. You know, because—*Hey*, where are you going?"

I get to my feet and search for the exact same box under the Christmas tree. This one with a tag that says, "To Asher, from Rosie". I hand it over to Asher and sit beside him. "*This* is what I got *you* for Christmas." I bounce in my seat, eager for him to open the box.

I feel several sets of eyes on us as Asher quietly stares down at the gift in his hands with a slow smile spreading on his face. It's sunshine and warmth and everything good in this world.

"You're kidding." He rips through the wrapping paper with an eager look in his eyes and opens the slim gift box underneath.

Asher and I burst into laughter as we realize we've given each other the same present: a glitter wand. Together, we pull out the clear plastic sticks filled with swirling colors and glitter—his blue, mine pink—and begin to move them from one side to the other, watching the confetti and colored bubbles inside mix together and sparkle, a riot of color.

"I can't believe we got each other the same thing." He *boops* me on the nose with the wand, and I swat at it, laughing.

"Well, I know it's a silly gift, but I bought it for you because of the stars." I shrug, trying not to jump up and down in my seat with excitement. He flips his wand upside-down again, and we both watch, a little entranced, as the confetti in his mixes with the blue liquid, creating a truly calming effect.

"I got it for you because of the confetti and glitter in it and, well, because it's pink and sparkly." He shoots me a heart-breaking smile. "And it just... It reminded me of you." Suddenly, we're in our own world, everyone around us forgotten. His voice drops down to a whisper. "Vibrant. Alive. *Beautiful.*"

My heart stops in my chest. It aches. It wants.

"Asher..."

"Sorry." He shakes his head, biting the inside of his cheek. "Alcohol. The kiss. Memories." And I get it, because, *same.*

We stare at each other for a minute, and I know he's waiting for me to say something, but I'm left completely at a loss for words.

I look down at my pink glitter wand and twist it around, watching how the sparkly confetti swirls with the fuchsia liquid. "Thank you for this."

He chuckles. "We got each other the same thing, Rosie. I think we did a total gift fail."

My head snaps up to meet his eyes. "Are you kidding me? It's beautiful. Yes, we both bought each other the same gift, but the reason we gave them to each other each have different meanings. You're a man of the stars—"

"And you're my lady in pink." He grins and my heart somersaults at his use of the possessive word.

I'm *his* lady in pink.

Chapter Fourteen

ROSIE

"You're getting it all wrong, and these need to be at the hotel in a couple of hours. Here, let me show you," Andrea tells me, her voice rising in exasperation. "You're supposed to put the map in the back of the basket *behind* the snow globe and the hot chocolate kit, not the other way around."

I sigh, wishing I could tell her where she can *really* put the contents of this basket. Instead, I hand everything to her and watch as she rearranges its contents.

We've been working together on building them for the past couple of hours since coming back from mass and I'm honestly over it. It's definitely not how I hoped to spend my Christmas Day—especially not after everything that's happened over the past 24 hours.

My mind wanders briefly over to Asher: to the glances we exchanged across the Wolff's dining table as both our families had breakfast together early this morning; the way he organized the chocolate chips in my pancakes into a smiley face, to the way he whispered, "Did you know that, in the US, the South consumes the most pancakes? It accounts for about thirty-two percent of total US consumption," as he handed me my plate.

My heart flipped in my chest, light filling me to the brim with his fun fact. The goofy grin that quickly spread across my face was impossible to control. I mean, it was all I could do to not throw myself into his arms.

God, I missed him.

Besides that brief exchange, however, Asher and I didn't speak much this morning. But it didn't change the fact that I would rather be spending the day helping him pack up the store instead of making wedding favors.

"Do you see now?" Andrea pushes the completed basket—white tulle bow and all—towards me to inspect.

"Yup," I say, popping my lips, not really paying attention to her.

"Really, it's not that hard. Diana and I are both speeding through them, and you've only finished five. What's with you?" She narrows her eyes at me.

"Nothing." I shrug, watching as Manolo plays with a small piece of tulle, tearing at it with his back paws, bunny kick style. "Just distracted, is all. Thinking about stuff."

Andrea smirks. "Oh, yeah? What stuff?"

"Work," I lie. "The promotion. I still haven't heard back."

My little sister snorts and shakes her head, pulling an empty basket towards her. "You sure you're not thinking about what happened last night?"

Diana lifts her head from her work. "What happened last night?"

I glare at Andrea because, *Jesus Christ*, does she have to provoke Diana? Andrea is the only one I've ever told about what happened between me and Asher, and I'd like to keep it that way.

"I have no idea what she's talking about." I glare at Andrea.

My little sister giggles but otherwise goes back to stuffing baskets with machine-like precision. A slow grin spreads across Diana's face. "*Oh.* Are we talking about that kiss last night with Asher?"

Andrea bursts out laughing, so I slap her shoulder. "Ow! *Jeez*, I didn't say anything. We all saw it happen."

"Yes, but you didn't have to bring it up! Plus, it was nothing. Not a big deal at all. Just a mistletoe kiss."

Yeah. The best mistletoe kiss that has ever existed ever.

"As if we don't all know that you and Asher had a thing growing up."

"*What?*" I screech, turning to Andrea. "You *told* her?"

"No one had to tell me anything. God, Rosie. It's so painfully obvious that at some point something happened. How could it not? Hormonal teenagers who spent all their time together? It was bound to happen. You think I never heard that guy climb up into your bedroom in the middle of the night?"

"*What?*" I repeat, horrified. "You—You knew about that?"

"Please," Diana scoffs. "Who do you think you're talking to here?"

Andrea covers her mouth to stifle a laugh with the back of her hand.

Traitor.

"I never got why you refused to publicly come out and tell everyone that you were dating, though. Were you two scared our parents wouldn't approve or something? Because Dad would've probably been thrilled."

"We never dated; we just—" I sigh. "I don't want to talk about this."

"They were never *really* together, but they did hook-up one time," Andrea clarifies, shoving another snow globe into the wicker basket.

How helpful of her.

"Seriously?"

"Wouldn't you rather she know the truth than make assumptions?"

"*No.* I'd rather no one know anything *or* make assumptions, thanks."

"I'm gonna try and not take offense at the fact that you chose to tell Andrea and left me in the dark." Diana scowls.

"I didn't *choose* to leave you in the dark. I chose to leave *everyone* in the dark. The only reason Andrea knows is because she was living with me at the time I had a small, alcohol-induced breakdown during quarantine," I explain. "Asher and I only had a one-night thing right after graduation."

A sudden wave of unease falls over me because reducing it to such simple terms feels wrong. What happened between me and Asher meant so much more.

"You didn't have a relationship, yet ten years later, you're still affected by a one-time hook-up?" she asks, with a raised eyebrow.

"Nine years," I mutter. "And it's not that simple."

"That's why you should pursue this thing. He's obviously the one who got away. How romantic would it be if you two got together again?" Andrea squeals, clapping her hands, almost floating away. "I mean, oh my god, it would be so cool. Just imagine it." Her eyes stare off into the distance, glazing over. "After all this time, she still loved him, and he always loved her."

"You're living in a fantasy world, acting like you're in your honeymoon phase when you haven't even gotten married yet." Asher wants to be friends—*just* friends—and even though the idea makes me want to throw up from the pain that runs through me, at least I know I have that. "It's not like that with him right now. He hasn't seen me in nine years. It's not possible."

Andrea snorts and shakes her head. "True love knows no time limit." I make a gagging sound and my little sister frowns. "That was mean."

"Don't get me wrong, sis—I love how happy and in love you are, but it's also kind of annoying," I tell her.

"If you don't believe me, ask Diana. She's been with Rodrigo forever. I'm sure she'll back me up," Andrea says confidently.

We both turn to look at our older sister, who just presses her lips together and walks over to the bar cart, opening a new bottle of wine and serving herself a glass.

"Dee?" Andrea asks.

"Yeah, sorry. What Andrea said." Diana forces a smile before taking a large sip of wine.

I check the time on my phone and frown. Isn't two p.m. a little early to start drinking?

I watch Diana's face as if finally seeing it for the first time since arriving. Dark circles under her eyes, hair messy, and... Oh god. She's lost a lot of weight. *A lot*, a lot. Her cheekbones have grown more pronounced, and her clothes fit one or two sizes too large. How am I just noticing this now? Her gaze stares off into the distance, dark brown eyes muted and sallow. It's like a light has gone off inside of her.

Andrea and I exchange a concerned look, seemingly realizing the same thing at the same time.

"You okay, there, Dee?" I ask.

"Yup." She tosses back the rest of her wine and pours herself another glass. "Super."

Andrea shoots me a look and mouths *"What the fuck."* I shake my head in confusion and answer, *"No idea."*

"Anyway," Andrea continues, pretending like everything's okay. "I think you should go for it. You guys have history. *Plus*, he's a Ph.D. who looks like he has a PHD."

"A what?" Diana and I ask at the same time.

"A Ph.D. with a Pretty Huge Di—"

"*Ooookayyyy*. We're done here!" I tell her, putting my face in my hands. I mean, from what I remember, she's not wrong. But I'm not about to tell my sister that.

"Gross, Andrea," Diana snorts.

"Come on, if you're neither gonna confirm nor deny my theory, you can at least admit that the guy is into you."

I snort. "He is not. He literally told me he wanted to be friends. *Just* friends."

"Oh yeah?" she challenges. "Then why the hell did he give you such a hot kiss in front of everyone, huh? That didn't look like a *friendly* kiss to me."

I bite my lower lip to keep myself from smiling just from the mere mention of the most incredible kiss of my life. The memory has my heart racing again. The way his hands slid into my hair, the scent of him filling me, fogging my head and clouding my judgment. How warm his body felt pressed against mine, how delicious he looked in that tweed blazer. The way his mouth moved over mine, and he breathed my name against my lips.

The fact that we were holding back because our families were present only made the whole thing better. It had my mind spiraling, imagining what it would be like if we had been alone.

"Look at you blush," Andrea teases me with a smug look on her face. "Now tell me again how it was just a friendly kiss."

I didn't say it was friendly for me, I almost tell her.

Ignoring her, I pull an empty basket towards me, haphazardly filling it with the stupid favors.

"You know, maybe we can try the mistletoe trick again this afternoon during the snowman building contest," she muses.

"How the hell are you going to hang a mistletoe bushel in mid-air, Andrea?" Diana asks.

She shrugs, unperturbed. "We can tie it to the porch roof or the aspen in the front yard or something."

"Crap. I forgot about the annual Christmas Day snowman building contest," I mutter under my breath.

"How the hell could you forget about that?" Andrea flashes me a smile and says, "Anyways, I'll get Alex to tie a little bushel somewhere to recreate the moment. Don't worry about it.

Maybe then we'll be able to finally determine *how* friendly of a kiss it was." I glare at her and toss a map of the Aspen-Vail area at her. She dodges it with a big smile and flips her long dark hair over her shoulder in a show of victory.

"You wouldn't." I glare at her.

Not that I wouldn't mind kissing Asher again. I just don't want it to be in front of my entire family like last night. I press my thighs together and try to clear my head before it starts fogging over with more fantasies of me and Asher, very alone and very naked.

"You're right. I wouldn't do that to you," she interrupts my daydreaming. "But I know other people who would."

Chapter Fifteen

ASHER

As we wait for instructions from the two women in charge—my mother and Julieta—I sip happily from my thermos. Hot coffee keeps me warm as I survey the crowd gathered in the Castillos' backyard for our annual snowman-building contest. A tradition that began sixteen years ago (fuck, am I old), it's not one any of us takes lightly.

"Hey." I hear Rosie come up behind me. "I'm so pumped for this. Aren't you?" she asks, buzzing with emotion.

Unable to help myself, the light in her expression brings back an excitement and fondness for this family tradition that I had lost long ago.

"I haven't built a snowman in forever. Well—not one of *this* caliber, at least."

I grin at her. "Get ready, because people have been upping their game these past couple of years." And I'm not lying. This snowman-building competition started off when we were kids, when they were just your classic two- to three-ball shaped little people with some type of prop associated with the theme. But by the time we were in high school, the whole thing had evolved into an insane, practically realistic snowman-building competition. There's no explanation for how a bunch of teenagers became magically adept at building these almost lifelike snowmen, but I'd bet every last cent in my bank account that it came from sheer, overwhelming competitiveness for this otherworldly—and completely useless—talent.

"Oh, I'm ready." Rosie rubs her gloved hands together, a villainous look in her eyes. "Ready to bring you and everyone else down."

I scoff. "*Please.* You're out of practice, and I've been doing this almost every Christmas Day for the past sixteen years. I've been an undefeated champ for the past five. Plus, I've always been able to beat you."

She mock-gasps and brings a hand to her chest. "You have *not*. I am way better at this than you are, and you know it. Need I remind you of Christmas of 2011?"

I throw my head back in laughter at the memory of how hard she beat all of us that year with the most amazing snowman in the shape of a polar bear. Rosie had found an actual fish from her mom's freezer to place in its mouth and beat us all by a long shot. "I will admit that was pretty sick." A current of electricity courses between us as we tease each other, our competitive nature coming out, proving that maybe this friendship thing can be possible.

Though having Rosie back in my life as a friend has me cautiously elated, the whole thing is bittersweet. The more time we spend together, the more I think about how this is all temporary, and how badly I suddenly find myself wanting it not to be.

Plus, the kiss last night didn't exactly help my jumbled thoughts on the matter.

"*Atención!*" Julieta claps her hands loudly to get everyone's attention. Rosie rolls her eyes at me before we both turn to receive instructions. "Welcome back to the annual Christmas Day Snowman Building contest hosted by Jaime and myself."

My mom nods once, looking out at the crowd as if this were the most important thing ever.

"To the first timers—and the ones coming back from hiatus—let's have a repeat of the rules. First: once we reveal the theme of the contest, you will have a total of *one hour* to complete your task. Five minutes to discuss what you're going to build, five minutes to collect props and tools from your car, inside the house—wherever—and fifty minutes of build time."

"Second," Julieta starts. "No copying other people's work. Third, *no sabotaging* other people's work." She glares at the two of us, pointing her index finger in our direction. "I mean it, you two."

Rosie tries to elbow me in the side, but I narrowly avoid her with a smirk. "I still maintain that your snowman tipped *itself* over," I whisper.

"Scoundrel," she murmurs back at me. But when I look down at her, I'm met with her full lips stretched into a vixen-like smile. My chest tightens and something inside me twists. The feeling is so intense, I almost wince in pain.

A sudden chilling breeze blows through, filling me with her scent, enveloping me with memories and snow flurries at the same time. Bringing back thoughts of what the delicate skin under her ear felt like under my lips, how warm her body was against mine, the way she whispered my name that night as I made her come.

With big effort, I look away, not allowing myself to get even more wrapped up in her.

"Whoever wins receives a prize," Mom continues, waving a white envelope in her hands. "Which will be revealed at the end of the competition."

"Now," Julieta continues, "because we are so many more this year thanks to our lovely future in-laws, whom we are very happy to have here," she smiles at Alex's parents, "we have decided that this year's competition will be carried out in pairs."

"*In pairs?*" Rosie, Andrea, and I whine in unison.

Julieta and my mom shoot us an angry look, silencing us.

"Wait, who's going to pick the pairs, then?" Andrea pipes up. This is vital.

"Well, let's see..." My mom and Julieta turn to each other, squinting and looking way too innocent. "I guess each girl will have to be with one of their parents, so Rodrigo and Diana will have to split up."

Julieta nods. "Yes, they'll definitely have to split up."

Diana flinches slightly as Rodrigo takes a step away from his wife, guilt clear on his face.

What the hell is going on there?

"Yay! I want to be with *Mami!*" Emiliana says.

Diana smiles down at her daughter and takes her hand, instructing Camila to go with her father, who eagerly leads her a few feet away from his wife.

Not my circus, not my monkeys.

"I think Andrea and Alex should be together, since they're getting married. It would be a great exercise to teach them about partnership and working together through tough times."

Andrea groans in frustration. "Are you serious? I'm the *bride*. Shouldn't I get to pick?"

"Hey!" Alex looks down at her, hurt in his voice.

"I'm sorry babe, but this is literally your first time seeing snow. Saying you lack experience in this area is an understatement. I really want to win this and I'm going to assume that I'll be carrying most of the weight here."

We all chuckle and Alex's cheeks redden. "I'm going to forgive you for that, but only because I love you so much."

Rosie makes a gagging sound, and I laugh. She looks up and

grins at me, and my heart tightens as I feel something shift inside me.

I think I might die before this competition is even over.

"This really isn't up for negotiation, love." Mom smiles at Andrea who crosses her arms in front of her chest and stomps her foot, powdered snow spraying her fiancé.

"Anyway, I think coupling up Diego and Alex's dad, Sam, would be a good bonding moment, as well. As for Alex's mom, we thought it would be cool to have her join us up here to drink mulled wine and gossip since we're the judges of the competition."

"Oh, thank god. I'm freezing my butt off here." Alex's mom half-jogs up the porch to meet our mothers with a relieved look on her face.

"And I guess that only leaves—"

"Wait, no. No, no, no, no. *No.* That is not fair. You can't have both of them on the same team." Andrea points in our direction. "It's not fair!"

Rosie and I look at each other, her hesitant excitement matching my own, I'm sure. Out of all of us, we're definitely the two best snowmen builders. Setting us up on the same team gives us a 95% chance at winning.

But it's not the increased probability of winning this year's prize that has me suddenly elated (last year, the "grand" prize was a sticker book—winning this has always been purely about bragging rights). It's the fact that I now have an excuse to spend the next hour working side-by-side with her, doing something we both love, working together as a team.

Unlike yesterday at the store, today's physical labor will be more fun than emotionally exhausting. Though wary of what spending so much time with her might do to me, I also can't help wanting to dive into these situations head-on. Rosie, on the other hand, looks somewhat hesitant.

This—*this moment*—is an opportunity to make things right between to two of us. I just hope she can see that.

"It's the most logical way to partner up." Julieta's voice is hard and final. Andrea crosses her arms in front of her chest, seething, while Rosie and I stand up straighter, predicting our basically assured win.

"Alright, we will start counting time as soon as we announce the theme of this year's competition which is... Best of *The Office!*"

Rosie and I immediately glance at each other, broad smiles on our faces.

"Holy shit, we've got this," I whisper.

She jumps up and down in place, hands on my chest to balance herself. "We *so* have this, Asher."

Chapter Sixteen

ROSIE

"Okay, let's decide what we're doing first," Asher says, words rushing out as quickly as possible. The way he's whispering—so low and urgent—makes me feel like a spy on a mission.

"I think we should do something with Dwight," I say.

"*Definitely* something Dwight-related." He nods seriously.

"Earlier seasons? Something everyone will know. I don't think my mom made it past season five."

"Mine didn't either." He frowns, shaking his head. "Why the hell did they pick this as the theme anyway? It's like it was *made* for us."

I wave my hand dismissively. "Who knows? They're both insane; they know we watched hours of *The Office* together." He laughs softly.

"If we're doing Dwight, we need glasses..." Asher looks back at his house. "I think I can get away with stealing my grandpa's reading ones. They don't look the same, but they'll get the job done, and I know where my mom keeps them."

"Sweet." I nod enthusiastically.

"What about hair, though? I don't think we'll be able to pull off a great hairdo. Can you manage being that detailed with snow?"

"No need. I have an old wig from that Halloween we went as JT and Britney in all denim? I think it'll work if we trim it."

He groans. "Please don't remind me of that costume. I cannot believe you made me go dressed like that to Lauren Nicholls' Halloween party."

I laugh just as we hear my mother yell, "*Un minuto* until you have to go find your props and then start building your snowman!"

"Okay, okay. So we've settled on this, then?" he asks anxiously.

"Yes, this is going to be great! I'll deny I ever said this, but you're better at the structural stuff than me—and definitely Andrea—so we have the upper hand there."

"Yeah, but you're amazing at detailing. That's where you used to get me." He winks, and my heart fills with light again. I feel like I'm glowing. Can he not see it?

"Okay, everyone," Jaime calls out. "You can go find your props and tools in three...two...one...*Go!*"

Andrea, Asher, and I shoot off like crazy, while the others slowly putter into the house. Diana pulls a spare scarf and hat off a hook by the front door, whereas Rodrigo has to be dragged by his other daughter to even consider picking a few things for their own. Dad and Sam look at each other and shrug, choosing instead to immediately start building their snowman without the use of props.

I locate the wig and a pair of scissors in my bedroom in record time and carefully barrel out into the yard.

"Two minutes before you have to start building!" my mother yells. "And remember, *both* partners need to be there to start the building process."

I groan anxiously, as I crane my neck looking for Asher, keeping my eyes on the front door of his house as I wait for him to run out. After a few seconds that feel like hours, he shoots out. "I've got them!" He waves the glasses in the air. "But I also got something else," he says, his breathing ragged.

He hunches over, panting, and passes me a stuffed animal in his right hand. "Mr. Stripes?" I ask, raising a brow at his sister's ginger tabby.

He nods, wheezing a little. Finally pulling himself together, he stands and looks down at me, cheeks flushed, glasses askew. Smiling, he says, "I thought we could use him as a prop for Sprinkles, Angela's cat. Let's just not tell Jess about it. She's still weirdly attached to her childhood stuffed animal."

"Oh my god. That's genius." He smiles back at me with that half-smile of his and I feel my knees turn to Jell-O. "I could kiss you!"

He inhales sharply at my words, but I stop breathing altogether.

It's just an expression. He knows that, right? He knows I don't *actually* want to kiss him, right?

Except that I really, really do, though.

He opens his mouth to speak, and I tense, bracing myself.

"Rosie, I—"

"Time's up! Get to building!"

"We're going to win. It's so freaking obvious we're going to win," Asher says, grinning widely. We snicker as he pats Snow Dwight's legs and I use a spoon to trace the outline of his shirt pocket.

"Let's not count our chickens before they hatch, okay?

There's always a chance of something catastrophic happening. Remember that one time Diana accidentally spilled hot chocolate over her snowman and the whole thing melted?" I ask.

"Yeah, but she was never going to win. Diana is great and all, but she's a shitty craftswoman." He looks up at me and grins. "Plus, it's basically just us against Andrea. I mean, I think Alex is a cool guy, but he's just standing there watching your sister work. And everyone else... Well."

I snort and nod.

Emiliana and Camila both only built regular snowmen with their parents, so they were never really going to win (but it's fine because I'm sure Mom has a consolation prize for them), and Dad and Sam quickly gave up after my mother informed them that the "*desk*" they had been trying to build for half an hour did not fit into the theme. "I meant *The Office* as in the television show, not an *actual* office."

With a groan, my dad had looked at Sam and simply said, "Drink?" before stalking off back into the warmth of the house.

"There's no way we're losing this, unless they're building something insane."

I laugh and survey the yard, watching Andrea and Alex bicker over how compact the snow needs to be. "Based on the tie around the snowman's neck that's been cut straight across and the mistletoe being used as a boutonniere, my guess is that they're building Jim the day of his wedding."

I guess she decided to use the mistletoe for other things, then, I think to myself, trying very hard to suppress my disappointment.

I do not succeed.

Asher leans over and squints at their Snow Jim from far away. "It's not bad... But I still think ours is better." We laugh as he pats Snow Dwight's butt and curves his hand around to shape it. I smirk at him, and he rolls his eyes at me without being able to help a smile. "Stop," he complains with a laugh.

Seemingly out of nowhere, Jaime's voice breaks through. "Five minutes! Five minutes to finish your snowmen!"

"*Jesus,*" Asher mutters under his breath, increasing his speed. "Let's start putting the finishing touches." Asher slides a stick into Snow Dwight's torso and carefully rests the stuffed cat on it. "Ta-da! I give you Sprinkles, pre-death."

I laugh and shake my head. "Right," I say, carefully placing the glasses on Snow Dwight. It takes a little maneuvering and a fine touch, but I eventually get them to fit on his face. With shaking hands, I reach for the wig and place it on his head, before grabbing the scissors.

"You got that?" He asks as he notices me struggle to cut the wig's hair with my thick gloves.

"Yeah, it's fine," I say. But as I attempt to part my Britney wig down the middle, Snow Dwight's head almost rolls off. "Shit!" I catch it before it falls, my stomach dropping.

"Fuck. Hold on—don't move an inch. Keep it still while I help reinforce it, okay?" I barely nod out of fear of ruining things as Asher moves around Snow Dwight, packing a bit of snow at the snowman's "neck" at the back. "Check it now. *Very lightly* let go of it and see what happens."

"Two minutes!" Jaime shouts.

I chew on my bottom lip and gently ease my grip on Snow Dwight's head but feel it immediately start to shift. I catch it between my gloved hands again before it gets the chance to roll off. "Nope, nope, nope. I need more snow here."

"Okay, okay." He comes around behind me, his chest pressed against my back, my head tucked beneath his chin.

Heart racing, adrenaline shooting through me as his scent fills my head, it throws me off balance a little.

"I'm gonna pack it on the sides from here while you hold it. Just don't move, okay?"

His arms cage me between his hard body and Snow Dwight,

and I wonder why the hell he would think I would ever want to move away from here. Sure, it's getting cold now that the sun is setting and the wind is picking up, but the heat radiating from him, from me, from *us*... The feeling of his hips against my backside lights a fire beneath my skin that overwhelms me, makes me wonder how it's possible I haven't melted our snowman yet.

I force myself to focus, to settle down, but just as I feel like I've gotten a hold of myself, a gust of wind blows around us. Asher's scent overpowers me, fogging my brain, loosening every joint in my body, causing me to slip and lose my footing on the snow and ice.

Before I can fall and topple the fruits of our many labors, his right hand flies to my hip to keep me steady, holding Snow Dwight's head with his left.

"You okay?" He breathes into my hair, the feel of his hot breath on my cool skin raising goosebumps. A small whimper escapes my lips when I feel him press even closer into me, the memory of him kissing down the column of my neck as he stripped me down to my underwear flashing before my eyes.

His nose grazes my jaw, which makes me grateful for the sudden knot in my throat and my inability to speak. Because I want to ask him whether he's doing this on purpose, whether the way his body is touching mine is intentional, whether he *wants* me to lose my goddamn mind with thoughts of him doing exactly this, in the privacy of a locked room, completely naked.

I clear my throat and focus on the fact that, whether intentional or not, we most definitely aren't alone, and this isn't a good time for daydreams (or, given its haunting nature, daynightmares).

"Yeah. I'm good. Just... Slipped a little."

I feel him nod once, a small *hmm* on his lips. With deep concentration, he works carefully to secure Snow Dwight's head, grunting once in a way that causes heat to start building low. As if by their own will, I push my hips back slightly into him, and Asher's hand freezes on the snowman.

"Sorry," I say. "I—I'm sorry. I didn't mean to—I was just trying to adjust my position and—"

"It's fine," he mutters before clearing his throat above me and pulling away. I feel the loss of his body against mine in a painful way.

"I think we're good now," he says in a tight voice. "The scissors? We have less than a minute to cut his hair."

I hand them over to him in a trance-like state, and he quickly does a better job at snipping the fake tresses into something resembling Actual Dwight's hair.

Once he's done, he turns to me, looking down with a question in his eyes. His gaze flicks down to my lips for a second before he adjusts his glasses on his nose, red from the cold. He takes a step closer to me, and he's so tall I have to crane my neck just to keep my gaze locked on his. Our breathing comes in a little harder, a little faster. I fight the urge to touch him, to run my hands all over his body and feel every plane and muscle. In an effort to restrain myself, I reach up to my hair and begin to braid it, keeping my hands busy and away from where they really want to be.

He stops my movements with a trembling hand. With a wondrous look in his eyes, Asher takes a pastel pink lock and wraps it around his gloved finger.

A sharp inhale, and I stop breathing altogether.

At the sound, Asher's amber eyes flash to me once more, darkened with a need and hunger that makes my toes curl inside my boots and my core heat even in this moment where the temperature is dropping by the minute.

"*Rosie*," he mouths, looking down at me like I'm something to eat.

I love it.

He tugs on my hair a little, opening his mouth to say something—
"Time's up!"

Chapter Seventeen

ASHER

"It's a masterpiece."

"I've truly never seen anything like it."

"They'll talk about it for years to come."

"Fanfic will be written about it."

"They'll write epics about it, passed down through time, performed in theaters *and* studied in classrooms all over the world."

"Oh, *shut up*, you two," Andrea hisses, crossing her arms in front of her chest. Rosie and I burst out laughing, a lasso tightening around my heart. Rosie slips, and I move quickly to catch her, holding her up as she damn near collapses from laughter. Her breath catches as I pull her up and, not being able to help myself, pull her briefly into me before letting her go. She looks up at me with a smirk, dark brown eyes scanning me for any hint of what I might be thinking.

I suspect she knows exactly what's going through my mind. Or at least part of it. And from the looks she's been giving me, I don't think I'd be too far off in saying that she isn't feeling something similar.

"This stupid contest was rigged." Andrea pouts, pulling Rosie and I away from our silent exchange. "You put *both* of them together *and* practically chose a theme made for them." She points accusingly at the two smug matriarchs standing on the top of the porch steps.

"Come on, Andrea. Your mother and Jaime would never do such a thing. Why would they rig the contest anyway?" Diego asks.

We all turn to look at our mothers expectantly, only to have them stare back, daring us to challenge them.

We don't. Naturally. It doesn't take a Ph.D. to know you should never cross two determined matriarchs—especially when they're my mother and Julieta. The first, a single mother who suffered deep losses and struggled to balance supporting her two kids *and* running a small business at the same time. The latter, a woman who followed her husband's career, giving up her own, to a new country with limited knowledge of the language, losing every bit of the large support system they had back home. Two strong women who found each other, support each other, and consequently take no shit from anyone in life.

No, sir. You do not question Jaime Wolff or Julieta Castillo, regardless of how suspicious they've been acting.

"I don't like your attitude, Andrea." Julieta narrows her eyes at her daughter before passing her a cup of hot chocolate from a tray. "And you seem to be the only one complaining."

Andrea huffs and takes the mug from her mother but doesn't press the issue further. Meanwhile, our mothers innocently hand a cup to everyone else in the group, giving Emiliana and Camila the ones with "super duper extra marshmallows."

I guess once you hit a certain age, you stop getting extra marshmallows, then? I look down at the three mini ones floating in my hot cocoa—practically needing the James Webb telescope to do so—as they quickly melt. "Adulting sucks," I mumble.

"Preach," I hear Rosie whisper next to me, lifting her own mug in understanding.

My heart warms in my chest, and it's not because of the marshmallow-deprived chocolatey goodness I currently plan on mainlining after standing in the snow for over an hour. It's her smile and the look in her eye right before they called time. I wanted—*want*—to take her by the hand and pull her away and leave everyone behind so I could just *be* with her. In any way she'll have me. I just want time alone with her.

"Can we get this over with? I'm cold, and I don't want my wedding guests—" Alex clears his throat and Andrea's eyes flash to him—"*Our. Our* wedding guests to wonder why I'm suddenly walking down the aisle covered in frostbite over a stupid, rigged contest."

Alex face-palms himself and groans, shaking his head. "Don't you think you're being a bit dramatic about this whole thing?"

"Nope."

With a sigh, both moms begin to survey Andrea and Alex's Snow Jim, and it's not half bad. It's made up of two large rectangle-esque pieces for the legs and torso with carved out details. You can tell that real effort went into it, but that the base looks a little flimsy. Atop the two larger pieces sits a round one, meant to be Snow Jim's head, with a cut tie wrapped around its neck (or lack of it, because Snow Jim has no neck).

"Is that my tie? Did you cut my tie just for the contest?" Diego asks, raising his voice.

Andrea just rolls her eyes and waves her hand dismissively at him. "I'm the bride, *Papi.*" As if that should clear her from all crimes from here until her wedding day.

Rosie and I both snort and glance at each other.

Julieta and Jaime go over to Snow Jim and scrutinize it in whispers, pointing at the hairdo Andrea tried to replicate using leaves attached to the head by sticking twigs through them like pins (a genius move I'll have to use for next year, if you ask me).

The detail work is so good that, for a second—*half* a second— I wonder whether they've got us beat.

But then they move on to our snowman and both our moms grin widely at Snow Dwight.

"This is incredible," Mom says. She looks up, her eyes bouncing between Rosie and me with a tender smile on her face. "You know, you two work really well together. *Look* at this. You make a fantastic team." I don't miss her meaning as she grins broadly and inspects our snowman closely with Julieta. Hoping Rosie didn't catch that, I run my fingers through my hair, trying so hard not to look at her. Finally, I cave and chance a look, catching her staring up at me, cheeks flushed.

We stare at each other in silence while the others discuss our snowman, and the urge to ask her whether she wants to get out of here becomes almost unbearable. But just seconds before I feel myself succumb to my need, I'm pulled back to reality.

"After much consideration, Julieta and I have made our decision," Mom starts.

"Can we do this inside? I'm freezing," Rodrigo asks.

"No!" we all bark in unison.

"Diego and Sam were obviously disqualified, and aren't placing at all. Tied for third place are Emiliana and Diana and Camila and Rodrigo." The girls cheer, jumping up and down in excitement, while we all clap for them. "Please come over here to collect your prize." The girls run up to the porch to meet their grandmother and my mom and immediately proceed to rip open the bag they're each awarded, its contents full of different types of candy and chocolate. (Definitely gonna sweet talk the girls into giving their favorite Uncle Asher one of those Twix.)

"And in second place..." Mom eyes us carefully with a knowing smirk. I can practically feel Rosie vibrating as she chews on her bottom lip, anxiously braiding and unbraiding her pink hair.

"*Jaime*, come *on*," Andrea whines.

With a smile, Mom's gaze drops to me and Rosie as she says, "Second place is for Andrea and Alex, which means Rosie and Asher win first prize."

"Yes! We won!" With a laugh, Rosie jumps into my arms.

I catch her legs as they wrap around me, her hands laced behind my neck. I bounce her in the air, laughing, unable to control the joy surging through me.

"We did it, Ash!" She says, looking down at me. Her radiant smile is breathtaking; I can't help the way it makes my chest constrict.

"We fucking *nailed* it, Rose." She bites her lip and burrows her face into my neck as I close my eyes and try to remember this moment, this feeling, for when I go back to being all alone. I'd love to deny I want her, but having her like this in my arms, her frame wrapped around my body... Even *I* can't lie to myself.

I *do* want Rosie. I want all of her.

But she'll never want me—not in the same way—which is why I desperately hold on as long as I can. That is, until we both seem to realize at the same time that: A. the way we're touching each other is wildly inappropriate, considering our history; and B. It is *especially* inappropriate when you're surrounded by other family members and friends.

She pulls away, and I help her slide down my body. I take a step back and adjust my glasses, while laughing awkwardly, trying my hardest to play it off like everything is perfect, like it's completely normal that she just jumped into my arms like that. I try to pretend like I currently *don't* feel the blood rushing to my dick with need, try really fucking hard not to think about what that would've felt like if we'd both been naked and how easy it would have been to just slip in her and—

Jesus Christ.

A throat clears behind us, and we both snap out of whatever trance we were just in.

"So, um, the award?" Diana asks, clearly trying to relieve some of the tension.

"Ah, yes." Julieta pulls a white envelope from her pocket and waves it in the air before opening it. "Two vouchers to the spa at *The Inn.*"

Andrea groans in frustration, and Alex wraps an arm around her waist, kissing her temple. "It's okay, babe. I'll book you a reservation."

She smiles up at him with a tender look in her eyes, shaking her head. "It's not that. I already have us both booked for the day before the wedding. That's why I'm upset. because we've been competing for something my parents already gifted us." She shrugs. "We could've spent the day together, alone, instead of doing this." Alex's face softens and he bends to kiss her sweetly on the lips.

But while everyone watches the tender moment, I shoot my mother a look. This is all too odd. Why would Julieta pick two tickets to the spa, already knowing that Andrea had reservations? I mean, what if she had won the contest? Would she have gone twice during the week of her wedding?

"So, here you go, guys." Julieta hands the tickets to me. "One for each of you. The appointment's already scheduled for tomorrow."

"Wait, what? How is it already scheduled if you didn't know who was going to win?" Rosie asks.

"It's, uh, under my name," she replies. "It'll be great, I promise. Be there by one, and then it's massage, facials, treatments, hot tub—you know, the works."

I look down at the thick gold and navy voucher, running my thumb over the embossed logo. "I might just give this ticket to my mother, Julieta. I have a lot of packing to do and she'd appreciate it more."

"No! It's non-transferable."

"Huh? I thought you said the reservation was under your name?" Rosie asks. "Are you okay? Are you feverish or something? Is the cold getting to you? You're probably already at that age where—"

"*Do not* finish that sentence, *hija. Cuidado.*" She glares at her daughter.

"Thanks for the offer, Asher, honey. But strangers touching me? No, thanks." Mom waves her hands. "And you don't need to be at the store in the afternoon. The movers will be coming in then to take the furniture away, so you're free to go. Enjoy the massage—you've been moving a lot of heavy things lately. Take a minute before having to go to the joint bachelor/bachelorette party tomorrow night."

I open my mouth to protest but then rub the spot where my neck meets my shoulder, feeling the tight knot already forming there. I figure if I'm going to be forced to socialize with drunk people tomorrow night, then it would be nice to have a good massage and therapeutic soak. It *has* been several days of moving and sexual tension. I definitely need to relax before I either collapse or spontaneously combust. Whichever comes first.

I look down at Rosie, a soft smile on her face. "We can get something to eat after?" I don't know where I get the courage to say the words, but they shoot out before I can even stop them. I hold my breath as she stares up at me, her lips parted. She's quiet for a beat as I feel our mothers' interested eyes on us, waiting for Rosie's answer.

After the longest ten seconds of my life, she seems to gather herself and whispers, "Yeah."

Chapter Eighteen

ROSIE

I SHIFT UNCOMFORTABLY IN MY ROBE, SITTING ON ONE OF the cream couches in the spa waiting room. I'm supposed to be relaxing, but honestly, I don't see that happening. Not after having to wear this *minuscule* bikini I was forced to buy at *The Inn*'s spa gift shop for today. I mean, okay. The only person that's going to be seeing me in this is the massage therapist and the person who'll take me to my private hot tub for the relaxing "detox" soak after. But still.

I stick my hand in my robe, shifting the tiny triangles of fabric to try to cover as much of my boobs as I possibly can, but it can only stretch so far. It's not like they're massive—I'm a solid B, maybe a C on a good day—but it's more that the bathing suit is really that small.

Suddenly, a throat clears, and my head snaps up, hands still cupping my breasts, only to meet Asher's wild gaze.

"Uhhh, what are you doing?" he asks, looking the picture of comfort in his own robe and swim trunks. It's a valid question, since I guess it *is* kind of weird for me to be rearranging my tits in the middle of a spa waiting room.

"I..." My voice trails off as I catch a brief flash of something in his eyes. He recovers, though, and I immediately pull my hands from my robe, closing it tight over my chest. "Sorry. Just... Shifting things around?"

"W-what? What does that even mean?"

I feel the heat of a blush spread throughout my body, and suddenly look down at the floor, searching desperately for a hole to throw myself down so I can disappear forever and ever and ever. I groan, putting my face in my hands. "My bikini top. I had to rearrange my bikini top."

He laughs and, when I feel the couch dip, I free my face from my hands and look straight into his eyes shining bright with humor.

"Don't worry. I'm not wearing my glasses and I was too far away to see anything, so it was all a blurry mess."

I laugh, relieved that he's not making it awkward. But, in all honesty, the fact that he saw something and is acting like it was nothing is giving me mixed feelings. What the hell?

"I think I *am* a blurry mess," I murmur.

Choosing not to dwell, I try to steer the conversation over to him and to a safer space than my boobs (which honestly, shouldn't really be that difficult)."How goes the packing?"

He shrugs, causing his own robe to shift, revealing a smattering of dark hair on his chest. "Pretty good. We're actually almost done. Although, we've decided to temporarily keep a few things for the next couple of days so your sister can take some of the bridal party skiing. Other than that, most of the furniture and stuff were taken away today to storage until mom's ready to sell and ship everything off that hasn't been sold."

"Whoa," I breathe. "I still can't believe that the store is going to just..."

"Disappear? Be turned into rubble only to have a condo building built where it was?" he asks, a hint of bitterness in his voice.

There's a pause while we both process this. "I'm so sorry, Asher. If it makes *me* really sad, I can't even begin to imagine how *you're* feeling."

He shrugs, looking out the frosted window. "It doesn't feel great, obviously. It was my grandfather's store and where I spent most of my afternoons as a kid. Before you showed up, that is," he says, turning to smile at me. "Later, as a teenager... I should have memories of how annoying working there was or whatever. But... we had a good time, didn't we? As faithful employees of *Seymour's Outdoor Sporting Goods,* I mean." The tone of his voice makes me believe he isn't asking a hypothetical question.

Is he really doubting how much our time together meant to me?

Although, can I really blame him after everything I've done?

"Are you kidding? We had so much fun." The corners of his mouth quirk up, but he turns back to look out the window, deep in thought. "I actually have this super fond memory of you and me in the storage room—"

His head immediately turns to me. "Our first kiss? You think of that, too?"

My breath catches in surprise, all the oxygen in the room having been sucked out. I don't even know how to respond to that.

After a pause, Asher seems to realize that I was not, in fact, referring to that moment. "Oh. You weren't talking about... God, I'm so sorry."

"No, it's... Um, actually... I was, ah, talking about the morning after Lucas Gold's party? The first time we got drunk together. We were super hungover, but we both had to work the next day. Your mom was out of town, so we took a nap on top of some sleeping bags in the storage room when there were no customers around?" I ask in a small voice.

"Oh, yeah," he says solemnly, looking down at his feet. "Sorry about that. I didn't mean to—I didn't mean to make things awkward. To bring that stuff up. We agreed to be friends and start new the other day. I just... I guess since Christmas Eve and the whole mistletoe thing, and with the store closing, that memory's kind of..." He grimaces like he doesn't want to say the next words, but can't help himself. "It's one of the memories that's been playing on a constant loop in my head lately." He squeezes his eyes shut and runs both his hands through his hair, lacing his fingers together behind his neck for a moment.

I try not to get too stuck on the use of the words "one of the." As in, there is more than one memory?

"Sorry. I shouldn't assume that you think about this stuff, too."

I watch him closely for a few seconds as he struggles with some internal conflict. Eventually, he places his elbows on his knees, heels of his hands over his eyes.

"*Fuck,*" he whispers.

"I don't," I say in a quiet voice. And because I've apparently lost my mind, I say, "I don't let myself think about you too much —or at least I try not to—because whenever I do, it tears me apart. Every time I let myself think about us and what we did to each other... It takes me back to the day it happened, fills me with regret, and the pain comes back fresh and raw. My heart breaks all over again, and... Then it takes me months to get back to a place where it doesn't hurt every time I breathe, where I can live with the dull pain." I pause, my breath stuttering. "No. I don't think of you often. I can't let myself."

Slowly, he sits up and pulls his hands away from his face, meeting my wide eyes with his. I struggle to inhale.

"Rosie," he whispers just as my eyes begin to sting, tears forming.

"I'm sorry. I shouldn't have said anything." I get up and tighten my robe, ready to leave this place and never come back. "You didn't—And I—I need to—"

But he reaches for me and wraps his large hand around my delicate wrist, getting to his feet. "No. No, don't. It's—"

"Welcome!" A low, but enthusiastic voice breaks through the tension. A woman in black scrubs, and a tight, sleek high bun with vibrant red hair walks in on us. "The lovely Rosie and Asher, correct?" Asher, still holding my wrist, nods to the woman. "Fantastic. My name is Birch. I'm the head of the wellness spa at *The Inn*."

I murmur a weak hello, avoiding making eye contact with Asher.

"Shall we get you settled in, then?"

"Actually," Asher says. "Would you mind giving us a minute or two? I just need to have a word with—" He turns to me, but Birch puts a hand on his shoulder, stopping him.

"I'm sorry, sir, but we're unfortunately running a little behind already, and the couple's treatment is pretty long. It would be best if we get started with your sensual massage class right away."

"*Our what?*" Asher and I ask in unison, our voices bouncing off the cream walls.

"Shh!" Birch admonishes us, looking around the waiting room, making sure it's empty. "Please. We have guests who are trying to relax. Our relaxation pods aren't fully soundproof, unfortunately."

"Wait, no. What are you talking about a couple's treatment? This is supposed to be an individual experience. *IN-DI-VI-DU-AL,*" I enunciate. I just embarrassed myself to an extreme level with Asher. I cannot—*will not*—spend the rest of the afternoon half-naked with him doing couply things after I just confessed my pathetic secret.

Birch physically recoils, clearly not used to someone with so little Zen energy. I've been living in New York City for the past nine years, lady. There is no such thing as finding your *zen* there. And if there is, I'm sure it's exclusive and *very* expensive.

"I'm sorry, but the appointment that was made was for a *couple*'s experience—not for an individual one," she says with genuine concern.

"But we aren't a couple," I retort, quickly flashing a look to Asher, who has gone suspiciously quiet. Why isn't he complaining?

"Listen," I exhale. "A mistake was made. Can we just have the individual treatment package, then? Is that okay?"

"Unfortunately, no. All treatments have been booked, and I do not have any free personnel or extra rooms available to split these treatments between the two of you." Birch's gaze bounces between the two of us as she worries her lower lip. "We could just cancel the treatment altogether?"

I say, "Yes," at the same time Asher firmly replies with, "*No.*"

We look at each other—me slack-jawed, him with an intense look in his eyes I can't quite pinpoint.

"It's fine," he says, shrugging casually, trying to mask whatever emotion seems to be wanting to break through. "We're fine," he tells Birch. "We can handle the couple's treatment thing, right, Rosie?"

I swallow the hard knot in my throat and try to ignore the way the light in my chest keeps growing, stretching, making me feel like I'm about to burst. I can't decide whether he's okay with it because he *wants* to do these couple activities with me, or because, in his mind, we're friends now and thinks it's going to be all platonic.

Worst of all, I don't know how to feel about either of those options.

"Rosie?" He asks again, his voice breaking through the fog. "Is that okay with you?"

I clear my throat and force a smile at both Birch and Asher. "Yeah. Absolutely. Let's do this."

Chapter Nineteen

ASHER

I'VE NEVER BEEN TO A SPA OR EVEN HAD A PROFESSIONAL massage before, so I was pretty excited to be able to experience this, especially after all the packing and heavy lifting I've been doing. After several days of physical strain and stress, the tightness in my neck and shoulders has gotten worse, and I was looking forward to having someone work through them. But now, as Rosie and I follow Birch down to "our room," I'm not sure how I feel about this. I don't know what to expect from the whole experience, but my mind is racing with possibilities of what this would entail. Will there be touching, or is it just sort of a side-by-side massages and treatments situation?

On the one hand, I'm done lying to myself about wanting her, so I'm not gonna deny that the thought of having my hands on her, feeling her soft skin beneath my fingertips, doesn't have my skin heating. On the other, this woman has been the axis of every single one of my fantasies, and, despite the fact that I'd spent nearly a decade building a protective wall against her, she's managed to bring it crumbling down in a matter of days. The fact is, Rosie Castillo has the potential to rip me to shreds —*again*. So I'm not so sure letting my guard down like this is such a great idea.

But what she just said...

"Please remove your robes and hang them on the hook behind the door. Once that's done, please lie on the tables face-down until I bring in your massage therapist and relationship guru," Birch says, a soft smile on her face.

Relationship guru?

Bile rises in my throat, and I chance a look at Rosie who is determinately *not* looking at me, her toasted skin flushed crimson. In all the years I'd known her, I don't think I've ever seen her look this uncomfortable. I wait for her to make a move, to call the whole thing off or take her robe off. She does neither, only plays with the belt, fidgeting with it while I imagine pulling it myself, unwrapping her like the best Christmas present.

"Should we—? I mean, is it okay if *I...*?" I let the question hang in the air until she can finally muster up the confidence to look at me. Is it the whole couple spa thing that's making her uncomfortable? Or the fact that she just revealed some information that I'm frankly still trying to process myself?

Both, maybe?

"Yeah, sorry. Yes," she says to her white hotel slippers.

One minute we're fine, joking around, and the next it's as if we're just waking up the morning after a one-night stand. I don't want to be doing this. I want to talk about what she said. I want to ask her what the hell is going on. We agreed to be friends, but I can't be the only one feeling this, right? If I were, she wouldn't be saying those things or acting this way. We *need* to talk about this because, if there is a chance—even just a microscopic chance in hell—that she's feeling this, too, well... I surprise myself by deciding that I won't let the opportunity slip away.

With my heart in my throat after coming to this monumental decision, I shed my robe and hang it on the hook before turning to her and offering my hand. "I can take your robe and hang it for you, if you want."

"Um, actually," she says, her eyes on my chest. "Would you mind just closing your eyes or something? Or lying facedown?"

I give her a look.

"I'm, ah, not wearing much underneath this." She blushes beet red, but I feel myself pale. The idea that she'll be... what? Almost naked? Just two feet away from me suddenly makes me a little lightheaded.

I grit my teeth, trying hard to control my expression. I nod and walk over to my table, lying face down on my stomach, and carefully fitting my face through the padded hole.

Rosie breathes a sigh as I watch her slippered feet as they walk to the hook on the door. She takes off her robe and hangs it up while I battle between avoiding the two things I should probably not be thinking about right now: what she told me right before the spa attendant showed up, and whatever the hell she's wearing under that robe that has her so self-conscious.

"*...not wearing much underneath this.*"

She walks to her table and lays herself down into position right before the door opens again.

"Good afternoon," a low, breathy voice enters the room. My entire body tenses as my imagination runs wild going over what awaits us this afternoon. "I'm Meadow, and I'll be the one guiding you through the massage."

Meadow and Birch? Really?

"I see you're already in position. But would you mind sitting up for a moment?"

Rosie makes a choking noise, and I hear her quickly shuffle on her table, the rustling sound alerting me to her movements. After a few seconds, I push myself up and swivel around to sit on the edge of the massage table, facing her. She hugs a sheet to her chest, covering most of her body. Only a smooth, tan leg pokes out on one side. Rosie gazes up at the attendant, who I barely even notice, with wide, dark eyes. She's so beautiful with that messy pink bun at the top of her head and tan shoulders, I think I stop breathing.

"Rosie, Asher."

I look at the attendant for the first time, a woman in her mid-fifties with long white hair down to her waist, as she brings her hands together in front of her chest as if in prayer. She bows once with a soft smile on her face, and I suppress the urge to roll my eyes.

"Welcome to *The Spa at The Inn*'s Couple's Renewal Experience." She looks up at us, eyes bouncing between the two with a smirk on her face. "This afternoon, we'll be working on reconnecting as a couple—physically and spiritually."

I swallow hard as Rosie and I look at each other in concern.

"We'll begin with the physical reconnection process by first teaching you some massage methods to use on each other. Nothing too out there, but since you aren't certified, I'll monitor for safety. This will help with rekindling physical intimacy."

"We don't need to rekindle physical intimacy," Rosie says, her voice shaking slightly.

Meadow gives Rosie a look. "We don't ever *think* we do, honey, but you're here, which means that there is a disconnect between you and Asher." I mean, she's not wrong. "In any case, it's always good to spice up the relationship."

"No! I mean..." She stares at me, frustrated. Her look says, *Why aren't you helping me stop this?*

The answer is so simple: I don't think I want to.

But if she really hates this, I won't force her. I lock eyes with her, trying to convey the message just with my expression alone.

I'm not going to let anyone make you feel uncomfortable.

"What she's trying to say is that we aren't a couple. We aren't *together* that way," I tell Meadow, raising my eyebrows.

Finally, after a beat, she seems to get the message. "Oh, no.

Did no one tell you what the couple's spa package entailed?" she asks, dropping her mellow voice front.

Rosie and I both shake our heads. "No one," I tell her. "We were told these were for an individual experience. Rosie and I are just friends." It pains me to say the words, but I say them just the same for her benefit.

"Oh, wow. That would've been real awkward. Our exercise for rekindling a spiritual connection would have entailed a few tantric positions and deep introspective work."

Rosie and I glance at each other again, the word *tantric* doing things to my body.

"Clothes on, of course."

Meadow places her hands on her hips and looks out the foggy window, thinking for a second. "I mean, we could skip all the romantic stuff and just do the massage? Honestly, you'll thank me for it."

"We asked for individual massages before, but they said you were fully booked," I tell her.

"We are. I just meant we can do *just* the massage class instead of that *and* the tantric training, and everything. After the massage, we can just lead you to the hot tub to chill. Or get hot." She laughs once at her own joke.

Rosie and I are quiet, both waiting for the other to say something—to oppose, to agree—anything.

Sensing the tension, Meadow speaks up once more. "It shouldn't be an issue, right? I mean, if you guys are friends, then..."

"Right, of course," Rosie says, nodding. "We're friends. We can handle massage lessons, right?" Her voice is about four octaves higher than it usually is, but if she's game, so am I.

"Sure," I say, trying not to focus too much on the fact that I'll get to feel her bare, smooth skin beneath my fingertips, her warmth. "Let's do this."

"Rosie, please put the sheet down and lay on your stomach, your face comfortably in the hole at the top of the table," Meadow instructs her. Rosie shuffles on the table, trying to keep her body covered as she does. Since it's obvious she doesn't want me looking at her for some reason, I keep my eyes on the ceiling, giving her some privacy.

"Okay. Now, Asher, please step over here on this side of Rosie's table." I walk over to where I'm instructed and try not to focus too much on the fact that Rosie's nearly-bare back is right in front of me, laid out on the table like a meal ready to be had.

"Hold out your hands, please," Meadow tells me, so I do. She pulls a bottle from the white sideboard under the window and pops the cap, squeezing scented oil onto my palms. I wince at the texture, feeling it start to get everywhere on me. "Now place your hands on Rosie's back near her neck and massage the oil into her skin, using the light and energy within to transmit every single feeling you have towards your friend."

Er, no, I'd rather not, thanks.

"Sorry, what?" Rosie squeaks.

Meadow rolls her eyes at us. "Just put your hands on her. How are you going to massage her without touching?"

"She's got a point," I mutter. "But we can end this here, if you like," I tell Rosie. I don't want her to feel pressured into doing something she doesn't want to.

With a frustrated sigh, she turns back onto her stomach and settles in. "Just get it over with."

Just what every man loves to hear...

"Oh, yes, see how tense she feels? You're definitely going to benefit a lot from this massage sweetie," Meadow tells her.

I snort when I hear Rosie mutter a "whatever" under her breath, but otherwise proceed to put my hands on her upper back. But the second my oiled fingertips touch her skin, I realize I've made a mistake. I wanted this so bad, but the surge of electricity between us is blindsiding, overwhelming. And from the sharp inhale I hear coming from her, I know she feels it, too.

Immediately, I lift my hands off her.

"No, no, no," Meadow says, grabbing my hands and placing them on Rosie again. This time, she doesn't let go. Instead, she holds my wrists and moves my hands over Rosie's body, the oil smoothing her skin, feeling her beneath my fingertips. "Follow this motion," she says, letting go of my hands.

And so I do.

I let my fingers press into Rosie's skin as I lose myself in her, feeling how soft she is. My mind clouds as I apply pressure in circular motions wherever I feel a knot, trying not to focus too much on how hot her little moans are. My breathing starts coming in faster, skin heating as my hands drift lower down her back and I fight the urge to let them fall to the sides, to skate over the sides of her breasts. I do my best to stop myself from leaning over and untying that bikini top with my teeth, not letting my mind wander to what it would feel like to pull the strings in one fluid motion.

When my thumbs move over a big knot in her back, Rosie releases an involuntary moan and it's all I can do to not come in my pants. It's deep and louder than the other smaller sounds that were already driving me mad. I'm suddenly rock hard, trying to hide myself from Meadow and the girl of my dreams by tilting my hips to the side.

After another small whimper from Rosie, though, I decide I can't do it any longer. I clear my throat and drop my hands because I doubt I can take another second of this. "We done?" I ask, my voice breaking.

Meadow looks at me like I've lost my mind, which I'm sure I have. "No, we are not done. Put your hands back on her. I'm going to teach you how to address her sciatic nerve now."

Sorry, what?

"Sciatic nerve." She blinks at me.

"Isn't that...?" I'm pretty sure that's the butt region, is it not? If she makes me massage Rosie's ass, I swear to god I'm going to combust. The Big Bang will have nothing on me.

Jesus, this is hell.

"Lower back. Humans carry a lot of tension in their hips and lower back—especially women. And I'd bet my last dollar that our Rosie here has some tension there."

"Hey," she whines.

With a puff of air, I put my hands on Rosie's lower back and follow the instructions of the massage therapist. That is, until there's a knock on the door and Birch peeps her head in. "So sorry to interrupt your treatment," she says. "But would you mind if I borrow Meadow? It'll be quick."

I nod, and Rosie mumbles a yes, and I think, *thank god*, because I need a break. But just when I think I'm in the clear, Meadow turns and says, "Please continue massaging her while I'm away. Lower back near the hips, circular motion." She pantomimes the movement I'm supposed to follow and then finally leaves.

Once she's gone, I take a step away from Rosie and tell her, "Don't worry. I'll stop."

There's an awkward pause where we're both quiet until she says, "You don't have to."

Excuse me?

I cough once. "What?"

"I mean, you don't have to stop if you don't want to. It felt... nice."

"Nice?" I hate that word. *Nice*. I don't like being *nice*. I was *nice* for so long, and look where it got me. No. *Nice* isn't something I want to be. Kind and good to her, yes. But when it comes to this? To this tension we *both* feel, if I'm reading her physical cues right—fast breathing, racing heartbeat, flushed skin—I don't want to be *nice*. I want her to want me as much as I want her. And if she doesn't want me, then that's fine; I'll step away. But I'm over this tiptoeing around our feelings, holding back from telling her and showing her how I feel.

If there is a small chance that she's into me the way I'm into her, then you can bet your ass that I'm going to take it.

So I walk back over to her table where she settles comfortably. She can't see me as I stare hungrily down at her, need filling me to the brim. I put my hands back on her with slightly more pressure than before, feeling more at ease because we're alone, and revel in the satisfied moan she breathes at the rougher contact.

I suck in a breath, marveling at the fact that she's definitely into this now. "This good?" I ask, my voice a little gravelly as I put more pressure on her back, a small whimper escaping her lips.

"Yeah. Yes," she says breathily.

I run my index finger slowly down her spine, barely touching her skin, and watch as goosebumps cover every inch of her back. With a satisfied smirk, I pour some more oil onto my hands, rubbing it between my palms to heat it up, before bending over to place my mouth close to her ear. "Tell me if this is too rough," I whisper. Rosie shivers at my closeness—or is it the words that come out of my mouth?—but otherwise pretends like this isn't affecting her at all.

She nods once, and I put my hands back on her, hands massaging under her bathing suit straps, running my finger under the strings, teasing her. Her breathing gets louder, and I can feel the skin beneath my fingertips heating and—god, I've never wanted anything more than I want to lean over and plant a kiss in the middle of her shoulder blades now.

"Don't stop," she breathes—suddenly tensing at her own words.

"I won't," I tell her between gritted teeth, letting her know it's okay to want to lose herself here, because I want to, too.

I add more pressure into her back, taking a chance and letting my fingertips skate slightly over the sides of her breasts. My eyes fly to her face, hidden by the table, to gauge her reaction and read her body language. "Again," she whispers.

Holy shit.

My heart beats loudly against my chest, the pulses so strong I can barely hear our breathing over it. It's racing, racing, trying to catch up to what I need, which is to touch Rosie all over. To *feel* her all over.

Again, my hands press into the side of her breasts and slide down her body. I use my thumbs to apply pressure in circular motions, living for each and every single sound that escapes her lips—each one shooting straight to my dick.

Unable to help myself, I press too hard on one of them, but she doesn't complain. Instead, a loud moan bursts from her, followed by my name.

"Fuck, Rosie," I say, unable to help myself. After watching how she squirms beneath me, the sounds she's making, I wonder whether I should run to the door and lock it. I don't know what's happening here, but I sure as hell don't want to stop because we're interrupted by another nature-named spa attendant.

When I make my move towards the door, however, she wraps a hand around my wrist and lifts her face to give me a horrified look in her eyes. "What are you doing? Don't stop," she whines.

I open my mouth to explain, when I catch her gaze dropping to the tent that's been pitched. At first, I blush, mortified. But then the pleading expression in her eyes turns to one of hunger.

"Asher." She pulls me closer.

I suck in a breath, gaze locked on hers, before moving back to her back, where I lower the sheet covering her ass in a slow, measured motion. My hands skate slowly on either side of her back until they reach her hips, where I let my thumbs hook into the two strings tied there. With one hand, I lightly tug at one of them—not really wanting to untie them, only wanting to tease her, to make her feel half as desperate as I do right now. With a groan, she slightly lifts her hips off the table and I take it as an invitation, letting the fingers of my right hand slip under the minuscule piece of black fabric barely covering her ass, both of our breathing ragged, blood boiling and—

"How are we doing over here?" Meadow's cheerful voice cuts through the tension, killing the moment I had been dreaming of for almost a decade.

Chapter Twenty

ROSIE

What am I doing? What the hell *am I doing?*

What the hell was I thinking asking him to keep going? God, I'm such an idiot. He asked to be friends. *Friends.* And there I was, encouraging us to pursue whatever the hell happened as soon as Meadow left us.

Thank *god* she interrupted us when she did. Honestly, I don't know what would have happened had she not done so. Where would we have ended up? His hands had already traveled over most of my body, sending shivers up and down my spine...

It was too much.

Seriously, Meadow walking in, telling us that they had found two other staff members to give us individual treatments, was a godsend. I could barely look Asher in the eye as we were led to our separate rooms, where I proceeded to be slathered and soaked in a multitude of products as I begged my heated skin to cool down. I was supposed to be relaxing, but I was so tightly wound by what had just happened that every touch by Sage (seriously, what is up with these nature names? Are they some sort of requirement to work here or are they fake? Are they the wellness equivalent of stripper names?), the new aesthetician

144

assigned to me, has been as uncomfortable as sitting on a spiked bed.

"You doing okay, hon'?" Sage asks.

"I'm okay, thanks. Just... a little anxious."

A little wrinkle forms between her brows. "This is supposed to be relaxing, honey."

I've hated every moment of it—a true travesty, considering I will never be able to afford something this luxurious ever again. I'm sure my father gets a discount, but really, how big could it be?

"I know, I'm sorry. I'm just not into all of this." A lie. A total lie. I would've killed for something like this two weeks ago. But how can I tell her that I was nearly caught doing something really inappropriate just a couple of hours ago by one of her coworkers and I'm still not over it?

"Are we done?" I ask.

She narrows her eyes at me and purses her lips. "Just about. Need to wipe this aloe healing mask off you." I bite back a sigh as she wraps up my last skincare treatment.

"Thank you so much. It's definitely not you—it's me."

"Oh, I know." She smiles like she knows it could *never* be her. Man, I'd love some of that confidence. "Let's take you over to the hot tub for a final soak."

I get to my feet, sliding into my fluffy complimentary pink slippers which I will definitely be taking home with me, and follow Sage down the hallway with newfound excitement. The hot tub, I can deal with. No one touching me, no one to feel forced to talk to—alone, letting the hot water soothe me as I try to process what just went down between me and Asher.

Finally, we reach the end of a dark hallway where Sage pushes open a large glass door with a soft smile on her face. "Here you go, honey. I hope this helps with whatever's been bothering you all day." I smile tightly at her, kicking off my slippers by the door, removing my robe before turning to the tub, and—

"*Jesus!*" I bring a hand to my chest when I see Asher in it. "What are you doing here?" He looks just as surprised as I feel.

"I didn't mean to scare you! I thought this was going to be a solo session, too."

"It's fine," I sigh, realizing just then that I'm standing in front of him in the world's most itty bitty black bikini ever. Thinking quickly, I realize there's only one of two options I can go with here. Either I pull the robe on to cover myself up again—risking making this whole thing even more awkward than it already is—or I can just say *screw it* and get in the hot tub with him. At this point, after that weird moment in the massage room, how much weirder can it get?

Spoiler alert. It can get much weirder.

Though it's true that Asher's vision is blurry when he's not wearing his glasses, I can tell that the closer I get to joining him in the luxurious stone hot tub, the better he can see me. I can tell by the way his eyes widen, the way they flicker for half of a second to my chest, and the way his throat bobs as he swallows hard with restraint right before he forces himself to look away.

I can't blame him. This bathing suit is ridiculous, and I hate it.

Because I want to die a little bit in embarrassment, I move quickly into the tub, thinking that at least the water and the bubbles will cover my body. I try to move fast as I wade into the hot water, but end up slipping, falling directly into his arms.

"I swear I'm not doing this on purpose," I say, a little breathless, despite the fact that I'm still holding on to his shoulders with a tight grip.

Asher's hands tighten briefly around my waist before pushing me carefully away. "No worries," he says, the corner of his mouth quirking up. He's smiling, but there's caution in his eyes. He looks away again, suddenly every muscle in his body tight. "I don't exactly mind."

I feel bad he never got that massage. He could've used it.

Asher looks to the side and leans his arms on the edge of the tub, exhales deeply, lost in thought. I move backward until I feel my knees hit the tub bench.

Taking advantage of the fact that he isn't paying attention to me, I take a minute to look at him—*really* look at him. My eyes drink in the profile of his nose, broken, yet sexy; his dark, curly hair, damp at the nape. The way his muscular chest rises and falls with each breath makes me wonder when he finds the time to work out between all the research he does. He looks utterly delicious and perfect. So much so, that I have to actively fight the urge to lean forward to lick the beads of water running down his shoulders.

Instead of doing what I really want to do, I play with my fingers under the water, trying to focus on anything *but* Asher, now—though he makes it difficult to do when I feel his eyes on me. I should be stressing about my promotion, shouldn't I? Isn't that what a normal person would be doing right now? Shouldn't I be freaking out because it's almost the New Year and I haven't even heard back from work?

Instead, all I can think of is him and what comes next between us. Not my future, not my goals. Nope, just Asher.

"I'm sorry," he whispers, finally breaking the silence between us, tearing me away from my train of thought. "I got caught up in the moment back there. I shouldn't have done that."

I look up to meet his repentant eyes, brows pulled together.

"What are you talking about? It's not like I didn't play a role there or anything."

"Still," he says, bringing his arms back into the water, staring down. "I shouldn't have done that. Made you feel uncomfortable."

"You didn't make me feel uncomfortable. You made me feel... other things," I admit, because honestly, there's no denying it.

He looks up at me, curious. "Okay. Well. I just wanted to make sure you were okay. I don't want to ever make you feel weird or... I don't know." He sighs.

"Thanks. That's sweet of you to be concerned. Really, it is. But I promise we're good. I—I enjoyed it. It just wasn't a good idea."

"No. Definitely not a good idea." He shakes his head solemnly, a frown plastered on his face.

"It's fine, Asher. Really. You were just following the massage therapist's orders." Can we stop talking about this now? But he looks so guilty, I can't stop myself from blurting, "Besides, I was the one who asked you to keep going."

We're quiet for a moment as we both process my words; my admission of guilt.

"Why?" he asks, his voice lower.

"Why what?"

"Why did you ask me to keep going, Rosie?"

I chew on my bottom lip, and shut my eyes tight as I shake my head, wishing I could escape. I feel him wade across the hot tub, though, moving in front of me. The heat radiating from his skin is much higher than the hot water we're currently in—both physically and metaphorically speaking. I know he won't let me off the hook.

"Why didn't you want me to stop?" he asks, his voice closer this time, almost a whisper.

I slowly open my eyes and meet his—amber, gold, sweet, so inviting. Filled with longing and something else I can't name yet.

"Tell me."

After a moment's hesitation, I say, "You know why." I take a deep breath, hold it for a few seconds. "Because of what I said before. And because... It felt good."

Asher dips a little lower in the water, lips briefly disappearing. He's quiet as he studies me, seeming to consider something. Before he can do or say anything, though, I stop him. "But it was wrong. We agreed to be friends and that wasn't a friendly thing to do."

He smirks, his eyes lighting up with humor. "I disagree. It was a very, *very* friendly thing to do. And I thought it felt good, too."

My breath hitches. "Yeah?" I ask ever-so-eloquently, voice breathy and shaky as he comes closer and closer.

"Yeah." Slowly, he wades toward me until our faces are just an inch apart, our breaths mingling.

I want to press pause and ask him what's going on. I want to press fast-forward to get to the good part.

I should stop this, for both our sakes. He asked for friendship, and the way he's brushing the pink tendrils off my face, the way his eyes keep looking down at my lips, the way he runs his nose down mine...

Well, this is definitely not something that normal friends do.

"The entire time," he says against my mouth, lips brushing mine, "the entire fucking time I was fighting the urge to kiss your shoulder the way I remember it made you moan."

Oh my god.

It's the first time he's ever directly brought up what we did since first seeing him again. And I don't know what to do, because that feeling I've been trying to repress? The one that keeps clawing itself back up my chest, wanting to burst through?

Yeah, it's telling me it really wants Asher to kiss me. And it really doesn't want him to stop there.

"*Ash*," I beg. But I honestly don't know whether I'm asking him to stop or keep going. Kissing him would prove to be incredible in the short-term, I'm sure. But it also may very well rip me apart as soon as I'm back in New York, all alone in my apartment without him.

"I love it when you say my name like that," he groans, presses his lips to my shoulder. My eyes involuntarily slide shut, a whimper escaping my lips, my body already a slave to his.

But still, I try to fight it. "L-Like what?" I tremble, almost convulse with the days—*years*—of accumulated need and hunger for Asher Wolff and it is absolutely killing me.

"You know how." He kisses my neck this time, following it with a delicate bite right where his lips were. "Like you want this just as bad as I do."

And in the blink of an eye, Asher grabs me by the waist and shifts us so that he's sitting on the bench where I was, and I'm straddling him.

"How did you do that?" I ask, a little breathless, a lot turned on. Though I'm not really looking for an answer, considering the second I settle on top of him I can feel just how hard he is.

More on instinct than by actual, conscious decision, I rock my hips forward on his lap and we both make noises we can't control. I feel myself start to fill with light, my chest expanding.

"This okay?" he asks, looking up at me with actual hesitation.

I press my forehead to his and laugh, clasping my hands at the nape of his neck. "You're asking me this *after* you pulled some ninja stuff and I somehow ended up on your lap with your cock under me and your hands on my ass?" For a moment, my stomach turns at my brazenness, scared that he'll reject me. But he chuckles, one side of his mouth lifted in amusement. "Yeah, I guess that's what I'm doing."

I stop laughing and kiss the corner of his mouth, letting my lips rest there for a beat. And I know I should be thinking about the negative repercussions, but right now all I can think about is how amazing it feels to be back in his arms like this; how we never should've stopped.

Something within me snaps, and it's like every filter and protective wall I'd built over the years comes crumbling down when I say, "You read me better than anyone. You know it's okay. It's how you knew I wanted you to grab me like that. How you know to call me on my crap." I pull away and make sure he's listening to me as I speak. "You *know* me, Asher Wolff. So, show me what I want to happen next."

With an almost guttural sound, Asher pulls me closer into him, finally—*freaking finally*—pressing his lips to mine. He nips at my top lip, then my lower one—tugging, teasing me with his tongue. With a moan, I part my lips for him and let him explore every inch of my body with his hands.

My fingers find their way into his curly hair, holding him tightly to me. I rock an unsteady motion in his lap, feeling every inch of him, his left hand slipping below my bikini bottom and gripping my ass. And when his fingers tease my cleft, I shiver in anticipation. I inhale sharply at his touch, but his right hand travels up my side, up my arms, over to my neck, and wraps around me. He squeezes softly there for barely a second before pulling my lips back to his.

My skin is on fire as liquid pleasure builds within me, so much so that I'm starting to ache.

"Fuck, Rosie. *Fuck*," he says against my lips, our breathing coming in rushed and frantic. Asher's eyes are on my lips—which now feel swollen and raw—as he seems to consider something. His hands tighten on me and he grits his teeth, as if he's fighting off something momentous.

Mortification floods my system. What if he's regretting this? I mean, his dick definitely isn't, but what if, emotionally and intellectually, Asher's realized that this probably wasn't the best idea?

I wouldn't be able to handle that kind of rejection. Not now. Not after this.

"Asher, I—"

"Hush," he whispers before placing a rough kiss on me. "I'm going to make you feel so fucking good, Rosie."

"Oh my god," I mewl as he moves his lips to my neck, teeth nipping at my soft skin.

The hand on my ass moves to one of my breasts, where he proceeds to push my bathing suit aside. Asher leans forward and kisses down my chest, over my breasts, all the way to my nipples where he kisses them and licks them until the pressure starts to build between my legs and I feel like I'm about to lose control. I'm filling more and more with light, climbing high, and my breathing is coming in harder and harder as he whispers my name over and over again and I rock on him and I'm so close I'm so close I'm so close.

I'm so fucking close

I cry out, "Asher, oh my god, I'm gonna—"

"*EXCUSE ME!*"

Asher and I both turn to the sound of a—understandably —*very* upset Meadow who just caught us in the middle of what can only be described as the best (and possibly only?) dry humping experience of my entire existence.

"Oh my god," I flush beet-red and adjust the small triangle barely covering my body.

"'*Just friends*', huh?" She crosses her arms in front of her chest, scowling. "This isn't *that* kind of spa, you know. We don't give out those types of happy endings."

"Jesus," Asher breathes, closing his eyes and leaning back against the wall of the tub, pulling away from me. The pain of the loss of the contact of his skin on mine is almost visceral.

"I'm *so* sorry, Meadow," I tell her. I attempt to move my legs to dismount Asher, but end up losing my balance, falling straight into the water with a big splash.

I straighten myself out and turn to look at Asher, expecting him to apologize as well. Instead, I find him holding his face in his hands, and my heart breaks because just like he knows me, I know him. And I can read his body language.

He's regretting this.

I choke back a sob, and get out of the tub on shaky legs, my skin buzzing. "I'm so, so sorry," I say, my voice cracking. My eyes sting as I fight back tears and walk quickly to the door, stopping only to slip into my robe and slippers, before running past Meadow straight to the locker rooms and back home.

Chapter Twenty-One

ASHER

I've been sitting at the bar for the past thirty minutes—though in truth it feels like ten hours—struggling to keep my wits about me. The joint bachelor/bachelorette party has already started, but of course the girls are fashionably—aka, *torturously*—late. Which means it's just me, Alex, Rodrigo, and Alex's friends.

Though Alex is a really nice guy and honestly great for Andrea, the members of his bridal party are complete idiots. Add Rodrigo to the mix, and you have the world's most obnoxious group of men I've ever met.

The quality of conversation—or lack thereof—has me believing I've joined some type of caveman group for the night, where the only thing on their minds is beer, women, golf, and... Nope. That's about it.

But it's fine. Necessary, even. I'm not here for them or to get drunk—I'm here to see Rosie. I'm here to talk to her after whatever the hell happened earlier today. After that incredible kiss, after hooking up, after *almost* making her come.

Jesus, I can't believe how incredible that was.

I've tried calling her many times—even stopped by her house before heading home—but she's avoiding me. Try as she may, though, there's no way she's missing her sister's bachelorette. So even if I have to deal with a few idiots for the night, I'll do it.

I run my fingers through my hair and knock back the last of my beer. Waving the bartender down, I ask for another, even though I should be pacing myself.

The things I want to say—*need* to say—they require me to be sober. I already know what I want, and it's her. It's always been her.

Despite still feeling a bit terrified, I'm ready to forgive and forget in order to do this—if she'll have me. I'm not ignorant to the amount of work and patience it will take, to how we'll probably need to ease into things. But I'm ready if she is. I just need some answers, because dry-humping me in the hot tub and then running away practically screaming sent a few mixed messages my way.

God, those lips of hers. Just thinking about them now makes me want to—

My thoughts are (thankfully) interrupted when I see a huge group of women wearing bright pink feather boas, sashes, and penis headbands walk into the pub. Among them, of course, is Rosie.

I can't help the smile that spreads across my face or the way my stomach lurches at the sight of her. I can't help the way I instinctively feel like hopping off this barstool and walking over, taking her into my arms. And I sure as shit can't help the way I want to tell her how I feel.

But, patience.

I don't want to scare her away.

From a distance, she catches me staring at her and waves gently with a bashful smile on her face. Not one for confrontation, I start to wonder how she'll want to handle what happened between us earlier today. She ran off, not even staying for that bite to eat we agreed to, so will she try to pretend like nothing happened? Or will we talk about it?

I watch her exhale deeply and, while all the other women head over to the party, she walks over to me.

"Hey," she says, her voice small, her smile even smaller. Though it's been years since we were best friends, I can still read her body language as if it were in size 50 font, all caps: she's fucking terrified to see me.

But she's here, talking to me instead of heading over to join everyone else. Which means she also can't stay away.

"Hey." I smile, not even trying to pretend I'm not ecstatic to see her.

"So..." she starts, looking down at her feet. "How you doing?"

"Is this how it's going to be? We're going to pretend like nothing happened?" I grin, watching as a lovely blush spreads across her cheeks.

Patience, Asher. Don't push. You'll get your chance to talk about it.

I laugh once and nod in understanding. "Okay, okay. I got it. No hot tub talk."

"*Thank you,*" she murmurs.

And though it might seem like I'm giving up, I'm far from it. I know that she needs to feel comfortable with me before I even attempt to touch the topic of us together with a ten-foot pole. So if she wants to not talk about it, I can put it off for now. I can play along. I can let her believe like this afternoon was nothing more than hormones taking over. It's the only reason I wave the bartender over and tell her, "Lemme get you a beer, then."

"You want another one?" I ask, looking around for the bartender.

"I'm good for now, thanks."

"Alright." I smile and just take a minute to stare at her—to just soak her in—because I finally have her all to myself.

She finishes off her drink and sets the empty glass on the bar with a satisfied look in her eyes. "It's been ages since I've had a good beer."

"I can tell," I laugh, pointing at her upper lip. "You've got some foam—"

"Oh, god." Even under the dim pub lights, her cheeks visibly blush as she reaches for a bar napkin.

"Here." Before I even know what I'm doing, I surprise myself by reaching out to cup Rosie's jaw and softly run my thumb over the foam above her mouth, my finger grazing her soft lips in the process. Her eyes widen at my touch, hand fisting around the napkin, crumpling it up into a ball. At my touch, she gasps softly, the sound almost making me groan.

Flashes of earlier today flit through my mind—of licking droplets off the delicate skin of her neck, of her hands in my hair, the sound of my name on her lips whispered against my ear in a low moan—and it's all I can do not to pull her into me again, crash my lips on hers and beg her to let me taste her everywhere.

PA-TIEN-CE.

My gaze moves from her eyes to her mouth, still cupping her face in my hand. "Sorry," I whisper, running my thumb over her lips, remembering how incredible they felt against mine—soft, plump, full. "Can't seem to help myself when I'm around you."

Dark chocolate eyes widen, lips part beneath my fingertips. A shiver runs through my body as my imagination floods with images of her. Before I lose all control and lean in to kiss her, I drop my hand. Immediately, I miss the warmth of her soft cheek against my palm. The urge to just grab her hand and take her home with me is enormous—almost over-whelming.

Now that we've reconnected, I need *more* with her.

Officially having opened the door to what I *really* want to discuss, I inch closer in my seat, our knees touching now. "Rosie, I—"

"Please," she says quietly, an ache in her voice—the same one that I feel in my chest. Neither of us can help the gravita-tional pull between us.

Why can't we just talk about it?

I see the fear in her eyes—the panic—and a flash of her kicking me out of her room when we were 18 momentarily blinds me, of her running away earlier today, both reminding me that we need to go slow. I can't scare her off—not this time.

"I know today and Christmas Eve were weird what with the mistletoe and the massage and then—" she swallows, squeezing her eyes shut. "Let's just—" A pause. A deep breath. "Let's just talk about something else, please." She looks away and begins to weave her hair into a braid.

"I think I'll take that other beer, though, if you don't mind," she murmurs, looking up at me through full lashes.

"Fair enough," I laugh and wave the bartender over to order another round.

"So if we're not going to talk about what happened today, what *can* we talk about?" I flash her a teasing smile, hiding my disappointment. "The weather?"

Relieved, she nods with a grin. "Seems safe. Okay—I'll start. Did you miss the snow while you were in California?"

I take a sip from my beer before answering. "I did. But then I moved to Massachusetts for five years where it snowed at least once a week during the wintertime."

"We rarely get any snow in New York unless it's because of a blizzard or something. And it only lasts about a day or two until it turns to sludge."

"Yeah, the snow gets pretty intense in Cambridge. So, despite having grown up here where we get a million feet of snow a year, I'm ready for a break. I'm thinking it's definitely time to go back to California." The words come out of my mouth, but I regret them as soon as they do. The urge to move back to the West Coast has somewhat dissipated since seeing Rosie. The idea of heading off to California while she's still in New York, of being separated by such a distance, is almost painful.

It suddenly hits me that, even if she does feel the same way, there is still so much to figure out together.

Is history about to repeat itself?

Shit.

My mind's a mess, my brain a couple of cracked eggs someone's scrambling in a bowl. I can't focus.

I know I want her any way she'll have me, but... What does she want?

"So, when do you find out about your NASA postdoctoral fellowship at Caltech?"

I smile half-heartedly. "They usually don't announce these things until the spring." But I don't tell her that it's basically a done deal for me. That my mentor is the one running the show and I'll probably get the official letter within the next couple of days. "I think I have a good shot at it, though." I shrug and take another sip of my beer, trying to hide the expression of disappointment on my face. This postdoctoral fellowship is everything I've been working toward since high school. And now? Now I'm wondering whether it's the right path for me.

I've spent almost a decade throwing myself into work, but it's only served as a way to distract myself from how utterly lonely and miserable I've been. It's been years of going on mindless dates, feeling like something's missing. And, of course, it's been her. It's always been her.

Is this the part where I give up my career to be with the woman I love? Because I'm scared I might actually do it.

"I'm sure you'll get it, Asher. I wouldn't worry about it. They'd be crazy not to take you." She smiles and rests her hand on my knee, and my heart jumps in my chest at the touch.

"Thanks," I mutter, feeling a bit guilty. I know how many people want this fellowship, and here I am thinking about all the other options and programs I still have time to apply to so I can be near her when we aren't even a thing, for Christ's sake!

"Look at us, all grown up with jobs and stuff. So official."

I chuckle. "Yeah. I definitely have you to thank for it, if I'm being honest. You're the one who gave me the book that inspired it all."

She smiles at me, sitting up in her seat. Rosie's hand unconsciously tightens on my knee, but I try to ignore it. "*Really?* That cosmos book? The one I gave you for your fifteenth birthday?"

I snort, because "that cosmos book" she's referring to is one of the most important scientific books of all time. Carl Sagan's masterpiece has been the spark—the *ah-ha!* moment—for so many to get into so many different branches of science—especially astrophysics. She doesn't know that the second she gave me that book, she opened my world up and changed who I am to the core. From the second I read the first sentence—"*The cosmos is all that is or ever was or ever will be*"—I was hooked. There was no going back.

And she gave that to me.

"Yeah, Rosie. That cosmos book." I quirk my mouth and shake my head.

"Well, if you're going to give me credit for your stellar career —haha, get it?—" I snort at her terrible joke. "—I think you should know that you're responsible for mine, too, in a way. You gave me the courage to apply to FIT and move to New York in the first place."

My heart stops.

"*Me?*"

Her smile is breathtaking as I process that *I'm* partly responsible for her leaving me? "Yeah! You pushed me to believe in myself. I would've ended up studying finance or business or whatever like my dad wanted."

"Wait, I don't understand." I squeeze my eyes shut and rub them beneath my glasses.

"Well—I wouldn't have had the courage to stand up to my dad and everyone else if it hadn't been for you. I would have *never* applied to that scholarship and gotten a full ride, I would've gone to Berkeley like you said, and I would have never gotten that promotion." She smiles, shifting excitedly in her seat. "Which I did, by the way."

Is she saying that if I had been less supportive, she would have taken that spot at Berkeley she got offered? Was *I* the one responsible for what happened?

I'm trying to catch up with my feelings, but I'm finding it difficult to get my thoughts in order. My heart rate spikes as I think everything over, until—no. Her going to New York was only half the problem, if that.

I want to be angry with myself for having pushed her to follow her dreams instead of the alternative, but I can't bring myself to do so. Rosie's happiness has *always* been my priority, and based on the expression on her face, she looks happy about the promotion.

I think.

"Congrats!" I force myself to say. "When did you find out?"

"A couple of hours ago, actually. Right after, um... " She clears her throat once. "Well, you know. *After.* My boss called me to give me the news." Her smile is bright, but it doesn't completely reach her eyes. It's as if she's holding something back. "It was my Christmas gift from the universe, I guess."

"Well, congratulations, Rosie. You deserve it," I manage, pushing myself to look as excited and happy for her as I possibly can. But I can't help the feeling of being punched in the stomach because she's made her choice. She's taking this job, officially tying her to New York.

Again.

I shouldn't be shocked or feel hurt—I mean, she lives there. *Has* lived there for several years. But something about us being here, the familiarity of it all, and feeling like it's all happening again is a bit crushing—hitting too close to home.

"Thanks." She chews on her bottom lip, not meeting my eyes. "I need to be back at the studio in New York on the third, which means I'm cutting my trip short. But it's good news." Her hands fly to her hair again, braiding and unbraiding it over and over again.

"So you're leaving on the *second?* Of January?" I ask, all the oxygen suddenly leaving my lungs. Because *no.* That's not enough time. *No.* How am I going to convince her that this thing with us isn't terrifying? That it's worth something? So she's staying in New York. Whatever. We can make it work, somehow. It's different now. We're adults.

"Yeah, it's soon. But the new season starts end of February, so we need to start building out concept designs and everything with the team as soon as possible."

"Right," I nod, a little dazed. I have less than a week to work with, here.

Difficult, but not impossible.

We spend the next hour discussing *Buffy the Vampire Slayer,* particularly the whole Angel vs. Spike thing (one of Rosie's favorite things to debate about). It's a little girl-talky to be honest, but I love watching her mind work as she rationalizes which man is better for the lead character of one of our favorite shows to watch together (it's the right amount of supernatural and Sarah Michelle Gellar for me, and the right amount of romance and comedy for her).

After an intense debate, she reaches the same conclusion she does every time: "Sure, Angel was almost perfect for her. But, hello! They would've never been happy. I mean, they couldn't even boink."

"Boink?" I burst out in laughter, but she ignores me.

"And then Spike was so cute and amazing to her once he got his soul back. Plus, he was hilarious and they had all that banter, whereas Angel was all broody and offered literally no comic relief. But then again Spike *did* do a lot of messed up things. So I don't see how you could ever get past all the terrible ways in which he tortured Buffy and her friends. Then he died all heroically and we realized the poor girl is just destined to be alone forever."

"*That's* bleak." I mutter, a little buzzed by now. "You just doomed one of our favorite fictional characters to a lifetime of loneliness."

Rosie snorts, shooting beer all over her. I burst out laughing and she starts to dry herself off with napkins. "Oh, god. It's down my shirt." She pulls her light pink sweater away from her skin and looks down her chest. Unable to help myself, my eyes follow hers to the soft swell of her breasts. "I need the bathroom," she says, getting up. "Be right back."

Taking a deep breath, I resolve to finally tell her everything once she gets back—to stop being scared and stop talking in half-truths.

I'm over it.

Just as I lift my hand to order another beer, I feel a slap on my back.

"Wolff boy!" I freeze, back ramrod straight. I recognize that voice, and it's definitely not one I want to hear right now. "How's it going, man? Long time no see."

I take a steeling breath, and turn to face Tyler Wesley—Rosie's ex. "Hey, man," I try to keep my voice as neutral as possible. The sudden anger that seems to light my skin on fire is unexpected, seeing as it's been almost ten years and I haven't given him a single thought since graduation.

"Saw you're here with our girl." He wiggles his brows, and I have to force my hands to grasp the edge of the bar, white-knuckling it. "You guys *together*-together, now?"

I want to tell him yes. I want to tell him to back the hell off. I want to tell him that neither she nor I want him here, especially after all the shit he put her through in high school.

But she's not mine. Not yet, anyway.

"Nah, man. Just friends."

He laughs once, unkindly. "Forever stuck in the friend zone, I see." He snorts and shakes his head, his eyes bloodshot. "She still around? Might give it another go with her."

The same sense of protectiveness rises within me. "No offense man, but what makes you think she'd ever get with you after what you did to her in high school?" Hoping he gets the message to get the hell out of here, I turn around in my seat, facing away from him.

In the reflection of the mirror behind the bar, I watch Tyler snort and cross his arms in front of his chest, looking way too smug for my comfort. "Only the fact that she and I finally slept together the New Year's after graduation?"

Once more, I freeze, hands fisting, because *no*. There's just no way she would do that. *No. Way.*

Except...

"It took a few years to get her into bed, but I definitely got farther with her than you ever did, apparently." My blood runs cold as he cackles, slapping me on the back again.

"*What* did you just say?" I turn slowly to face him, gritting my teeth. "Is this another one of your stupid rumors, Wesley? Same guy you were in high school, I see. Can't get a girl to sleep with you so you have to lie to everyone about it?"

He drops his arms and squares his chest, adjusting his stance. He's done playing, and frankly so am I. "No need to lie about this one, *Wolff*. I gave it to her, and *she. Fucking. Loved it.*"

Before I even know what I'm doing, I push my stool back and tackle him to the floor, the crowd separating as I straddle him and hold him to the ground. I'm not the lanky eighteen-year-old I once was, and Tyler Wesley has definitely let himself go since high school. This time, I have the advantage to kick his ass.

And that's exactly what I plan to do.

Rage overtakes my whole body, blinding me, turning me into an irrational being. I pull my fist back, ready to let him have it, when I feel two small hands holding it back.

"Stop!"

Chapter Twenty-Two

ASHER

18 Years Old

I CAN'T BELIEVE HE CAN JUST STAND THERE, LAUGHING WITH his buddies by their cars like nothing happened. Like he didn't just humiliate his on-and-off-again girlfriend—my best friend—of over a year in front of the entire school.

Doesn't Tyler care? Doesn't he give a shit about the fact that Rosie's been crying all day? That people have been whispering and looking at her every time she walks by?

Truth be told, I never liked the guy. Not from the second she came up to me and told me he'd asked her out. I warned her, told her all the things Tyler Wesley said about other girls and how he acted, but she said he was different with her, that he really cared for her.

Now, I don't know if that's true, but I do know that you don't make up some story and tell every guy in school that you slept with your girlfriend. And you definitely don't describe in full detail what she did and what you did to her. You don't let your buddies chant really inappropriate, messed up things at her as she walks by on her way to class in front of the rest of the school.

I watch as Tyler says something to his equally moronic cohort and they all burst into laughter.

The image of Rosie crying in homeroom earlier today, hiding her face behind a curtain of black hair while she softly sobbed, rips through me. And with that, the anger becomes impossible to control.

I tried to cheer her up by passing her a note, making sure she knew how amazing she is, and then subsequently spent the rest of the day checking up on her every so often.

But it wasn't easy.

Do you know how idiotic high school is? How mean people can be? Between the girls in our class calling Rosie a slut and the guys yelling lewd comments at her, it took everything in me to keep her from breaking down publicly, which would have ultimately made it worse.

"Wait 'til we get home," I kept telling her. "Wait 'til we get to your place, and then you can break down."

So here I am, waiting for her in the parking lot so I can give her a ride home, while I watch the idiot who hurt my best friend laugh it off like she doesn't mean anything to him.

But she means everything to me.

All of a sudden, the rage bursts through and, before I even know what I'm doing, I stomp off towards him and his buddies.

"Wesley," I call out. Tyler and his friends turn to look at me with skepticism. They cross their arms in front of their chests just as I belatedly realize that I'm about to pick a fight with the captain of the hockey team and his teammates.

Real smart, Asher. Prepare to be pummeled.

But my anger is bigger than my fear, and it's reached a boiling point that's definitely thrown me over onto the irrational side.

"What the hell do you want, Wolff?" He calls out, his jaw tight.

There's never been any lost love between the two of us.

I stop right in front of him, grinding my teeth, fists clenched at my sides. For a brief moment, I hesitate. But then I remember her telling me how he pushed her and tried to force himself on her when she refused. How he broke up with her and called her a prude, only to find out the next day that he'd told everyone they'd slept together anyway. That she'd spent the night at his place because his parents were out of town and he'd fucked her in every single position imaginable. Most people believed him, but I sure as hell didn't. Because she spent the night with me. She spent the night in my arms, crying softly as we watched hours and hours of The Big Bang Theory *even though I hate that fucking show.*

But I couldn't help it. "I watch it and it makes me think of you," she told me last night. "Of who you'll be after you finish getting your degree and your Ph.D."

"You expect me to be like Raj and not be able to talk to girls?" I asked her, feeling slightly annoyed.

She smirked at me. "No. But I like to dream of you getting everything you want, and I know that includes being a kick-ass astrophysicist, working at an amazing place like Caltech. Just like Raj."

Her words made my heart ache. I wanted to tell her that I wanted that, too, but that the thought of us going off to different colleges next year was killing me. I wanted to tell her that what I wanted was to be...together—though I couldn't quite figure out what that meant. I just knew I wasn't looking forward to not seeing her every day.

Tyler's expression morphs from one of anger and defensiveness into one of smugness. "Ah. You here to defend your precious Rosie's honor?" He and his group of idiots burst into laughter.

"You know what you said is bullshit," I say through gritted teeth. "You owe Rosie an apology."

He raises his hands in the air and shrugs. "Hey. I only spoke the truth, my man. It's not my problem you're jealous I made it into those pants before you did, you chump."

I'm gonna kill him.

I don't know exactly where I get the strength to do so, but I suddenly find myself tackling Tyler Wesley to the ground.

Despite having the advantage of the element of surprise, I only get one good punch in before he rolls us and sits on my chest. With a smile on his face, he holds me down with one hand and punches me right in the face with the other.

My head hits the pavement so hard, the pain so intense, I barely make out her screams, barely hear her calling out my name, begging him to stop hitting me.

At the sound of her voice, Tyler stops pounding on me, and jumps quickly to his feet. "Rosie. Babe."

Seriously???

"Babe, he started it." He whines, pointing a finger in my direction.

For once, he isn't wrong, though.

"Shut up, Tyler. I don't want to hear it," she snaps back, her voice a far cry from the small, beaten down one I've heard all day. I smile through the pain, because there she is. My girl is back.

Warm liquid gushes down my face as I look around, my eyes searching for hers. But the asshole's punched my glasses right off and I can't see anything.

As if reading my mind, I feel her scramble around beside me. "Here." She hands me my glasses, her voice low as she says, "Be careful. I think the creep broke your nose, because it's gushing blood."

In the background, I hear Tyler making up all kinds of excuses, begging her to talk to him, but we're in our own world now.

"Can you stand?" she asks, taking my hand in both of hers. "Sit up carefully first." So I do.

I gently put my glasses on, wincing at the pain on the bridge of my nose. "Yup, definitely broken." I try to act cool, like it doesn't hurt that bad, but the blow to the head makes me dizzy, and I almost fall right back.

"Okay, so I'm definitely driving you to the hospital. Where are your keys?"

My eyes widen. "You're going to drive?"

She glares at me. "I'm your only choice right now. I promise not to get us in an accident."

For a brief moment, I pause and just look at her—at the concerned, yet determined, look in her eyes. At how she's just taking charge of the situation, wanting to take care of me, and in that moment I know.

It's so goddamn glaringly obvious:

I love her.

I'm in love with her.

And it only took taking a punch to the face and a blow to the head for me to realize it.

Chapter Twenty-Three

ROSIE

"Wʜᴀᴛ ᴛʜᴇ ʜᴇʟʟ ᴅᴏ ʏᴏᴜ ᴛʜɪɴᴋ ʏᴏᴜ'ʀᴇ ᴅᴏɪɴɢ?" I ᴘᴜʟʟ him off Tyler by the shoulder, screaming at him over the drunken, rowdy crowd.

After some resistance, Asher finally releases my ex and gets to his feet, ignoring me completely.

"*Asher*," I plead, watching his angry face as he picks up his coat from the stool and stalks off, wrapping his scarf around his neck.

I look helplessly around, as if waiting for someone to give me some answers, but no one can deliver them. I watch the bartender round the bar and run over to Tyler, helping him to his feet.

"That motherfucker," he slurs. "He just fucking *tackled* me! *Again!*" Once steady, Tyler pushes the bartender's hands off him in frustration.

Shocked, I search the crowd for Asher and see him making a run for the exit. Tyler notices him at the same time I do and starts towards him, but is pulled back by the bartender. "Dude, just let him go. He didn't even punch you."

Wordlessly, I thank the bartender before picking up my things, leaving my ridiculous bachelorette regalia behind, and head off through the swarm of people in search of Asher.

I run after him as he pushes the front door of the bar open, slipping my coat on. The cold night air bites at my cheeks as I call out his name, stopping him before he can make his escape back home.

He freezes and mutters something under his breath.

"Asher, what *was* that?" I think back to the crazed look in his eyes as he held Tyler down, as he readied himself to hit him. I've never seen him like that—eyes wild, teeth clenched.

"How could you do it?" Asher's voice—venomous, cold—cuts through me. He turns to face me, and even in the low light from the lamppost I can tell his eyes are blazing with rage.

My stomach turns, and I pale.

He knows. Tyler told him, and now Asher knows.

"I—I—" I can't think of anything to say. I already know how low I stooped that New Year's Eve night.

Asher laughs once, humorlessly, digging both of his hands through his dark curls. "I don't get how you could sleep with him after everything. Forget about the fact that he broke my goddamn nose. You don't care about how he messed me up? Fine. But what about what he did to *you*? What about how he basically assaulted you and tried to force you into sleeping with him? What about all the shit he spread about you when you said no?" He drops his hands and looks at me with disgust. Bile rises in my throat and I have to swallow it down. "Don't you have any self-respect?"

I inhale sharply. Suddenly, *I'm* the one enraged. *I'm* the one fisting my hands at my sides. Trying to control the sudden urge to slap him once across the face—*hard*—I straighten and glare at him. "Don't you *dare* talk to me like that."

"I just don't get it. How can you just hook up with him? How could you just forget about everything we'd been through and just go to *him*? Did you do it to hurt me? Was that it? Because, if so, mission accomplished."

Now I'm *really* upset.

Fire courses through my veins as the image of him and that leggy mystery blonde pops into my head. "I went to that New Years' party for *you*, wanting to make things right with *you*. But it wasn't just about that—I wanted to *be* with you. To fix what I'd broken. I was there because I wanted us to figure things out and *be* together. And I looked and looked for you, only to find you hooking up with some random girl on our bench—which *you* admitted to doing to purposefully hurt me, by the way. So why would I even think what I did with another guy mattered even a little bit to you? How dare you make yourself the victim here when you didn't show one ounce of interest in me anymore? You made me think you'd moved on with someone else, so I tried to do the same."

His face falls, his brows furrowed in confusion. "You were there to make things right? To get together? Not just to fix our friendship?"

"I already told you this. I was there looking for you to *be* with you."

His eyes widen, and he shakes his head. "You didn't say it was to—"

"And then I found you. I found you, and there you were. Hooking up with someone else, making eye contact with me, showing me that you were the one who clearly didn't care anymore. So, yeah," I throw my hands up in frustration. "Yeah, I slept with Tyler because you had moved on and I hadn't. I slept with him because I was sad and pathetic and heartbroken and it was a mistake. You were so clearly trying to show me we were done. That you were completely over me. So what the hell do you care?"

Horrified, he shakes his head. "I—I wasn't *over* you, Rosie."

"Well, the fact that you had someone else's tongue down your throat certainly made it seem that way." I roll my eyes and cross my arms in front of my chest, trying to hide the ache where my heart is. Just remembering that night almost brings me to my knees. To this day, I've never felt a pain so visceral, so intense.

"I'm not proud of it, but..." Asher exhales, his warm breath visible in the cold night air, and he puts his hands on his hips, staring down at his boots. "Yes, I knew you were there. And... I was so hurt, Rosie. I admit I had a bruised ego, and having to see you after you rejected me the morning after the party was the hardest thing I would do. I wasn't over you, but I didn't want you knowing that. So, yeah. There was this girl and..." He shrugs, guilt spread clearly on his face.

A pause. "You are such a goddamn hypocrite, Asher." I can tell my words slice through him as he physically recoils, his widened eyes growing even larger. My eyes begin to sting and a sob catches in my throat. "You were intentionally trying to hurt me." My voice breaks on the last word as I try to hold myself together unsuccessfully. I feel the first tear slide down my cheek, so I bring my hand to my face to wipe it quickly away.

He winces, scratching the back of his head. "I—I was hurt. It's not an excuse, but it's why I did it." He shrugs, opening his mouth and shutting it again. "And I felt awful, because I knew it was wrong on so many levels. I told you this already."

I put my face in my hands and hunch over as the tears come freely now. I feel him reach out and place a hand on my shoulder, but I shake him off. *"Don't touch me,"* I hiss.

Yes, we talked about it. But things have changed over the past couple of days, and he knows it. My walls have come crumbling down, old wounds have been reopened, and try as I may, I can't keep repressing the lingering feelings I have for him.

Because they're there. Boy, are they fucking there.

"I would never *intentionally* hurt you, Asher. Yes, I messed up after graduation. I was stupid and selfish and thinking about myself. But it was never about purposefully hurting you. I was doing what I thought was right for me at the time. And I realized I had messed up the second I got to New York. I called you a thousand times, but you never picked up the phone. You refused to talk to me!"

"*Because you broke my fucking heart!*" He yells, his voice bouncing off the stone buildings in the empty street. "You fucking broke it!"

As if called upon by our combined rage, snow flakes begin to fall, swirling all around us, isolating us from the outside world. It's just us and our heartbreak in this snow globe.

Neither of us says anything for a moment, the silence enveloping us as we stare at each other, gauging what the other will do next. After a moment, his expression shifts and he stares at me with a desperate look in his eyes.

"Rosie." My name is a plea on his lips. "I admit that I was trying to make you feel shitty, but I was young and a kid, and that's how you handle things when you don't know any better. With immaturity and lack of forethought. It was an emotional response from an immature and heartbroken guy who wanted to look like he wasn't hurt and suffering every day of his goddamn life because you left him." He takes an impassioned step towards me, his gaze intense. Asher towers over me, standing so close his scent floods my brain, fogging my mind, his words making my head spin.

"I wasn't over you." He scoffs like the idea of him not caring about me is absolutely ridiculous. "But why *him*? Why did you have to pick the one guy I truly hated? The one I had to watch date and treat you like shit before my very eyes every day for almost two years. How could you still want him after everything?"

I realize all of a sudden that I don't care anymore. That I just want to come clean. "Do you think I slept with Tyler because I *wanted* him?" I scoff, shaking my head at how dense he can be.

"I was hurt, too, Asher. So I did something stupid that I regretted the second after it was over. Except I wasn't trying to hurt you like you were trying to hurt me. I did it because I was heartbroken and looking for comfort. Which is immature of me, as well, but still." I take a deep breath. "I did it because I thought we were through, and I was still in love with you."

The words hang between us, neither of us daring to say anything.

He steps closer, lifting his hands to cup my face, dragging his thumbs over my cheeks, wiping my tears away. My skin tingles, and that sparkly feeling in my chest resurfaces ever so slightly. "Rosie," he whispers, pressing his forehead to mine. "I'm so sorry."

I sniffle and place my hands on his chest, feeling his cold jacket beneath my fingertips, aching for all the time lost between us. "No, don't. It was my fault. The way I left—" I choke, shaking my head and squeezing my eyes shut. "I was wrong. So wrong. I wasn't thinking about anyone but myself and how angry I was at my dad. It was a reactionary response from someone who was terrified and didn't think twice about who she hurt in the process and there's not a day that goes by that I don't regret how I handled things before I left."

He shakes his head, frowning. "You already apologized."

"I know." I sniffle. "But it's not enough. It will never be enough. We'll never get back to that." My heart—it aches. Saying the words aloud is dangerous, but I can't keep repressing it anymore. After this afternoon, I don't think I can. I don't know if today was just a physical thing for him, but it definitely wasn't for me. Slipping back in love with him in a matter of days has been as inevitable as gravity.

But how does he feel?

"Rosie, I'm sorry. I wasn't ready to talk to you after you left. But, you're right—I shouldn't have run away from you or hurt you like that on New Year's. At the time, I wasn't sure..." He hesitates. "I wasn't sure about anything."

I can't look at him. So much has happened between us, so many mistakes were made—by the both of us. My heart's been dropped in a blender, pulverized, and turned into nothing so many times by him, it feels like a medical miracle to still be alive.

"But I'm here. I'm here now and I want this so fucking bad, Rosie," he says, an ache in his voice. "So *please*, Rose... How can we get past this? How can we get past all the stupid stuff that's happened between us over the last nine years?"

I stare up at him, heartbroken. My breath catches in my throat and I wipe under my eyes, the ache in my chest expanding. "I don't think we can."

Our breathing is ragged as I watch his eyes land on my lips, hands still cupping my face—gentle, but supportive at the same time. My hands fist on the lapels of his open coat, pulling him closer to me.

He swallows hard, slowly shaking his head. "I know that isn't true. *You* know that isn't true. We belong together, Rose. Always have. Always will."

"Ash." I feel a tear roll down my cheek, which he brushes away with his thumb. His large hands hold me tenderly, watching me with that look in his eyes...

"I'm here. And I'm not going anywhere. I'm here until you send me away."

For the first time in nearly a decade I feel safe. I feel like I'm exactly in the right place at the right time.

I tilt my face up towards his and push up onto my tiptoes, our lips less than an inch apart.

"Ash," I say again, conflicted. But I also know that I've waited nine years—even more than that—for this man, and, despite feeling absolutely terrified, I'm not about to let this opportunity slip between my fingers. Not if he wants it, too.

I'm scared—I've *been* scared—but I know I can do this now.

Suddenly, the tender look in Asher's eyes is replaced with one of conviction. He drops his right arm and wraps it tightly around my waist, pulling me roughly into him. My breath catches as I stare into his amber eyes and trip forward, one of my hands sliding under his jacket, pressing it right over his heart. I feel it beat rapidly beneath my palm, his chest moving quickly up and down as his breathing speeds and turns shallow.

With a pained voice, he murmurs, "I've missed you so much," before pressing his lips to mine with a relieved groan. And even though we've seen each other every day for the past couple of days, I know exactly what he means.

I whimper as he walks me backwards, pressing me with his body against the wall beside the pub door, trapping me between the cold brick and his hard chest. My pulse races and I can barely catch my breath as the spark inside my chest ignites like fireworks, bursting light through me, my heart squeezing in my chest. His lips move enthusiastically over mine, teasing them with his tongue until I open for him with a moan.

Asher's right hand travels to my hair, grasping it hard it a fist, pulling my head back. With his other hand, he removes my scarf from my neck, throwing it haphazardly on the snow by our feet. For a split second, it distracts me, but every thought in my brain is obliterated once his lips land on my neck, sucking on my skin. He groans into the spot where my shoulder meets my neck and nips me lightly, using the grip he still holds on my hair to maneuver me however he wants.

His other hand slides down to my lower back, where he pulls me even closer to him, his hand grazing the bare skin that's been accidentally exposed. He tightens the hand in my hair, and I moan loudly. Embarrassed, I blush and pull away. "I'm sorry, I —" But the hungry look in his eyes tells me everything I need to know: he loved it.

Asher's lips come down on mine once more, and I feel myself melt against him, because nothing will ever feel as good as his lips on mine, as the sensation of having his body pressed against mine.

Heat pools between my legs as the need to feel every inch of his body grows substantially with every kiss, every graze, every touch. Barely able to contain myself, I run my hands underneath his jacket to feel the muscles of his back, seeking his warmth, needing to be as close as possible to him. Wishing I could push his jacket off his shoulders and climb him like a tree, never wanting to stop for one second.

As if he could read my mind, he bends at the knees, sliding his hands behind my thighs, and lifts me to him, wrapping my legs around his waist. He holds my ass tightly in his hands and presses me up against the brick wall again. Asher pushes his hips into me, letting me feel the hard shape of his cock through his jeans, making me moan.

"Need you," he practically growls against my lips. His words vibrate through me, all the way to my core. Desire pools between my legs, which I tighten around his waist.

I dig my fingers into his hair, scratching his scalp with my nails, biting into his lower lip—*hard*. He hisses, goosebumps covering his neck, making me smirk.

An overwhelming feeling of light bursting inside me, makes the words "Missed you" slip from my lips.

He pulls away, gazing at me lovingly, my heart aching in my chest. I run my fingers through his mess of curls as he plants sweet pecks on my nose, my cheeks, my neck—anywhere he can reach.

Still a little drugged, still panting, I kiss the bridge of his nose, exactly where it was broken nine years ago.

"No foggy glasses this time." I grin, remembering our first kiss in the store stockroom.

He shoots me one of his lopsided half-smiles, and my heart flips. "Anti-fog lenses."

"In preparation for this moment?" I tease.

Asher grins down at me, nipping my lower-lip again. "I'd love to think I was that smooth. But no." He smirks, going in for another kiss—this one soft, seductive, but not hungry. As if we had all the time in the world to enjoy this—to enjoy *each other*.

Asher pulls away and presses his forehead against mine, our breaths mingling as I wonder idly how he's able to hold me to him for this long without his arms tiring.

I love this. I absolutely love this. I don't ever want to leave his arms ever again. I want to live here. Make myself a home here. Spend the rest of my life here.

Wanting to resume our make out session, I go in for another kiss—only the pub door bursts open with a loud noise, a young woman spilling out of it, falling to her hands and knees in the snow. Asher immediately sets me on my feet on the ground, as we look down on the heaving figure.

"Oh my god. *Andrea?*"

Chapter Twenty-Four

ROSIE

I drop to my knees beside my drunk sister, just as Diana appears behind her. "What the hell happened?" I guide Andrea into the pine bushes nearby and hold her long hair back, grimacing and looking away as she finishes throwing up.

"They were doing shots," my older sister grits out.

I shake my head in confusion. "Shots? Andrea doesn't *do* shots."

Diana's jaw ticks. "Well, she let herself be talked into them by Rodrigo." She scoffs, and looks off into the distance, her anger palpable. "They both did."

As if summoned, Alex stumbles drunkenly out of the bar, unfocused eyes searching for his fiancée. "Andy," he breathes. He attempts to kneel beside her, but instead slips on unsteady feet directly onto his bottom.

Asher moves quickly and helps Alex stand, while Diana and I do the same for our little sister. Outside in the fresh air, the smell of hard liquor is anything but subtle. They've definitely been hitting it hard.

Asher looks expectantly toward the door. "Rodrigo?"

"Not coming," Diana says tartly.

"Not coming? He's just going to stay at the bachelor/bachelorette party while his wife leaves to take care of her drunken sister?" I can't help asking.

"Let's just get these guys home," Diana bites back.

Holding my future brother-in-law by the arm, Asher says, "I'll take Alex to the hotel; it's just a couple of blocks away. Can you manage Andrea, or would you prefer to wait here while I drop him off?"

I adjust my little sister's arm around my neck, my hold around her waist. My height definitely has me at a disadvantage here, but her waif-thin figure is my saving grace. "We got this. Thank you, though. But how will you get home?"

"I'll have *The Inn* call me a cab or something. It's no big deal; I promise."

He frowns at me for a second, the wicked, yet still goofy, smile on his face just a memory burned into my brain. The intense look in his eyes tells me exactly what he's thinking— especially since I'm thinking it, too.

I wish more than anything that we hadn't been interrupted. I hate this for us right now. I want us to go back into our bubble.

"Please text me when you get home," I swallow hard, my heart breaking for the opportunity lost. "Just to make sure you get home safe." I pause. "You still have my number?"

Asher gazes intensely at me. "You kidding? Got that memorized." Using his free hand, he taps his finger to his temple and smirks.

Mourning what could've been, I shoot him an impish smile. With a final look over his shoulder, he turns and makes his way to *The Inn.*

Andrea asks about Alex, desperation in her voice. "He's fine," I reassure her as we walk to the car. "He went back to his room. You'll see him tomorrow."

"I love him so much," she sniffles as we strap her into the backseat. "I love him so much, and he doesn't know how awful I am." Andrea places her face in her hands and starts to cry, while Diana and I stare at each other, exasperated.

"I guess she's a weepy drunk." She shrugs nonchalantly, rounding the car and getting into the driver's seat.

The drive back home takes less time than it does for us to *quietly* carry our sister up the stairs. Frankly, it's a little infantilizing, if you ask me. Here we are, three grown women, shushing each other, trying not to get caught by our parents.

We change our sister into her jammies and have her slowly sip some water while she looks up at us with a miserable expression on her face.

"He doesn't know that I'm terrified," she whispers guiltily as we help her into bed.

Diana and I exchange a confused look.

"Alex. He doesn't know that I'm terrified of getting married."

"Jesus," Diana mutters under her breath, bring her palm to her forehead. "Are you saying you don't want to get married?"

"No!" My little sister sits up quickly and sways, catching herself on the bedside table. "No," she whispers. "I do. I do want to get married. I'm just so, so scared. How is he not scared? I don't want things to change. Why do they need to change?"

"Andre," I tell her. "Things aren't really changing. You're already living together. You're just... making the thing official. Just getting a piece of paper that makes it legal." I sit next to her at the edge of the bed and run my fingers through her dark hair. She nods, rubbing her hands under her eyes, wiping her tears away.

"Yeah, no, I know. I just love him so much, you know?" She

takes a deep breath and looks up at Diana. "How did you know Rodrigo was The One?"

My breathing stops and I look up at my older sister with questioning eyes. Diana stares anxiously down at the two of us, crossing her arms in front of her chest, nibbling on her lower lip. "Well?" Andrea presses her. "How did you know?"

"Andrea, marriage is—*can be*... overrated."

My little sister's eyes widen and her face pales. I scramble my brain to figure out what to say, what words will help save this situation. "What Diana *meant* to say was that putting a label on it—having a piece of paper—isn't going to change things." Andrea looks at me with hope in her eyes. "Isn't that what you meant to say to our little sister who is supposed to be getting married in less than a week?" I glare at Diana, wanting to kill her for throwing her insecurities and whatever the hell is clearly going on in her marriage at Andrea. Anyone with two eyes can see that Alex and my little sister are totally gone for each other, and that Diana and Rodrigo's relationship is on the rocks. "Right, Dee?"

Diana swallows hard and looks away. "Right. Everything will be fine, Andre."

My little sister sighs and looks down at her hands, frowning. "So you think it's all in my head?"

"I think it would be incredibly naive of you not to be a little scared, because it's a life-changing decision. But you love Alex, right?"

"Can't imagine my life without him." She sighs lovingly. "He's incredible. That's why I'm so scared."

"Don't be. You picked a good one." I smile and pat her hands, glad that she's calmed down some. "Now, go to bed. You have to spend the entire day with your in-laws skiing tomorrow."

Andrea groans and dramatically throws herself back on the pillows.

"G'night," I say, kissing her forehead.

"Night-night," she mumbles, already half-asleep.

I lead Diana out the bedroom, turning off the lights as I do. In the hallway, I turn to my older sister and glare at her. "What the hell *was* that?" I whisper-yell. "She's supposed to be getting married in five days and you're putting your shit on her."

"*Excuse me?*"

I sigh, rubbing my eyes in frustration. "C'mon. I'm sorry, but it's obvious you and Rodrigo are going through something." There's an uncomfortable pause where I wait for her to confirm my suspicions, but she doesn't budge.

"You know you can talk to me about it, right?"

She inhales sharply, assessing me carefully. "It's—It's not—" She exhales, her eyes suddenly devastated. "It's not something I'm ready to talk about yet. But you're right. I was... *putting my shit* on Andrea when I absolutely should not have been."

I frown, and take her hands. "When you're ready, I'm here to listen."

"Thanks," she mumbles, wiping a tear away. "Not tonight, though. I'll see you tomorrow."

I sigh as I watch my sister walk back to her childhood room, closing the door softly behind her with her head hung low.

Feeling conflicted, I remind myself that there's nothing I can do for my big sister right now. She needs to come to me.

Plus, after such a long day all I want is to slip into bed and wonder what could've been had Asher and I not been interrupted. I groan as I take my jacket and sweater off, not wanting to think about how damn frustrated and *bereft* I feel.

As I pop my jeans open, my phone vibrates in my back pocket.

ASHER

You home right now?

ROSIE

> Yeah. Just put Andrea to bed. You get home
> safe?

I see the dots bounce on the screen, waiting for his answer, only to have them disappear again. I frown down at my phone, waiting but nothing comes up. Just as I give up hope on receiving another reply, I hear a loud tap on my window.

"Jesus!" I nearly jump out of my skin at the sight of the top of Asher's head, dark curls on full display. The initial shock, however, disappears as the memory of me running my fingers through his hair while practically mauling his face about half an hour ago makes me shiver. He grins widely when my eyes meet his, though I can tell he's struggling to hold on. I move quickly to slide the window open, bringing with it a wave of chilling air.

"Holy crap," he whisper-yells. "How the hell did I used to do this all the time?" I watch as he transfers his grip from the trellis to the window ledge.

"You getting old? Not as spry as before?" I tease as he pulls himself through the window.

He laughs once, still struggling. "That and the fact that that trellis is about five minutes from breaking apart. I swear this thing is almost fully rotted. It's a miracle I didn't just fall to my death."

I snort as he lands in my room head-first with an ungraceful thud.

"*Shhh.* You're going to wake everybody up." But I'm laughing, thrilled at this surprise. I feel like I'm back in high school, sneaking around after curfew with my best friend. Except this time, I can't help thinking about what he's hiding under all those layers.

Asher gets to his feet and adjusts his glasses on his nose,

before sliding the window shut. "I thought I was going to die there for a minute."

"I'm happy you didn't." I stare up at him in awe. I can't believe that we're back here after nearly a decade. "It's been a minute since you climbed through my bedroom window. Any particular reason why?"

He smirks, taking a step closer to me. One of his arms winds around my waist, pulling me roughly into him. I inhale sharply, my hands flying to his chest.

Damn it, Rosie. Be cool, dude.

But my heart beats so loudly in my chest, I swear to god it reverberates through the entire house. I wish I were the type of person that can play it cool, but there's no denying that I'm seconds away from ripping the clothes off his body. I have no poker face.

As if reading my mind, Asher gives me a mischievous look and leans down, placing a soft kiss on my neck, then another higher up just below my jaw.

Struggling to keep my breathing steady, I fist his cold jacket in my hands, steadying myself as his right hand cups my face. I feel my body shiver, but it's not from the winter bite of his cold jacket.

"I felt as though we had some unfinished business to discuss," he murmurs in my ear.

Chapter Twenty-Five

ROSIE

"Yeah? What kind of things?" Heat pools between my legs as my brain goes foggy. Blanketed by the darkness of the bedroom, the scent of citrus and detergent overpowers me, weakening my knees.

His free hand digs into my hair, using the strong grip to tilt my face up towards him. Asher watches as I toy with my lower lip like a hawk, his gaze dark and hungry. He tightens his grip in my hair, his hand so large his thumb comes around my neck. Another gasp as he squeezes lightly, because gone is unsure and hesitant Asher.

I stretch up on my tiptoes, shortening the distance between us, slipping my hands under his jacket to feel the hard muscles of his chest. With winter layers on, he doesn't look like the type of guy who's built. But as I run my hands over him, I can feel the chiseled shape of his pecs, his abs, his shoulders, all hidden under the soft fabric of his sweater.

Asher isn't a cartoon of a scientist, one of those clichés you see on TV who live for their discoveries and the Marvel universe. He isn't a cruel stereotype of a nerdy person, with absolutely no social skills, lanky and pasty. He's passionate about his research, yes. But he's also just a guy who looks to the stars for answers with a normal interest in superhero movies, helps strangers pull suitcases from baggage claim carousels, runs, and is *perfection* underneath those layers of winter clothing.

His lips hover over mine, his breath tasting like hops and sweet, sweet memories. "Ash—"

He groans, and I feel the rumble of it under the palms of my hands. He nips at my bottom lip, gentle enough for it not to hurt, but hard enough to let me know he's on the edge of losing control.

The sparks in my chest reignite—burst—as his lips fall on mine, kissing me with newfound desperation. Locked in my childhood bedroom, it's just us, completely unfiltered, our need for each other unhidden. We're done pretending like we don't want each other anymore.

It's liberating.

Asher slides a leg in between both of mine and I moan, the sound of my need unleashing something within him. Practically growling against my lips, he takes his jacket off in one swift movement, throwing it behind him.

"Need you right fucking now," he says against my lips, greedy hands flying to the hem of my sweater, pulling it off. It feels so natural to want him like this, I don't even give any of it a second thought.

I slide my hands under his sweater, under his thermal, and start to pull them off at the same time. But his impatience gets the better of him and he removes the layers himself.

Through half-lidded eyes, he watches me as he throws the bundle of clothing to the side, where it lands on my desk lamp. In hushed laughter, he pulls me closer still.

I reach out and fix his glasses, askew from kissing, and he shoots me a tender smile. Suddenly, it's like a veil of tension disappears, evaporating into nothingness, leaving me only with the feeling of joy that I'm here, half-naked with my best friend (former best friend?), about to do something I've dreamt of for years.

Asher stares down at me with a smile on his face, the skin-on-skin contact driving me a little crazy as his hand pushes my pink hair away from my face. "You're so beautiful. I always thought you were so beautiful."

I feel myself blush and I have to look away.

His fingers go to my chin, and he guides my gaze back to his. "Don't. Please don't do that."

"Do what?"

"Run away from this." He swallows hard. "Not yet. At least give me tonight."

I open my mouth to protest, to ask what he means exactly by that, but he silences me by putting his mouth on mine with a moan, obliterating every other thought in my mind. All I can focus on is how his fingers are pulling the zipper of my pants down slowly, torturing me inch by inch with anticipation.

With one arm looped around his neck to support myself, I manage to unbuckle his belt and pop his jeans open with the other. My hand slides into his boxers and we both stop breathing as I feel the heat of him.

"*Fuck*, Rosie. *Fuck*." His fingers dig into my hips as if his grip on me is the only thing holding him on this earth.

Asher spins me and pulls my back into his chest, the contact absolutely delicious. With one hand, he pushes my hair to one side and nuzzles my neck, kissing down all the way to my bare shoulder. His tongue plays against my skin as one arm grips me tightly against him, feeling his hardened cock against my lower back. My stomach clenches at his touch, and I suddenly feel painfully self-conscious. The fog of lust clouding my mind has cleared enough for me to realize that the last time this man saw me naked I was 18, several pounds thinner, had considerably fewer stretch marks, and gravity had not yet taken its toll on certain parts of my body. Asher, on the other hand, had always been my cute best friend. But now, as a *man*—grown, solid like an oak tree, his handsome features more mature—he's irresistible.

Talk about a glow-up.

I lean back into him, letting him support my body as my legs turn to jelly. His fingers slip under the waistband of my underwear, just teasing. I feel the light touch all the way to my core as he trails his fingers back and forth under the elastic. The feeling is so exquisite, it makes me whimper, my eyes sliding shut.

But for a moment, I hesitate. I've spent the past twenty-four hours eating like a glutton and the night drinking beer—I'm bound to be bloated. I look down at myself and grimace. Panic spreads through me as I try not to go to an insecure place, wishing my body looked the way it did when I was 18. I'm all about self-love, but even the best of us has our weak moments.

"Shouldn't you, ah—" He bites my skin and I feel it between my legs. But I don't let it derail me. "Shouldn't you take off your glasses?" I whisper, my voice shaking a little.

I feel him shake his head against me, his nose in my hair as he inhales deeply. "I want to—*need* to—see you."

"B-but—" I stammer. "But won't you ruin them or something? Your glasses, I mean."

"Stop it," he murmurs against my skin, taking my bra strap between his teeth and letting it snap against my shoulder when he releases it.

"What do you mean?" My voice is nearly inaudible as he continues to trail his mouth up to my jaw.

"You're beautiful and soft and perfect and I've been waiting *years* to see you like this again. So please. Stop it. I'm not taking my glasses off—you're gorgeous and I want to see all of you. You have nothing to worry about." The fact that we're so connected, that he can read me so well—even now, while our minds are clouded with this hunger for each other—makes my chest tighten. The already-difficult task that is breathing becomes nearly impossible.

I feel safe; this is right. Of course, there will be consequences to deal with tomorrow. But right now, all that matters is being with him like this.

Asher trails the back of his hand down my side, raising the hairs on the back of my neck. He slips a hand under my bra, cupping my left breast in his hand. We both groan at the contact, and he whispers, "You feel incredible." His teeth graze my neck, my body yielding to him, arching to give him better access.

One of his hands drops to my hip, while he slowly drags the knuckle of the other tantalizingly down my spine, pausing only to unhook my bra. Gently, he presses another kiss to my shoulder, slowly lowering my bra down my arms, fingers grazing my skin.

After helping me wiggle out of my jeans, Asher grabs me by the waist and tosses me onto my bed, where I land with a gasp and a bounce. I scoot back on the mattress, watching as he undresses. With a predatory look in his eyes—a slight smirk that says, "*Now I've got you*"—he prowls toward me.

My heart races as I tremble in anticipation, watching with disbelief as his hands travel up my knees to the inside of my thighs and back again, his nails scratching my skin slightly.

"I've waited so long for this," he says, his voice low and guttural.

It's impossible to hide the ache in my voice when I reply, "I know; me, too."

"*Jesus Christ*." His gaze travels slowly up and down my body, his fingers tracing the lines of my lace pastel pink underwear. He ducks, pressing his lips to my right hipbone, then the left. Pressing open-mouthed kisses in between both my legs, over the pink fabric of my lace underwear, my back arching off the mattress. Asher climbs up my body, kissing what seems like every inch of it.

"Asher." I bow off the bed again as he sinks his teeth into my shoulder, following it with a soft kiss.

"You want this?" His voice is gravelly, deep. And if his question weren't absolutely ridiculous, I'm pretty sure it would've made me melt into a puddle.

I snort at him. "Are you kidding?"

"I need you to say it. I need you to say that you want this, too."

"I want this. *God,* do I want this."

He flashes me a heartbreaking half-smile and kisses me softly on the lips, laughing into my mouth. "Just checking." He tugs at my lower lip, soft kisses turning into heated ones.

The next thing I know, Asher's kissing his way down my body, his hands on my hips. He hooks his fingers under the elastic of my underwear, licking me once over the fabric in a slow, languid movement. I inhale sharply; my heart stops beating.

I moan, my eyes rolling into the back of my head.

"I want that, Rosie." His voice is gravelly—assertive. "But not right now. I've waited nine years to be inside you again and I can't wait a second longer." I feel his warm breath against my wet skin as he slowly pulls the last piece of clothing between us.

He climbs over me once again, kissing what seems like every inch of my body, stopping at my breasts for just a moment, before settling comfortably between my thighs. Arms looping around his neck, legs wrapping around his waist, hardness rocking against where I'm ready for him. The feeling of him sliding hard over where I'm wet and soft, is exquisite. We both groan at the feeling, Asher's back muscles tightening underneath my hands.

One part of my brain wants to beg him to stop teasing me, to do it already. But the other, smarter side overrules it. I want to lose myself in him, drown in this sensation, live in his arms and—

"Protection. I—I don't have any," I groan, feeling terrifyingly close to having my head explode.

Asher smirks, amber eyes shining in the darkness. "I, uh, may have made a pit stop on my way here."

This man.

He pushes up off me with a smile on his face, pecking me on the lips once before running over to his jacket faster than the Road Runner could ever have dreamed of.

He rips the gold foil in his hands with the words *Magnum* emblazoned in bold on it. It's only then that I gain the courage to actually look down *there*, just to mentally prepare myself. Watching in awe as he rolls the condom on, I gasp as I realize just how much of a glow-up Asher *really* had.

Once he's done, he comes back over me and pulls my left thigh tightly over his right hip. I stare up into his frantic, yet low-lidded eyes, digging my fingers into his hair. Suddenly, the weight of this momentous thing we're about to do hits us both just as he lines himself up. "Asher—" I choke.

He nods once, swallowing hard. "I know," he whispers, kissing me deeply as I cant my hips up to him. "I'm right there with you, Rose."

I wince as he pushes in, his size and the fact that I haven't slept with anyone in years making it nearly impossible. But I'm turned on enough that it takes just a few small thrusts and a little patience. He peppers sweet kisses on my neck and chest and when he slides in to the hilt, we groan in unison, pausing only to enjoy the feel of each other's bodies.

How is this happening? How did we get here?

He goes slow at first, with tiny thrusts made to help me get used to his size. But it's tight and his jaw is clenched in self-restraint, his muscular arms shaking as he holds himself over me.

Asher shifts his weight to his left arm, his right hand traveling to where both our bodies are connected. His lips come over mine, tongue licking into me as his thumb starts to circle my clit in quick, precise movements.

I whisper his name against his lips as both our breathing grows even more ragged. The speed of his movements increases, the stretch less painful. I wonder idly how he could be so coordinated, thrusting into me like that, holding himself above my body, all while getting me to where I need to be with his fingers.

I feel the pleasure build between us, the heat and light fill me to the brim right before I explode all around him. Breath catching against his lips, my mind goes blank. I feel the wave of pleasure fall over me and spread through every inch of my body. Vaguely, I feel him press his mouth to mine again, muffling my cry as my back arches off the bed once more and my nails dig into his shoulders.

The orgasm lasts for what feels like hours, my mind so foggy that I don't even notice that he's hooked my legs over his arms, spreading me.

"You're fucking unreal. *This* is fucking unreal," he growls, his voice low.

Asher comes over me, my legs spread wide, and shifts his hips forward once more. I cry out because I can feel every perfect inch of him this way. He shushes me and presses a hand over my mouth, silencing my moans as his hips start to rock into me with a punishing rhythm.

Gone is the careful man. Out of control Asher is here for the remainder of the night.

The feeling of him moving inside me is so good, I struggle to keep my eyes open through it. But I want to see him—*need* to see him. To see the wildness in his eyes behind the lenses of his tilted glasses. To see how much he wants this, me—*us*.

Despite the look in his eyes, the change in his demeanor, I

can tell he's holding back. We're *both* holding back because it must be around 2:00 A.M. at this point, and we're in my twin-sized childhood bed, in a house filled with sleeping people, and I just want to scream his name.

The urge to lose our minds with each other is strong—I want him to go harder, faster, scream my name—but every time he tries, the headboard knocks into the wall and we have to pause.

He shifts my legs up onto his shoulder and moves down to kiss me, bending me in half.

"I love that you're so flexible," he pants against my temple. "Does it hurt?" he asks, half concerned, half distracted.

"Yes, but—*ah*—in a good way."

"Good," he growls, shifting his weight onto one arm so he can wrap a hand at the base of my throat. "Next time," he whispers against my ear, "I'm going to fuck you so hard, you're going to beg me not to stop."

"I don't want you to stop now," I complain.

He laughs in my ear, a breathless, choppy laugh. "I know. But you're about to come, and so am I," he says through gritted teeth.

I open my mouth to object, when he pulls up onto his knees, wrapping his left arm around both my thighs, holding them to his torso. His hair is a mess and his glasses are falling off his face as he thrusts into me.

He's so good, this is so good, and I never want it to end.

The speed of his hips increases and I'm so close again, and he's so close, and I can't keep my eyes open a second longer as they roll to the back of my head and I pull a pillow over my face because—

I come harder than I've ever come in my life, my skin igniting, dewy and flushed. My sounds are muffled as I let the final wave of pleasure wash over me, leaving me a trembling mess.

And just as I start coming down from my high, I feel his hold tightening around my legs as he succumbs to his release.

He pulls the pillow off me and tosses it aside, lying on top of me with a groan, burying his face in my hair.

Panting, I try to wrap my mind around what just happened. But I push it aside, wanting to enjoy this moment for what it is, without having to think about the consequences. Not now. Not yet.

"Rosie," Asher whispers in my ear. "I don't—" I hear him swallow hard and readjust himself over me.

"What?" I ask, muscles locking, bracing themselves for rejection.

He blows out a puff of air and pulls out, still hovering over me. He fixes his glasses over his nose—smudged from what we just did—and looks down into my eyes. "I have to say that... I don't think there's *any possible way* that no one heard what we just did."

We burst out into whispered laughter and he rolls off me, running his fingers through his hair. He turns to look at me with a half-grin and pulls me into his chest. With a sated smile, I burrow closer into him and feel the press of his lips against the top of my head. The last thing I remember is my eyes drooping as I feel his arms wrap tightly around me, holding me to himself.

Chapter Twenty-Six

ASHER

The weight of Rosie's arm as she rolls into me—legs unconsciously tangling with mine, face snuggling into my shoulder—wakes me. My chest swells with emotion, the feeling so incredible I actually have to do a mental double-take to make sure I'm not dreaming.

But no. After taking a few minutes to run through everything that happened last night and taking in the very real way in which my left arm seems to have fallen asleep due to the weight of her on it, I come to the conclusion that I'm not dreaming at all. This is real. Last night was real.

I grin stupidly at the ceiling before my eyes land on her, admiring how the early morning sun creeping in from the window lands on her naked back, making her skin glow even more radiant than it usually does. I move my fingers softly over it, writing my name over her ribs with my fingertips, laying claim, feeling incredibly possessive of her.

Even though I absolutely have no right to be.

She's never *officially* been mine—I know that. But it's getting harder and harder to deny how much it feels otherwise.

I reach over to the nightstand with my free hand to retrieve my glasses and phone, moving carefully enough so I don't jostle

Rosie and wake her. I don't *think* she'd kick me out of her room, but I also don't want to leave unless I absolutely have to.

The time on my phone tells me it's 6:00 A.M—which means I've only slept about three hours. I can't help my grin as I think about the two incredible, mind-blowing, life-altering rounds of sex that kept us up that late.

Last night was us fulfilling a physical and emotional need; reconnecting after nearly a decade's worth of hunger that we've kept suppressed. There was no battling the gravitational pull between us. We didn't focus on what it all meant for us; all we did was go by what we were feeling—what we've *been* feeling.

Now that we're no longer in the moment though, I need to take a minute and ask what we're doing, what this all means, and what the hell we're going to do once the holidays are over.

I grimace, just imagining Rosie's rejection. I don't think I would be able to handle that again. Not after last night.

Just as I'm about to set my phone down, I read the banner notification underneath the time and my stomach drops. A huge knot forms in my throat and my heart beats a loud drum while my eyes remain laser-focused on my lock screen:

From: Space Telescope Science Institution
Subject: Your Application to the NASA Hubble Fellowship
Program
Date: December 26th, 12:03 am PST

Hands shaking, I unlock my phone and click on the email, swallowing hard.

Dear Mr. Wolff,

We are pleased to inform you that you have been accepted into the

NASA Hubble Post-Doctoral Fellowship program to be completed at CalTech University pending your completion of your Ph.D. program by Spring of this year. We...

I stop reading after the first sentence, unable to continue. That's it. I knew it was already pretty much a done deal, but now it's official. Rosie accepted her new job and is staying in New York City, and I'm headed back to California to continue my research.

Chest cracked wide open, I try to envision a world in which we don't happen, in which we both go back to our old lives and leave this night behind. I struggle to breathe, to keep my heart beating as I feel the ground shake beneath us. But then I feel Rosie snuggle closer into me, her pink hair shifting, falling smoothly off her back and it gives me hope.

She sighs softly as her arms tighten around me, and I know just with that movement that she's only a few seconds from waking.

I stare down at the woman who's had my heart for most of my life and am filled with emotion. Four years of undergrad and five years of graduate school have all led to this one career-making moment, and I'd give it up in a heartbeat if it meant I got to be with her.

But is that even what she wants? Would she even take me? I'm prepared to beg.

God, I'm so pathetic.

I twirl a strand of her hair tightly around my index finger, wanting to tie myself to her permanently.

No, I won't let this be over. After all these years, all this pain, we can't leave things like this. We can't have had what we had last night and just go back to our normal lives.

I won't go down without a fight.

With a deep breath, Rosie stretches over my chest and

smiles, the feeling of her naked breasts moving against me causing other parts of me to stir.

"Hey," she yawns softly, her smile breaking through my panic.

I smile, helpless, and bring my hand to cup her face. "Morning."

She blushes deeply, struggling to meet my eyes as I sit up in bed. The ache to feel her all over again is so strong, I don't even wait for her to reply before I kiss her.

I can tell I've caught her off guard, but then she deepens the kiss, standing up on her knees, wrapping her arms around my neck to kiss me more comfortably.

"Mmm," she hums before pulling away. "What time is it?"

"Six-ish. I should leave soon," I whisper against her lips, wrapping an arm around her waist and pulling her closer to me, taking us both down onto the mattress.

Rosie's lips part for my tongue, and soon we're lost to each other again, my hand cupping her ass as she hooks a leg over my hip.

"God, you feel amazing." I mumble, already dizzy and out of breath.

She giggles and pecks me chastely. "You said that last night." The memory of being inside her almost breaks my focus.

I burrow my face into her hair, inhaling the scent from her neck. "You smell incredible." Like coconut and home.

"You said that, too." I chuckle as she nibbles on my bottom lip, her hand traveling down my chest at a painfully slow pace. I want her to touch me again, but not right now.

I grab hold of her wrist before she reaches her wanted destination and bring her hand to my lips, kissing every knuckle. "Turn around," I command.

She stares up at me for a second, wordless. "Turn—?"

"Turn around," I cut her off without further explanation.

Rosie pouts for a second, her bottom lip jutting out for a moment. I smirk and she smiles playfully up at me, but ultimately listens and turns away.

I wrap an arm around her waist, pulling her back to my chest so hard, it's a wonder either of us are still breathing. But it's like I can't get close enough to her to be satisfied, like nothing will ever be enough.

The idea of having to let her go in just a few days' time makes matters worse, and only makes me increase my grip around her. If I hurt her, she never says anything about it, but I can tell the atmosphere in the room has shifted from one of playfulness to one of desperation. It's like we both know this could be the last time we're together.

I mean to kiss her shoulder once like I know she loves, but the overwhelming need to enjoy this moment before it's gone leads me to sink my teeth into her soft skin, possessive.

I can't lose you again.

I desperately want to say the words, to make sure that everything will be okay. But if this is going to be the last time I'm with her like this, there's no way I'm risking it with conversation about whatever the hell this means.

Instead, I practically growl the all-encompassing words, "I want you," in her ear. Like last night, an involuntary shiver runs through Rosie's body, raising goosebumps all over her soft, tan skin.

"I want you, too," she breathes, her voice barely audible.

I suck softly on her neck, lips grazing up to her jaw as I cup her breasts in my hands, feeling the tight nipple under my palm. I squeeze her hard enough to elicit a gasp—the sound of it shooting straight down my spine, making me want her more. My right hand wraps softly around her neck before moving slowly down between her breasts and over her stomach. When it stops just under her bellybutton, my beautiful girl starts to squirm uncomfortably.

"Not my stomach, please."

I hold her tighter still, my lips to her ear. "You. Are. Beautiful." I punctuate every word with a kiss under her ear. "I. Love. Every. Inch. Of. Your. Body." Rosie inhales sharply as my hand travels further down, her body tensing with anticipation.

I smirk, because, after last night, I know exactly how to turn her pliant.

I kiss her neck once more, open-mouthed, and feel her shiver against my body with a soft hum that drives me to the edge.

I tighten my arms around her. With a low and commanding voice, I whisper, "Get on you hands and knees."

With my arms still wrapped around her, I kiss slowly up her neck. Relishing in the slickness of sweat between my chest and her back, we both try to catch our breaths.

I don't want this moment to end, but here we are yet again.

I nuzzle her neck, anticipating the conversation I really don't want to have—but also really do.

"That was..." she breathes.

"Yeah." I press my lips to the ball of her shoulder once more, which is rapidly becoming one of my favorite places to kiss, too.

She looks at me over her shoulder, her pink hair a mess underneath us both, a frown on her face. There's a question in her eyes, but she doesn't dare ask it. Not out loud. And I think it's because neither of us knows how to answer it.

Yet.

Instead of putting pressure on the situation, I give her a soft kiss, letting her know it's okay if we don't talk about this now. But when I pull away and gaze at her happy, loving expression, my heart tightens in my chest and this time I feel myself frown.

"What is it? Is it us?" Panic causes her face to pale, which makes me ignore the sudden rush that courses through me at her use of the word *us*.

"No. *No.*" I rush to turn her body to face me head-on, cupping her face in my hands when she does.

"Because if—"

I kiss her quickly again, stopping her from saying something neither of us wants to hear right now. "No. It's not that. It's—" I wrack my brain, trying to think of what to say, what logical excuse I could come up with. "It's—"

Fuck, Asher. Think faster.

"Is it the post-doc thing? Is it because you haven't heard back yet?"

Bingo.

"Yeah, the post-doc fellowship has me really stressed out. Sorry." And it isn't even a lie—it's just for different reasons than she thinks.

She lifts her hand to run her finger through my hair, smiling softly at me. "You're so smart and amazing. I can't imagine why anyone ever wouldn't want to have you."

I know she didn't mean anything specific by it, but her choice of words makes my chest ache, the pain of what the future holds pulling me out of this perfect moment, sinking its teeth into me.

Pressing my forehead to hers, I squeeze my eyes shut. I mumble a thanks, but otherwise bite the inside of my cheek, trying to keep myself from asking her questions I might not be ready to hear the answers to yet.

She kisses my chin, and I open my eyes to meet hers. Taking in her beautiful features, the curve of her full lips, her dark brown eyes, I bask in the knowledge that I've loved this woman for almost my entire life and will likely continue to do so regardless of whether we end up together or not.

And in that moment, I know I've made my decision. I know what I'm going to do.

ROSIE

THE SNOW CRUNCHES BENEATH MY BOOTS AS I MAKE MY way to the shop. It snowed pretty heavily last night, but the town is good about keeping the streets clean and the sidewalks salted, so the walk there isn't too bad. Which is good, since what happened last night between Asher and me has me so distracted, I've already tripped about three times just on my own two feet, never mind the black ice.

I can't get the memory of us out of my head, the words he grunted and whispered into my ear replaying over and over again—*coming* and *been wanting this for so long, so fucking long* —culprits of the constant shivers running up and down my spine all morning.

Less than a week ago, I was dreading coming back home, knowing that there was a chance that I might run into him despite having been told he wasn't going to show. And when I saw him at the airport, standing there, looking delicious? My heart broke all over again for the missed opportunity of what could have been our relationship. I thought he still hated me. I thought he wouldn't want to speak to me ever again. I broke our hearts and thought I'd never get another chance at repairing them.

But after last night, I'm beginning to question whether all is lost. Does he want to actually give this a shot with me? Or was it just something fun, just a fling for the holidays?

I realize that this is a conversation we probably should have had earlier this morning when we were still in bed, but one thing led to another and we were lost in each other.

With the exception of that thing with Tyler, I'm not someone who jumps into bed with just anyone, but I don't think I need to have had a lot of sexual experiences to understand that last night was special—that it was otherworldly.

Even my first time with Asher didn't come close to what last night and this morning turned into.

By the time we were done this morning, sounds of stirring were starting to come from the other bedrooms in the house. Asher had to leave quickly, tiptoeing out the front door to avoid getting caught. We didn't get a chance to discuss what had happened or how we were going to move forward.

Honestly? Even now, as I make my way to *Seymour's* to have this conversation, I have no idea what I would say. I mean, I feel like I've loved Asher most of my life. If I haven't been able to shake him off after all this time, I hardly think I'll be able to after what we shared last night and this morning.

But what does that mean? Does that mean jumping into a relationship? Is that something we should be doing? Is that even what he wants? What *I* want? If all goes to plan, he'll be moving to California in just a few months to pursue his postdoctoral fellowship at Caltech. And I... I'll still be in New York. Doing my own thing. Working at *Celebrity Dance Battle*—same as I've been doing for so many years now.

I pause at a stoplight and groan, squeezing my eyes shut. It's like high school all over again, both of us heading to different parts of the country, starting another phase of our lives without the other in it.

It's like someone knocked all the air out of my lungs, leaving me paralyzed with fear. My head is a mess, and I want to cry. I don't want to talk to him, but we need to eventually address it all, and it has to be away from the prying eyes of our family members.

When I get to the shop, I pause with my hand on the doorknob, steeling myself. I watch Asher through the storefront window as he moves some ski equipment to the front from the back, his curls a mess.

I'm briefly distracted by his disheveled hair, reminding me of how I ran my fingers through it all night as he kissed every inch of my body. Reminding me of how I held on to it several times just from what he was doing.

My breathing speeds as a sudden image of Asher above me pops into my head, his neck snapped back, telling me how he's been waiting for this very moment for years—*for fucking years, Rosie.* It blinds me. An electric current runs through me and my skin heats.

Shit.

I try to rein in my emotions and push the door open, the bells atop the door jingling.

Asher's head lifts from his work to look in my direction. Immediately, the concentrated look in his eyes shifts to one of happiness, and for a brief second I think everything will be okay.

That is, until I remember all the reasons this might not work out.

Maybe his smile is just a friendly one. Maybe it's his way of saying it was a one-time—okay, *three*-time—thing. Maybe he just wants to be friends and forget about it all. Which would be... okay? I think I could live with that. I could live with him wanting to remain friends. It would mean having him in my life even though I won't... you know... *have* him in my life. But I'm pretty sure I'd rather be friend zoned and never have him care about me the way that I oh-so-clearly do, than have Asher regret what we did last night.

But there's no way he didn't feel what I felt, right? I mean, can experiences like that be completely one-sided? Did I really hallucinate how freaking incredible it all was?

God, I'm a mess.

"Hey." Asher grins broadly at me, setting the clipboard and pen in his hands on the counter behind him. My eyes land on the rolled-up sleeves of his sweater, his strong forearms in plain sight, making my heart tighten in my chest.

What is it about men and forearms? Is it just me?

"How are you?"

I walk deeper into the store, wondering how to even start talking about this. How much painful small talk will we have to endure? But when I accidentally word-vomit, "Sore," I realize that I pretty much just saved myself minutes of awkward chit-chat leading up to the big one.

Asher chuckles bashfully, his cheeks tinged with my favorite shade of pink. "Yeah," he coughs into his hand. "Me, too." It's his shy, but still playful smile that tells me that things aren't so bad— that it's likely he *doesn't* regret what happened in my bedroom earlier this morning and late last night. I don't know what his smile means exactly, but I can tell his expression and body language aren't dripping in regret.

Good. That's good. I wouldn't have been able to handle this otherwise.

I stare at him intently, trying to figure out what he's thinking, but I come up short. It's like my insecurities and nerves have interfered with the telekinetic powers he and I have sometimes.

"So I'm supposed to help everyone out today with equip-ment for the wedding party ski day, but after that we can hang out together while they're out? Your mom asked me to help with the in-laws and the party and stuff, since some have never skied, but I'm sure I can disappear."

He looks happy and relaxed, and I'm... not. How could I be? What we did meant so much to me. Does the fact that he's so chill mean that he doesn't think what we did was a big deal?

I feel the panic creep over me, my breakfast rise in my throat.

Asher's face falls and he runs quickly over to me, holding me up by the shoulders as the room begins to spin. "Hey, what's wrong?"

I don't even know where to begin.

I press my lips tightly together, hoping it will help to prevent the word vomit that seems to want to explode from within me. I have absolutely no control over what will come out of my mouth, especially since I have no idea what I'm feeling.

"Rosie, come on. What is it?" His eyes bounce anxiously all over my face, trying to read it.

I give him a *What do you* think *is wrong?* look, and his expression falls. "Oh."

"Yeah," I manage to whisper, exhaling a breath I didn't even know I was holding. "*Oh.*"

One of his hands reaches up to cup my face, my skin heating. He holds me with such tenderness, it makes my heart ache. I want to ask him what's going on here, but I'm terrified of what he'll say. Maybe not knowing is better than knowing.

"C'mere." He pulls me into his arms, wrapping an arm around my waist. I nuzzle into his chest, inhaling his scent—the one that's now on my sheets, on the pillow I cuddled after he left, the one I hugged all morning as I replayed every second of our time together while I lay awake, naked in bed.

"What are we doing?" The words come out fast, too quick for me to stop them before they're spoken.

I feel Asher inhale sharply once, followed by a hard swallow. When he doesn't immediately answer, I pull my face back and look up at him, straining my neck a little. "Asher?"

His expression pained, all signs of the happy man from just a few moments ago gone. "I don't know how to answer that."

I nod quietly and press my forehead to his chest, committing his scent to memory, relishing in the feel of him after all these years. No matter what, right now, this moment right here, standing with our arms wrapped around each other in the store where we grew up together, my chest so filled with light and joy, might make all of it worth it.

No matter what he says, I'll always have last night, this morning, and this feeling. This *perfect* feeling.

"I'm still going to need you to answer the question for me, though," I whisper against him.

He sighs and pulls away, cupping my cheeks with both hands.

Asher tilts my face back to look me straight in the eye, and murmurs, "I don't know what we're doing, Rosie. But I know that talking about things yesterday was amazing. I know that what we did was amazing."

"That's an understatement." I smirk, trying to lighten the mood.

It works because he chuckles a little and smiles, wrapping his hands around my waist again. I sigh happily, placing my right hand over his heart where I feel it beat beneath my palm.

"So tell me what *you* want."

I stare up into his golden eyes, my eyes trailing over the bump in his nose, which he got from fighting for me. They trail over his perfect lips, the ones that did so many incredible things to my body last night. I reach up and run my fingers through his hair, my mind reeling, completely mesmerized by the fact that this brilliant, kind, loving, *gorgeous* man is here with me, holding me, asking *me* what I want.

But I'm a little coward.

I squint up at him and ask, "What if what I want isn't what you want? I don't want to go first—it isn't fair." The words come out in a teasing tone, but I am one thousand per cent serious.

Asher flashes a wide, happy grin in my direction, thumb tracing my lower lip. "Cards on the table, Rosie? I'll take whatever you'll give me." He frowns, his eyes boring into me.

My lips part as I try to read his face, but there's nothing there to find. He's being sincere. "What are you saying?" I manage, barely able to breathe.

He takes a deep breath and kisses my forehead with the softest pressure. "I'm saying that I don't want to be just your friend or your neighbor. I want us to *be* together."

"I'm going to need specifics here."

He pulls me into him tighter still, tipping my face closer to his. Asher leans down and I rise up on the tips of my toes, our lips just half an inch apart now. "Rosie." I feel the heat of his sweet breath on my tongue, the ache in his voice matching the one in my chest. "I want to take you on a date and give you my sweater when you're cold. Hold your hand as we cross the street and take you back to my place where I can hold you on my couch while we talk. I want to kiss you and fuck you and make you come, leaving you sated, but still hungry for more. I want to hold you afterwards and kiss every inch of your body, making sure you know how fucking beautiful you are." He presses his forehead to mine and tugs softly at my lower lip with his teeth, brushing his lips over mine. "Or..." he pulls his face back a little, a lopsided smile on his face. "Or we can go back to being friends. To talking. To being in each other's lives."

"Friends? You want to be friends?" I frown, looking up at him.

He puffs out a gust of air, laughing. "Did you not hear the part where I said I wanted to kiss you and fuck you? No, I don't want to be just friends. But if, uh... *being* with me like that again is too much for you, then I'll take friendship. I'll take whatever you give me. Except going back to not talking. I won't do that. Anything but have you disappear from my world again."

I stare up at him in wonder. "Okay, but to clarify...? Are you saying—"

"That I would drag you into that storage room right now and have a repeat of last night? Yeah." His voice is rough and gravelly—no longer dripping with that playful lasciviousness. "I want you." He presses his lips to mine, not waiting to deepen the kiss, throwing himself into it before cutting it off after a few seconds. "I haven't been able to stop thinking about you and what we did since I left your bedroom this morning," he tells me, panting.

"Me neither," I whisper, my lips grazing over his as I speak. "But—"

Asher groans, going in for another kiss, turning us while he walks backwards, guiding us toward the storage room in the back of the shop. Once we make it into the dark room, he pushes me against the shelves, kisses trailing up and down my neck. This is my shot to ask him whether it's just something we're doing for now or whether his intention is to keep this going after the holidays. He kisses down my neck, whispering words about how wonderful I feel against him, how he wishes he could spend all day, every day like this with me. How much he loves the feel of my curves in his hand.

My brain fogs as his hand travels to my knee and he hikes my leg over his hip, leaning into me, pressing the hard ridge of his cock against my most sensitive part, making me moan.

I know I should be asking about a million questions right now. Like whether he means this to be a temporary thing, just for while we're here. I gather all my strength and focus to open my mouth and ask the right question—

But then his hand travels under the four layers of fabric covering my torso, thumb skirting the underwire of my bra, and my mind goes blank. It's like all reason has disappeared from my brain, and logical thinking is just not a feature this version of my body comes with.

"Take off my jacket," I beg, feeling like I'm burning up. "Take it off now."

Asher pulls away and fights with my zipper, which gets stuck on my scarf. "*Fuck.*" His fingers shake as he struggles with the jacket, tugging and wiggling it until it breaks free. "Finally." He breathes a sigh of relief.

Asher's lips fall back on mine as he pushes my jacket off my shoulders, letting it fall to our feet like a pink, poofy cloud.

"God, you feel so good." He groans, his thumb skimming over my nipple under my bra.

Need overpowers my overthinking, eager hands flying to the hem of his sweater, pulling his shirt up, admiring every inch of skin I reveal, wanting to lick up his chest—

The bells over the store door jingle, and the sound of several people's footsteps flood the store. "*Asher?*"

Asher and I pull apart, staring wide-eyed at each other as realization breaks through the fog. "Fuck," he mutters under his breath, pulling away to adjust my wrinkled sweater while I pull his back down. With a frustrated smile, he mouths, "*Later.*"

I heave a sigh, cursing the universe for always having someone interrupt us. It's like it has an edging kink, for Christ's sake.

I slip my coat on, leaving it open, and follow Asher out of the stockroom. Once we turn a corner, I freeze, mortified, as the store fills with our family and the bridal party. My cheeks heat and I know—*I just know*—what everyone is thinking.

Thankfully, no one says anything. Both our mothers, however, meet our gazes with smirks on their faces.

"Well," Jaime smirks. "What were you two doing in there?"

Asher shrugs once without looking at his mother as he picks up the clipboard he left on the counter. "Checking to see whether we had any more hand warmers. Rosie's a little cold."

I hear my mother and Jaime snicker as I try to be subtle and make my escape.

"Really? Because she looks quite flushed to me." They look eagerly between us, as if waiting for us to crack.

"Was there something else you needed, Mother?"

"Yes. I know we said you could bow out from skiing, but we really need your help. Turns out we have more newbies than we thought."

Asher's face falls, and I try to hide my disappointment. We were supposed to go on a date.

"Can't you hire an instructor? I—ah—I actually already made plans, so I can't—"

"Oh, really? With who?" Jaime asks, shooting me a glance.

I press my lips together, looking everywhere except at her.

Asher scratches the back of his head. "I—Some high school friends." Not a lie, necessarily, since I was pretty much his only high school friend. We've been doing a lot of "technically not lying" lately. "I'm busy."

"Regardless of your...*plans*," Jaime eyes me, "we need you. Please stay?"

With a resigned nod, he agrees.

"Sorry," he murmurs as soon as his mother walks away. "I guess lunch will have to be dinner? Can you manage to escape your family then?"

I fight the urge to reach out to him, to run my hands up and down his chest.

"Andrea and my parents are going out to dinner tonight with

Alex and his parents. And I think Rodrigo and Diana are taking the girls to the movies so... Yeah, I don't think anyone will miss me tonight."

A wide grin spreads across his face. Asher looks once over his shoulder, checking to see whether we have any eyes on us. Once he makes sure the coast is clear, he reaches out, his finger trailing down in between my breasts, down my stomach, hooking at my jeans, pulling me a little closer.

"Date night, it is." he whispers, his face dangerously close to mine.

"Okay," I whisper, chest tightening in anticipation. "I'd love that."

Chapter Twenty-Eight

ASHER

"The Blue Elk?" Rosie smiles, looking up at me curiously.

I squeeze her hand and laugh once as I open the restaurant door for her. "What's wrong with this place? They make the best pizza in the area."

She laughs and nods, twirling a strand of her hair around an ungloved finger. "I guess so. I just think it's funny. It was *the* date spot in high school."

"Exactly," I tell her, pulling her by the hand over to the hostess stand. "Once I realized I liked you as more than a friend, all I wanted to do was take you out to dinner here. So I decided I'm going to live my teenage fantasy tonight." I laugh and try to make light of it despite the painful memories of having to watch her do the thing I wanted most with someone else.

"I'm sorry we didn't have the chance to ever do this. But I'm so happy we get to do it now," she says in a low voice.

One of her hands digs into my hair, which she uses to help pull my face to hers. I stare down at Rosie's perfect red lips and feel the same pull increase in power. Not being able to bear it any longer, I bend down to press my lips to hers, almost shivering at the small moan that escapes her lips when I tease her tongue with mine.

The hostess clears her throat behind us and I start to think that we've been cursed; that fate is constantly out to interrupt us just as things get good.

I turn back to the annoyed hostess and apologize before requesting a table for two near the window (prime real estate for its fantastic views of the face of the mountain). I pull out Rosie's chair and catch a whiff of her perfume, the scent of it bringing with it a wave of memories from last night, making me dizzy.

Barely recovered, I take a seat across from Rosie and smirk at her shy expression as we both slip our coats off.

"What?" she asks, cheeks red and flushed. Her hands fly to her hair, and she starts to weave it. "Is there something on my face? In my hair?"

I chuckle and shake my head. "Nah. Just thinking about how lucky I am. To be here with you, like this," I say, a soft smile on my lips.

She grins up at me and lets go of her hair, reaching across the table to hold both my hands in hers. After a few seconds of silence, she stares up at me, anxiety in her eyes.

"Hey," I say softly. "What is it?"

"I just..." She hesitates and shakes her head, closing her eyes. "I don't know what we're doing. What this is. And I'm scared of what comes next."

I try to swallow the knot in my throat and look out the window. That pang in my chest is back—painful and impossible to ignore—so I do my best to breathe through it. Because while I find myself ready to go all in so quickly after reconnecting, I know she's a little skittish. If I want this to last, I *need* to take this slow.

I turn my gaze back to hers and offer her an encouraging

smile. I decide to tell her the truth, just like I did at the store. "I'm scared, too. But I know I want this. Do you?"

My heart races in the split second that I wait for her answer.

Rosie bites down on her lower lip, trying to stop a slow grin from spreading on her face. She flips one of my hands and starts to trace the lines of my palm with her index finger. In a soft voice —almost a whisper—she says, "Yes. Yes, I really, *really* want this."

I laugh once in relief, and bring her hands to my lips, placing a kiss on them. "Good. Now let's get some pizza."

As I pull out of the restaurant parking lot, I feel Rosie press her lips to my shoulder. "Thank you for the date. It was amazing, and the food was delicious. I forgot how much I missed that sweet corn and chorizo pizza from there."

I smirk at her odd choice in toppings and pull out onto the highway. "I'm glad you enjoyed dinner. But the date isn't over."

"Oh? It's not?" She raises an eyebrow at me.

"No." I laugh softly at the confused look on her face. "That was just the first stop. Next up, we're going stargazing at the lookout point."

"What?" She grins up at me. "Really?"

I nod, my heart tightening at the excitement in her voice. "Yeah. Just like we used to."

"Well, I hope not just like we used to." She smirks, and my heart tightens in my chest. "But aren't we going to freeze? It's like twenty degrees out or something."

I laugh at her. "You've been gone way too long if you think that's going to stop us from stargazing. We don't let silly things like below-freezing temperatures get in the way of nighttime outdoor events here in Colorado. Plus, I have a comforter and blankets in the back seat, along with two insulated travel mugs full of hot mulled wine."

"Oooh, fancy."

She beams as we reach the lookout point and I back-up so that the truck bed is facing out over the cliff. I move quickly to set up everything for us, unrolling two thick sleeping bags over the truck bed as a makeshift mattress, and pulling out the heavy comforter and a few pillows I took from home. Once I'm done, I pat the truck bed and shoot her shocked face a smile.

"Ready?" I wrap my hands around her waist and help her up on the truck bed, handing her the comforter for her to wrap herself with.

I grab the two travel mugs and hand her the one I bought today specifically for her. When she notices, I revel in her gasp. Rosie reaches carefully for the pink bedazzled travel mug, the one I found by happy accident earlier today at one of the local gift shops. It cost an arm and a leg, but honestly, just looking at the expression on her face, makes it all worth it.

"Is this for me?" she breathes, her voice full of wonder as she stares at the pink tumbler, sparkling even in the dark of the night.

"Yes." I laugh, climbing easily up onto the truck bed. "You like it?"

She shoots me a look of disbelief. "Like it? I freaking *love* it, Asher. This is incredible."

I settle in next to her under the comforter and wrap my arm around her shoulders, bringing her closer to me. My chest fills with pride at how happy I've made her. I just want to make sure she knows how much I *see* her. How much I hear and know her. That no one knows her or understands her better than I do.

There is no amount of time or space or drama large enough to change that.

I will always know her. She will always be a part of me.

I'm done denying it.

I feel the last brick of my wall crumble as I kiss he top of her head and then her cheek. She turns toward me and cups my face, bringing my lips to hers. We kiss, slow and deep, our breathing growing faster, our hearts beating harder. When she shifts under the comforter next to me, I swing her legs over mine and pull away to stare deep into her eyes.

"I love this," I say, my fingers in her pink hair.

"My hair?"

I chuckle. "Yes, that, too. But I meant that I love being here with you like this."

"Me too," she whispers, biting her lip. "I mean, I'm freezing, but this is incredible."

I laugh and pull us both back against the pillows, staring up at the night sky. I sigh happily as Rosie readjusts herself and places her face on my chest, her hand directly over where my heart is beating furiously under my coat.

Together, we fall quiet and look up at the stars, thousands of stars visible in the clear night sky, an endless world before us.

Bliss, pure fucking bliss as I hold her in my arms and we quietly admire the Milky Way, as I marvel at how amazing life can be that I can bask in the two greatest passions of my life at the same time.

I don't think I've ever been happier.

"I missed this. Though we *definitely* didn't cuddle like this when we were teenagers," she whispers, as if not wanting to disturb the perfect silence of the moment.

She doesn't know her voice is all I craved to hear for the past nine years.

"Mmm," I kiss the top of her head and inhale her addicting

scent, a soothing balm to the nerves building within because I don't ever want to let go.

"We did our fair share of cuddling. In your bed," I smile into her hair as she laughs softly.

"Yeah, but it was never like this." And she's right. I never got to feel her body wrapped around mine, her hands on me like I do now. So I slip my right hand from my glove and dig my fingers into her hair to hold her to me; my other hand wrapping around her thigh, lifting it higher up on my body.

It's in this moment that I realize everything I said to save face the other day in the store after she apologized was true. If it had been this way, if we had ever reached this point in our relationship before going off to college, things would've been completely different. I don't think I would have been able to manage being so far away from her. I would've transferred or something just to be near her. Or I would've begged her to do the same.

Would we have stayed together? Would she be happy with her work like she says she is now? Would I have the career I have? Almost any door I want open for me to walk through?

I don't know. I don't have the answer to any of those questions. But one thing I do know, is that I'm not going to let anything come between us again, no matter what that is.

"You know," I tell her, my voice in a whisper. "Every time we'd come out here, I'd have to fight the urge to kiss you crazy. After that insane first kiss in the stock room, it's literally all I could think about sometimes."

She snorts a little, and burrows into me. "Well, why didn't you? Kiss me, I mean."

I laugh once, my eyes still on the stars above us. "I never stood a chance. You were with that idiot, Tyler, on and off again all the time and I valued our friendship more than I valued my need to—Well. My need to *be* with you."

Rosie tenses, so I pull her away a little to get a good look at her face. "Hey, what's wrong?"

"I'm sorry about everything." Her voice breaks.

"Stop. We talked about this already. It's over. Let's just enjoy this moment and move on, okay?" She doesn't answer, her eyes on my chest. I lightly grasp her chin and use it to tilt her face up to me. "Hey, I'm serious. Don't." I bend to kiss her, and put every bit of myself into it. I want to clear her head of bad memories; to have her focus only on the present and what it could mean for the future—*our* future.

Soon, though, the kissing escalates into something more—something heated and fueled by need. I roll us over, one leg in between both of hers, hovering over Rosie while my tongue explores her mouth. I move my lips to her jaw and push her scarf away, wanting to feel the warm and delicate skin beneath it.

"Ash," she moans, squirming below me as I tug on her ear lobe. Suddenly, she shivers, but I don't think it's from the cold. "Let's move this somewhere else. Take me home."

And so I do.

Chapter Twenty-Nine

ROSIE

THE PAST COUPLE OF DAYS HAVE BEEN A WHIRLWIND OF kissing and sex and love and feeling so luminous and bright and shiny that I feel like I could burst. It's been surreal and exhausting and I'm sore in places where I didn't even know I *could* be sore.

As I get ready to sneak out of the house and avoid my family and wedding activities *yet again*, I run my fingers delicately over my collarbone in front of my mirror. My eyes close, remembering the sweet way Asher kissed me there this morning before sneaking back out of the house through my bedroom window.

It's been a few of days since our first real date. Though we're still hiding it from everyone, there's no denying we've been getting a bit sloppy. Last night, for example, I ran into Andrea in the hallway as I walked to the bathroom wearing only Asher's shirt. I froze, my hand on the door handle, as she took in my appearance—sex hair and all—and whispered, "You owe me a story."

I simply nodded and went in to pee. By the time I was done, she had gone back to her room, and I just slipped into bed next to a sleeping Asher.

Avoiding her is key, so I sneak out into the hallway, doing my best not to make a peep. I don't want to alert my family, currently working on folding programs, to my presence.

I tiptoe carefully down the stairs, but just as my foot reaches the final step, I trip over Manolo, who runs away with a howl.

"Rosie?" I hear my mother's voice.

Suppressing a sigh, I call back and walk into the kitchen, which looks like it's been hit by a bomb of ribbon and expensive card stock. "Hey, guys. What's up?" I ask, though it's clear.

"Um, hello? Where are you going with your purse and your coat on? We were all supposed to meet before the rehearsal dinner to help finish up the programs. The wedding is tomorrow," Diana says, her voice haughty.

"I was just going to *Seymour's*. To see Jaime. I'll be back in time to shower and change for the dinner."

My dad narrows his eyes at me. "Didn't Jaime go to the airport to pick up her daughter? I thought Jessica was flying in today, wasn't she?"

Shoot.

That's right. Asher did mention that.

"Uh, yes. But—" I stammer, looking to Andrea for help. Eyes wide, she shakes her head and shrugs her shoulders. "I—"

"I was sending her to meet Jaime there," my mom interrupts, her gaze locked on my own as she speaks. "I asked Rosie to go help Asher with the last of the packing since they only have a day left to wrap everything up because of the wedding." What the hell is she talking about? When did we even discuss this? "Didn't I, Rosie?"

Mouth agape, I stare at her for a beat. Is she... Is she covering for me? Does my mother *know*?

Holy crap.

"Yes. I was just doing what Mom asked," I tell the room.

Dad doesn't buy it, though. He sets the program on the table and shoots me a look. "You don't think you should be helping your sister, instead? You don't think *your* family and the wedding activities you've missed come before him? You haven't been to any wedding events in the past two days, Rosario."

"Diego," my mother intercedes. "*I* asked her to help *my* best friend. This isn't about her."

"Plus, *Papi*," Andrea speaks up, "we don't really have much to do. And all the things she, uh, *missed* were more for out-of-towners. Rosie isn't an out-of-towner."

"May as well be," Dad mutters, almost inaudibly.

He looks from my mother to my little sister and nods before addressing me again. "Fine. Just be sure to be back tonight for the rehearsal dinner. The entire family is coming; your *tía* should be landing later this afternoon, along with your cousins."

"Carla?" A hopeful smile spreads across my face at the prospect of seeing my favorite aunt. My father's sister took me in when I moved to New York the summer before college, before I had a dorm. She took me in when I left and felt like I had no one.

To say it caused a rift between the two siblings is an understatement. Dad wasn't happy with anyone who seemed to approve of my lifestyle change. According to him, he didn't move his entire family to another country just to have me pursue the arts. In his opinion, it's, "an empty, meaningless, fruitless endeavor that only a child could dream up."

My aunt, an artist herself who had been living in the city for almost as long as we'd been in the US, did *not* take it well.

In all honesty, I'm surprised he even wanted to invite her after how that whole thing went down. But I guess after nine years, if Asher and I can get over our shit, my dad and his sister can get over her giving me refuge in a strange city before starting college at a school my father didn't approve of.

"Sure. I'll be back in time for dinner." Before my father can stop me from leaving, I turn and walk out of the room, practically making a run for the front door.

"Have fun!" my mother calls out.

"Holy..." I breathe, looking around the bare walls and couple of boxes strewn around what *used* to be Asher's grandfather's store.

Asher pops up from behind the counter, hair a mess. "Hey," he says, walking around it and heading over. He cups my face in his hands, tilting it up to his, and places a sweet kiss on my lips. "I was hoping you'd show soon." He presses another kiss on my lips, but releases me, moving out of my eye line so I can fully take in the store. "So what do you think? Depressing, right?" He grimaces as he looks around the store.

My heart aches as I take in how bare and empty the shop looks, how it feels like all the amazing memories I have of this place have been ripped from the walls and packed up, leaving an unrecognizable room in its stead. I'm so taken aback by it, I barely notice how delicious he looks in his fitted red henley. "I— It's so much worse than I thought it would be." My voice breaks, a wave of grief, of an ending, crashing over me. "It's really over," I whisper.

Asher comes up behind me, wrapping his arms around my waist and tucking my head under his chin. He kisses the top of my head and buries his nose in my hair. "Yeah, I know."

"This is..." I choke. "This is *awful*," I tell him.

"Yes, but also no, Rosie. Selfishly, I want to keep this store as is. To keep the memory of my grandfather alive, to keep my own childhood memories alive—and yours, for that matter. *Ours.* But... I also want my mother to be able to retire. She can't handle this on her own anymore. And now with Jess and I living so far away, she can come visit us more often, you know?"

I turn in his arms and look up at his handsome face. "Yeah. It's just a shock, is all."

"I get that." He kisses my forehead. "But it's a new beginning for her, cheesy as it may sound."

I smile and kiss his chest, resenting my coat for not letting me get closer to him. "What about you? What about *your* new beginning?"

"What do you mean?"

"Your fellowship. Have you heard anything yet?"

His arms tense around me. "Uh, I should have more news soon."

"I'm so sorry, Asher," I say. I rise up on my tiptoes and stretch to kiss him lightly on the lips. "I know how important this is to you. I'm sure you'll get it."

He smiles down at me and kisses the tip of my nose. "Don't worry. I have backups on the East Coast, too."

"Yeah?" I ask, intrigued.

"Yeah, some teaching positions."

My eyes widen. "Whoa! You'd bypass research and go straight to teaching? That's amazing!"

A shadow passes over his face, an expression I can't quite pinpoint. "Yeah, Rose. It's... It's great."

Heart racing as I think how easily I could transition this conversation into asking what will happen after the holidays. What are we going to do? Are we going to keep doing this— whatever *this* is? Is this a relationship? And if so... Are we going to try long-distance? And what are the East Coast positions he's talking about? We've been hanging out together—if that's what you call it—for a few days now but haven't really talked about what comes next.

If this were someone I'd just met, I wouldn't even dream to think about making this something more long-term, right? But with Asher... I've known Asher for over sixteen years, if you count the ones where our relationship was on hiatus (which I do). He's not just some guy I met on Tinder that I've been on three dates with.

I can feel myself pale as the realization that I'm leaving in just a few days and we don't have anything figured out starts to fall over me.

Asher notices the second I'm close to losing it. His expression shifts to one of concern, his brows furrowed, eyes bouncing between both of mine. His hands come up to cup my face as he asks, "Hey, what's wrong? What's going on?"

I shake my head, not knowing how to start. My eyes begin to sting with unshed tears. "Asher, I—"

"*Yoo-hoo!!!*"

Chapter Thirty

ASHER

"WELL, HELLO THERE!" ROSE AND I PRACTICALLY JUMP AT my sister's voice. "What's this?" Jessica says, eyebrows raised in surprise, a slow grin spreading on her face.

"Uh..." Not knowing how Rosie wants to play it, I stay quiet, watching her struggle with the words.

"Hi, Jess." She walks over to my sister to embrace her.

"It's been too long, sweetie."

I watch as Rosie nods, eyes squeezed shut. "I know. I missed you."

Jess pulls away first, putting her hands on Rosie's shoulders. Her eyes bounce between the two of us. "So tell me. What the hell did I just walk into?"

Rosie heaves a big sigh and puts her hands on her hips, resigned. "I mean, I could say 'it's not what it looks like,' but it so obviously is." Rosie half-smirks, half-looks away in embarrassment.

Try as I may, there is nothing anyone could do about the fucking gigantic grin spreading across my face.

Fuck yes.

Jessica flips her dark hair over her shoulder and removes her gloves. I can see the wheels turning in her head, and brace myself for the teasing that's to come.

But I honestly couldn't give a shit. Rosie just acknowledged that there's something going on between us aloud and I. Am. Elated.

Jess snickers. "This is incredible."

Rosie puts her face in her hands and shakes her head. She sighs, her voice muffled. "Would you mind keeping it to yourself for now, please?"

"Yes," Jess chuckles. "Don't worry about it. I know the second this gets out there will be *a lot* of invested people. I totally get you guys wanting to keep it hidden for as long as possible."

My stomach tightens and I swallow the hard knot that's suddenly formed in my throat. I don't need Rosie to be reminded of how complicated this will be. I'm scared she'll cut and run if it's too much.

"I think you're exaggerating," I tell my sister, who just snorts at me.

"I don't know what to say, except... It's about time?" She smiles proudly, eyes bright with excitement.

I choke. "Excuse me?"

She laughs and walks over to wrap us both in her arms. "You guys are such idiots," she says, without elaborating.

An uncomfortable pause passes through us, broken only by Rosie's deep sigh. "I should probably go; leave you guys to catch up."

"Don't mind me!"

"It's not a problem. I have to get back anyway. Mom bought me some time, but I think I've sufficiently pissed my family off today. I need to help them fold programs before the rehearsal dinner," she says, rolling her eyes.

"Fun!" Jess exclaims with false enthusiasm.

"You have no idea." We chuckle as she heaves another sigh and moves to kiss me on the cheek.

"See you later?" she whispers, to which I just nod, a little shellshocked she just publicly displayed affection like that.

Jess and I watch Rosie walk out of the store, and I silently thank her for waiting until she's gone before the inevitable teasing begins.

We watch Rosie turn onto Main Street before Jess turns to me with a face-splitting grin.

"Don't," I tell her before she begins. "It's—"

"Are you seriously trying to tell me '*it's not like that?*'" She laughs once. "Please. I basically caught you two in the act. Plus, I've been watching you pine over that girl since before you even realized either of you were in love with each other."

"We're not *in lo*—" I start.

Jess cuts me off with a scoff. "Don't even try to deny it. It's so obvious." I raise my eyebrow at her, shooting her a look. "Fine, maybe not to you two idiots, but it's definitely been obvious for everyone else in the world. I mean, I think we all had bets going from when you two would end up together. But then, I don't know, did you guys get into a fight or something? Because you kinda stopped talking to each other, right? At least I stopped seeing you two together. And you stopped mentioning her."

"Jesus Christ." I throw my hands in the air in frustration. "You have been *way* too involved in my life if you've been able to notice this," I tell her.

"Asher, literally *everyone* noticed how you two must have had a falling out—"

"Who the hell is '*everyone?*'"

"—so seeing you like this again *must* mean that you've fixed things? Or that you're *together*-together, now?" she asks, her voice hopeful.

For a moment, I consider telling her the truth. Getting someone else's advice on the matter—especially from someone who knows us both—would be invaluable. On the other hand, telling my sister about my love life doesn't sound like fun.

In the end, though, I recognize how in need of advice I am. When it comes to Rosie, there really is no thinking straight.

So I exhale sharply and stare her down before saying, "We had a falling out after senior year, yes. Didn't speak for several years. And then..." Jess squeals, jumping up and down. I roll my eyes as she claps her hands. "*As I was saying...*" I put my hands on her shoulders to stop her from bouncing into the ceiling. "We ran into each other here, obviously, and we've been... hanging out."

"Ew," she says, scrunching up her nose in disgust, but still with a smile on her face. Her enthusiasm for this relationship is contagious, which makes me realize how cautious I've been.

"What? I just said we were hanging out."

"I know what that's code for, though."

I snort and shake my head at her. "I will neither confirm nor deny." But I can't help the grin that spreads across my face.

"Gross," Jess says, following me as I head into my grandfather's old office to make sure the last of it is packed. "*Buuut*," she starts, a smile in her voice. "I gotta say this sounds incredible. And, oh my god, Mom's gonna be so happy."

I laugh almost giddy with excitement. I pick up a box and walk out to the front of the store with it, lining it up next to the few left that will go into storage tomorrow morning. "Yeah, I think she and Julieta have been trying to set us up this entire time, to be honest. The weirdest shit has been going on ever since we got here." As I voice my suspicions out loud, I begin to believe them even more. "There was this thing with the mistletoe on Christmas Eve, and then the snowman building contest, and—Jesus Christ—then this whole thing at the spa where we just…" I laugh at myself and run my fingers through my hair. "I mean, I'm pretty sure they even booked our airplane tickets to land at the same time, since my Christmas present from Mom was the flight here."

"*What?* She only got me a stupid scented candle for Christmas, and you got a *plane ticket?*"

Laughing, I tell her, "Yes, but she wasn't trying to set you up with your estranged best friend, Jess. You have your little happily ever after in Germany. How is Nick, by the way?"

"He's fine," she says, waving her hand dismissively. "But don't try to change the subject. What's going on with you two, then? Are you just hooking up, or…?"

I turn to face her head-on, a pained expression on my face, I'm sure. "I don't know," I say, my voice almost a whisper. "I mean—fuck—she's even more amazing than I remember. And it's been incredible to see her again. And I told her I wanted whatever she'd be willing to give me. But we still haven't yet determined what that is. And… Well, the last time we saw each other, things didn't exactly end on good terms. I've forgiven her and I'm pretty sure she's forgiven me, but…" I sigh heavily. "I don't know. I don't know why I can't shake this feeling that she's five seconds away from running again. Like she's just going to disappear into thin air, and I swear to god that just the idea of that makes me fucking sick, Jess. Like, it literally hurts to think about." I force myself to inhale deeply, stretching out my suddenly tight chest.

"Sorry," I whisper. I squeeze my eyes shut and rub them with my fingers. "It's… been a lot of new and old feelings lately. And, well, it's a lot to handle."

Jess just stares at me, eyes soft yet filled with concern. "So, you're scared to talk to her about what comes next then?"

I nod, and look away.

"Well, it's understandable that you're scared. I don't know exactly what happened, but I get being afraid to lose the person you love, you know. I've been there more than once. Losing Dad and Grandpa weren't enough; I had to go and marry a man who literally leaves me for months on end with little to no contact."

I wince and look back at her, never processing up until now what loving someone in the military is. Fucking brave.

"But you can't go on like this, Asher. You need to figure out what you're going to do. The holidays are almost over, and you don't want to get your hopes up if nothing is going to come of it. You need to know where you both stand."

"I know where I stand," I tell her with confidence. "I'm ready to give it all up for her. Everything. If she asks me to, then I'm ready to do it."

Jess pauses for a beat, eying me carefully. "What do you mean?" she asks, concern lacing her voice.

"I got the NASA fellowship," I say. Her eyes widen and brighten with excitement.

"Asher! Oh my god! That's so—"

"But I'm not taking it, Jess. I swear to god. I know that it's something I've always wanted, but I want her—*need* her more. I've lost her before, and I—I don't think I can handle doing it a second time."

She frowns at me, skepticism in her eyes. "You make your own choices about your professional career, Asher, but... If you're still wondering what comes next after the holidays, if you're scared that she's about to run away, then... I mean, do you even really have her?"

My stomach rolls, and I feel myself pale as adrenaline starts coursing through my body because... Because she's right. Because I *don't* have her. Right now, all I have are these new amazing memories we made while reminiscing over the old ones.

Right now, all I have are a past and a present, and no guaranteed future.

Right now, I have jack shit.

Rosie and I need to figure things out and do so soon.

Chapter Thirty-One

ASHER

18 Years Old

I CAN'T KEEP THE SMILE OFF MY FACE AS I WATCH ROSIE *tipsily sway to her favorite song. With a red Solo cup to match her short dress, eyes closed, hips moving from side to side to the beat, I wonder whether she's ever looked this free in her life.*

"I'm soooo fancyyyy, you already knooooww..." she sings off-tune and I can't contain my laughter any longer. We're in a house full of our former classmates celebrating the end of high school, but all I see is her.

Over the loud music, she yells, "Hey! Don't make fun of me!" But her smile is wicked and her eyes shine bright like they have ever since yesterday afternoon at graduation. "I'm celebrating, still!"

"I know. You deserve to."

"We both do."

She smiles up at me before taking my left hand and pulling me forward, wrapping my arm around her waist. My heart stops beating immediately, breath catching in my throat at the feel of her.

Holy shit.

"Dance with me? I'm so happy I feel like I could float away any second now. We just graduated high school and get to go off to college, away from this place."

My stomach turns at the thought of leaving her, of us going to different schools. Sure, we'll be close by, but it's a far cry from living next door to each other.

For now, I let myself enjoy this moment and use both arms to bring her into me. "Sure, let's dance. Celebrate that we're done with this place. That we're moving on."

"That I'm done with Tyler and you and I are gonna spend the summer together traveling around the West Coast." She grins.

I grin because, fuck yes, that idiot is out of the picture and it's going to be just me and her for three months, alone. And this time, I'm not going to let anything stand in my way. This time, I'm going to tell her how I feel.

"Then you're off to college at Berkeley, and me at Stanford." I say. But as soon as the words leave my mouth, her cheerful expression slips slightly.

"What's wrong?"

Rosie hesitates, takes a deep breath. "I just... Berkeley? Econ? I don't think that's where I belong, Ash."

I frown and nod sympathetically. "I know, Rose. I'm sorry. I know you wanted to go to that art school. I know it was super fucked up for your dad to say he wouldn't support you in any way if you went down that path." I try to manage as much genuine sympathy as I can, but it's a bit hard to feel bad for her. I'm in love and the last thing I want is for her and I to be three thousand miles away from each other. "And I'm sorry you don't get to pursue your dreams." That is something I can genuinely say. "But at least we get to be close by in the fall, right?" I smile encouragingly at her.

I watch as she struggles to do the same, but it doesn't reach her eyes. "Yeah. Yeah, that's going to be awesome. You're right."

"Okay, then." I nod, gathering strength from somewhere inside me to smile down at her and say, "You look beautiful tonight, by the way. Have I mentioned that?"

Her eyes widen as a broad smile spreads across her face. "No, you haven't." She bites her lower lip and raises an eyebrow. "Since when do you tell me I look beautiful?"

I shrug nonchalantly on the outside, but am exploding with happiness on the inside. "You're always beautiful. I've always thought so. Sometimes, you're so beautiful it makes it hard to breathe."

Her breath catches and we suddenly stop swaying side to side, the music and the crowd of people disappearing into a nebulous background.

"What?" she breathes.

I take a steeling breath and slide a hand up her side, traveling over her shoulder and neck, threading my fingers into her raven hair. "Just thought it was time for me to actually start making myself very clear. I'm done hiding how I feel."

"Ash..." she shakes her head, eyes wide with fear. They mirror mine, knowing that I'm on the ledge and whatever reaction she might have to the words that are uncontrollably spilling from my lips will forever change our relationship.

"Just... Just listen. I've loved you—pretty much singularly—since the moment I met you. It took me years and a punch to the nose to figure it out, but I do. I love you. I'm in love with you." I use one arm around her waist to clutch her closer to me, another to cup her face. "I love you and I think you love me too."

Rosie looks away, but she can't hide the tears as they start to build in her eyes. Hands trembling on her body, my heart gallops for what feels like several painful minutes as the fear of losing her overcomes me.

Just as I begin to curse my existence, my inability to recognize that of course she never loved me and she never will, her hand reaches up to wrap around my wrist. At first, my heart drops, anticipating her rejection. But when she turns her face to kiss the palm of my hand, I feel it begin to soar.

Through her lashes, her dark brown eyes peek up at me, cheeks crimson, lips trembling. But she doesn't say anything. She keeps quiet, my heart on the line, as she searches for something in my eyes.

Whatever it is, I'll give it to her. Anything for a shot at her.

"Rose?" I ask, a little breathless. My heart has begun to hope, and I don't think it could take her telling me to go.

"I'm so angry with you," she says, voice breaking as she closes her eyes. Tears start to fall from her eyes, and I move quickly, brushing them away with my thumbs.

Crushed, I nod, feeling the knife slice and quarter my heart into small pieces. "I—I'm sorry. You're right. I never should've told you. I shouldn't have said anything. And now I've ruined our friendship and—"

"I'm so angry with you because you made me believe for so many years that you weren't interested." She opens her eyes and finally looks up at me, a small half-smile on her face. "And now you're saying we could've spent all this time together-together?"

I freeze. Open my mouth to say something. Freeze again. "But... Tyler?"

She rolls her eyes at me, pushing my hands off her face. "Was someone I dated because I thought you only saw me as a friend. I liked him, but the reason we always broke up was because I was so in love with you. I wanted you. And he was so possessive and annoying. And I just wanted to be with you. I tried to push it away, Ash. But how could I not love you? We're always together. I preferred spending time with you over him, most of the time. This sounds horrible, because I did like him, I did have feelings for him. Of course I did, or I wouldn't have dated him. But he never held a candle to you." My breath catches as I stare down at her, lips parted. "No one ever will."

"Rose... I had no fucking idea up until a couple of weeks ago when I started to suspect it."

She sputters a laugh, running her hands up and down my chest. "Me running to you, begging you to kiss me over a year ago wasn't enough of a hint? Me asking you to spend almost every night with me wasn't enough? Always picking you over him?"

"I... don't know what to say."

Her hands slide up my neck and tangling into my hair, using her grip to pull me down. "Kiss me, then," she begs, the ache in her voice mirroring the one in mine.

Without having to ask me twice, I bend down to meet her halfway, and when our lips finally meet, I swear nothing else matters.

In an instant, our kiss evolves into something incendiary, burning my chest from the inside out. I feel, more than hear her moan as I come at her lips from another angle, and force myself to remember that we're in the middle of a party, in front of our entire senior class. I couldn't give a shit about what they think, in all honesty, but Rosie's just coming off a couple of weeks of bullying after her ex slut-shamed her, and I don't want to bring any more unwanted attention to her.

As if reading my mind, she pulls away suddenly, eyes low-lidded. I stare down at her kiss-bruised lips, aching to have them back on mine, to see them wrapped around me.

"You're so beautiful," I tell her again, because she is. "I've wanted to tell you how beautiful I think you are every day since the moment I met you." I squeeze my eyes shut, pressing my forehead to hers.

"And you're perfect. And that kiss was..." she breathes, her voice barely audible over the beat of the loud music.

"Yeah," I say back, fingers toying with the zipper at the back of her dress, skating just above to feel the bare, smooth skin of her back. I feel her shiver beneath my fingertips as she looks up at me with fire in her eyes.

"I'm tired," she says suddenly.

"Oh." Disappointment washes over me like a bucket full of cold water, and I pull slightly away. I had dreamed about taking her to our looking point and holding her as we gazed at the stars. But if she's tired, then—

"Let's go home?" Rosie raises a suggestive eyebrow at me and almost immediately the heat is back, coursing through me like wildfire.

"You mean... together?"

"Yeah. Together. To my room." I watch as her breathing goes ragged, chest raising up and down to the beat of my quick-racing heart.

I cup her face in my hand and run my thumb over her lower lip, swollen from our kiss. "Rose. Are you sure?"

"I've never been surer about anything in my entire life. I love you. Take me home."

And with those words, I press my lips to hers, and pull her out of the party and into my truck, where we drive back home together.

Chapter Thirty-Two

ROSIE

Nine years ago, I fell in love with my best friend. And in less than twenty-four hours, I loved and lost him, breaking both of our hearts in the process. Part of me keeps telling myself that if Asher has truly forgiven me as he says he has, then I should be able to forgive myself as well.

But the fear of having caused absolute irreparable damage, or the fear of doing it once more, has been haunting me ever since our mistletoe kiss. It's like I've been at constant war with myself, wanting more than anything to *be* with him, to *have* him, to *never let him go*. Whereas another side keeps telling me to run, telling me that I'm going to get hurt again, but, most importantly, I'm going to hurt *him* once more.

And I just can't have that. Not again.

My mind and heart and soul are a jumble of thoughts and emotions and I feel like I won't be able to breathe until I determine exactly where the hell we stand. I'm afraid to find out, but I don't have the luxury of fear anymore. I don't even think it has a place in love.

And yes. I know I just said *love*. Because that's what this is. And it's why I find myself at the shop an hour before my sister's rehearsal dinner. I don't think there's a better place to make things clear between us than *Seymour's*. The store held special meaning for our relationship and would be the perfect place to determine either our end or new beginning.

I push the store doors open with determination, my eyes automatically landing on the man who's had my heart for nearly a decade. Maybe even longer.

Asher looks heartbreakingly perfect as he stands there in a suit and tie, his black curls styled to perfection, glasses fitting perfectly over his nose as he reviews a stack of paperwork.

My god, this man really has the potential to rip my heart out.

His amber eyes fall on me as he hears me enter, his expression shifting from one of concentration—deep-set furrowed brows, thin lips—to one that I can only describe as joy—eyes bright, wide smile, taller stance. It's as if I'm the only thing he sees. And just those few seconds when our eyes meet cause a seismic movement inside my chest, breaking through the nerves and fear, because all I can wonder is how I ever lived one second without this incredible man. How will I ever live without him?

There's no question in my heart or head or soul that what I want most in life is him—*us*. Now I just have to be brave enough to ask for it—even after all the shit I put us through.

"Hey," he says in a soft voice, walking over to me. He reaches out and wraps an arm around my waist, placing a soft kiss on my forehead. Asher runs a hand through his hair, messing up his styling in the process, but leaving him looking even more delicious—something I didn't think would even be possible. I mean, Asher Wolff in a suit? Ten out of ten, would recommend.

"Hey," he says again. "Shouldn't you be with your sister helping set up or whatever? I don't want you to get in trouble again for hanging out with me."

Hanging out?

My stomach rolls once more, but I try to remind myself that he's just using it as an expression. Right?

Right?

My hands go to my hair and, though I spent hours curling it to perfection, I begin to weave it into a perfect side braid without my control. "I won't, I don't think. The rehearsal dinner is at a restaurant, so there isn't much to do. They're basically in charge of everything."

"Good." For some reason, an uncomfortable silence falls between us. Not knowing what to say next, I continue to stare down at my sparkly pink shoes, the same ones I wore for Christmas, the ones that make me the happiest. Right now, though, I feel like my heart is beating out of my chest. I'm caught between wanting to run out of the store and asking questions to get the answers I came here for.

Asher rushes over to me and takes me in his arms, wrapping them tightly around my waist as he bends down to press his lips to mine. I clasp my hands behind his neck and slide as much as I can with these heels onto my tiptoes to make it easier on his back and my neck. Sweet kisses quickly turn heated, and soon we're panting into each other's mouths and I'm feeling him hard, pressed against my stomach.

"God, I missed you," he says, forehead pressed against mine, eyes closed tight as he pants against my mouth.

I can't help the big goofy smile that spreads across my face. "It's only been like, five hours," I whisper, kissing him lightly on the lips once more.

He shakes his head softly, frowning. "Five hours too long."

Light starts to build in my chest, pressure mounting inside it. There's little room left, but I seem to be filling more and more as the seconds tick by.

This is it. Now's the time!

But I chicken out, not wanting to ruin this perfect moment. I need to keep it together.

"You're wearing that red lipstick I like," he growls into my neck, biting me softly before kissing me in the same spot. I try to let go, to enjoy this moment, but I'm too tense.

Reading me perfectly, Asher senses something's up almost immediately. "Hey, what's wrong? Was that too much?" His hold on me loosens and suddenly I want to punish myself because, my god, I'm such an idiot.

"No, no!" I say desperately, pulling him back to me, slapping a forced smile on my face.

Asher sees straight through me, so he reaches behind his head to take hold of my wrists and gently releases himself from my grasp. "Hey, talk to me," he says calmly.

I try to hold strong, to keep the fake smile across on my face, but the void forming in my chest is too strong, the stinging in my eyes too sharp. I can't hold this in any longer. Feeling like I'm about to come unhinged, I struggle to take a breath.

"Rosie," Asher says, his voice more distressed than before. "Hey, take a deep breath for me, okay? Please take a deep breath."

Desperately, I clutch his hands as I try to regulate my breathing through the panic attack, but I can't seem to get ahold of myself as warm tears streak over my cheeks.

Asher's hands travel all over me, rubbing soothing circles on my back, cupping my cheeks and kissing them as he begs me to slow down my breathing, as he tells me he's got me. Finally, he grabs my hands and puts the palm of them over his heart, just as I feel myself begin to lose the strength in my legs. He wraps an arm around my waist and holds me to his torso as the other presses my hands into him.

"Feel my breathing," I hear him say, his sweet voice breaking through the panic. "Feel how my chest moves." He exhales deeply. "Try to match it." And so I do. I press my hands harder into his chest, his hand over mine, holding me to him as my breathing slows, and my tears stop. After a few minutes, I drop my hands from his chest and hold my face in them, ashamed. Weak and exhausted, I ache for my bed and comfortable shoes.

"I'm so sorry." I hiccup. "That hasn't happened to me since..." *Since the morning after I slept with Tyler Wesley; the morning after I saw you with the blonde.* I shake my head, not wanting to go there again. "I'm sorry," I say again, my voice small.

"Don't. Stop," he pleads, bringing my hands to his lips and kissing them softly.

"Can we sit somewhere?" I ask, feeling considerably less weak than I did a few minutes ago.

Asher nods. "The office." I turn to start walking there, but he swings me into his arms as easily as he picked up that duffel at baggage claim just one week ago. He takes me into the office and settles me onto the desk, reaching into one of the open boxes for a box of tissues. He pulls a few out and hands them to me to pat my face dry. Thank *god* I chose tonight to wear waterproof liner and mascara. I had a feeling tonight would be emotional, but for wholly different reasons.

"My makeup?" I ask, because I'm due for a lot of family photos tonight, and I don't want to have to go back home to get it redone.

"Your makeup is fine. Intact. *You,* on the other hand..." He sighs and cups my face with his hands. They're big and warm, and I feel safe and happy between them. My hands come to his wrists and I hold him there as I turn my face to kiss both his palms.

After a few moments of just staring at each other, he asks, "What was that? A panic attack?" I nod, looking away. "Why? What's going on?"

I look up into his gold eyes, filled with concern and something else. His thumbs caress my cheeks as he waits patiently for me to articulate everything I want to be brave enough to say.

"Talk to me, Rose. Please." His hands move into my hair and he tilts my head to press his lips to mine. I sigh happily, feeling the tension leave my body as I give into him. After a few minutes of slow, deep kisses, he whispers another plea against my lips. "You can trust me."

"Are—" I sniffle, wiping my nose with the back of my hand. "Have you heard back from the fellowship? The NASA one in C-California?" I wince, waiting for his answer, looking down at my hands to avoid his eyes when he tells me he's leaving, when he tells me that he won't be able to do this after the holidays.

I feel him tense and shift uncomfortably from one foot to the other. "Yeah." He clears his throat. I brace myself for confirmation. "And it's not happening."

I gasp. I don't need to be an expert to know that Asher is top in his field. I just *know* because he's brilliant and he's always been an academic overachiever.

"Are you serious?" I ask, a little slack-jawed.

Asher presses his lips together, but doesn't elaborate, and though him not getting into the program is disappointing for me, too, since I want him to get everything he deserves... Selfishly, there's a part of me that's excited for the possibilities that await us. Now that he's not going to California for his dream job, that gives us the chance to figure things out, right? To see whether we can make this work outside of the holidays, outside of Avon.

That is, if he wants to, too.

Which leads me to my next, and very important point...

"We need to talk," I say with more courage than I feel. "About us."

Chapter Thirty-Three

ROSIE

ASHER IMMEDIATELY DROPS HIS HANDS AND PULLS AWAY from me, face pale.

"Are you breaking up with me?" he asks, a little breathless.

"Breaking up?" I ask, a little bewildered, the words burning my throat. "We're together?" I ask.

Asher's eyes widen as he physically recoils. "We're *not?*" The pain in his voice slices through me and creates some of my own. "Are you saying that this entire time we—Are you saying that—" He stops mid-sentence, shaking. "Jesus Christ, Rosie. At least in *some* regard, right? I mean—"

"No, no, no," I say, pushing off the desk, going to him and taking his hands in mine. "That's not what I meant. It's just, we've never talked about where we stand. Officially. And that's all I wanted to clarify. I want to talk about *us*. About what we're doing. But more importantly, what we're *going* to do, Ash. I need to know. I need to know before I lose my mind, because I cannot —*I just cannot*—do this one second longer without knowing where this is leading. Because, I—I—" I gasp and stop myself before revealing too much. I feel the four walls of the small room cave in on me. I try to inhale slowly, but it's like my lungs have stopped working. I'm losing my footing, but before I let myself

249

have a second panic attack in less than an hour, I force myself to stop.

Closing my eyes, I recall a breathing exercise Barbara recommended.

In for five seconds. Hold for five seconds. Exhale for five seconds.

Throughout it, Asher waits patiently.

"You what?" he asks finally after a moment of silence. "What were you going to say?"

I squeeze my eyes shut and look away, shaking my head. I know what I was going to say, but it's insane to say the words now. Not because I feel like it's too soon—because it's been years in the making.

No, I stopped myself because I'm terrified the second the words *I love you* come out of my mouth, all of this will go away. Because I don't deserve it. Any of it.

"What were you going to say, Rosie?" he asks again, reaching out to me, placing one hand on my waist and the other on my side, just over my ribs. He rubs his thumb over the soft pink satin of my dress right under my breast, making me shiver as he brings his face to mine. Our lips hover over each other's for a few seconds before they come together in a slow, deep kiss that makes me weak in the knees.

"Say it," he commands, a little breathless. "Say the words I've been waiting for you to say to me for almost a decade." He swallows hard, his Adam's apple bobbing visibly, just as I feel more stinging in my eyes.

"Asher," I plead, my voice cracking.

"Say it, Rosie. If you feel it, *please* say it. I need to hear the words, even though I know you feel them." His voice is pained as he begs, and my heart races.

I want to, but saying them without knowing where we stand

officially feels like jumping without a parachute out of a plane. How am I supposed to land without crashing?

But when I look up into his eyes and see my love for him reflected in his, I decide to leap into it. I realize that for the first time in years, I can stop being scared. I can admit how I feel about him. I can forgive myself—truly forgive myself—for what happened because here we are now, after all these years. And I know it's going to happen—*us*. *We're* going to happen. And Asher won't let me fall. He won't let me crash and burn.

So I bring my hands to either side of his face and kiss him for a few seconds, dipping my tongue in his mouth, tugging at his lower lip with my teeth.

"I love you," I breathe against his lips. "Of course I love you. I think in a way I've *always* been in love with you since the first second I met you and you told me that silly thing about wolves."

Asher inhales sharply just as his grip tightens around my waist and his lips crash over mine. He makes a sound, low and deep in his throat, that can only be described as a growl, and walks me backwards, sliding me over the mahogany desk, trying to fit himself in between my legs. Frustrated with the material of my dress, he pulls away and starts pushing the hem of the skirt up my legs. As I pant in eagerness, I shimmy over the desk, helping him gather it at my waist. Asher makes room for himself in between both my thighs, his fingers digging into my hair as we kiss, drugging and hypnotic kisses that have us forgetting who we are, what we're doing, and where we are.

"God, I love you so much, Rosie," he whispers against my ear, one of his hands traveling to the front of my panties, trailing the elastic with his fingers.

I shiver at his words, at the warmth of his hands on my body, at his scent filling up my head, clouding it. I clutch at his blazer desperately, needing to hold on as he bites my neck, making me moan and call out his name in the empty office.

He pulls me closer to the edge of the desk, pressing the hard ridge of his pants right where I'm wet and swollen and need him the most.

"*Ash.*" A sharp inhale; an electric current up and down my spine. "Please." And I don't know exactly what I'm begging for, but he seems to know perfectly well what to do.

One of his hands travels to the outside of my thigh, hooking it over his hip as his lips trail kisses down my neck. He pulls down the straps of my dress, leaving me in just a light pink bralette that, by the looks of it, he *really* seems to like. With his teeth, he carefully pulls the cups over my breasts, his rough five o-clock shadow scratching against my delicate skin. But I love it. I love feeling him hard and rough against me in every way. It makes me feel alive and present and I don't ever want to move from here.

He pants, breath coming in quickly, wild eyes trailing all over my body as he pulls away.

Asher drops to his knees between my legs and places a kiss over my underwear, right where I need him most. With careful, yet determined movements, he pulls my underwear off and tosses it over his shoulder. He stares into my eyes before taking off his glasses and setting them next to me on the desk. Tightening his grip on my thighs, he pushes them as wide open as they'll go, and leans forward to lick me in one long, slow, deep movement right over my core.

"*Fuck,*" he groans, his lips grazing my overheated skin. His tongue runs up and down my slit once more, a little more out of control this time. "Fuck, you taste so good, Rosie."

I whimper at his words and at what his tongue does next, moving in circles around my clit, never quite doing what I need it to do. I hear myself beg, call out his name, ask him to suck on me. But he just laughs once, the feeling of it rumbling over me exquisite.

The noises we both make as he brings me closer and closer to the edge with each swipe of his tongue are almost obscene, bouncing off the empty walls of the office that used to belong to his grandfather, and mother after that.

But I don't care about that now. I don't care about any of it. Because all I can think about is how his lips have locked around my clit and he's sucking in delicious pulses that have my entire body shaking in anticipation. Suddenly, I can't hold it any longer, and I explode into one of the most incredible orgasms I've ever had in my life. Blinding and overpowering, like the brightest star, my fingers fisting in his hair, holding on as I ride it out.

"You're amazing," Asher says, getting to his feet and kissing me, his tongue dipping into my mouth in the same hungry way it did before. I taste myself on him, and it's heady and mind-melting, and *my god* I need him now.

"I need you inside me," I say, my voice barely audible over the loud beating of my heart in my chest. My hands fly to his belt, and I make quick work of it and his zipper, pulling him closer into me. I manage to pull him out, kissing his neck as I feel him hard in my hand, pumping him a few times. Asher groans in my ear, his hand coming up into my hair to grip it tightly, forcing my head back so he can kiss me again.

Together, we work to remove his blazer and unbutton his shirt.

He pushes my hands away and lines himself up, ready to push into me, but he stops just as the tip is inside. "Condom—" he pulls his face away in a panic. "They're—*shit*—they're in my car. We used up the last one I had in my wallet last night. Do you—"

I shake my head, bring his lips back to mine. "My purse. In my purse." Asher reaches quickly for the clutch I set on the desk, hands working at lighting speed as he rips open the packet and rolls the condom over himself, eyes never leaving mine.

"Need you," I say, reaching for him, wrapping my legs around his waist.

"Jesus Christ," he moans, kissing me and lining himself up against me once more. He runs the tip of his dick up and down my wet folds first, before finally pushing inside and knocking the oxygen out of me.

I'm still not used to the tight feeling of having him inside me, filling me so much I feel it all the way to my toes sometimes. He pulses once as if reading my mind, and I lose all conscious thought, my shoes dropping loudly to the floor, as my fingers lock behind his neck.

It doesn't last long, but as we lose ourselves in each other, calling out each other's names in pleasure, I realize I never want to be without this man ever again. I realize I would do anything for him.

Come hell or high water, I will always love Asher Wolff.

We come together, clawing at each other as if terrified someone would dare come between us and pull us apart. Desperate to be as close as humanly possible, his dewy skin pressed against mine.

"You know," he says, chuckling a little and breaking the silence. "I kinda wish we'd have done this on this desk earlier, before packing things up." I pull back and frown at him in confusion, adjusting my bra over my breasts. He kisses the tip of my nose. "Like in the movies. So that I could do that whole, cool pushing everything off the desk thing."

We laugh like giddy idiots, and he presses a kiss over my heart. "It would've been a hassle to clean up."

"Meh. Would've been worth it."

He presses soft kisses anywhere his lips can reach, expression buoyant, radiant. "You love me," he whispers, staring at me with a half-grin.

"I do. And you love me, too," I say with confidence, not able to help the smile quickly spreading across my face, the tingly electric current coursing through my body.

My heart flutters at the expression on his face, at how he looks *almost* as in love as I feel. "I was already so happy before the words came out of your mouth, but it's nothing compared to how I feel now. It's like seeing the James Webb telescope images versus the ones taken by Hubble. It doesn't even fucking compare." He kisses me deeply. "I'm James Webb telescope happy."

I snort and shake my head, elated. "You are such a nerd."

"*Your* nerd."

MINE.

He kisses me on the lips and hums, eyes closed, completely naked aside from the trousers around his ankles. I press myself closer into him, our dewy skin warm from exertion. "So, is it safe to say then that we are, in fact, *together*-together? Like, actually a couple, then? Because I'm so done pretending this isn't happening, that we aren't made for each other."

I smile broadly, my heart racing with excitement. Is this really happening? "You want to do this? Even if it's going to be long distance? At least for a few months while you figure out what your next steps are." My stomach rolls at the thought of having to be away from Asher after having the most incredible week of my life. I want to be supportive, but I can't deny that just thinking of us being thousands of miles apart feels like tearing my heart in two.

"Well, we don't know exactly *how* long-distance it's going to be yet until I find out exactly where I get a job and stuff. I mean, I could still find a job in New York City or something. But for now, yes, long distance. You in New York while I'm in Cambridge. We'll finally be able to tell everyone and stop hiding, and our families will be so happy—you know they will." I laugh and nod, just thinking of my mother's reaction to this news; of what Andrea will say once she finds out all my pining is over. At how happy Dad will be that I'm dating someone he loves and respects.

I watch his guarded expression carefully, asking myself the entire time whether I'm living in some fantasy land or something. I mean, *what the hell is my life?* How did I get here? Just last week I was miserable, worried sick, running every possible worst-case scenario pertaining to seeing this man again after so long through my head. And now? Now it's nothing short of everything I've ever dreamed of having, but never dared to ask.

I don't deserve him. I don't deserve any of this.

But I'd be a fool to say no.

"Well?" he asks a little impatiently. "Are you in? Can we do this?"

I cup his face between my hands and pull him down for another kiss, pouring every single one of the words I'm too choked up to say now.

"Yes, I'm in. I am so freaking in."

It's finally our time.

Chapter Thirty-Four

ASHER

I knew that misleading Rosie about the fellowship was wrong; I knew that letting her believe that taking a teaching position right out of grad school was a good thing and not career suicide was shitty. But if telling her the truth was the only other alternative, I still would've done what I did.

It had to be done. If I had told her the truth, she would've made me go. And then what? What would've happened to us? She was coming to me to define our relationship and I had already decided there was nothing I was going to let get in the way of us.

So I did it.

I wasn't going to go back on my decision now, so I knew I had to move quickly to withdraw my application. I didn't want her finding out somehow and forcing me to take that path. I wanted to burn each and every available bridge down. Which is why I immediately emailed my mentor a short, yet respectful email thanking him for the opportunity, but rejecting it all the same.

It took all of three minutes before I received a response back from him.

From: Dr. Emile Rousseau
Subject: Re: NASA Hubble Fellowship
Date: December 30th, 6:14 PM

Asher,

I am extremely disappointed to hear this. Not sure what's made you change your mind all of a sudden, but I am going to ignore this email and take it as a momentary lapse in judgment. Please take the new year to get your head on straight and get back to me by the 5th.

Best,
Emile

French people are so temperamental.

Frowning, I slip my phone back into my pocket and try not to think about how I might have offended one of the most important people in my career. But when I look up and my eyes land on Rose's smiling face, my heart lifts, and I know that I've made the right decision for myself. I refuse to let her go after everything we've been through—the good, the bad, the beautiful, and the ugly.

Rosie and I are going to happen. Are *happening.*

The feeling crashes over me in a wave of happiness and light. And I just watch her in complete awe, ecstatic that I get to call her mine now.

As my mind idly wanders to thinking of our future together, I overhear Diana say, "Ugh, couldn't you have saved your sister's wedding pictures from your pink hair phase and dyed it back to black for the occasion? Seriously, Rosie. How old are you?"

I scowl at her from afar, wanting to speak up for my *girlfriend* right now.

Diana has been acting bitchier than usual lately, but this is next level.

And this thing with Rosie's hair isn't a phase. She's expressing herself, finally having the courage to show everyone in her life who she is. Will she have pink hair forever? Who knows. But right now, this is what makes her happy. Why can't her family understand that?

The way they speak to her or about her sometimes brings out a fierce protective side—even during those years when we weren't on speaking terms. My love and devotion for Rosie never went away—*never*—even though my old self would love to have believed otherwise.

"Okay, just the sisters and mother in the photo now, please," the photographer cries over the loud voices.

Looking relieved, Diego walks away from the photo session and over to me. I go back to watching Rosie with a smile on my face, only to feel his heavy gaze on me.

The tension is palpable, and I wonder whether he knows about us, too. It's clear at this point that our mothers do, but what about Diego?

Though it's not like keeping it a secret will matter much anymore. We plan on telling people tonight in a *subtle* way, not wanting to steal Andrea and Alex's thunder.

"Diego? Is everything...okay?" I ask after a few more seconds of uncomfortable silence.

He doesn't take his narrowed eyes off mine as he continues his intimidating glare, watching me with skepticism. Another uncomfortable stretch of time and, "So. Asher."

Ah, he absolutely knows. Here we go.

"Yes?" I ask innocently.

"Are you still planning on going to that post-doctoral fellow-ship for NASA at CalTech you told me about this summer? The one you've been dreaming of doing since *undergrad*?" He glares at me, crossing his arms in front of his chest. And suddenly I get it. He's concerned that I'll break his daughter's heart if I move to California.

"No, Diego." I smile, trying to reassure the man who helped raise me through my teenage years. He wasn't the warmest man, but he was the strongest male role model I had. The one who taught me the value of hard work, of setting goals and achieving them.

His story and professional growth are what inspired me in the darkest times. A man who, as a high schooler, fought tooth and nail to gain a full ride scholarship to an American college—Cornell University. A man who took his education and was able to revamp a hotel chain in an almost-failed country through non-corrupt ways. Diego Castillo—a no-nonsense man of integrity who caught the eye of famous hotelier Jean-Luc Dumas—was the man who took over as my role model after my grandfather died and someone I did not want to disappoint.

"The fellowship isn't happening. I'm staying on the East Coast next fall." I smile encouragingly and pat him on the shoulder, trying to tell him that I've got this. That I'm not going to hurt his daughter by leaving.

But instead of looking placated, Rosie's dad gapes at me. "What do you mean you're staying on the East Coast? Asher, you can't be—"

"Diego," I hold my hand up to stop him. "I know what you're trying to tell me. And I just want to say, I'm not going to hurt her. I'm going to look for jobs in New York City. Or maybe extend my Ph.D. or something so we're close—or at least in the same time zone. I'm not going to abandon her or let something as small as distance get in the way of our happiness. What we have is real, and we're going to do this the right way. I promise you."

Diego's eyes widen, looking mildly horrified—which completely throws me off balance. I thought he'd appreciate it; I thought he'd be happy I'm trying to make it work with his daughter.

His dark brows furrow and his mouth twists. "Asher, you cannot seriously—"

"Diego!" Julieta calls. "We need a picture of you and me with Alex and Andrea. Quick!"

Rosie's dad looks from me to his wife, his expression torn. Julieta grows impatient and pulls him away by the hand. He points his index finger at me, and says, "We're not done. We need to discuss this."

"What was *that* all about?" I hear Rosie ask beside me. Not caring about being subtle anymore, I wrap an arm around her waist and kiss the top of her head, closing my eyes to inhale the scent of her, letting it soothe my suddenly anxious body.

"I don't know," I say into her hair. "I think he was just checking up on us."

Rosie looks up at me with a sweet smile, and I feel that familiar gravitational pull. We're already touching, for Christ's sake, but it never feels like enough. She gives me an odd look and gnaws on her lower lip.

I laugh at the way she clutches the back of my blazer, pulling me closer. "What?"

She shakes her head with a soft smile. "Nothing. I just—" she huffs. "I really want to kiss you."

My heart nearly explodes; overjoyed, it beats wildly against my chest. I'm suddenly overcome with this need to pull her into my arms and kiss her like I never have before. But we can't, can we? Not in public—not yet.

I look around the restaurant event space, filled with the bride and groom's family and bridal party. The low light has definitely set a romantic tone thanks to the several candles lighting each of the four tables. In the middle of the room, there's a small space where a few people have begun dancing to the soft, Bossa nova music playing in the background.

"Dance with me?" I ask, my voice betraying my need to feel her in my arms right now.

Without another word, she grabs hold of my hand and leads me to the middle of the room, letting me wrap my arms around her waist. When her hands slide over my chest to meet at the back of my neck, I shiver, needing to suppress a groan. She presses herself up closer to me and looks up to meet my eyes, beaming.

I beam right on back.

"This is it," I whisper, not even giving a shit at the looks we're getting from some curious family members. "We're doing this."

It's not a question, but just in case, she whispers, "Yes. Absolutely, yes, we're doing this."

A little breathless as we sway to the music, I bring my face down to hers as she stretches higher onto her tiptoes to meet me halfway. No longer caring about the people around us, we let ourselves get lost in the feeling of our lips molding to each other. I revel in the taste of her tongue in my mouth, the little sounds she makes, only audible to me, and how it awakens things in me that should be dormant in a public setting. I use a light grip to pull her slightly back and get a good look at her. She makes a small sound of protest and, with half-lidded eyes, pouts. I chuckle and shake my head a little, our faces still close enough that our noses graze against each other.

"Why'd you stop?" she asks, her voice a little pained.

I give her a peck on the lips, which she tries to deepen unsuccessfully. "Because," I tell her, my grip in her hair growing a little sharper, but still unnoticeable to anyone else. "I need to tell you that I love you."

A slow smile spreads across her face, her cheeks reddening.

God, do I love her.

"I love you, too."

And not giving a crap anymore about the fact that we're in front of all of our loved ones and are supposed to be keeping this a secret, I slide my fingers into her hair at the base of her neck and bend to kiss her, putting every single ounce of love and loyalty I have for her into it. I'm in this for the long run, and I want everyone to know.

Chapter Thirty-Five

ROSIE

"Shh!" I whisper-yell, half laughing as Asher trips down the last step of the stairwell. "You're going to wake everyone up!"

He bends down to kiss me on the lips, an arm wrapped around my waist while the other holds his coat and blazer. Asher smiles against my mouth, unable to keep his enthusiasm from radiating outwards—just like me.

I don't think I've ever been happier. Honestly, the only thing causing me distress right now is the fact that he has to leave my bed at six a.m. after having spent one of the most incredible nights of my life. That and the fact we still haven't figured out the exact details of how this is going to work moving forward. He'll be in Cambridge while I'll be in New York City—but that's only until May. We still haven't discussed what comes after, even though I know we'll make it work. Somehow.

Last night was everything, and though I tried really hard to concentrate and be present for my sister's sake, it was nearly impossible to focus. Without the restrictions of hiding our relationship, Asher's hands were always on me. The way he grazed my shoulder while talking to his neighbor at the dinner table, tracing soft patterns on my exposed skin. The way he placed a possessive hand on me as we listened to the Best Man speech.

The way he wrapped his arm around my waist as we mingled with the crowd, knees buckling as he whispered how beautiful I looked, how much he wanted to kiss me... The way his lips felt on mine when he finally did, right there, in front of everyone.

It wasn't long after that that we Irish-exited the hell out of the rehearsal dinner and came back here.

"You need to go," I whisper against his lips, pushing him towards the front door. A risky move, of course, but the only way to get him out after the trellis fell in the middle of the night.

"We're gonna get caught," I murmur. The last thing I want is for him to leave, but it won't be long before my family starts to wake.

"I don't care." He kisses me once more before releasing me.

Honestly, I don't either, but I don't want to start off our public relationship by getting into an argument with my dad about what's "appropriate" under his roof.

"Maybe the trellis falling in the middle of the night was a sign that we made the right call coming out last night. It's the universe's way of telling us that we don't have a use for it anymore because we don't ever have to sneak around again."

"I think you take the universe way too seriously," I whisper, teasing him with a soft kiss. I open the front door as quietly as possible, signaling for him to leave.

Asher laughs and nods. "Okay, I'll go. But you can't make fun of the universe, Rose. I love it almost as much as I love you." His words make my heart soar, my face split into an uncontrollable grin. So I fist his shirt in my hand and pull him down for another kiss, a low moan escaping my lips right before it turns too heated.

"Now, get out of here," I smile, a little dizzy.

"Yes, ma'am." But he barely makes it off our lawn before turning and jogging up the porch steps, his cheeks and nose already red from the cold air.

"Just wanted to ask you something real quick," he says with a smirk. "Will you be my date to your sister's wedding?"

I laugh softly, and nod. "Of course, you idiot. I'll be your date to all the weddings."

"Oh, yeah? So not just ours, then?" A soft gasp escapes my lips at his comment, his teasing smile falling just a little at the corners before recovering. He holds it tightly, waiting for my response.

I try to control my breathing, but he just put the idea of us officially together for the rest of our lives in my head, and it makes my brain spin. It's not that I don't like it—it's the opposite. Even after making this official and being surrounded by wedding talk 24/7 this entire time, I haven't even let myself associate Asher and me with marriage. The fear of losing him once more is so deeply ingrained in me that I haven't allowed myself to even think about the topic.

But he's opened the door to it—even if it's barely ajar—and now it's *there*.

He watches me with expectant eyes, growing more and more anxious with every second that goes by. After a long, uncomfortable pause, I watch as he begins to regret it. And I hate that.

"Not just our wedding, Ash," I say finally, sliding up onto the tiptoes of my pink slipper-covered feet to kiss him once more on the lips. "I'll be your forever date to everything."

Asher inhales sharply against my lips, his forehead pressed against mine. "Forever, then. I like the sound of that." He smiles, his face radiant, before kissing me once more until I need to lean on him for support.

Gently, he pulls away and walks back to his house without another word or glance in my direction. Once I manage to make my legs work again, I shut the door with care, and tiptoe toward the stairs to get a few more hours of sleep before I need to get up for my sister's wedding day.

"Rosario," a deep voice behind me stops me in my tracks.

I turn slowly to face the dark figure by the kitchen doorway, my blood pressure dropping. "Dad."

"Come have some coffee with me." His voice is calm as he walks back into the kitchen and I follow reluctantly.

He gestures toward one of the chairs at the kitchen table, and I take it, mentally preparing myself for whatever lecture he's prepared.

I get that it's his house and we need to follow his rules, but it's not like I'm a teenager anymore. He can't ground me or anything. I'm a grown woman, and I can totally have premarital sex if I want. This is America.

Still, why am I so nervous?

Because you hate disappointing him. And, sometimes, it feels like that's all you ever do.

I keep quiet as I watch him prepare our coffee, and he doesn't volunteer anything either. By the time he finally hands me a mug filled to the brim, I start to believe I'm going to get off easy.

But, of course, I'm wrong.

"So," he starts, blowing into his piping hot coffee. "Asher."

I grip the mug tightly with two hands. "Yup."

"How long has that been going on?"

"Um," I lift my eyes nervously to meet his—dark, narrowed. "This time around? Since seeing each other at the airport, I guess." Kind of. "And in high school for a couple of days." I don't know why I go into details. Maybe it's the intimidating way he looks at me or the way he asks the question like an FBI agent interrogating a suspect.

Dad nods once but is otherwise quiet as he stares into his coffee. He takes a tentative sip, checking the temperature, I suppose, while I leave mine untouched. I watch as he gears himself up for one of his speeches, but I don't know why. Is it really such a big deal he caught his twenty-seven-year-old daughter sneaking out a guy he's known and loved for over fifteen years? I get that my dad is super Catholic and has the whole *machista* "I'm the man of the house, so my word is to be respected" thing going for him. But *come on.*

"I know you and I haven't agreed on much over the years—"

I snort, crossing my arms in front of my chest. "An understatement."

"But contrary to popular belief, I *am* proud of you and all the work you've done. Of your accomplishments."

I sit up in my chair, raising an eyebrow at this sudden unexpected turn of events.

Definitely not where I thought he was going with this.

"Over the years, I haven't really understood why you've chosen to take certain paths above others I thought were more... *practical.*" A euphemism for "smart," I'd bet. "But," he continues, "I'm not so stubborn that I can't see your achievements and be proud—admittedly in a limited capacity."

Jesus, there always has to be an asterisk next to every good thing he says about me, doesn't there?

Dad sighs and looks out the window for a moment.

"I know I wasn't easy on you and... maybe some day, when you have your own kids, you'll understand what it's like as a parent. What it's like to love your child that the fear of them getting hurt or living an unhappy life can become crippling. You want them to go off into the world and make their own path, whatever they may choose. But you love them so much that when they pick a path unfamiliar to yours, it scares you to death and makes you react in unreasonable ways."

My heart beats loudly against my chest, mouth slightly slack-jawed. We've never really had this conversation outright. Not since that horrible fight right before I left. We didn't even have it when I came back for the holidays that break. Dad and I just kind of slipped into a tense relationship that has gotten progressively better over the years—at least in a let's-brush-this-under-the-rug type of way.

"After you ran off to New York, though," he continues, "I told myself I wasn't going to try and interfere anymore. I told myself that, even though it would take time—and a hell of a lot of patience—I would try to be..." He grimaces, searching for the right expression. "I don't know. Somewhere between 'approval' and 'tolerance'. The former sounds too accepting, and the latter too harsh." He shrugs, taking another sip of his coffee before continuing. "I wasn't quiet about my opinions, but I promised myself that I wasn't going to try to change your mind anymore. That I wouldn't get angry and try to pressure you into doing what *I* would do. Because we're different people. I wanted to know more about this life you were living so far away from us. So I tried to be more involved."

At first, I want to laugh in his face. How dare he say that? Of course he's always been against everything I've done. Of course he's always pushed me down or not taken my career seriously.

But then... I think back to the past couple of years, and am a little taken aback. He's right. He hasn't been *vocally* support-ive, but, in his own way, Dad *has* been making an effort. He's asked about work and how it's going. He's asked what my career progression looks like. Every time, I thought he was using it as an opportunity to put me down, but he wasn't. He was trying to be more involved in my life. And I just didn't see it.

He didn't go about it the right way, but I guess that was him giving it the ol' college try?

"I—I—" I shake my head, at a loss.

"You don't need to say anything yet. Just let me finish." He sighs. "I figured if I kept pushing too hard to get you to listen, to do things my way, one of two things would happen. You would either, A, *actually* listen to me and go into business or finance and lose that spark of yours I love so much. Or, B—the more likely of scenarios—I'd push you hard enough that you'd never speak to me again." He shrugs once. "Either way, I'd lose you. And that's something I'll never be willing to compromise on.

"So, yes, I said I'd never get involved in your life again. But, *hija*... Today, I need to break that promise." I stiffen, suddenly on high alert. I can basically *feel* my body gearing up for a fight with my dad, and I resent him for it. He's about to ruin one of the most blissful mornings of my life. I just know it. "And it's not for my sake or yours, but for the man who spent the night with you."

"What?" I finally speak, confused out of my mind. "What are you talking about?"

He looks down at his coffee for a moment before speaking again, measuring his words. "Did Asher tell you about the NASA Hubble fellowship?"

I frown, confused. "The one at CalTech? Yeah, he told me about it. He got his rejection letter yesterday," I frown. "How did you know about that?"

"He's been talking about it for years. Dreaming about getting the chance to participate since he heard about it his first year of grad school."

I'm overflowing with a mix of emotions: jealousy that my *father* has known more about Asher's life over the past few years than I have and absolute and total heartbreak that the man I love most couldn't get into the program he's dreamt about for that long.

"I didn't know," I say.

"Yes. He's been preparing for this *literally* years in advance. And when his favorite professor and mentor moved over to CalTech he was overjoyed because he knew—despite the panel of people reviewing his admission—that it would give him a leg up to have a recommendation directly from the man he'd be working with."

"Wow. I didn't know all of that." He must've been so heartbroken when he got the rejection letter, then. Much more than he led on.

Dad nods several times, finally locking eyes on me. "Now, tell me, Rosario. Knowing Asher—knowing how intelligent, dedicated, and hardworking he is... Knowing everything that you know about him, how can you really believe that he was rejected from the program?"

I physically recoil at the question, sitting back in my chair. "What?" I ask, my voice small, like I'd had all the wind knocked out of me.

Because I'd never really thought of it before.

"Do you really think *anyone* would say no to him?" he asks, his eyes narrowed at me. And I can see the anger and disappointment boiling under his skin. Except I know it's not aimed at me, this time. Not specifically.

I shake my head, helplessly trying to find the words. "But if he's dreamt of this so long, why would he—?"

Dad raises an eyebrow, looking at me like I'm dense. And I am. I am *so* dense. But... He wouldn't give up his dream just for me—for *us*—would he?

I start to open my mouth and object to my father's suggestion, but then something stops me. A flashback of our conversation that first day in the shop. The day we decided to bury the hatchet, so to speak. The day he said it was probably a good idea that we broke up, because he would've been too distracted by our relationship to be able to do well in school—to get as far as he has.

"Oh my god," I whisper, putting my face in my hands. "No. He can't," I say, looking up to meet my dad's eyes. "He can't—I mean is he—?" I groan, my breathing getting faster. "Is he an idiot or something?"

Dad looks at me with something akin to pity. "Not stupid. Just... in love, I suppose." He waits for me to verbally acknowledge it, but all I can do now is nod.

"All I'm saying—all I'm *asking*—is for you to think about what you're doing. Asher is an incredible man with a brilliant young mind. It doesn't take a genius to understand that that man is capable of absolute greatness. And while, as a father, I am happy you have found a man who loves you so much he's willing to give up his entire career for you—because that is what he's doing, by the way, he's committing career suicide—I'm asking you to reconsider.

"I worry that it will not only affect him and his place in his profession, but it will inevitably affect your relationship in the long run. It will affect your long-term happiness. Maybe I'm just exaggerating and he won't ever resent you for it—you didn't ask him to give it up, after all—but I don't want that for you. I love you, so please don't take this the wrong way, but you're being unknowingly selfish. Staying with him, knowing that he turned down the opportunity of a lifetime to do life-changing research so he can be near you while working at a dead-end teaching job instead... Well, I would argue it'll be the most selfish thing you'll ever do. And neither of you deserves that."

With a sad look in his eyes, Dad gets up from his seat as I look out the window, unable to focus on anything through the tears that have suddenly formed in my eyes. Because Dad is right. Asher lied. Rejecting the fellowship is totally something Asher would do just for us to stay together. And there's no way

I'm going to let him do that. I need to tell him to go to CalTech, to make sure that it's not too late for him to accept the fellowship. I mean, we can do long distance; we can—

We can what? Try and make our relationship work through my new job and him having to finish his grad school? Maybe that'd be fine.

But then what about after he moves to Pasadena? I haven't started my new role at work, but I *know* it's going to be draining and so, so time-consuming. And he'd be starting a new job he's going to have to focus on in the fall, as well. It would require all his dedication and focus. But I know Asher. He'd want to travel here every other weekend, or want me over there, taking time away from what's important to him—school, work, *a life*. He even admitted it himself.

On top of the travel, we'd have the time difference to battle with and three thousand miles between us... And how long is that supposed to last? My contract with the show is four years, and his will probably be two? Three? How long do these fellowships last? And then what? What would be his next career step? Probably *actual* NASA in Houston. Or maybe stay at CalTech. Or fuck, who knows!

But I can't let this end. Couples survive long distance dating, right? Some of them do. And if Asher and I were able to love each other through these past few years, then we can definitely continue to do so after this week.

I just need to confront him and push him into the right direction: his fellowship program. I know that deep down it's the right thing to do—I *know* it is. But then, why does it feel so bad?

Chapter Thirty-Six

ASHER

I WATCH HER FROM A FEW FEET AWAY AS SHE LINES UP IN front of the church, taking pictures with the other bridesmaids. Her hair is up, leaving her neck exposed to the cold winter air, and I get lost in it. I get lost in visions of earlier this morning when I dragged my lips and tongue over the delicate skin.

A gust of biting wind blows through, making me worry for her. Is that short, faux-fur jacket all the bridesmaids are wearing keeping her warm enough? The cold air gives her tan nose and cheeks an extra tint of red to them, making her look so cute I can barely control the grin spreading across my face.

She looks so beautiful. And she's mine.

Fucking finally.

Once they're done taking photos of the bridesmaids and they move on to the groomsmen, Rosie catches my eye from afar. She shoots me a hesitant smile and power-walks over to me, heels clicking on the pavement.

"Hey," she says, the smile on her face not quite reaching her eyes. I frown in confusion but decide not to press her for info. She's probably nervous for her sister. That's normal, right?

I take her face in my hands and bend down to kiss her deeply, inhaling her signature scent as I do. I feel the tightness in my chest, the blood racing through my veins, and relish in it. Kissing her like this, in public, is an absolute rush. We're together—finally together after all these years—and we can finally tell everyone.

I lose myself a little in our kiss but get pulled back to reality when I feel her hands on my chest, pushing me away. I open my eyes to meet her gaze with confusion, only find her going through some internal struggle.

"Hey, what's going on? Is this about kissing in public? I thought we resolved that last night at the rehearsal dinner. Pretty sure everyone knows by now and is pretty ecstatic about it. I mean, I even spoke to my mom and sister about it when we were wrapping up everything in the store this morning." I genuinely think I have never seen my mother or sister happier for me. Not that I needed their validation, but it was nice to know that at least my family's on board.

"No, no. It's not that," she shakes her head, cringing. "I mean, it's nothing, really. We can talk about it later."

I wrap my arms around her waist and pull her closer into me. "Hey, talk to me. Don't shut me out, please." I swallow the knot in my throat, the feeling that she's slowly slipping through my fingers starts to creep through my body.

No. No way. It's not happening. Not again.

Rosie and I are solid. We've *both* wanted this for far too long for her to just suddenly change her mind. This is happening.

She fists my coat lapels in her hands and presses her forehead against my chest before taking a deep breath. "You smell amazing," she says in a soft voice.

"Don't try to distract me. Tell me what's wrong, please."

"What *really* happened with your NASA fellowship?" she whispers the question into my chest.

I tense, my arms wrapping tighter around her waist. "I told you. It's not happening."

Slowly, she raises her face to look me straight in the eye. "And why's that?" she asks. "Is it because you didn't get in or because—" She swallows hard once. "Or because you rejected it?"

I take a beat before answering, because I know what she's going to say and I don't want to hear it. Instead, I go for an obvious deflection: "Who told you?"

"Ash," she says, her voice small, beautiful dark brown eyes wide.

"Was it your dad? Did he tell you? Or was it Jess? Or my mom? She can't keep a fucking secret to save her life."

She pinches the bridge of her nose and squeezes her eyes shut for a moment, processing my words before speaking again. "You mean to tell me all these people knew—*my dad* knew—before I did? Jesus, Asher."

I sigh and look away. "It's not a big deal. I decided the program just wasn't for me."

"Not for you?" She pushes away from me completely, and I feel the loss of her body against mine like a gut punch. I reach out for her once more, trying to keep her near, but she dodges my hands, pushing them away.

"*Rose*, please," I beg.

"How can you say the program isn't for you?" she asks, her voice rising, causing a few people to turn in our direction. She glances furtively around us, and lowers her voice when she says, "It's all you've ever dreamt of."

"Untrue," I tell her with one hundred percent honesty. "*You* are all I've ever dreamt of."

She scoffs, and I wince. "You don't mean that, Ash."

"Yes, I really fucking do, Rosie," I growl.

"You've wanted this for so long," she says, her voice breaking. "And I'm not taking this away from you just so we can be close by."

"What are you saying?" I ask, my stomach rolling over and over again.

"Long distance. Let's do long distance." She exhales, her bottom lip shaking.

"I don't want to do long distance," I tell her, pouring every bit of energy and resolve into my voice so she can get it through her thick skull.

She's. Fucking. *It.*

And I'm not taking any more chances with our relationship.

"We would already have to do long distance while you finish your Ph.D. program at MIT anyway, so I don't really see what the difference is."

"Exactly. Exactly that. We would be away from each other for five more months while I wrap up my program. I don't know about you, but I know it's not something I'm looking forward to. I finally have you, and I'm not about to throw it away over a *job*," I spit out.

"You and I both know it's more than a job," she whispers, her wide eyes red-rimmed. "I still remember how excited you get every time you talk about your research. This *job*... It's your dream."

I swallow the lump in my throat and shake my head softly, trying to deny it. But she knows me. I would have every resource at my disposal to do life-changing research. And she knows that, too.

"What about us, then?" I ask, fear overtaking my system, keeping me from physically being able to reach out to her like my body craves. But Rosie hears my need for her touch and walks over to me, taking my hands in hers.

"We stay together. We do long distance. We see each other when we can and—" Someone calls out Rosie's name, cutting her off. We turn to look as people start going into the church, while the bridal party lines up outside the church, waiting for the bride to arrive.

She looks back at me and smiles weakly. "You have to do it. We both know that you do. Email whoever the hell you need to and ask for your spot back."

"Rose, I—"

"I have to go," she says as we hear her mother calling out to her in the background. She gives me a quick peck on the cheek and jogs off clumsily to the rest of the group, leaving me dumbstruck at the foot of the church steps.

I don't know exactly how I get to my seat, but I suddenly find myself sitting next to my mother in the second row of pews on the bride's side of the church. I watch as Rosie gracefully walks down the aisle in her red dress, and never, not for one second of the entire ceremony, take my eyes off her.

She leaves the day after tomorrow. *Two* days. And then I'm back to lonely cold nights at the lab in Cambridge while she works in New York for hours on end. Where we won't get to see or speak to each other as much. Where we'll get frustrated and inevitably start fighting—as one does in long-distance relationships. Call me a cynic, but it's true.

None of it would have mattered—not really. Because it would've been temporary. It would've had an expiration date. I would've moved to New York or at the very least somewhere closer after completing my Ph.D. Maybe Princeton?

But if I take the NASA fellowship at Caltech... There's no way of knowing how long the separation will last. Because what happens after I finish the fellowship? Where will I go? It's not like the research I chose to do is something I can pursue anywhere in the world. It's very specific and requires equipment, knowledge, and resources that can't be found at just any university or research center—even the best ones. And California is so far away...

My mother elbows me in the side, momentarily pulling me away from my downward spiral. She gives me a questioning look, but I shake my head, trying to contain my expression, before looking back up at Rosie. I want to soak up every moment I have with her before our inevitable separation.

I watch her as Andrea and Alex exchange vows, watch as she's moved so much by her sister's wedding, it brings her to soft tears. And then all of a sudden, a wave of crippling fear falls over me, knocking me breathless. I catch myself on the pew in front of me as I try to recover from the image of her doing this with someone else—standing at that altar, marrying someone that isn't me—almost brings me to my knees.

I'm scared that if I take this job, that's exactly what will happen. I'm scared that if I listen to her, we'll end up breaking up in a messy, horrible way, and I'll lose her forever.

But I'm also scared that by not taking the fellowship, I'll be betraying myself and everyone around me. Because she's right—it's been one of my biggest dreams to do so.

But not the biggest.

Another vision pops in my head just then: one of *both* of us standing at that altar one day, making this official. Of us making a life together. Of waking every morning in the same bed—*our* bed—being able to laze around in it as much as we can. And suddenly, the answer is clear.

I don't care what she says, what her dad says, what *anyone* says. My dreams are bigger than the universe, and I'm not taking that fellowship.

Chapter Thirty-Seven

ROSIE

Asher and I haven't spoken since before the ceremony. Not about the fellowship and definitely not about our relationship. We just haven't had a chance to do so given all the pictures that I needed to pose for, the family friends I had to say hi to.

And thank god for that.

I know that deep down inside neither of us wants to face the fact that what's coming—whatever it may be—because it sure as hell won't be easy.

He *needs* to take that fellowship, but the way he talked about it earlier today made it clear that he had no intentions of doing so. Which makes me wonder what in the hell I'm doing and whether my father was right. Am I really going to be so selfish that I let Asher give up his dream just to make it easy on our relationship? Although, another side of me keeps reminding me that he is a grown man, capable of making his own choices. And if he chooses to pass up this amazing opportunity, then—

No. No way. He has to take it.

It's why I've spent the entire night stuck to his side, only leaving it once for post-ceremony family pictures. I'm anxious and scared, and I take comfort in the fact that I don't seem to be the only one in this relationship currently feeling this way. The way Asher wraps his arm around my shoulder possessively at the dinner table, or how tightly he holds me as we glide across the dance floor tells me that he's freaking out just as much as I am. I'm leaving in a couple of days and we haven't really resolved any of the big picture questions looming over us, not quite letting us enjoy this moment.

Every smile is a little strained, every kiss a little desperate.

But even though I know—we *both* know—that it's something we should probably address sooner rather than later, neither one of us wants to ruin the night by bringing it up. Not after how painful our conversation outside the church was—and that only lasted a couple of minutes. I could see the panic in his eyes, and it took everything in me not to capitulate to what he wanted. But there is no other option—he's going to California. I won't have it any other way.

And so now, as he twirls me around the dance floor with the ease of Fred Astaire, I do my best to memorize every single detail about tonight. I make sure that this moment, his arms wrapped around me like he never wants to let go, the way his scent fogs my brain, clouding every thought I could possibly have that isn't of him. I memorize the way his fingertips feel at the base of my spine, of the sound of his breath. And I memorize the sweet way in which he whispers the words "I love you" in my ear right before he takes my face in his hands and kisses me.

A half-smile spreads across his face, the first genuine-looking one since our conversation before the ceremony. "And I have a surprise for you."

"Oh, yeah?" I smile, threading my fingers into his thick curls at the base of his neck. "What's that?"

He brings his lips to my ear, his breath tickling. "I got us a hotel room," he says, wiggling his eyebrows suggestively. I chuckle and kiss his chin. "But, under a different name, of course. Didn't want your dad finding out that I plan on locking you up in one of his hotel bedrooms all night." He presses a kiss under my ear, and I shiver.

"But it's almost midnight," I say, not really caring. "I need to eat twelve grapes as soon as we hit the New Year! I don't want any bad luck following me into the next three-hundred-and-sexy-five days."

"*Sexy*-five? How many drinks have you had?" He laughs and kisses my nose.

I roll my eyes, but can't help the smile on my face. "You know what I mean. It still doesn't take away from the fact that I need to eat my twelve grapes at midnight."

"While I value your Venezuelan tradition—ridiculously superstitious as it may be—and I don't want to be disrespectful to it—"

"This is you not being disrespectful?" I snort.

He kisses his way from beneath my ear all the way to the corner of my mouth. "I propose something new. I promise you'll get to eat your grapes at midnight—but they'll all be while naked and in bed. And it'll have to be one after every orgasm."

I laugh. "Twelve orgasms in one night? That's ambitious."

"The way I'm feeling right now? I'd say it's realistic." He smiles slyly before pressing his lips to mine, his kiss deepening. "I need to make up for lost time."

A little breathless, I ask, "What about the balloons? It's *also* tradition to tie a wish to the other end of a balloon's string and release it into the night sky at midnight. That one is more of a hotel tradition, but it's still significant to me. To *us*."

He laughs a low laugh that I feel to the tips of my toes. "I don't need it. I got the one thing I wished for every single year right here in my arms."

Pulling back slightly, I narrow my eyes at him. "What are you talking about?"

He shrugs and smiles innocently. "Just that I used to wish for one thing exclusively every year since we were probably sixteen—with the exception of that awful New Year's where I hooked up with that one girl—and I have it now."

"You mean—" I stammer, tongue tied.

"I wished for you every single year. I wished for you to like me, at first. Then, to come back into my life, more specifically. But if I was feeling especially greedy, I would wish for this—for *us*. And this year, I get to say it came true."

I can't breathe. I can't breathe and it's because my chest feels like it's expanded to insane proportions, my heart not able to take this in. "You're telling me that even after everything, you still wanted me?"

"Of course I still wanted you, Rosie." He takes my face in his hands, all the humor in his eyes gone. "I've always fucking wanted you. And I will always want you. You are a permanent part of my soul," he says, his voice almost a growl. And without another word, he bends to press his lips to mine, one of his hands sliding to the back of my neck, holding me in place. His other hand travels down my back, fingers skimming my spine, stopping only to rest just above the curve of my bottom. Losing my balance, I grasp his biceps tightly, nails digging into the fabric of his blazer.

By the time we pull away from each other, we're both a little breathless, I feel the uncomfortable, yet all too familiar ache build between my legs, and his hardness presses against my stomach.

"Let's go," he says, his voice rough, eyes low-lidded. "I need you naked and below me now."

Feeling more brazen than usual, I whisper, "I'd rather have you behind me tonight."

"*Fuck*," he groans, pulling me in for another rough kiss. He pulls away quickly, pressing his lips together as if he can still taste my lips on his. "I'm gonna go check-in. Get our room key. You say goodbye and goodnight to whoever you have to, because I'm not letting you out of our room until they make us. And I asked for late check-out."

I laugh as I watch him walk away from me, off the dance floor, heading for the front desk, looking uncomfortable from his hard on as he does.

Once I've said my goodbyes and congratulations to the bride and groom, I search for my parents, who are nowhere to be found. I find Diana, however, at a table alone, staring sadly into her champagne glass. And though I know I have somewhere I desperately want to be, something tells me now is the right time to ask her about what's been going on with her.

"Hey," I take a seat beside her; she jumps just a little in surprise.

"Hey," she answers back, her voice breaking. It's only then that I notice she's crying. Mascara-streaming-down-your-face crying.

"Oh my god, what the hell happened?"

"Just caught Rodrigo making out with one of the bridesmaids outside," she says, matter-of-factly.

"*What?*" I shriek. "Are you kidding me? I'll *kill* him." I push out of my chair, ready to commit murder. But Diana stops me by wrapping a hand around my wrist, pulling me back down.

"Stop. Don't be ridiculous."

"Ridiculous? What the hell are you talking about? You just caught him cheating on you! At your sister's wedding! With your sister's bridesmaid! Who the hell was it, by the way? I'll murder her, too."

Diana snorts and wipes her nose with the back of her hand.

"I'm loving this sisterly protectiveness, but it's not necessary. It's also not the first time I've caught him cheating on me, anyway."

It takes me a minute to process what she just said.

"What the hell are you talking about?" I manage.

Diana heaves a sigh, her exhaustion coming through. "I mean that... I mean that Rodrigo and I are separated. Have been for a while. We're getting a divorce."

Chapter Thirty-Eight

ROSIE

"I'm sorry—*WHAT?*" I ask, in complete disbelief. "What do you mean you two are getting a divorce? How is that possible?" My sister, always so emphatic about family values and putting your needs second in the name of your husband and kids, is getting a divorce? "I don't understand. When did this happen? *How* did this happen?"

"Well." My sister takes a long swing of champagne. "It could have something to do with us growing apart after getting married so young. Or with the fact that his *girlfriend* of two years finally outed him after giving him an ultimatum, where he chose her over me and the girls."

"*What?*"

"Although, I don't know how the girlfriend's going to feel about the bridesmaid situation," she says, ignoring me. Diana shrugs, and looks over her shoulder out to the patio, lost in thought for a moment. "Once a cheater, always a cheater, I guess."

"Diana... What happened?" I ask, my voice softer now. I reach out and take hold of her hands in both of mine, squeezing them.

"We just... I don't know. Grew apart. And then he started traveling more for work. I was constantly home alone with the

286

kids. And then the trips became more frequent and longer, and then one day... One day, I get a call from this woman." She scoffs, shaking her head. "Telling me that she was my husband's *girlfriend*, that she had stolen my number from his phone so she could call and let me know that he was in love with her and she was in love with him. She told me all about how they met on a flight and—" She swallows hard once and squeezes her eyes shut. I repress the sudden urge to vomit.

I cannot believe this actually happened.

"I confronted Rodrigo after that, and he didn't even put up a fight when I kicked him out. I swear I could see the relief in his eyes. He didn't have to be the bad guy who abandoned his family for a hot piece of ass, because I had been the one to tell him to go. Though, if you ask me, he abandoned his family way before that, when he stopped coming home as often, completely forgetting about his kids."

"*Jesus*," I breathe, trying to process everything. "When did this happen?"

"About three days before Andrea got engaged. Which is why we hid it so long. I promised to put up less of a fight during divorce proceedings if we pretended to be together one last time for the holidays. First, so that Andrea wouldn't freak out about marriage; second, so the girls could have one last Christmas with their dad, since I have a feeling they'll be seeing *a lot* less of him in the future." Her mouth contorts in pain, and honestly I can't blame her. "And third... Well, selfishly, I didn't want everyone in the family to look at me with pity over the holidays. I didn't want to be the bride's sad sister going through a divorce while everyone is happy and in love." Her eyes well up again, but she moves quickly, wiping them away before they can streak down her cheeks.

"I'm so sorry," is all I can think of to say.

"It is what it is. Now I'm just this soon-to-be divorced

woman in her mid-thirties, with no career prospects or anything because I didn't even finish college. I just dropped out when I got married to take care of my husband and start a family. And while I am so happy that I was able to be there for my girls, now I'm left with... Well, with nothing. I don't know what I'm going to do, how I'm going to support myself or my daughters. I mean... we'll get child support checks from Rodrigo, according to my lawyer. But they're nowhere near what we'll need. Which, honestly, I don't get. They're his *daughters*. And that money is supposed to be for *them*. I don't get how he could fight me so much on it. I need to find a job and a new life and I don't even know who I am anymore. My whole life became my family, and that's fine, but I feel like that was my entire identity. And it sounds pathetic and horrible, but now that our entire family dynamic has imploded... What am I supposed to do next?" She puts her face in her hands, really sobbing now as my heart breaks for her. "For the longest time I thought the most important thing in the world was to get married, have kids, and put them over everything. Which is how it should be—but to an extent. I forgot about myself. Being a mom and a wife became such a big part of my personality, that now I don't know who I am, Rosie. I don't even have any hobbies! I gave up the entirety of my twenties to take care of a man who can't even make himself a PB&J sand-wich. Now what? I have to rebuild myself and... and... just *start from scratch*, I feel like."

"Diana, my god," I say, rubbing circles on her back as she sobs into her hands. I feel horribly guilty for not noticing earlier, for not being there for her. "I'm so sorry this happened to you, but just know that you are one of the strongest people I know. Right now, it seems like you have nothing, but it isn't true. You have your kids, and your sisters, and your parents who will support you, and you *will* find yourself again. It won't be easy, but you'll be able to do it."

She drops her hands and sits up, looking me straight in the eye. "I know that. I know that I'll be able to. But—and I feel totally guilty for saying this—I just wish I hadn't given everything up for someone. I had an entire career ahead of me, and I just... I'm just saying, if I'd kept going, I'd have at least one thing for myself at the other side of this."

My stomach rolls again just as a cold, anxious current creeps up my spine and neck.

"I wish I hadn't given everything up for someone."

Is that what's going to happen between me and Asher? Will he grow to resent me one day? If we *do* decide to do long distance, will we argue and fight and grow frustrated until one of us fucks up and ends up ruining every single good memory we had? If he picks me—*us*—over his dream, then will he grow to resent me or regret us the way Diana has? And if I just pick up and go with him to Pasadena, give up this huge opportunity with *Celebrity Dance Battle*... Will it be the same thing it was with Diana?

"I'm sorry, Rosie. I can't be here anymore. I'm going to duck out early, take the girls home before they see their dad whoring around." She pushes away from the table and gets up, taking her purse with her.

"But—"

"Please don't tell anyone. Not yet. I'll tell Mom and Dad tomorrow morning, and Andrea when she gets back from her honeymoon."

And without another word, Diana disappears into the crowd, leaving me sitting there, shellshocked, by myself.

"Hey," I hear Asher's voice behind me. "I've been looking for you everywhere. I thought we were going to meet up in the lobby after you said goodnight to everyone."

"Yeah, sorry," I say, getting to my shaky feet. "I was just resting my feet a little; my shoes were killing me," I lie.

He smirks and wraps an arm around my waist, leading me out the door of the hall towards the elevators. "Let's get you to bed then. Though I can't promise I'll let you get much rest."

I don't remember the elevator ride to our floor or even how we made it to the bedroom. All I know is that one second I'm in the reception hall, being pulled away by Asher, and the next I'm standing in the middle of a beautiful suite, all gold and cream linens. Asher stands behind me, arms around my waist, kissing my neck and bare shoulders. I sink into him, loving the way his fingertips feel over my skin as he undresses me, as I stare out the window at the little town of Vail, readying itself to ring in the New Year.

I feel Asher's warm lips against my neck, and I can't help it when my eyes slide shut. I want to succumb to the pleasure, to forget about everything my sister said, to forget about how Asher is going to give up a once in a lifetime opportunity only to resent me for it later. I want to forget about my promotion or the fact that in two days we're about to go back to living in different places and not speaking as often.

I want to forget everything and anything that isn't him and me right now.

So I let him slowly pull down the zipper of my dress and let it fall at my feet. I revel in the gasp that leaves his mouth when he sees what kind of underwear I'm wearing underneath.

He sets his glasses gently on the bedside table, before coming back to me, where I make quick work of undressing him—despite the fact that he seems to be physically incapable of keeping his lips off of my body.

As he gently pushes me onto the bed, I try to forget about how, in less than 48 hours *everything* is going to change—and not in a good way like we'd hoped.

Asher seems to sense some of the finality as well—or at least shares the same feeling of dread that's come over me now. His hands shake as he climbs over me, covering my body with his. On instinct, my legs find themselves wrapping easily around his waist. Bringing him closer still between my thighs. Feeling him like this, so close and intimate, fills me with both relief and torture. I want to be like this forever, but I also need to never see him again.

Without another word, without wasting another second, he's inside me—nothing between us. It's the first time we do this without protection, and we both realize it at the same time. He forces himself to stop, and looks down at me with questioning eyes, his brown furrowed in strain.

"Should I—?" he pants, our faces only inches apart.

"No," I say, my voice cracking. "I'm on the pill and clean." And a part of me wants to feel him fully before I take myself away from him.

And with those words, Asher loses all sense of control over his body. He groans loudly and starts moving in fast, hard, *desperate*, motions. Like he can't get closer to me fast enough. And I feel how scared he is of losing me as his fingers dig into my skin, his grip hard on my thigh, my shoulders, my breasts, my hair.

We're making love and I'm telling him goodbye, and he's inside me, moving in ways that can only be described as fighting to keep me.

And I want to stay. I want to keep him, keep *us*. But I can just feel our relationship disintegrating in slow motion over the next couple of months. It'll start with missed calls, then missed trips. Jealousy and resentment will slowly infiltrate our relationship like an infection we can't get rid of.

Eventually, we'll both be exhausted of fighting, and everything will fall apart. He'll blame himself, maybe even quit. And I can't let him do that. He needs to stick it out.

I want to put my face in my hands and cry, letting the grief wash over me. Because I know what I have to do. And it hurts. It physically hurts. Because this love we're making—I'm about to shatter it.

Tears fill my eyes as I feel my heart break for us. Hiding my face in his neck, I try to hold on to the last few moments that we have. I cant my hips up, trying to get a better angle and call out his name when he hits exactly the right spot. I let myself get lost in the moment, in the way he loves me, the way he knows my body.

If he notices my tears, he doesn't say anything. He merely presses his lips to mine, and kisses me with complete abandon as we fall together.

When it's over, he rolls over to his back, pulling me onto his chest. I feel the remnants of him inside of me still as I press my forehead to his chest, letting his scent calm some of my heartbreak. I want to remember everything about us, memorize the way the warmth of his skin feels against mine.

Asher's arms tighten around me, pressing against the top of my head. "I love you," he murmurs. "I will *always* love you."

I look up at him and do my best to smile, but I can feel it come out a little mangled. "I love you, too, Asher. Forever."

No matter what, right now, this moment right here, with our arms wrapped around each other, my chest so filled with light and joy at just having been able to spend time with him, might make all of it worth it. No matter what happens, I'll always have this past week and this feeling—this perfect feeling.

Chapter Thirty-Nine

ROSIE

18 years old

I GROAN AS THE SUNLIGHT COMING IN THROUGH MY WINDOW *wakes me, cursing it for ruining what must've been the best dream of my entire life. It wasn't a new one, that's for sure, but it certainly felt real. I squeeze my eyes shut and pray I can fall asleep once more to get back to my favorite fantasy: Asher and me together. But when I try to pull the comforter up and over my head, I feel resistance, a tug from someone else.*

Another groan, but this time, it isn't mine.

With a gasp, I sit up in bed and turn to look down at the man beside me.

Asher.

My heart somersaults in my chest as I watch him slowly wake, look up at me with bleary eyes, face adorably wrinkled with sleep.

"Hey," he whispers, his voice thick. It's not the first time I hear his just-woken-up voice, but it's the first time it raises goose-bumps over my bare skin.

His groggy smile is heartbreaking as he reaches for my naked body. In one fluid movement, Asher manages to pull me down onto the mattress beside him and wrap me in his arms. "You feel so good." He turns my body to face away from him and pulls me into his chest, kissing my bare shoulder before burying his face in my hair.

"Oh my god," I whisper, biting my lower lip, trying to keep my face from breaking in half with how big I want to smile.

I feel him laugh softly into my skin before pressing another kiss to my shoulder. "I know. Last night was amazing."

"Mmm." I attempt a stretch, wincing at the foreign soreness between my legs and rest of my body. It feels like all of my joints have come loose, like my body has lost some of its tension.

And it feels fantastic.

"You okay?" he asks, hand skating over me like he can't get enough.

"Me? Oh my god, yes," I turn in his arms to face him, to reach up to cup his face in my hands and run my fingers through his sleep-rumpled hair.

"You look adorable like this," he breathes.

"Like I just woke up? Need I remind you that this definitely isn't our first sleepover?"

He smirks. "No. But it's our first sleepover of this kind with each other." He wiggles his eyebrows. "First time for other things too. At least for me."

"Duh. Same."

"Yeah?" He asks, looking back at me with a hesitant smile.

I roll my eyes at him. "Of course. Don't you think I would've told you if I had? You're my best friend."

He shrugs before giving me a soft kiss on the lips. I try to chase it but he pulls away, smiling. "So you never did this with Tyler, then? Or anyone?"

"God, no," I snort. "And you didn't do it with anyone else either?" I ask, suddenly very scared that he'd been living a secret life I didn't know about or something. Maybe he and Kissy Missy made it farther than I thought?

"No." He laughs.

"That's surprising."

"Surprising?"

"You just... seemed like you knew what you were doing last night. And doing it really well." I blush and cover my face with my hands, too embarrassed to go on.

He chuckles softly. "Thanks. You too. Hence, the question about you and Tyler."

"Ugh, please don't say his name anymore. I don't want him associated with this perfect moment."

"Perfect, huh?" Asher wraps his arms around me, the giddy energy in the room filling me with bright light.

"Perfect. Everything was perfect. You're perfect."

His eyes soften before speaking the three words I'd been waiting years for him to say to me. "I love you."

I press my forehead to his bare chest and whisper, "I love you, too," like it's the most dangerous secret.

"I can't believe I finally get to say it to you. In a non-friend way, of course."

His arms tighten around me before pulling me up to kiss me, rolling me on my back. He kneels between my legs as he kisses my neck and chest and suddenly I feel him there again. I blush crimson at the feel of him, heating every inch of my body, remembering all the incredible ways we lost ourselves in each other.

"God, and now we get to travel for the next three months on our own. We can't tell our parents about us until after the trip, though, obviously. I mean, your dad would freak if he knew we were together and going on a trip by ourselves. And then we're gonna be in college, which sucks because we'll be separated, but we won't be so far away so—"

Every muscle in my body tightens at his words, the hope laced in them. Because he still doesn't know, because I still haven't found the courage to tell him.

Sensing the change in my demeanor, Asher pulls away, rolling onto his side beside me. "What's wrong?" He pales, his voice shaking slightly. "Shit. I'm sorry if I'm being presumptuous about us being together, I just—"

I place a hand over his mouth to silence him. "No, stop. Of course I want to be with you."

"Then what is it?"

It's wild, but even after everything that happened last night, he still looks like he doesn't think this is real.

I take a deep, steeling breath and stare up at the ceiling, measuring my words carefully.

How do you tell your best friend, the man you're in love with, that you've been lying to him and everyone you know for the past month? That you're not planning on going to the West Coast anymore because you got a full ride to your dream fashion school in New York City? That all the plans you made together and the excitement about not being far from each other have all evaporated into thin air?

Not being able to tell him has been killing me inside, but I just couldn't bring myself to do it. I knew that eventually I would've had to, but my plan was to wait until the end of our trip. Now though... I can't talk about making plans and doing this long-distance when I know for a fact that I'm leaving.

It's time I break the news to him and my parents. My god, they're going to be so angry. Dad is going to flip, give me a speech on how I'm wasting my life and I should be pursuing more practical things. And Asher... He's going to be so hurt I lied to him for so long. We tell each other everything, but this was the one thing I couldn't manage to bring up, despite all the chances I had to.

It's just my luck that after years of loving him, I finally find out the feeling is mutual as our paths begin to diverge.

"Hey, what's wrong?" He cups my face with his hand, catching a tear with his thumb. "Rosie, talk to me."

I reach for him, letting him pull me into his arms as I kiss up his neck, jaw, lips.

"If you're worried about going away to school, don't be. Okay?" I hear the panic rise in his voice, feel his heart race in his chest beneath my fingertips. "We'll work it out. Stanford and Berkeley are so fucking close, Rose. We'll see each other on the weekends and talk on the phone every night and text and—"

"Rosario? Are you up?" The sound of my father's voice causes Asher to scramble out of bed, search desperately for his clothes as I dig furiously—and quietly—in my dresser for clean underwear and pajamas. I wipe my face clean of my short-lived tears, and check my reflection in the mirror, hoping the wild sex hair I'm sporting can pass off as regular old bedhead.

"Shit! Shit, shit, shit!" He whispers, struggling to hop into his jeans.

"You need to get the hell out of here. Now." I point in the direction of the window and he nods, quickly pushing it open, tossing his shoes out before climbing out.

"Hey," he stops, head poking in. "I love you."

I smile back at him standing only in panties and a bralette. "Love you too." My heart flips in my chest at his grin. "Come by later?"

"Absolutely," he whispers just before making the climb back down.

In just a few seconds, I manage to dress in my pajamas and robe, and go downstairs for breakfast where I'm met in the kitchen by my parents.

"Hey, good morning," I greet them cheerfully. The cloud I'm

walking on has me feeling fifty pounds lighter, floating around the kitchen. As I reach for the coffee pot and pour some orange juice into a glass, I lose myself in a flashback from last night. So much so, I barely miss the tension in the room.

Until...

"Rosario Cristina. Siéntese, por favor."

Oh shit.

He just first-and-middle-named me. And used the formal third person in Spanish.

There's no equivalent to the formal "you" in English, but it's something used mostly in business settings as a sign of respect or when speaking to strangers—at least in Venezuelan Spanish. In my father's case, it's also used when he's about to lose his utter shit.

Chills run up and down my spine as I brace myself for what's coming, every muscle in my body suddenly tense.

My father has called me by my first and middle name and used the formal third person at the same time only twice before in my life. The first, when I was grounded and he caught me sneaking out of the house to go to Jasmine Miller's fifteenth birthday party. Dad was so pissed he added two more weeks to my punishment and took away cellphone and computer privileges, completely isolating me from everyone else (except for Asher, of course, who kept sneaking into my house late at night to hang out and watch videos on his phone and iPad).

The second time he lost it on me, was when he was teaching me how to drive. I had my driver's license test the following day, so Dad took me to an empty parking lot away from other cars and potential dangers to practice. Still, I somehow managed to crash his Honda Civic into a wall, destroying the front bumper and scratching the entire left side of the car as he screamed his head off at me.

"¡Rosario Cristina, si usted vuelve a chocar mi carro la voy a castigar por un año!"

Yeah, no. It was terrifying.

So when I hear my name roll of his tongue in that icy tone of his, I know he's about to ruin the best morning of my life.

Trembling, I set my juice down on the kitchen counter before looking to my mother for support—a failed Hail Mary, since her eyes are locked in on the kitchen table steadily avoiding my gaze. A frown plastered on her face, fear radiating from every inch of her I watch as she nervously gnaws on her lower lip—a habit I've inherited.

"What's up, Pa?"

"I know," *is all he says.*

I stop breathing, heart galloping in my chest, pounding loudly against my ribs as it attempts to escape my body. Probably in an attempt to avoid what's coming next.

Smart.

Dad knows about last night, about Asher and me and what we did upstairs. But I pretend like I have no idea what he's talking about: "What do you mean? Know about what?"

I should probably cave and admit to my very Catholic father that yes, I had sex last night, that I'm sorry. But I'm not sorry. And it's not like it's some random guy. It's Asher. Asher. We all love him, right? And last night wasn't about lust—it was love. Plus, we're both eighteen, so it's not like he can do anything, right?

But I know from the fire in my father's eyes that he won't listen to my reasoning. I know from that look that I'm screwed. But just how screwed am I?

"You know what, Rosario. I know about FIT."

Oh, shit. So, I'm *really* screwed then.

I feel the stinging behind my eyes build, feel the way my body shakes, a sheen of cold sweat beginning to blanket my skin.

"H-h-how did you find out?"

"*Just saw* this *in the mail.*" *He pulls a large white envelope from on top the table. Between my morning panic, I hadn't noticed it was there.*

"*I opened it and—*"

"*You opened my mail? How could you?*"

"*I can open your mail if I want to! You live in my house and you're my daughter, and so long as you live here, I do whatever I want.*"

I flinch, taking a step back.

Mom reaches up to gently put a hand on Dad's lower back, but he pulls away.

"*It says here this is your acceptance package with your schedule and living arrangements. Meaning you already said you'd go?*"

I press my lips together, biting back all the awful things I want to say right now. All the horrible names I want to call my father.

"*So did you? Say you'd go?*"

I hiccup and nod. "*Yes.*"

"*Well, you're not going. I already sent a check to Berkeley, and I'm not paying for you to move to New York in the fall to pursue some childish dream. I didn't make all these sacrifices, work this hard, and move us all here for you to study something that's going to take you nowhere.*

"*Do something practical with your life, Rosario. Los sueños son solo sueños.*" Dreams are only dreams.

"*Papi, I'm good at this. Really good. I mean, I must be if they offered me a full ride, right? And it's what makes me happy. Don't you want me to be happy? Can you see that?*" *I plead, but he just shakes his head.*

"*You're going to Berkeley and you're going to major in Economics. Then you're going to get your MBA and you'll do something in business. Or study pre-law and then go to law school. That's valuable. Design isn't valuable. It won't put food on the table."*

I suppress a scoff and everything about how art is valuable, how I'm talented and I'm not going to be wasting my time. But I know he won't hear any of it.

"You get your undergrad degree and then your grad degree and then you don't need to worry about anything else in life."

Instead of telling him how having all the graduate degrees in the world can't guarantee happiness or financial security nowadays, I choose to give him the bottom line: "I'm not going to Berkeley. And you don't have to worry about your check to Berkeley or FIT. You're getting a refund from the former, and I got offered a full ride for the latter." I feel the tears streaking down my face, the disappointment I feel from my father's lack of support draining.

My mother gasps, hands flying to her mouth. Dad lowers his face to level with mine and bites out a, "What did you just say?"

"I'm going to FIT whether you like it or not. I'm an adult now, and it's my choice." I do my best to keep my voice level, not letting it waiver. "You can either be happy for me or not. But I'm going to FIT in the fall. And I'm going to be amazing."

"Then you need to leave. You're going to waste your life pursuing these stupid dreams of yours? Fine. But I'm not going to watch you do it. Either you call Berkeley and ask for your spot back, or you get out."

"Diego!" My mom gets up from her seat.

"No, Julieta. This is for her own good. She says she's an adult? Then she knows how to take care of herself, right? She doesn't need us. So, I want you to leave. Until you come to your senses, I don't want you to come back."

"You want me gone? Fine. I'll be gone by the end of the day." I wipe my nose with the back of my hand before turning back to my bedroom. Behind me, I hear my mother scream at my father in

Spanish, but I don't care. I lock the door to my room, pull out my suitcase from under my bed, and get to packing.

As I throw stuff into my bag, I pull out my phone and look for the one number in my contacts belonging to someone I know will help me out of this one.

My aunt Carla.

Chapter Forty

ASHER

18 years old

I GET TO ROSIE'S HOUSE JUST AN HOUR AFTER SNEAKING OUT *of her window, grin forever plastered on my face.*

I'm so happy, I don't see how I'll ever get over this giddy, drunk feeling currently overtaking my body. In all honesty, I struggle not to pull the front door of its hinges with how excited I am to see her again.

But when I walk through the doorway, I feel like I've walked into a funeral home. From the corner of my eye, I catch Julieta softly crying into her hands at the kitchen table as Diego stares blankly at the wall. If either of them hears me walk into the house, they don't acknowledge it.

Not wanting to interrupt whatever the hell is going on, I tiptoe up the stairs to Rosie's room. I knock softly, a sense of unease flooding my system. It's like a dark cloud has fallen upon this house and a feeling of dread begins to spread through me.

From the other side of the door, I hear movement—lots of it. Things being thrown around, clothes hangers sliding over a rack, cutting through the eerie quiet of the house.

"GO AWAY!" I hear her scream in a rage when I knock a second time.

"Rose?" I pale. "It's me. Asher."

The ruckus on the other side of the door stops allowing me to hear her deep sigh, the frustration behind it a punch in the gut. Does she not want to see me anymore?

After a brief pause, I hear her quick footsteps before she opens her bedroom door, pulling me inside, before softly shutting it behind me.

"I really can't talk right now, Asher. I'm busy." Her cold and curt voice is a stark contrast to the one I woke up to this morning, the one that seemed to unfurl every tense muscle in my body, relieve every single insecurity and doubt in my mind because she said it back, she said she loved me back, and suddenly the world opened up for us, with so many possibilities.

"Busy? I thought we—" But then my eyes land on the two suitcases on her floor, filled almost to the brim in clothing and art supplies. And my stomach drops, because it knows. It knows that something has gone incredibly wrong.

Even still, I hope for the best, hope that my instincts are off, and ask, "Why are you packing for our trip now? It isn't until next week."

But with a frown on her face, hands on her hips, she turns to face me on an exhale. "I'm not going on our trip, Asher."

I swallow once, bracing myself for what's coming. I don't know what's going on but I know her, I know Rosie and I know that whatever it is that's wrong isn't some silly thing.

"I saw your mom downstairs. She looked really upset. Was crying and everything. And your dad—"

"I don't care how my dad is doing. He can think whatever he wants." And with that, she goes back to pulling things off hangers and haphazardly folding and tossing them into the largest suitcase.

I bob my head, nodding, trying to control my breathing and keep my voice steady as I ask, "So, can I ask where you're going, then?"

Her hands pause folding her Sunnydale Class of '99 t-shirt, eyes glued to it as she takes a deep breath. "I'm going to New York."

I run my fingers through my hair, struggling to keep my voice even. "Is that all I'm gonna get? You're leaving for New York? Will you be back in time for us to go on our trip or—"

"I told you—I'm not going on our trip anymore." She goes back to folding as my heart beats furiously against my chest.

I swallow the knot in my throat and squeeze my eyes shut, willing my heart to slow down so I can hear her response to my question: "Is this about last night?"

"No," she answers simply. "But last night can't happen ever again."

Pain. Pure, white-hot pain shoots through my veins, burning every inch of my body, making it impossible to breathe. My mind spins as I try to wrap my head around the words coming out of her mouth. An hour ago, I was in absolute bliss. Now, I feel like I'm on the edge of the abyss, one millimeter away from total doom.

"What?" I manage to push out using whatever oxygen is left in my lungs.

Rosie gets to her feet in one quick movement, dark eyes cold and flat. Lush lips that kissed every inch of my body last night now pressed flat. I brace myself, because I can tell the next words out of her mouth are sure to eviscerate me.

And yet I can't make myself leave, give her the space I know deep down she needs.

"Last night was a massive mistake that should have never happened. I thought I felt something, but it was just the nostalgia of us graduating and going off to college so far away. It meant nothing."

So few words, some more painful than others, but for some reason my brain chooses to focus on the ones that weren't said to purposefully hurt me. "So far away? Berkeley and Stanford aren't far from each other. What do you mean?" I ask.

"Yes. That's the other thing. I'm not going to California for school. I'm going to New York. I applied to FIT in the fall, and I got in. My acceptance letter came in a little over a month ago. I just never told you because I knew you'd make a big deal out of it and try to convince me to stay."

I would have never convinced her to stay. I love her too much to put my needs before hers. Would I have been devastated? Absolutely. But best friend or lover, I would have always encouraged her to go. I've always known it's her dream.

The room spins, drains of any available oxygen and I can't fucking breathe. Her words derail me, and I physically stumble as I take an instinctive step toward her. Desperate. "But school doesn't start until the fall. You're leaving now? We can spend the summer together. You don't want to be with me romantically? Fine. But we're still friends, right? We can still be—"

She holds a hand up in the air to stop me as the panic begins to overtake me. I feel the cold sweat trail down my back, my hands shaking as they ache to reach out to touch her, to double-check that she's real and this isn't a nightmare I can't seem to wake up from.

"Asher," she starts. "I don't want any of this. I think maybe you misread the situation."

White hot rage replaces the pain as her words finish shattering me. "Misread the situation?" I ask, voice shaking in anger. "You mean misread you when you said you loved me too? Misread you and I sleeping together? What did I misread it for, exactly? What were you trying to say? Because I can't think of any other meaning behind those words and actions. I thought everything from last night and this morning left things pretty fucking clear."

Through red-rimmed eyes, Rosie stares back at me, chewing on her lower-lip to hold back what she really wants to say.

"I'm going to New York. I'm going to prove to everyone that I can do this."

I throw my hands in the air. "Fine! Go to New York. Go to New York and pursue your dreams. I'm not trying to stop you. I'll never stop you from trying to pursue something you love, something I know you are amazing at. But can't you go to New York and have us still be together? At least be fucking friends?"

She hesitates, and for a moment, I begin to hope.

"You just don't get it. I've thought this through, and you'd only be holding me back. I don't want to be with you. I don't want us to be together. I have things to achieve and prove and accomplish."

I stand on the edge of the crumbling cliff, too scared to make a move even though I feel it collapsing beneath my feet. I want to plead with her, to beg her to reconsider, to stop her from saying all these awful things. But her hard eyes tell me she's serious, that there's no beating her resolve.

"You're just standing in my way, Asher."

Every bit of air leaves my lungs, head spinning faster and faster every time as I process just how fucking done we are— before we even got to start.

Not knowing what else there is to say, I nod once trying to keep my composure, willing the stinging in my eyes to hold until I make it back home. "Alright then," I push out. "Have a nice life, Rosie."

Her frown deepens, and for a split second I think I see a hint of the woman from this morning in her eyes. But then the dark cloud overtakes her once more, and she's gone in a flash.

In a trance-like state, I slowly leave her room and walk out of her life.

Chapter Forty-One

ASHER

THE BOUNDARY OF NO ESCAPE IN BLACK HOLES IS CALLED the event horizon. It's what we call the point at which the gravitational pull from this astronomical phenomenon is so strong, there's no going back.

And that's where I'm at.

I'm at the event horizon with regards to my feelings for Rosie. I'm in love and there's no fucking way I'm going back—no matter what she says. We will make it work. We have to make it work.

We *will* make it work.

Last night, we left things unresolved. She didn't say it outright, but I knew she was second-guessing us progressing with our relationship. I could feel it in every word spoken on her lips, every look in her chocolate brown eyes, and every single soft touch of her skin.

As her body yielded to mine in the late hours of the night, I felt as though she was telling me goodbye in a way. And it terrified me. Pulling her tighter to me, putting every ounce of love and energy I felt for her, for us, and for our relationship in every word whispered into her ear and every single touch... And yet still feeling like she had one foot out the door.

She can say whatever the hell she wants about me and my career, but there's no way I'm going to let her make this unilateral decision to break things off. There's no way I'm going to let her destroy what is meant to be just out of fear.

I open my eyes and look over at her, pink hair fanned over her pillow like some kind of deity as she sleeps peacefully, completely unaware of the gut-wrenching anxiety her words caused last night. Trying not to wake her, I wrap my arms around her waist and pull her back to my chest, burying my face in her hair, inhaling deeply as I let her scent come over me like a soothing balm.

Yeah, there's no fucking way I'm letting her go.

With one last slow, deep breath, I let myself be pulled back into a blissful sleep with the woman I love in my arms.

The bed jostles, waking me from my deep sleep, but it isn't until I hear the sound of her zipping up her dress that I open my eyes to see her fully clothed, pink hair loose and wild around her bare shoulders.

"Hey," I say, my voice thick with sleep. Reaching over to the nightstand to pull my glasses on, I ask, "What time is it?"

She turns to look at me with guarded guilt in her eyes. "Um, it's seven-thirty," she says, looking at her phone.

"Seven-thirty? Then what are you doing up? Get back in bed," I say, pulling the covers over and patting the mattress with a smile. "Late check-out isn't until noon."

But she doesn't move.

Suddenly, I realize what she's doing, feel her pulling away. *Shit.*

I sit up in bed, my eyes roaming her for any chink in her amor. But it kills me to see that she's already made her decision.

"Rosie," I say, moving to the edge of the bed as quickly as I can. "Rosie, *no*."

"I have to, Ash," she says, her voice breaking.

I get quickly to my feet, taking her hands in mine. It's freezing and I'm fully naked, but I don't care. She's trying to leave me again and I'm not going to survive this time around.

"Rosie, *please*," I beg, feeling the stinging behind my eyes. "*Please* don't do this to us. Please stay. We'll figure it out. I'll go to the stupid fellowship and—and if you really are okay with us barely seeing each other or talking to each other then—*Fuck*, I don't care. Let's do it. I'll have any part of you you'll give me. Just please—*please*—don't end this. We can do this."

"Asher. We can't do long distance," she says, eyes watering. "We both know that."

"No," I say, angry now. "We can do this, Rose. I know we can."

She cups my face in her hands, and I place my hands over hers, holding onto them as much as I can.

I can't let her go again.

"You said it yourself just a few days ago, Ash. You said it was a good thing we didn't do long distance in college. You said I would've been a distraction. You said that our love would've ruined you. Would've ruined us."

I groan, my grip growing tighter on her hands. "That's some stupid shit I said to save face because I was still fucking heartbroken over you running away. I didn't mean it."

"But it's true," she cries, tears streaming down her face. "You're right. I would've ruined your career. The way you put it made so much sense. And I'm not going to do that to you, Asher. I might have done it last time out of selfishness, but I won't do it this time around. And I'm definitely not going to risk ripping us, what we have—*had*—apart."

"We were straight out of high school, Rose. Just kids. It was just college," I growl. "It's different now. *We're* different now."

"Exactly," she says, pulling her hands away and taking a step back. "The stakes are higher this time around. And I'm not going to be held responsible for being the one to ruin your career and kill your dreams. What if we don't work out, huh? What if we make all these sacrifices and we don't work out and then all we'll have is hatred and resentment toward the other. I don't want that. I don't want us to hate each other. I don't want you to have to give up anything for me."

"This is bullshit!" I yell, not giving a shit about waking the other hotel guests. "Pure and utter bullshit. I would give up every star in the universe for you, Rosie. Every planet, every galaxy, every goddamn blackhole. I would give up anything just to be with you. All you have to do is ask."

"That's the problem, Asher. I love you too much to even dream of asking you to give something like that up. It's what you love."

"You're using the fellowship as an excuse because you're fucking scared of telling me the truth."

"And what's that?" she asks, jutting her chin out, her bottom lip trembling slightly.

"That you're picking yourself over us again. That you're picking New York and your career and your fucking glitzy lifestyle over a life with me. A *good* life that I can give you with a family and love every day for the rest of your goddamn life." My heart is beating against my chest so loudly, I can barely hear myself over it. The fear of losing her all over again has me breaking out into cold sweats.

I'm desperate, can feel my heart start to break inside my chest. I reach out and grab her by the waist, pulling her into me.

I grip her tightly, as if doing so will keep her from leaving me. "We can find a way to love each other," I tell her, trying to control my breathing. "It doesn't have to be like this—this *all or nothing* shit."

"Don't you get it? This *is* me loving you!" She throws her hands up in frustration, then pushes me away. "This is me telling you I love you above anything else. Because I'm willing to sacrifice what I want most in the world—a life with you—for what I know you actually *need*."

"No."

"Yes. Yes, yes, *yes*. I love you and I will not allow my love for you to be the reason you give up everything you've worked for since high school. I just won't. And I know us and I know you, and you will lose focus. We'll either fight and break up, or we'll travel so much eventually one of us is going to give up our career for the other and resent it."

"I would never dream of asking you to give up your career for me."

"Exactly! That's exactly what I mean. But you expect me to be okay with you doing it? To ask you to give it up?"

"You're not *asking* anything. I'm offering," I growl.

"No. Absolutely not. You're only offering because you're scared of losing me more than you would be sad about taking a shitty job." She's wiping the tears from her face, and I want more than anything to be the one doing it. But the anger and frustration I feel right now keeps me locked in place.

"That's my whole point!" I laugh dryly, throwing my hands in the air. "I'm picking the option I can live with the most."

"But then, a few years down the line, when you see your colleagues at the forefront of research, with their grants and their studies, and you're in a second rate job... And when the initial newness of me rubs off... *Then* you'll resent me and us and everything we had. It'll break us, and I don't want that. I want to keep the memory of what we had—this amazing week —intact."

"No," I say again, hands fisted at my sides.

"Asher." She blows out a deep breath. "You're going to the fellowship and I am not going to be the one to drag you down." She sighs deeply and walks over to me, taking my face between her hands again. She drags her thumbs over my cheeks and suddenly I realize that I'm crying.

"Rose." My voice breaks. "Please."

"I love you, Ash. I will always love you. But I'm scared loving each other will ruin us. You *deserve* to follow your dream at CalTech in the fall. This is too big an opportunity to pass up. And I—I have to take on that new job on *Celebrity Dance Battle.*" She reaches up onto her tiptoes and places a soft kiss over my lips. It's salty from our tears and sour from the heartbreak. I want to lose myself in it, but stop before it rips me apart.

Rosie pulls away first, turning to pick up her shoes by the foot of the bed, before heading for the door.

"Rose," I say, my voice cracking just as she opens the door. "Rose, I don't think I'm going to recover from this."

Her face twists in pain and she runs back into my arms, looping hers around my neck and bringing me down to meet her lips in another kiss. Desperate and sad and all-consuming. It makes the room spin and rips my heart to shreds.

She pulls away, her lips grazing mine as she says, "You will. And one day, when you're with your sexy scientist wife, you'll thank me."

All the air inside my chest seems to leave my body as she walks out, leaving me standing naked in the middle of the room.

The best thing that's ever to happened to me just walked out of my life and I'm just supposed to be okay with it?

Chapter Forty-Two

ROSIE

By the time I make it home, I'm done crying. Which is surprising, given that the pain of this heartbreak goes marrow-deep—a pain I would've never been able to imagine. Though, to be honest, I've cried so much over Asher Wolff that I might just be tapped out at this point.

My heart, it aches in a way that makes me wonder whether it's even still there. Then I realize I might have left it behind with Asher, in the hotel room where I broke his.

This place... it will forever remind me of us. Of us growing up, falling in love, and fighting—all for it to end in heartbreak. *Twice.* Although this time around, I can confidently say that I think I did the right thing by him. Asher deserves better than to let himself be dragged down by me. And I deserve better than to let myself helplessly fall in love with a man I'll only disappoint.

I tiptoe into the house, being careful not to wake anyone, but hear my mother call out for me to come into the kitchen. Mom and Dad are both seated at the table in their robes, looking a little worse for wear.

Dad stares at me with questioning eyes—which I ignore. I know what he wants to ask me, and though I have the answer he wants, I don't think I'm ready to speak the words aloud yet.

"You're up?" I ask my mother, avoiding my dad's gaze.

"Yes. We went to bed late, but waking up early is a hard habit to kick. Even after marrying your youngest off on New Year's." She smiles broadly.

"How about you?"

"Yeah, just getting in." *Obviously.* My voice sounds cold and detached, even to my own ears.

"Is everything okay? With Asher?" she asks, brows furrowed.

Part of me marvels at how my uber-conservative parents seem to be super chill with the fact that I'm *clearly* walk-of-shaming it right now and aren't giving me shit. But the other part of me realizes that it was my mother and Jaime who've been playing matchmaker to the two of us, so she's probably thrilled. Dad's concerns, on the other hand, lay more on whether we're still together or not.

I guess there's a time and place for decorum.

Very hypocritical, if you ask me.

I suppress an eyeroll and inhale slowly, forcing my chest to expand. Gathering some inner strength, I turn to my father and say the words he's been waiting to hear since yesterday morning: "It's done," I say. "*We're* done."

"*¿Qué?*" My mother raises her voice. "What are you talking about? What is she talking about?" She stares at my father accusingly.

Ignoring her, I address my father: "I'm going to change my flight for later today instead of for tomorrow. Will you take me to the airport?"

Dad nods, having the decency to look a bit sympathetic.

"Will you two answer me? What do you mean *it's done?* You cannot be *done,* Rosario. Jaime and I worked really hard to get you two idiots to realize you belong together for it all to fall apart before it ever really began! *Dios mío. No puede ser.*"

Receiving confirmation that our mothers had been colluding this entire time to get us together *almost* makes my mouth twitch with a smile. Everything that went on these past few days screamed meddling mothers. Half of me wants to yell at her for pushing us together, for indirectly being responsible for the worst pain imaginable. The other half, however, wants to thank her for giving me the most blissful week of my life. Without her and Jaime's obvious and at times, completely inappropriate involvement, Asher and I would never have gotten to experience that kind of love. And I know with every fiber of my being, that I will never get it again.

Love like that—it's a once in a lifetime thing.

"*Diego, ¿qué coño hiciste?*"

Dad gapes at Mom, unable to form a rational response. He knows he's in deep.

"You guys can settle this on your own. I'm going to get everything ready. See what the next flight out I can get is."

Mom starts laying into Dad in Spanish as I walk away, not caring about waking the others in the house. My parents can rip each other apart while I pack my bags, for all I care.

Feeling almost numb, I multitask, searching for another flight on my phone while doing a piss-poor job at packing everything up in my suitcase. Just as I click confirm on my ticket change for a flight out tonight (for the low fee of $1,200!), I catch sight of the pink magic wand on my nightstand. Biting my lip to keep from crying, I shove it in my carry-on, and let myself absorb this pain.

A sob catches in my throat, threatening to start the tears again. But I push them back down. It's for the best. I'm not worth anyone giving up their dreams. And I don't want to disappoint my parents now, more than ever, by not taking this promotion.

Asher and I are done. For good.

Chapter Forty-Three

ASHER

Two weeks later

I spin the cardboard coaster on its axis, watching it absentmindedly as my mind wanders. My body is currently at my favorite bar near campus, *Miracle of Science*, but my head and heart are back in Colorado. Or I guess New York?

Sitting alone at this bar isn't exactly a new activity for me. It's not like I'm generally an antisocial person—the opposite, actually. I have plenty of friends. It's just that this is where I like to come and people watch, have a nice beer, a good burger, and watch the beautiful Massachusetts snow blanket all of Cambridge while I make notes for my thesis or brainstorm when I'm stuck at a particular point in my research. It's my Fortress of Solitude, of sorts, where I come to be alone amongst the crowd.

This time around, though, I guess I'm hoping the bar lives up to its name. I hoped sitting here at my favorite table by the window, watching all the undergrads and grad students start piling in for a few drinks on a Thursday night, would help inspire me to find some sort of answers. Except not of the scientific variety this time.

I should be at the lab. I should be double-checking my cita-
tions, my formulas, all of my work for next week—my thesis
submission. I should be camped out in my lab like everyone else,
poring over data and making sure everything is perfect before
sending it off to the printers.

But I'm here, miserable, pining over a woman who has told
me time and time again that she *doesn't* want to be with me. A
woman who has done nothing but reply in barely one or two
word answers since last seeing each other over a week ago.

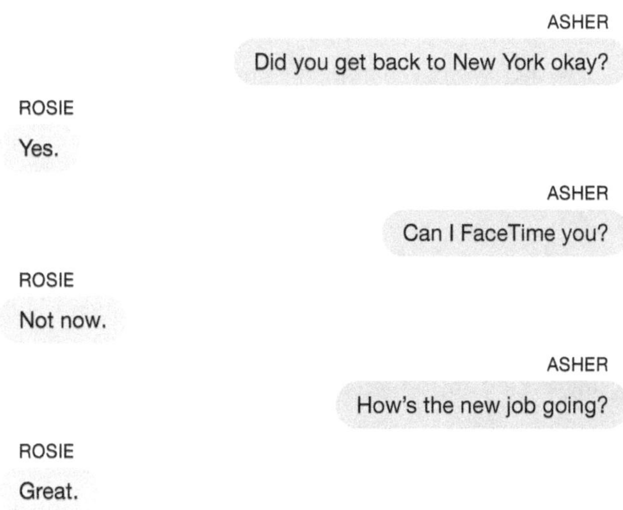

Even though it shouldn't have, it had been one of the
messages that stung the most. I knew she was excited about this
new opportunity. Still, it didn't feel amazing to hear how much
she was enjoying life without me.

Though that wasn't the most painful exchange we had. The
worst one came a few days ago:

ASHER

> I have a long weekend coming up for MLK. Can I come down to New York so we can talk things out? This whole thing is dumb. We should be together.

I had to wait two whole days for an answer, and when it finally came through, it wrecked me:

ROSIE

> Asher.

That was it. That last thing she said was my name. And I could hear her voice, the admonishing tone, even as I read it. I could hear the way she was shutting me down just by using my name. And it made me hate it.

For days after, I couldn't stand to hear it spoken from anyone's lips.

I should be taking advantage of this long weekend just like everyone else is. I should be prepping like crazy, focusing on my research, putting the finishing touches. I should absolutely not be losing myself in thoughts of the woman I love, the woman who doesn't want me. I should be memorizing every bit of information and preparing for my defense, which is just over a month away. But I'm here, drowning in thoughts of her and us and everything we could have had. I'm here thinking of ways to convince her to let me come see her.

Which is, of course, exactly what she said would happen. By texting her that, I'm proving her point all along, aren't I? I'm *not* at the lab. I'm *not* prepping myself for the defense. I'm here, drinking beer, sulking like a pathetic idiot, moaning over someone who clearly doesn't want me.

Because if she did, she would at least get back to me. She would at least—

My phone lights up beside me, and my hand flies to it

instinctively, hating the fact that part of me wishes it were her so much, the vibration of it makes my heart race in my chest.

I know it's anyone but her, though.

Still. A man can dream, can he not?

I pick the phone up and see that it's just my sister, checking up on me for the millionth time.

I wouldn't say that I've turned exactly into a recluse since New Year's Day, but... I also haven't been the easiest to reach person in the world.

JESS

Where the hell have you been? I've been calling and texting you for the past couple of days and you haven't gotten back to me. Are you dead?

ASHER

Deceased.

JESS

Bruh. Come on. What happened.

I sigh, finishing off the last of my beer and waving at the waiter for another round before answering.

ASHER

Nothing happened. Just busy wrapping up my research for my thesis.

JESS

I meant what happened with Rosie.

ASHER

I know what you meant. And nothing. Nothing is exactly what happened.

My fifth beer arrives, and I take a big gulp, settling in for the round of questioning that's about to follow.

JESS

I don't get it. You guys looked so happy
together at the wedding. And at the store when
I almost caught you doing gross things.

ASHER

Isn't it like 2 a.m. there? Shouldn't you be
asleep?

JESS

I have a baby. I never sleep.

Come on. What happened between you and
Rosie?

I felt like everything was finally falling into
place.

I sigh. It *was* falling into place—except it crashed and burned instead of landing gracefully.

ASHER

We're done, and that's all you need to know.
Now please let it be.

No need to get into the details.

JESS

Asher, come on.

I rub my temples with both hands, trying to keep the migraine I feel coming on at bay. They've been coming around more often these days, these migraines—something I've never had before in my life.

Stress, probably. Broken heart, more likely.

My phone buzzes incessantly, this time a call trying to come through.

With a groan, I curse my sister's name and swipe my finger across the screen to answer the call.

"*Leave me the fuck alone.* I already told you everything you needed to know. Which is nothing. It's none of your goddamn business."

There's a pause on the other end of the line as I wait for Jess to lose her shit on me.

Instead: "Mr. Wolff."

Oh. Shit.

"Dr. Rousseau." I clear my throat, automatically sitting up straighter in my seat. "I'm so sorry about that. I thought—I thought you were—" I catch myself. No need to get personal, here. "I apologize. How can I help you?"

"Well, you can start by accepting my offer for the post-doctoral fellowship. I gave you until the fifth to reconsider. It's the tenth." I pinch the bridge of my nose and squeeze my eyes shut as I listen to his stern voice. It brings back memories of my early years of grad school, of lectures that inspired me to explore the universe more deeply.

"I'm not taking no for an answer here, Asher," he says more kindly. "I know that for you to have said no to this program means that something significant must've happened. But this isn't something that I can just let you pass up."

I open my eyes and stare out onto the street, watching people walk by under the snow, wondering where they're headed to. Meanwhile, I'm sitting on my ass heading absolutely nowhere—figuratively because I don't know what my future holds after this semester, and literally, because I have four and a half beers in me, and I'm starting to sway a little, my eyesight a little blurry even though I'm still wearing my glasses.

"There has been a—" I measure my words, searching for a professional way of saying that I just got my heart ripped to shreds by the woman I think I'm supposed to spend the rest of my life with. Or rather *was*. Thinking that might be oversharing just a *little bit*, I choose to say "*situation*" instead.

"A situation?" he asks, his voice flat.

"Yes. I, ah, had a situation. And... And I'm not sure whether—"

"Do not. Do not tell me you are rejecting this offer, Wolff. We discussed it at length before I even moved here. Your research is brilliant, and everyone on the team is excited to have you here." His accent thickens in the same way Rosie's does when she's upset, making it harder to understand his words as they're yelled at me over the phone. "You'll have CalTech *and* NASA resources. You'll have a lab, and guidance from some of the most brilliant minds in the country. *Hell*, the fucking world! You loved the campus and the school, we even looked at neighborhoods together for apartments. How did that all change in a matter of days? If this is about compensation, I'm sure we can—"

"No, no. It's not about compensation," I clarify.

"If this isn't about compensation and your 'situation' as you call it is in the past, then what can we do to get you to be a part of this?"

I run the fingers of my free hand through my hair, sighing in frustration. There's a beat on the other end of the line while he lets me think.

"I—" I stutter, struggling to think.

"Asher," he says, his voice kinder now. "This is too big of an opportunity to pass up."

Hearing the same words Rosie used come out of Dr. Rousseau's mouth sparks some type of rage inside me. One fueled by frustration and hurt and rebellion. She thinks the opportunity of a *job* is bigger to me that that of spending a lifetime with her? Because if that's what she thinks, then I'm only just realizing now that maybe she doesn't feel as strongly as I do. That maybe she's scared she doesn't love me as much or enough to be able to make it last as long as I want it to. That maybe because she doesn't love me as much as I do, she'd feel guilty for leading me on or something.

I shove my fingers in my hair, fisting them to the point where my scalp starts to hurt and my chest aches. The void yawns again, the taste of hops and bile rising in my throat at just the thought of that.

But no. No, I know she loves me. I know she thinks she's doing right by me. She's just *wrong*.

Still. She wants me to go to CalTech? She wants me to continue my research on the other side of the country? She wants us to *not* be together and to throw everything we had into the trash? Fine. Fucking fine. I'll do it. I'll fucking do all of it.

"You know what Emile? You're absolutely right. Thank you so much for your patience. I was going through a bit of family troubles and not thinking clearly. I would love to take the post-doctoral fellowship."

Dr. Rousseau grunts appreciatively. "Good. Good. I knew if I called you I could convince you. Now, I need you to reply back to the original email, recanting your previous one rejecting the offer. I need you to clearly state some thing or other pertaining to personal issues, of course. I tried to stop the committee from offering the fellowship to someone else for as long as I could, so it better be good. Then explain that you have changed your mind and would like to accept the offer."

I nod my head, even though he can't see me. "Will do."

Once I get him off the phone, I immediately follow his instructions before heading over to Rosie's contact info. My thumb hovers over the screen, hesitating though I know what I need to do. She wants me to move on, but the temptation to contact her, to hold on, is too big right now. And I need it gone if I'm going to move on.

Slamming back the rest of my beer beforehand, I quickly move through the menu options and block and delete her number. I go into our messages and scroll through them one last time, my heart aching in my chest, stinging building behind my eyes.

Letting out a shaky breath, I delete our chat history, too, letting go of the last piece of communication I have with the girl I know I will always love, but never be able to be with.

I wave down the waiter and ask for another round.

Chapter Forty-Four

ROSIE

One month later

"You're doing that thing again," I hear Barbara's voice break through my day-dreaming.

"Huh?" I ask innocently. "What are you talking about?" But I know exactly what she means. I've been a total space cadet since getting back from Colorado, forgetting things, not listening to people while they talk, not eating or sleeping. Just kind of... existing while adjusting to my new job.

It hasn't been easy. It hasn't been easy resisting the temptation to answer when he calls or texts, begging to talk or to come see me. And it hasn't been easy not writing him back, asking where he is when he suddenly disappeared a month ago.

Though it breaks my heart to not hear from him, I hope he's finally focusing on school; that I'm not in his way anymore.

"That thing where you look off into dead space and your eyes glaze over and you look like you've been petrified." I narrow my eyes at her as she waves her hand in a flourishing motion and yells, *"Petrificus Totalus!"* Almost knocking over our drinks.

We're out at my favorite Latin restaurant downtown, where the dancing is amazing and the food is even better. I haven't been feeling particularly social these past couple of weeks, but when Barbara insisted we go out to "celebrate starting my new job" (i.e. "you look like shit and clearly need some cheering up"), I decided not to fight her on it. Knowing her, she wouldn't have left me alone until I gave in.

Bless her.

"I'm fine," I mumble, moving our glasses of *guarapitas* away from knocking distance. "Just tired. This new job is exhausting." And I'm not even lying, either. It's been long hours of boring fucking meetings discussing budgets and looking at focus group results. So far, my job has mostly consisted of kissing the network executives' asses, rubbing elbows with "the right people," and *definitely not* the creative side of things. I don't think I've been in a single "creative" meeting since starting this new role.

"How *is* the new job?" she asks, biting into a hot *tequeño*. "You kicking ass and taking names yet?" A string of melted cheese falls on her face, which she quickly licks away.

"Totally," I say, my voice flat. "Last night I stayed in the studio until one a.m. poring over spreadsheets and contracts and had the time of my life. And whenever I wanted to discuss the creative direction for the show costumes with some of the execs, they'd shut me down, telling me that the status quo is '*working fine*' now, so why fix what isn't broken."

Barbara's brows pull together. "I don't understand. Didn't they hire you because they *wanted* your input?"

I wince. "I—They hired me because the other person quit. And I'm beginning to understand why."

Barbara frowns, her eyes filled with concern. "Do you want me to talk to Rob? I can ask him what the hell is going on." Rob is the executive producer of the show—and Barbara's fiancé's best friend. Though her good intentions warm my heart, the idea of having her reach out to him on my behalf makes me cringe. I'm an adult—I should be able to handle this myself.

"Nah," I say, shaking my head. "It's fine. Thank you though."

"Babe. Seriously, I don't mind. I mean, if the job description is completely different from what you're doing now, I think it's fine to reach out and—"

"It's not," I tell her, my eyes locked on our food, avoiding her gaze. "Not different from what the job description said, I mean. Yes, I thought I would get more say in creative decisions, but I always knew it was going to be a *management* role. Which means *managing* things. People, money—that type of stuff."

"Wait. I'm confused. That doesn't sound like something you'd be into at all," Barbara says. "I thought you said—"

I sigh, cutting her off. "I know what I said. And I know that it doesn't sound like something I would do. But I was *asked* by the producers to apply. And it was a big deal. And I *did* think I would be able to get more creative. But I haven't even *touched* my sketchbook since last season. I have barely looked at the materials we'll be using for this upcoming season, except for when discussing them at a budget meeting." I finish off my drink and knock it down on the table a little more forcefully than I intended.

"Rose—"

"It's fine. I just need to get used to this new job. It's normal. Plus, it's not like I suck at it. I'm actually *good* at it." Fantastic, even. There's no doubt in my mind that if I had listened to my dad and gone into finance, I would've been extremely successful.

We're quiet for a beat, the sounds of the crowd and the music filling the space between us.

"You're miserable," she says simply.

I open my mouth to deny it, but what's the point? "I'm miserable for other reasons."

"Yes, Asher is a big part of this, but... But I think you need to reconsider your professional choices, as well."

"My professional choices?" I ask.

"Yes."

"Barbara. It's just a shitty start to what's bound to be a fantastic job. It doesn't mean I'm suddenly going to change my career."

"Yes, but you aren't happy with what you're doing. You looked *much* happier when you were on set for the movie."

"Well, yeah, because I got to work for myself. Collab with the studio and the team, of course, but basically I was working for myself based off a concept we worked together on as a team. But I can't do that at CDB."

"So why not go into feature costume design full-time then? You could move to LA and—"

I scoff. "Are you insane? Do you even know how risky that is? It would be impossible to find a job there. I mean, these studios work with well-establish companies and designers. I'm a nobody."

"You are *definitely* not a nobody, Rosie. You have a fantastic resume. And it's not like you don't have experience."

"I've done one movie."

"And managed an entire television show's costume department."

I shake my head before taking another long sip of my drink. "It's not the same and you know it. Hollywood is different. It's too much of a risk. *Phantom Fighters* only happened because of you. There's no way I'll ever be able to get a job like that."

She sighs and shakes her head, turning in her seat to search through her enormous purse. It takes a couple of seconds, but she manages to fish out her phone. Barbara scrolls through it for a bit, and hands it over to me.

"Here," she says, her eyes narrowed. I take the phone from her hand.

"What am I looking at?" I ask, before looking down at her screen.

"The producer for the *Phantom Fighters* movie sent me some preliminary stills. I think you should see them."

I scroll through her photos, feeling the involuntary tug at the edge of my lips. I've been sad for so long, I hardly recognize the muscle movements as I smile.

"They look *incredible*," I breathe, zooming in on Barbara's phantom fighting suit. "The costumes look fantastic on screen, don't they?" I ask, my voice a little distracted.

"You did a fabulous job designing them," she says. But my eyes are still on her phone screen as I dive deeper into the pictures, disappointed when there are no more left.

I shrug, smiling. "I had the original ones from the TV show to work off of and a fantastic team. But yeah, it was so much fun doing the whole movie." I hand her back her phone and call a waiter over while she stuffs it back into her bag. After ordering another round of drinks, I turn back to look at her.

"She asked me if you'd be willing to do her next movie, by the way."

"What?" I look up at her, my eyes wide. "Who?"

"Jenna. The director. She wants you to do the costume design for her next movie."

My jaw drops. "Jenna—" Barbara nods.

"That's nice of her. But I have this job here and—"

"Come on, Rosie! Stop with this. You hate this job. And even if you didn't, you definitely like it a lot less than what you were doing for the movie."

"Barbara, I can't just quit this job. It's a—"

"—huge deal, yeah, I know. You've said that a million times. But a huge deal to whom? To you? Or to your parents? Or to what you *think* your parents want?"

The air rushes out of my lungs as I watch my friend's eyes go fierce.

"You're living this life for someone else, and it's making you miserable. And I'm sorry, but I stand up for my friends when someone messes with them, and right now, you're doing that to yourself."

"What the hell are you talking about 'living for someone else'? If I were living for someone else, as you say, I would be working in finance right now, just like my dad wanted me to."

"You're doing the finance version of costume design and you know it. You idealized this job and now it's making you miserable. I'm pretty sure your mind—consciously or subconsciously—was like, 'Hey, bruh, this combines creativity and management; so maybe it can make my dad proud.' But it's dumb. You're being dumb."

"That's ridiculous," I snap, but something inside me starts to bubble because I know she's right.

"Is it? You didn't tell your daddy dearest you got a management position and were all happy when he didn't seem supremely disappointed in you? Part of you didn't jump at the first opportunity to take this role because you were seeing your family during the holidays and you thought it would impress them a little bit?" I swallow hard, tasting the bile I suddenly feel rising in my throat. I squeeze my eyes shut and rub the place over my heart where the ache never seems to fade.

"Stop it." But my voice is barely audible.

"And did you, or did you not, break up with the love of your life because you let your father convince you that loving you wouldn't be worth the potential heartbreak? That you weren't worth the risk? That loving you would fuck up Asher's life? I mean, who thinks that?! You're just using this stupid job as an excuse to keep yourself away from Asher, because you're scared your father is *actually* right. You're scared you're not important or special. You're scared that he'll one day live to regret abandoning his dreams for you. And you're scared that your dad is right, and that you would be making a huge mistake by taking a risk and making a lateral career move."

"I *like* my job. Me not quitting isn't about Asher."

She scoffs. "Sure it's not. It definitely isn't because if you quit your job, then you wouldn't have the excuse of anything tying you down here in New York. You wouldn't have an excuse not to pursue something new with your career. You wouldn't have an excuse to allow yourself to love and be loved by a guy who never stopped wanting you or thinking of you as the center of his universe."

"You are way out of line, Barbara."

She throws her hands in the air in frustration, just as I start to push my chair back to leave. "Don't," she says, wrapping her hand around my wrist. "I'm not trying to be mean to you, but you need to hear this." I don't look at her as she talks. "You're worth it, Rosie. You're worth everything. And I'm not the only one who believes this—but you seem to be among the very few who doesn't and that's fucking tragic. You need to live for yourself—pick where you want to work, trust yourself and take risks —in work and love. You *can* pursue something else professionally and you *can* be loved by the man of your dreams without ruining his life. I don't know how else to make you understand that you need to have faith in yourself, to believe that you are more than enough, and that you are capable of greatness. You need to start fighting for yourself, because you deserve more."

I look down at my hands as I feel the tears slowly fall down my cheeks.

"Now, be honest. Do you like your job? No more lying or sugar coating," she warns.

I snort, wiping my nose with the back of my hand, feeling the stinging behind my eyes intensify. "No. Not at all. I thought

I would. I thought it would be similar to what I did on set for your movie. I thought I would be able to have my own vision and execute it. Work with the studio on a concept, of course, but ultimately make the final calls on wardrobe and aesthetics. But it's none of that."

"Did you like working for the movie?"

"Loved it," I say, a little wistfully.

"What did you love about it?"

"Collaborating, but also having independence. The money and the ability to take breaks in between projects."

"Okay, so why aren't you doing that?"

"Well, for one, I can't do both CDB and freelance movie costume design. And if I focused only on the costume design... Well, I'd never have a stable income—at least not at first—and that's kind of terrifying. Plus, I'd have to move to California and —" I shut my mouth closed, stare wide-eyed at Barbara as a smile spreads across her face.

"I think you have the solution to both of your problems right in front of you, kid. You're just too scared to take a risk."

I take a deep breath before knocking back the rest of my *guarapita*, wincing at the intense alcohol and sweet aftertaste. As I run my fingers through my hair, I look up to see the couples dancing on the floor, my heart aching at the sight of one in particular who can't seem to keep their eyes—or hands—off each other. The scene drags me back to my little sister's wedding, to swaying in Asher's arms, the feeling of complete happiness, warmth, and protection overwhelming me.

"I miss him," I admit. "More than I ever thought I could miss someone. More than I ever missed him before."

"I know, babe."

"I can't do this anymore," I breathe, feeling the tears start to fall down my cheeks. I tear my eyes away from the happy couple to meet Barbara's. "I need to get him back."

"I know."

"But how? The last time he texted was in *January*. He's clearly done with me. He hasn't reached out since. After pushing him away so much, he's finally done with me," I sob, crying into my hands.

"I doubt that, Rose. I mean, the man was ready to give up a lot to be with you. That's not just something that goes away."

"Fine, maybe he still loves me. But he's probably furious with me. And I can't just show up without a plan. We'd be in the same position we were in before."

She reaches out and grabs my hands in both of hers. "Okay, so let's make a plan. How can I help?"

Chapter Forty-Five

ASHER

I should be nervous. I should be freaking out. I should be worrying about the fact that this is practically the most important moment of my career. It's been years leading up to it, and I cannot fuck this up. I should be focused on the fact that I've been working on this since high school by taking AP science classes, then college, and grad school, all throughout my Ph.D. program, and need to do well. More than nine years of prep have led to this moment right here where I will stand up in front of a group of my thesis committee—and others who want to see my presentation—and present five years of research. They'll listen and then drill me on it. They'll measure my ability to explain my findings, to defend their value and probability. They'll determine whether I deserve to be called *Doctor* Asher Wolff.

But I honestly couldn't give a shit about it.

My anxiety has never felt this bad, it's true. But none of it has had anything to do with my thesis defense, this life-altering moment.

It has everything to do with the woman I just saw walk through the lecture hall door near the back.

I know my research material and exactly what I'm going to present. I know every single slide in my PowerPoint presentation by heart. For five years I've focused on data analysis for gravitational waves signals, and I know my material better than anyone. There's no doubt in my mind that every bit of information I worked on for the last few years has value, and that I'll be able to defend it in front of my thesis committee behind closed doors after the public presentation.

What I don't know is what the hell Rosie is doing here. I don't know what this means. Is she here just to support me or is it something more, too? Is she here as a friend, or is this about *Us*, capital U?

As I stand by the lectern waiting for the members of the audience to settle comfortably into their seats, I watch the woman who ripped my heart to shreds—*twice*—stumble and trip through the chairs. An explosion of pink that makes my chest swell and stomach turn at the same time, and it takes every ounce of strength in my body not to go running to her.

Yes, she broke my heart. Yes, she ignored me and hurt me to the point where I had to block and delete her number and text exchanges from my phone. But she showed up, which means she cares.

Not that I ever really thought she didn't. When she broke up with me, I definitely questioned her sanity, but never, for one single second, did I question her feelings for me. There's no way anyone could ever fake the amount of chemistry and love we experienced—even if what she feels is clearly not as strong as what I feel for her.

Rosie settles comfortably into a seat before she looks up, eyes searching for me. When they finally meet mine, I can practically hear her sharp inhale. Cheeks blushing crimson, she raises a shy hand and waves, a small hesitant smile spreading across her face.

Slightly slack-jawed, I raise my hand in kind to wave back, the pull of her chocolate eyes on me stronger than any supermassive blackhole could ever dream to have.

"Wolff," my thesis advisor gently pulls at my blazer, distracting me from what *must* be a hallucination, right? "You ready?" She asks.

"Dr. Cho. Hey. Yes." I clear my throat and adjust my tie as I look down at the petite woman.

She smiles kindly, eyes crinkling beneath her grey-streaked black bangs. "I know you've been a bit distracted lately, but you've got this, right?"

"One hundred percent," I say, standing a little taller. "Nothing is going to distract me from doing my best in the presentation."

Except maybe the fact that the love of my life decided to show up to my defense after months of radio silence.

Although, in all fairness, I *did* block her number, so who knows whether she's tried to contact me lately.

"Good, good," Dr. Cho nods her head thoughtfully.

"Sweets!" I turn to watch my mother wave from the second row, right behind where my committee is meant to sit. She raises both hands and gives me a thumbs up with a nearly face-splitting grin. "You're going to do amazing!" she whisper-yells.

I grin, so thankful that she was able to make it all the way over here to support me in this huge moment. Though I was heartbroken when she sold *Seymour's*, I can't deny the positive effect letting go of that store has had on my mother. I suppose I've always seen her as a huge force, raising my sister and I basically alone (save for the Castillos' help) and never considered just how fucking *tired* she could be.

"*Thanks for coming,*" I mouth at her with a wave before turning back to Dr. Cho.

"I'm going to briefly introduce you, sing your praises, and then we can start, okay?" She smiles encouragingly at me, patting my shoulder. "After that, I'll take a seat over there with the rest of the committee and you can start presenting your work. We'll be ready to start in a few."

I nod and watch the crowd settle quietly.

Dr. Cho approaches the lectern to introduce me, but my eyes lock on the beautiful pink-haired woman in the back of the room and I can't listen to a word she says. Rosie mouths *"Good luck"* from her seat. Doing my best to settle the storm of emotion brewing within me, I grin back and thank her.

A round of applause rouses me, breaking the moment we shared.

"Okay, Asher. You're up." Dr. Cho smiles up at me, motioning for me to take her spot at the head of the classroom.

A research assistant from my lab dims the lights and shoots me a thumbs up. And with that, I look up at the title slide of my PowerPoint presentation, the one that contains every bit of relevant information I've collected over the past five years. I take a deep breath, switch on the mic, and rest both hands on the sides of the lectern.

"Good morning, ladies and gentlemen, members of the committee, and other faculty and fellow candidates. It feels surreal after all this time to finally be standing in front of you all delivering my public thesis defense. It's been a long time coming, and I certainly wouldn't be here if it weren't for so many people who have supported me and inspired me along the way. So before we begin, I'd like to thank you all for being here. This is incredibly special. And though I'd love to say more, I know none of you are here to hear me wax poetic about how much life and people have inspired me in my scientific pursuits—except maybe my mother. Hi Mom." I wave at my mother as the crowd chuckles at my joke. "So without further ado, let's get into it."

Chapter Forty-Six

ROSIE

An hour and a half later of what I understand as pure gibberish (but I'm sure is all brilliancy) and a fascinating question and answer session from the audience, I watch as Asher receives a roaring wave of applause and support after delivering his concluding remarks. It's emotional for everyone there—not just for him or the people he loves. It's like this entire place—his scientific community—are just as proud of him as Jaime and I are. He's respected and admired and I choke up as I watch the audience gaze up at him in admiration.

I am in love with this moment.

He exhales deeply, the relief of being done with this massive milestone in his career clear on his face. It's over, and if he passes his actual defense behind closed doors—which of course he will, because he's Asher—he's officially done with school.

Kind of. There's the whole fellowship thing of it all and the possibility of even more of them after that. I mean, *Jesus*, academia sounds like never-ending work.

Dr. Cho, a petite woman in her mid-sixties, shakes Asher's hand, congratulating him on his presentation. I watch as he pulls her into a hug, the woman's eyes widening in surprise. She pushes him away and pats his shoulder while he laughs, signaling for him to join his mother, who stands anxiously on the sidelines waiting for her son. Even from all the way in the back of the room, I can tell Jaime's ready to bounce off the walls, full of pride. Once he makes it over to her, she throws her arms around Asher's neck and holds him close. Jaime squeezes her eyes shut tight, trying hard not to cry. The moment is so tender, it claws at my chest, my own eyes watering.

"We will be taking a five-minute break, after which Mr. Wolff will need to defend his thesis presentation in front of his preselected committee behind closed doors. Friends and family can follow David, my TA, up to the Astrophysics department conference room. We will be hosting a small celebration there with some champagne and cake and the like," the petite woman says from the lectern. "On behalf of the department and MIT, we would like to thank all those who attended the public defense. We hope you have a fantastic rest of your day."

And with a ball in my throat, I grab my things and make it out of my seat to walk all the way to Asher.

He sees me approach and pulls away from Jaime, who smiles the second she sees me standing there.

"Rosie! I'm so happy you could make it." She envelops me in her arms, and I let myself sink into the love emanating from her. My second mother.

"Thanks for giving me all the info, Jaime. I really appreciate it." Over her shoulder, I watch Asher frown at my words, realization dawning on him.

Yes, your mother was the one who told me about this because you seem to have blocked my number and I needed to pull a Hail Mary out of my ass so I can come and tell you how much I love you and that I want you back.

Jaime pulls away after just a few seconds, taking a step away from us. "I'm just going to head up to the conference room while you finish your defense..."

Asher nods at his feet, staunchly avoiding both of our gazes.

"We'll see you up there." She kisses him on the cheek before leaving with a, "I'm proud of you, kiddo."

Once we're alone, he finally lifts his gaze to mine. "You're here," he breathes.

My first instinct is to say *"Of course, how could I not be?"* But then I realize I've essentially disappeared from his life, pushing him away—*more than once*. Why would he think for one second that I would be here to support him, regardless of how important this moment is to him?

Instead, I say, "Yes. I'm here."

He nods thoughtfully but looks away, lips pressed together.

"Unless you don't want me to be? I can leave now and—"

"No. No, I'm just surprised, is all. Last time we spoke you made it clear you weren't really up for having any type of relationship, remember? I texted about seeing you and you just... ghosted me."

I wince, clutching my purse and coat tight in my hands. "I want to talk about this. I do. It's why I'm here—besides wanting to see your defense, of course. But do you really want to do this when you have to defend the last five years of your research to a whole committee that will define your future?"

"The only future I truly, wholeheartedly, and desperately want is standing right in front of me. And just over two months ago, she told me I couldn't have it."

I swallow. "This can hold until later. I promise."

The wrinkle between his brows deepens when he rubs his eyes beneath his glasses, exhaling a sharp breath.

"Okay." He nods. "Okay. Will you wait for me? Will I see you up there? I should be done in twenty minutes." He chuckles, running his fingers through his hair. But I can see the fear behind his eyes, the anxiety the thought of me leaving him once more causes him.

And it wrecks me.

Even if he ever forgives me for running away, for being too scared to take a risk on us and myself, I never will.

"Yes. I know history has taught you to believe I won't, but I swear to god I'll wait. I'll be waiting for you with everyone when you come out."

"Okay, good."

"Okay." And with trembling hands, I place them on his chest as I reach up onto my tiptoes to press my lips softly against his cheek. He exhales sharply, wrapping a hand around one of my wrists, pulling me back into him before I even have a chance to roll back onto my heels.

Keeping his eyes on mine, he presses the palm of my hand to his face. "Seriously. Please be here when I'm done."

"I swear."

The petite woman from before comes up behind him and places a hand on his shoulder.

He drops my hand, but keeps our fingers intertwined as she says, "Asher, we're ready for you. It's time to say goodbye to your friend." She smiles briefly at me before giving us space to say goodbye.

"I'll see you soon," I promise, mustering every bit of resolve I can into my voice, hoping he trusts it enough to focus on his defense and not on whether or not I'll still be here when he's done.

He nods once and kisses my forehead before dropping my hand and walking to the front of the room. I slip out of the lecture hall and follow the stragglers to the department.

Jaime and I anxiously snack on sickening amounts of carrots and hummus as we wait for Asher's return to celebrate his successful doctorate dissertation. We meet his friends from the department, who gush nonstop about how brilliant and kind he is, his mother glowing with pride. Some of his female students approach Jaime with caution to sing her son's praises, clearly smitten with the pure hotness and undeniable attraction that is Asher Wolff. I would feel a bit more jealous that he's surrounded by brilliant women who seem to all want him in different ways, but I can't blame them. Asher is brains *and* beauty—there's no denying it. Add to that the fact that he's their teacher (kind of), so how could they not be attracted? Who doesn't love a little "falling for the professor" fantasy?

The elevator doors open into the hall and a flood of congratulatory words spill into the department. Asher strides into the cramped hallway full of people waiting expectantly for him with his committee members in tow.

"—fantastic—"

"—should be really proud—"

"—looking forward to seeing more from you when you're at—"

They praise him, but he ignores them, his eyes searching frantically for something—*me*.

"Rosie." He rushes over to me once he finds me, arms quickly wrapping around my waist, holding me tightly to him. "You're still here."

It kills me to hear the surprise in his voice. I've let this man down so many times... From this moment on, I swear to the universe that I will do my very best never to let him doubt me ever again.

That is, if he'll still have me.

I look over his shoulder at the group of people behind him, looking up at Asher with both admiration and fondness—something I completely understand. Being enraptured by his brilliancy, while getting lost in who he is as a person.

There is no one like Asher.

"I'm guessing it went well, then, *doctor?*" I ask low in his ear.

I hear his sharp inhale, feel his arms tighten even more. "That is the hottest thing I have ever heard you say, ever," he whispers so only I can hear. I laugh, feeling light, basking in the ease of our conversation. I know there's much to address and to get through, but it's nice to know we can celebrate this moment together without letting our baggage taint it.

"Shall we get to the champagne, then?" Dr. Cho asks.

I pull away, letting everyone else around him congratulate and shake his hand, commenting on his presentation and lamenting how much he will be missed when he leaves for California.

I make to move to the back of the room, but he quickly catches my hand, keeping me by his side.

Seemingly out of nowhere, two bottles of champagne appear on the conference room table beside a very large chocolate cake. From a large cloth tote, Jaime pulls out several dozen disposable clear cups and begins to line them on the table in neat rows.

Asher takes the first bottle in his hands and grins at me before popping it open with ease, the light in his eyes filling me with enough joy to last a lifetime. I blink back tears as I watch him pour the sparkling liquid into the clear plastic cups, making sure everyone in the vicinity gets one before he does.

I watch him with awe, my heart filled completely to the brim. There's no feeling quite like seeing someone you love achieve something they're passionate about, that they've worked on for so long. In my experience, it's even more gratifying than achieving something yourself because you don't have your own insecurities dragging you down. Watching Asher get all the praise, admiration, and accolades he deserves, that he's worked hard for, reminds me that I am one hundred percent sure he earned it all and more.

After making sure everyone's been served, both bottles empty now, Asher holds out the last glass for a final speech:

"Despite having spent the last hour and half doing it, I'm not really great at the whole public speaking thing," he starts, pulling a small round of chuckles from the rest of the guests. "But I'll keep it simple and sweet: Thank you. Thank you again to my mother, my friends, this incredible department, and everyone who managed to make it to the defense. I know we're all scientists here—well, *almost* all of us." He winks at me and his mom. "But it has been a thing of magic. So thank you again for your support. Although I'm sure the free food is a big incentive, given how poor grad school salaries are nowadays."

With a final laugh, we drink to Asher.

I pull away to help Jaime with the cake, passing paper plates around as the crowd mingles. When everyone seems to have a piece, I take mine and stand in the corner of the room, eating it alone, needing to take a beat, completely lost in thought.

"Thank you for coming." I jump at the sound of his voice, choking on my cake.

"Thank you for letting me be here," I say back, wiping off some crumbs with a napkin. He takes the plate from my hand and sets it on the table, pulling me quickly into his arms. We hold each other for a few moments in the corner, and I relish in the feel of him. Melting in his arms, soaking up every moment he gives me—I'll take every single one he offers for the rest of my life. My hands slide up his back, into his hair.

Being in each other's arms, the scent of him coming over me, overpowering all of my senses, is like coming home—something I haven't experienced in over a decade.

"Should we talk?" I ask because I'm a masochist, of course. I should be extending this beautiful moment, should let him enjoy his celebration, but instead I choose to cut to the chase because I'm desperate for the answer. And the question isn't whether he loves me—of course he does, just as much as I love him. The question is whether he can forgive me, whether we can be together, whether he'll take a chance on us, and whether he believes that I want this enough to fight for it every day if we have to.

"Yeah." He nods, pulling away to stand upright. "Let's— Let's talk." He takes me by the hand and pulls me out of the conference room, taking me through the maze of small offices to one in the back with his name on it.

"You have your own office?" I balk.

In true Asher fashion, he shrugs bashfully. "It's not a big deal. I share it with someone."

He shuts the door behind us and stands to face me, the strength I'd manage to summon suddenly gone from my body.

"So... Let's talk."

My throat constricts as I try to suppress a sob and I hate myself for it. I didn't want to cry.

He reaches out to cup my face and I lean into his touch. "Rose." Voice tight, pained.

"Okay. Okay. I'm just gonna... I'm just gonna say everything I want to say."

He nods and I clear my throat. "First off, I want to apologize for... *so many things*. I shouldn't have spoken to you that way the morning after our first time back in high school. I shouldn't have left the way I did on New Year's Day. I should've trusted you when you said that we could make it work. Trusted in myself to be enough for you, to not listen to my dad about me not deserving you and telling me breaking up with you was the best thing for you. Though, my god, you're so incredible it was hard not to instantly believe him, you know what I mean?"

"Your dad told you to break up with me?"

"Yes, but don't be mad at him. He loves you too, you know; he just thought he was protecting you, even if he hurt me in the process. And he was right that I shouldn't have let you take a bullshit position in New York just so you could be close to me. Of course, you weren't exactly forthcoming about the fellowship, but once I found out, I should've immediately searched for a compromise. The truth was, between what my dad said and then Diana announcing her divorce—"

"*What?*" He cuts me off.

"Oh, you haven't heard. Yeah, she and Rodrigo were actually pretending to still be together at the wedding for Andrea's sake, but they'd been separated for a while. She finally came clean to me at the party and... It was a whole thing. Well, in part, it's why I freaked out. I had just found out the truth about you being accepted into the fellowship, about how you were giving up this huge opportunity just to be with me, and then, right before us going up to the hotel room, Diana told me. She told me all about how miserable she was, how she gave up her career to be with him and start a family and now she has nothing to rebuild with. She was distraught, crying about how she didn't know who she was anymore, what to do with her life... And I didn't want that for either of us. In the end, in my mind, one of us would have had to compromise their professional life for their personal one. And I couldn't let that be you because I love you so much. And when I thought about leaving my job... I just couldn't do it. It felt like it was the first time my dad was *somewhat* okay with what I was doing because I was at least higher up. And even though I wasn't in love with it even before I started doing it, I liked the *idea* of it, the stability. I wanted to do more movies like the one I had done before the holidays, but I didn't trust myself enough to take a risk professionally. To give it all up, move to California for you and a new career, and then lose it and lose us. The thought alone was... debilitating, at best." I swallow, remembering the fear, the anxiety that this all brought on. "I was terrified of killing the best parts of us."

His hands come up to cup my face, and he takes a step closer to me.

"And now?" He asks, his voice shaking and low. "Are you still terrified?"

"Yes," I confess. He pales and drops his hands, looking away. But I go on: "Yes, I'm terrified. But mostly I'm terrified that if I keep holding on to how I'm feeling, if I keep trying to protect myself, to protect you, *us*, from the *possibility* of imploding, then... Then I'm scared I'll forever feel like my life has yet to begin. Because that's how I feel. When I'm with you, I feel like I'm on play, and any second we're not together, it's like my life is on pause. I feel like I haven't started—not really. Ugh, maybe this whole metaphor doesn't make sense,." I groan, shaking my head. "I mean, I could go back home and go on without you for the rest of my existence. And I know I'll be able to make something of it. It just wouldn't be a full life; it'd barely be anything at all. Instead—if you'll have me, of course—I was wondering whether you wouldn't mind terribly maybe giving us a shot? Maybe trying things out?" My voice comes out as a squeak, and it's only then that I realize there are tears streaming down my cheeks.

Asher's face splits into a grin. He pulls me into him and presses his lips to mine as my heart swells so much, I begin to wonder whether it will fit in my chest. His arms come around me, sliding down my sides to cup my ass and lift me off the ground in one fell swoop. Instinctively, my legs come to wrap around his waist, fingers digging into his hair.

It's barely a kiss, just two smiles pressed together.

"Yeah. Yeah, let's fucking do it." He presses his face into my hair, kisses the delicate skin under my ear. "Whatever it takes. Though," he pulls away slightly to look me in the eye, a frown taking the place of the beautiful, heartbreaking smile covering his face before. "I should tell you that I did accept the fellow-ship. And I'm pretty sure I'd burn a *huge* bridge if I retract my acceptance now. Would you be down to… to do long-distance?" He winces as if preparing for a physical blow.

I pretend to think about it as I feel his back and neck tighten beneath my fingertips. "Mmm, long-distance between Los Angeles and Pasadena will be hard. But I think we'll manage."

A small smile plays at his lips. "What?"

"I mean, it's what? Fifteen? Twenty miles away?" I whistle and shake my head. "I'll need to finally learn how to drive prop-erly and I heard traffic can be a nightmare, but it's okay. I'll do it for you."

"You're moving to L.A.?"

"I *told* you. I decided I need to take a chance on myself, too. This whole thing wasn't about my feelings for you. I *know* how I feel about you. I love you. It's also about my feelings for myself and whether or not I felt good enough for you, or even good enough to take a chance on myself. And turns out, I think I'm pretty awesome at what I do. And I think you love me, too. And yes, there's a lot to be scared of. But am I supposed to just live a bubble-wrapped life just because there's a small chance I can get hurt? A life where I'll be left wondering every day if I made the right choice, whether I'd still be happy, whether *you'd* still be happy? No, sir. It was time I took a chance."

"Second chance, actually. At least with us." He smiles his delicious half-smile before pressing his lips to mine.

"Yes," I whisper against his mouth once we come up for air.

"I need to apologize too," he whispers, turning to pushing me up against the wall. Asher drops his lips to my neck again before looking me in the eye. "I should've been more honest about everything going on and told you about the fellowship, about wanting to give it up to be with you. It was an unfair thing of me to do, because you're right. I would've been so fucking happy to move to New York to be with you, but realistically speaking, I think a part of me would've been extremely disappointed I never pursued that opportunity. I'm afraid I would've inadvertently ended up resenting you or us—at least some part of me would've."

I nod and place a soft kiss on his nose, grateful that we're finally speaking our truths aloud.

"So, what does this mean, exactly? I think I know, but see, I've waited over a decade for this—for *us*—and... *Fuck*, I need you to fucking spell it out for me in exact words, Rosie. Because I can't make assumptions anymore. I need you to tell me what it means when you say you want to do 'this.'"

"What it means is you and I are now a couple. It means, I will take on that contract my friend Barbara helped me get and move to Los Angeles full time, where I plan on taking on many more costume design roles for movies. It will be hard, but I know you'll be there to support me. It means you'll be at your fellowship in Pasadena, where you'll be working long hours doing kickass research that I totally don't understand but I'm sure is brilliant, and I'll be there to support you, too. It means that after a year, or honestly, maybe just a couple of months, we move in together. We try to slow things down because, from an outsider's perspective, it might seem lighting fast, but within just a couple of weeks of us moving into the same place, we're engaged. Next thing you know, it's Christmas, and you and I are getting married in a small ceremony with just our family and a couple of friends under the Colorado stars. And people will complain about the cold and how insane it is that we got married outdoors in the dead of winter, but we'll laugh and tell them it's how it had to be because it's where we fell in love: under the stars, surrounded by snow, in the warmth of our love."

I watch as he swallows, voice hoarse, eyes red-rimmed as he says, "That sounds pretty fucking great."

The End

352

Liked Rosie and Asher's story? Make sure you leave a review. :)

Also, make sure you check out Barbara and Theo's story in *Shall We Dance?* and Matt and Liza's in *Fall Into You* and *Happily Ever Disaster*.

Acknowledgments

This book... This book has been a beast. It was rewritten a couple of times, had to be set aside due to health issues—*twice*—and cut down by several thousand words. Usually, I write books in a relatively short amount of time, but because of everything life threw at me, it took about a year on and off.

Because of that, I sat with these characters for so long, I felt like I knew them better than any of the ones I've ever written. There were so many more things I wanted to include from the life I envisioned for them as they grew together in their new relationship, so many windows into their past that I wanted to show on-page, and all of the deliciously hilarious meddling Julieta and Jaime really did in the original outline (maybe I'll save that for bonus chapters). I know she's a big girl, but my heart couldn't take cutting out more from *Snowmance* (shout out to my QC girlies for helping title it).

Asher and Rosie's story was so beautiful in my head and heart and if I could, I would've probably written twice as much. I hope this was enough to convey how much these two people love each other and why they hurt each other so they didn't hurt each other even more. (Thank god they got their shit together and made it happen in the end, because I just couldn't with all the pining). So this is my thank you to you. For reading what might be my favorite book to date.

This book also reminded me why I love this community and what I do: because it constantly leads me to meeting new people and experiences. Once I decided that Asher *had* to be an astrophysicist, I reached out to a Ph.D. candidate who looked willing to sit down with me and discuss their experience. Thankfully,

Doctor Sylvia Biscoveanu—possibly the coolest person I know—did not think the email from a stranger inviting her out for a drink to talk about it all was creepy (thanks for not thinking I was a serial killer!). I was awkward and a little tipsy, but it worked out, and now we're real life friends! She was invaluable with the research she provided (I hope I didn't mess anything up; I apologize if I did), with the experiences she shared, and kind enough to invite me to her thesis defense—an emotional and fascinating moment I am honored to have been able to watch and celebrate with her friends and family. So thank you, thank you!

Additionally, this book would definitely never have been made possible without the help of my betas Ania, Barbara, Kristen, Jenn, and Tracey (especially T. I could not have written her without you.)

Writing can really be a lonely endeavor, and having a community is the most important thing in the world. I am eternally grateful to the entire community I have built, the new friends I make every day, and the support system I have from everyone in my life—Booksta or not.

K. Always, thank you. Your support means everything to me. I would not be here, doing what I love, without it. Not a second goes by where I don't feel grateful and honored for it.

I'm also going to do something out of the ordinary and thank myself. Yup, that's right. I'm going to thank myself for putting my health first, even if it meant delaying this book by a year. It was the right call. So thanks, babe. You're the best. Take care of you.

I hope you liked *Second Chance Snowmance.* I fucking loved it.

CAROLINE FRANK

Caroline Frank is an indie author and self-proclaimed shoe addict. She currently resides in Massachusetts with her husband and two crazy cats, Señor Kitty and Salem.

She spends her days reading, crocheting, crafting, writing, and biking. Her favorite things include the first sip of an iced-cold Coke and using self-deprecating humor to get through the day.

Though she always planned to eventually take over the world, she thinks writing fun stories every day is pretty freaking awesome and plans to continue to do so for the foreseeable future.

Seasons of Love Series (Open-Door Romantic Comedy):

Fall Into You (Book 1)

Shall We Dance? (Book 2)

Happily Ever Disaster (Novella - Book 2.5)

Second Chance Snowman (Book 3) - Coming November 23!

Second Chance
Snowmance

SEASONS OF LOVE:
BOOK 3

CAROLINE FRANK

Standalone Women's Contemporary (Open-Door):

In For a Penny

IN FOR A PENNY
TELEPHONE
CAROLINE FRANK